To Cat...
Enjoy...

Sincerely,
Jeanette Fratto
4-9-14

No Stone Unturned

Jeanette A. Fratto

Outskirts Press, Inc.
Denver, Colorado

Outskirts Press, Inc.
http://www.outskirtspress.com

ISBN: 978-1-4327-4553-0

Library of Congress Control Number: 2009934026

Outskirts Press and the "OP" logo are trademarks belonging to Outskirts Press, Inc.

PRINTED IN THE UNITED STATES OF AMERICA

To my late parents, who first instilled in me a love of reading and writing; and to my husband, who supports my efforts unconditionally.

Chapter One

When I look back at the last year, I might not have come to California had I known what lay ahead of me. I never was the adventurous type, favoring the sure thing over the unknown. I made sure I had all my ducks in a row, as the saying goes, before I left, but how quickly they moved out of line. I guess it's good we can't see the future. I could have missed so much. I can still see myself the day I left Detroit, waiting at the airport, deciding to buy something to read . . . . . .

I paid for my magazine, noticing that the lady behind the counter – hair pulled back, starched white blouse – resembled my high school English teacher, Miss Benton. This produced a flood of thoughts about my high school days, which weren't exactly pleasant. Miss Benton did not seem to have an existence outside the classroom. I often imagined her being put up on a shelf each night, along with her books, only to come back to life again at the dawn of a new school day.

Miss Benton's role as yearbook advisor made her notable in my mind. I could still hear her saying, not knowing I was within earshot, that she didn't think it was appropriate to put the caption "girl most likely to lead a boring life" next to my graduation picture. It wasn't that she didn't agree with it, even I did, but her sense of decorum, and fear of the principal's disapproval, prevented her OK. And so I became, Linda Davenport, the girl most likely to marry early and have six children. Not much difference really.

I stared out the window as the airplane taxied down the runway, reflecting on this unwanted trip down memory lane, courtesy of a Miss Benton look-alike. Age 28, six years out of college, previous employment – school teacher. Nothing in my life so far had altered the "boring life" prophecy. I did fool them on the marrying early/six children part.

As the terminal receded from my view, I eased back into my seat, eager to put distance between Detroit and me. Would Los Angeles be better? It couldn't be worse.

Aunt Martha said it was a bold move I was

making, with all the weird, un-Godly types in California. My mother just cried and wrung her hands. She stopped between tears long enough to remind me that if my dad were alive he'd certainly put his foot down on this wild notion of mine. He had gained more power in death evidently, since in life Mother never let him put his foot down on anything. My best friend Junie said she was proud of me even though she herself couldn't leave her hometown, caring so much for roots and family as she did.

So there it was, my sendoff. The consensus was that I was foolish, maybe even uncaring. The truth was I needed to save myself from slowly going crazy in a city that, like my life, was stagnating. I felt as though I was in a time warp. Mother was no longer alone, having moved in with Aunt Martha after Daddy died last year. They managed well even though they had only two things in common; being sisters and widows. While my mom and dad lived frugally in northwest Detroit on Dad's accountant's salary, with me their only child, Aunt Martha's husband Edward had provided a lavish lifestyle in a large Bloomfield Hills home, the fruits of his hard work as a lawyer for General Motors. Their three sons grew into successful professional men, two doctors and a lawyer. Just when Aunt Martha and Uncle Ed could enjoy some unencumbered time together, Uncle Ed suffered a massive heart attack while in the basement looking for his golf clubs. By the time he was found, slumped over his golf bag, it was too late.

Daddy, on the other hand, didn't have such a merciful demise. He lingered slowly and painfully, bravely fighting lung cancer, until he succumbed to its devastation two days before his 65th birthday. Aunt Martha, a widow for two years by then, didn't like rattling around in her large house alone, but wouldn't give it up, wanting a place for family gatherings. Mom didn't like living alone either. It didn't take too much convincing for her to sell our modest family home and move up, as it were, to Bloomfield Hills, even if the circumstances were sad; Daddy being lowered into the ground as she rose to life in a home he never could have provided.

The steady hum of the plane's engine relaxed me somewhat as I continued to ruminate on the life I was leaving. There were no regrets really, yet there was a tinge of sadness. As disappointing as Detroit had become to me, it was still my hometown, and Dad and Mom had done their best. They certainly taught me the value of a dollar – food coupons were clipped, clothes bought on sale, no frivolous expenditures, and bills always paid first before any recreation was pursued. We always had the basics but not too many frills. I saved my babysitting money and later most of my paycheck working part-time in a local department store after school and on weekends. I did this all through high school, a period in my life I could have gladly skipped.

I suppose everyone feels somewhat alienated during the teen years. I was sure the word was stamped in large letters on my forehead. Shy by nature and self-conscious about my plain looks – light brown hair and eyes, a nose a little too big, a mouth a little too small – I didn't easily integrate into a new crowd. Junie and I, best friends since first grade, stuck together like glue. We could laugh and joke, our special little party of two. On days she was absent I was forlorn. Puberty, a condition overtaking most of the girls in the 9th grade, had passed us by. Almost daily we checked ourselves for budding breasts and rounded hips and came up wanting. The boys passed us by too, so school dances and mixers were events we avoided.

As we waited for the bodies our mothers promised us would come in God's time, we found other ways to adjust. Junie was athletic so she signed up for every sport she could. I was mildly athletic. I did play some tennis in junior high, but I didn't like sweating that much. I was smart though, in the intelligent, well-read way that impressed adults and left those my own age cold. I found this appealed greatly to my teachers and I used it to my advantage. There was a certain respect accorded me when I finished a quote from Rudyard Kipling or identified the theme of <u>Madame Bovary</u>, while the rest of the literature class looked blank.

Thanks to Daddy, I developed an early love of books, and they were my key to the world. We made many trips to the main public library on Woodward Avenue, with me skipping along the stone terrace pretending the library was my own private castle. We'd come out with our latest supply of reading, ready to be transported to far off lands.

Eventually I developed physically, just as Mom said I would, but, by that time, I considered breasts and hips secondary to what my counselor called my fine mind. This fine mind earned me a scholarship to the University of Michigan, an opportunity I would not have had on Daddy's income.

College days are supposed to be great. People reminisce about them. Songs are sung about them. In truth, I was in awe of the school. I'll never forget my first visit there, on a rainy day in my senior year of high school. Ann Arbor looked so beautiful to me, rain dripping off the leaves of the trees, lights on in dorm windows that gave me a peek into a world I hoped to enter soon. When it did become my world the following autumn, the same magic was still there for me.

Safely ensconced in Mosher Hall, with a roommate from Chicago, I soon learned the diversity of my surroundings. People came to U. of M. from all over the world. There was a great education to be had outside the classroom as well as in it, and I partook of everything that was free or cheap. Although my scholarship paid tuition and living expenses, my spending money came from my meager savings. Once again I was on the no-frills plan but it was OK. The dorm meals were good most of the time and if I was invited out for a hamburger by some of my dorm friends, I could usually swing it. Other times I'd just say I had to study, can't afford to lose the scholarship you know.

Fall evenings were a beautiful time to take a walk. The leaves were turning to brilliant reds and golds, the air was crisp, and the smell of it was exhilarating. The streets with sorority houses held a special fascination for me. I knew it was a life I'd never be part of for two reasons; fear of rejection if I participated in rush week, and not being able to afford the extra costs of going "Greek", if miraculously I was accepted.

Occasionally my dorm would "cooperate" with one of the sororities, where several girls from each group would have dinner in the others' domain. I participated once. The large, elegant sorority house with its stately dining room was very impressive. The pork chops and applesauce tasted just a little better than if they had been served in the dining room at Mosher Hall. We were all treated politely but when this glimpse into sorority life ended we recognized it for what it was, a nice exchange to show how benevolent the more affluent half could be.

Still, life was good for me in Ann Arbor. I met so many interesting people, especially David. David! My eyes still fill up with tears if I think of him too long.

My reverie was broken by the loud acceleration of the engine as the plane sped toward take-off. At the same moment I was aware of a hand thrust toward me and someone saying, "Hi, I'm Carol Alder. As long as we're going to be seat mates for five hours I thought we should introduce ourselves." I hadn't noticed this lovely blonde lady next to me. She must have sat down while I was daydreaming.

"Hi," I responded, "I'm Linda …Linda Davenport."

Carol began chattering about returning to California after visiting an old friend who lived in Royal Oak. "I've never been to Detroit before," she continued, "and I must say it doesn't have much to recommend it."

Even though I agreed, she must have seen me flinch, a reaction not unlike someone talking about a member of your family.

"Oh, I'm sorry if I spoke out of turn," she stammered. "I did have a good time and I'm sure many nice people live there." Her voice trailed off and her face had that "please rescue me" look.

I started laughing. She relaxed when I assured her I was not offended, especially since I was leaving for what I hoped would be greener pastures. She settled back in her seat and I reached into my purse and pulled out the letter that started it all.

Dear Miss Davenport:

We are pleased to offer you the position of copy editor for our new subsidiary, Grenville Publishing. If you accept, your starting salary will be in the range discussed with you in your meeting with Mary Cappo. Your salary and benefits package will be finalized upon your arrival in Los Angeles, with starting date to follow thereafter.

Arrangements will be made for your travel to California. Please contact my secretary, Barbara Nelson, at 555-610-1839 at your earliest convenience. She will handle the details.

We look forward to you joining the Grenville team.

Sincerely,
Harold Thompson
Managing Editor

I refolded the letter and reflected on the day that triggered this major life change. It was only a few months ago that I traveled to Los Angeles for a week long teachers' conference that included workshops on innovative teaching methods. I had never been further west than Chicago. There was always a mystique to California for me, so I was anxious to take it all in, especially in February when I could be sure of cold, slushy weather at home. The conference gave me a legitimate excuse to spend money on what Mom called frivolity. Mom was sure the West Coast could offer nothing but decadence. She did respect my six years as an English teacher though. Sensible work, she called it. She also knew my head could not easily be turned. Mom's approval was still important to me, even though I had been self-supporting for years. I guess it was my respect for her more than my hovering insecurity.

I stayed in Santa Monica in an old hotel facing the ocean. A group of teachers were able to obtain a good rate, and the hotel was close to the conference site. The sun reflected off the ocean every day. People walked dogs and rode bikes in shorts. I was enamored.

One workshop featured a presentation on a new series of children's books designed to increase their vocabulary while also introducing them to great literature. The publisher, Grady Inc., had created a subsidiary specifically to focus on this new market. I loved the books and the approach.

Later that evening I walked to a nearby coffee shop to have dinner and almost collided with the workshop presenter, Mary Cappo. I complimented her on the wonderful afternoon. She invited me to join her for a quick bite and we ended up spending two hours discussing the sad state of the spoken and written word these days. She showed interest in my background and wondered if I'd consider switching careers. She was impressed that I not only taught English to junior high students, but emphasized writing skills too.

The new subsidiary, Grenville Publishing, needed

skilled copy editors. When I told her I established student essay contests locally which were so successful they expanded state-wide, her eyes flashed.

"I'd like to see some of your work," Mary commented, "examples of your guidelines for the essays, your judging criteria, things like that."

I told her I would put a packet together when I returned home. She gave me her business card, shook hands, and we parted.

"I think you'd like living in sunny California," she added, looking over her shoulder.

I was too excited by what just happened to return to the hotel. I walked instead to the nearby Third Street Promenade. Its bustling activity was a perfect counterpart to the buzzing in my head. I daydreamed that I was a successful copy editor, promoted to managing editor, living in an ocean view townhome. In another, I developed my own publishing company, handled successful authors, and lived in a penthouse.

An accidental jostle from a man hurrying by jolted me into reality. Linda Davenport, you dreamer! You've done only the most conservative things all your life and now you're going to give up everything you know for – what? Was that my mother's voice or mine in my head? I strolled along watching couples holding hands and children being enthralled by the street performers. Why wasn't this life possible for me? There's something in the air here. For once I'm thinking of a future that doesn't bore me. As I headed back to the hotel, I vowed to send my ideas to Mary Cappo. What did I have to lose?

After I returned home, Mom, Junie, even Bill Hanson, my school principal, noticed the spring in my step. They chalked it up to my West Coast experience. I didn't share the real reason with anyone. I didn't want Mom's displeasure or Junie's disbelief to dampen my spirits. If my opportunity didn't work out, I wouldn't have to hear "I told you so" or "It's for the better." I quietly packaged my work, sent it to Mary Cappo, and waited.

When six weeks passed without a word, I started to think maybe Mom had a point about all the insincerity in California. I hoped I'd get the courtesy of a return on my materials, at least. By the time the whole episode began to seem like a dream, I came home from school to find my phone message light flashing. As I kicked off my shoes and ran the messages, there was Mary Cappo's voice apologizing for her tardy response. Not only did she like my work, so did the managing editor.

Mary was coming to Chicago next week on business, and if I could work it in, she would fly to Detroit for a day to discuss employment possibilities. If I could work it in, I repeated, as I danced around the room. Oh yes, I could definitely work it in.

We met in her hotel room. My work was spread out on the table along with papers outlining the criteria that Grenville had established for the publishing they would undertake. Mary wasted no time in discussing the role that needed to be filled and the reasons why I was an ideal fit. When she spoke of salary range I had to keep from showing my eagerness. The starting salary was $6,000 a year more than I made now, with a great benefits package too.

"Now you'll find housing costs higher in Los Angeles, but you won't have bills for winter clothes or heating," she continued, "so it pretty much balances out. I can send you some rental ads so you can get a feel for your expenses."

My head reeled. What had been a vague hope for the last few weeks was now a concrete offer, there on the table, waiting for my decision. And I wouldn't be saying yes only to a new job. I'd be saying goodbye to a teaching career, my hometown, friends and family, everything that up to now defined me. My heart said I was ready; my head was doing "what ifs?" all over the place.

Mary, sensing the private war I was fighting, told me she realized this was something I probably needed to think about. She was returning to California the next day, and would talk to me before she left.

"Sleep on it," she suggested. "You can call me here before 10 am. I'm leaving for the airport then."

Sleeping on it was impossible. No sleep would come. Although I'd never envisioned myself as a teacher the rest of my life, I didn't expect to leave the field so soon. I could see the faces of Mom, Junie, my boss, my fellow teachers, when I told them of my plans. They'd be aghast. I wanted this opportunity, but could I stand up to all the head shaking that would go with it?

Thank God Mom was with Aunt Martha. I knew I'd feel guilty leaving her if she didn't have the new social circle to which Aunt Martha had introduced her. With every toss and turn my resolve grew. California wasn't outer space, after all, although Mom could argue that point. People phoned and planes flew. Mom could visit. The school could easily fill my position when I'd finished out the school year. As I drifted into a restless sleep, I knew my answer.

I could hardly wait to call Mary. At 7 am I dialed the hotel, hoping she was up.

"I'm on my second cup of coffee, just waiting for your call," Mary laughed. "I hope the early call is a good sign."

"If saying yes is a good sign, then it is," I exclaimed. Now that it was out, relief flooded through me. I'd always contended that making a decision wasn't tough, reaching the decision was. If this didn't reinforce that, nothing would. "I'll have to close out my affairs here and finish the school year. That's two months away. Is that all right?"

"No problem as far as I can see. I still have to get the managing editor's final approval...." she heard my groan, "no, no, it's just a formality. I was sent here with the authority to make you an offer if all the pieces fit. Officially though, it comes from Harold Thompson." We hung up after she assured me I'd be hearing something within two weeks.

I showered and dressed. As I drove to school I looked at all the familiar sights, soon to be memories. I decided I wouldn't say anything to anyone yet. I wanted time to plan my departure without unwanted advice or discouragement.

The next few days I felt like two people; the Linda everyone knew, and the Linda with a secret.

Every activity and conversation was shadowed by my knowledge that everything would be changing. I made lists – give my landlord notice, sell or give away my furniture, sell my car. I wanted to go to California light – a new life, new things. It seemed appropriate. When I had it all worked out in my head I would break the news. Mom would be first. She'd be the hardest. The rest would be downhill.

Mom cried. "Are you crazy?" she gasped between sobs. "You're so solid. That's what I tell everybody, you're so solid."

Yes, there it was again, that "boring, predictable" label disguised as solid.

"Mom, you know I've wanted more of a challenge. I feel stale. People all around me seem to have fulfilling lives. I feel like an observer. This change will be so good for me. You can visit me. It will work, you'll see." I sounded stronger than I felt.

More tears. I put my arm around my mother, holding back my own tears. Eventually she stopped, wiped her eyes, blew her nose, and gulped, "When?"

"The end of the school year, June. That's two months away. You'll have time to get used to it before I go." I sounded lame. I had dropped a bomb on my mother's neat little life and it would take more than two months to clean up the fragments of her despair.

The rest were easier. At least no one else cried. Bill Hanson seemed shocked. It was so unexpected of me and of course I was irreplaceable, he hastened to add. He'd said the same thing last year when another teacher left to have a baby. I guess we were all irreplaceable. At lunch the teachers' lounge buzzed with talk of what Linda was doing. I walked into the midst of it. After some nervous giggles the questions flew at me like a mosquito attack at a picnic.

"Whatever made you do it?" from Sarah.

"This seems so impulsive, not at all like you," Ellen chimed in.

"Not like you at <u>all</u>," from Karen and Peter simultaneously.

I was beginning to enjoy this. Everyone was dumbfounded. My announcement had shaken their perception of me and seemed to be shaping their reaction more than what I was actually doing. I could have announced I was signing on as an astronaut. No difference.

By the end of the week everyone knew. Junie, mother of two girls, didn't think she could get along without me, especially my common sense advice.

She frequently confided to me her insecurities as a mother and wife, yet she loved her family dearly. There seemed to be a glint of envy in her eyes that I had the freedom to pursue something new, but she had too much loyalty to her family to admit it.

The next two months went quickly. My confirmation letter arrived and Mr. Thompson's secretary Barbara was helpful with more than just making airline reservations. She gave me tips about the safest neighborhoods, even sent me ads. She offered to check out any that interested me. One, a bedroom and bath with kitchen privileges, in the home of a widow, looked promising. It was furnished and the price fit my budget.

Barbara was breathless when she called me back. "Linda, you'd have to live here to realize what a deal this place is. A beautiful old home near San Vicente Blvd. You can even walk to the office. The lady who owns it, Mrs. Carter, has been alone since her husband died and she's lonely. She doesn't need the money, she could get so much more than she's asking. She just wants some companionship."

"Why is it still available?"

"That's the best part," Barbara went on. "The ad I sent you ran just one day. Mrs. Carter was bombarded with calls and they overwhelmed her. She gave up on the idea and canceled the ad. When I told her about this lovely Midwestern lady coming to Los Angeles and not knowing anyone, and needing a nice homey environment......well, you can guess the rest."

"Barbara, now <u>I'm</u> breathless. I hoped to find a furnished place, and with no car, this is amazing," I exclaimed. "How can I thank you enough?"

"Invite me for dinner in that beautiful kitchen you'll be able to use," she laughed, "and send your deposit right away."

It was settled. While I wrapped up my affairs, my mind was in California. I sold most of my furniture, gave away the rest, and attended to a myriad of details that slowly disengaged me from life as I knew it. Scrapbooks, clothing, and mementos were boxed and sent ahead to my new address. Goodbye parties were given for me. It was really happening. I was leaving.

Mom became more upset as my departure neared. My old but reliable car went to her. She took it as a sign I'd be back and would reclaim it. Since this thought cheered her, I left it alone.

"Don't burn any bridges, Linda," Mom repeated each time we spoke. "Detroit might look real good to you some day."

I couldn't imagine what day that would be, but I didn't plan to burn any bridges either.

Mom and Aunt Martha drove me to the airport, with Junie in the back seat next to me twisting her fingers. I never knew silence could be so loud. After checking in I purchased a magazine, then rejoined the group. We stood around nervously until my flight was called for boarding, then the words held back came tumbling out. Amid tears, hugs, and "I love you's", I assured them it would be fine, then walked through the jetway, not feeling nearly so certain at all.

Chapter Two

We had been airborne about an hour. Carol hadn't spoken to me since take-off. The flight attendant was serving beverages to our row and as I reached across Carol for my coffee, she leaned forward and jostled the cup. Only a drop spilled but Carol was once again apologetic. Our eyes met, and we laughed.

"We have to stop being so serious," I managed to say.

"Yes, let's start all over. I'm Carol Alder. Nice to meet you Linda," she answered.

"Likewise," I murmured, my laughter subsiding.

We talked non-stop for the next two hours. Carol seemed fascinated with my story and assured me I'd done the right thing. She was one of those rarities, a California native, and had no desire to live elsewhere. "Why? It's perfect there!" she emphasized, lest I think she wasn't adventuresome.

"I feel so much better talking to you," I confessed. "These last few hours had me in turmoil. The tearful good-byes were hard enough but I had to relive my high school days in a sudden flash just because a magazine saleslady was a dead ringer for our yearbook advisor."

"Change is hard, even under the best circumstances. I admire you for taking the step. If I can help you get adjusted, just ask," Carol offered.

"You're my first California friend," I declared. I didn't count my new employer and staff. They had been wonderful, but it was business related. I looked forward to knowing Carol. She seemed sincere and genuine.

As we traded tidbits of our lives I learned that Carol was 30 years old, graduated from UCLA, and had her own condo in Laguna Hills, a small town in Orange County, south of Los Angeles. She gestured frequently with her hands and I noticed they were delicate, with short manicured nails. She wore only a simple gold necklace and hoop earrings which looked stunning against her green linen pantsuit. Her hair was slightly curly and cut to frame her even features. A natural beauty.

"Tell me what you do Carol," I asked. In all our

talk she had not mentioned her employment.

"I work for Probation," she responded, watched for my reaction, then continued. "I've been there since college graduation. I'm a supervisor overseeing a unit of officers who prepare adult sentencing reports for our local courts."

Although I was vaguely familiar with the word, I had a hard time believing that this pretty, lady-like person could be in such a profession. My contact with probation officers had been limited to two students who had stolen merchandise from a drugstore. Their officers, both burly types, checked with me on their school attendance and progress, regular attendance being an important condition of probation. I couldn't reconcile Carol with them.

Carol sensed my puzzlement. "I'm used to the look you're giving me. The truth is, not everyone working for Probation looks like a gorilla."

"Oh, no, did I have <u>that</u> look?" I laughed, a little embarrassed. "It's just that the only two probation officers I ever met were sort of tough looking."

"Well, in some assignments it doesn't hurt to have size and strength going for you. If you're on the street supervising gang members, it can be a plus. Most assignments though require common sense, knowledge of the law, and the ability to be balanced.

We have the power of the court behind us in all we do. We don't have to come on like gangbusters."

"What led you to this particular field?"

"The summer before my junior year in college I did some work with their volunteer program. Probation was looking for one-on-one visitors for kids at juvenile hall. I was majoring in psychology and planned on going into the people business but I still wasn't sure what form it would take. Volunteering turned out to be the greatest experience. The kids were troubled and needy. I worked under the supervision of their probation officers and learned the many ways they work with both children and adults."

"You mentioned you were involved with adults now, didn't you?" I questioned.

"Yes, for the past two years, right after I was promoted to Supervising Probation Officer," Carol clarified. "I started out with juveniles though. After that first summer I was anxious to volunteer again, so I repeated my efforts the following year. That cinched it. As I finished my senior year I felt pretty sure that I could satisfy my career desires by working in Probation. Lucky for me when I graduated the department was hiring. It was 1992 and Probation was growing along with Orange County."

"Was it a difficult process?" I interjected.

"Sort of. It lasted about three months. Each step eliminated a few more people, until it was down to 24 other candidates and me." Carol shifted in her seat, animatedly telling a story she must have told many times before, clearly enjoying it. "We formed class #42 and began a six month training period in October, learning all phases of Probation work. I learned during the selection process that we had to be prepared to transfer to any assignment. I've had three in the last eight years."

"Your work seems interesting. You still sound excited about it, too," I commented, thinking about the boredom that had set in for me after three years of teaching.

"You never know what each day will bring. There's always a challenge. Just about the time you think there's some sameness to your job, you're trans-ferred to an entirely different assignment. When I went to adult work, as a supervisor yet, I felt like I started all over again."

"Didn't you say that you learned all phases while in training?" I countered.

"Yes, but that was six years before. To tell the truth, when you supervise juveniles, that becomes your focus and you tend to forget all the other things the department's doing." She paused and seemed to be lost in thought. Her brow furrowed as though something unpleasant came to mind. Just as quickly her expression cleared and she went on. "I was so happy to be promoted. I'm at our headquarters in Santa Ana, but I visit the various courts during the week to speak to the judges and stay current on sentencing patterns."

"I hope my new job will prove as great for me as yours is for you," I murmured.

"Oh, it will. Have faith!" Carol answered, patting my hand.

We sat in silence then. The pilot announced that we'd be landing in an hour. I thought of everything Carol had told me. How sad it was when her parents were killed three years ago in an auto accident. She and her older brother, an attorney in Newport Beach, were the sole heirs. Although she didn't say it, she had the look of someone who didn't need to worry about money, and I suspected it was always that way in her family. Yet Carol was unpretentious, friendly, approachable.

I wondered if she'd ever clipped a coupon, chuckling at the thought. My upbringing had made me conscious of every dollar earned and spent. It was ingrained in me, but I wasn't sorry. I had a comfortable savings account, now in the process of being transferred to a California bank, and a growing investment account. I had no debts. It felt good. Frugality pays off, I reasoned.

My excitement grew as Los Angeles loomed in the distance. I anticipated seeing my new digs. Mrs. Carter (call me Edith) and I spoke on the telephone twice; once to become acquainted, and the second time to confirm the arrival of my belongings and discuss when I would arrive myself. I planned to use an airport shuttle service Barbara Nelson had recommended. Mrs. Carter – Edith – said she'd have a light meal for me.

We prepared for landing. Carol looked over at me. She seemed almost wistful. "I'd like to give you my telephone number so we can stay in touch," she offered. "After all, I'm your first California friend so I'm obligated to check on you from time to time," this with mock seriousness.

"I'd love that. As soon as I have my own phone I'll give you my number too. It shouldn't be too long."

We gathered our belongings and exited the plane, heading for the baggage claim. Carol's bags arrived almost immediately. We hugged good-bye, she wished me luck, and handed me her business card. Her home number was written on the back. I watched as she went through the doors. She hadn't mentioned how she would reach home, but I didn't expect to see a black limousine pull up and a chauffeur alight and nod to Carol. He opened the door for her to enter the back seat. I briefly glimpsed a man's pant leg before the door closed behind her. Her luggage was placed in the trunk, the chauffeur went back to the driver's seat, and the limo quietly merged with the airport traffic, disappearing in the distance.

As I puzzled over this I realized my bags were part of the few still circling the carousel. I grabbed them and headed through the doors toward the shuttle bus area. It was 3 pm and slightly overcast. Common for June in California I'd been warned. It still seemed beautiful. Palm trees were silhouetted against the sky, their fronds looking like green fireworks against the blue of the sky. Flowers blooming everywhere gave off a heady perfume. I found my bus and boarded.

Traffic was heavy as the shuttle pulled out of the airport onto surface streets. I tried to picture Edith Carter. She sounded 70ish on the telephone. From what Barbara had told me she was a sweet gray-haired lady who would probably mother me to death. A little mothering would be OK, but I'd need to set some boundaries I decided.

The driver turned onto San Vicente, a wide street with large homes on either side. I loved California architecture and the homes on San Vicente were a visual feast. Soon we turned onto a side street, turned again onto Crescent Lane, and stopped in front of a large two story Spanish hacienda. It reminded me of a small hotel. As the driver retrieved my luggage I took in the view. A stone walkway through a spacious courtyard led to the entrance, framed by massive double wooden doors. A fountain gurgled in the center of the courtyard. Balconies surrounded the upstairs. Music could be heard, but faintly. I couldn't tell where it was coming from. The home sat at the end of a cul-de-sac, and bespoke elegance and privacy. The other homes on Crescent Lane, although architecturally different, had their own quiet elegance. I was flabbergasted. Barbara hadn't prepared me for this.

I thought of what Mom's reaction would be. Up to now Aunt Martha's home had been the standard of envy in our family, and her house didn't come close to Edith Carter's. I stood gaping, then realized my bags had been brought to the door. An outline of a small woman was visible in the doorway. I hurried up the walkway feeling like a hick. I handed a tip to the shuttle driver as he passed, and greeted Edith Carter as she walked out to meet me.

Sweet was the word that immediately came to mind when I saw her. Her silver hair was styled in an attractive short cut, which set off her soft gray-green eyes. She was trim in a dark blue slack outfit and sandals, and looked to be at least 70. We shook hands warmly.

"Linda, I'm so happy to finally have you here. Come in, come in. Let's have some tea and get you settled. Oh, do you like tea?" she added as an afterthought.

"No, I mean yes," I answered. "I'm sorry, my brain cells don't seem to be working as a team." I felt heat rising in my cheeks.

"You're tired, and this is all so new to you. Let's just relax for a while. There's a nice pot roast in the oven. You'll feel better after you eat something."

I noticed that my luggage was no longer by the entryway. Edith saw my blank look and explained, "Charlotte, my housekeeper, took your bags to your room. She'll unpack for you if you don't mind. She's already hung the clothes you sent ahead. If you'd rather do it yourself....." her voice trailed off, waiting for an answer.

"No, of course, I'd appreciate it. Thank you." I sat there. I'll wake up any minute and still be in Detroit. This is surely a dream. Edith picked up her chatter.

"I hope you understand you're not obligated to have meals with me, but I always have extra, so feel free. Charlotte cooks as though my family still lived here. You can use the kitchen whenever you want, if you'd rather cook."

"Thank you. I don't want to impose. You've been so nice. It's really more than I expected, your home and all," I babbled. "I'm trying to fit this all in."

Edith laughed a warm, deep laugh that put me at ease. "Oh Linda. You're almost as I pictured you. A little taller maybe. Since that nice lady, Barbara I think her name was, came to see me about the room and told me about you, I've been looking forward to your arrival. It will be so nice to have a young person in the house again. My three children are out of state. Their lives are so busy I see them only for rare visits. When my husband died last year this house seemed so empty. I couldn't bear to give it up though, too many good memories." She looked around the large room at the pictures grouped on the walls and tables. Happy, smiling faces caught in all manner of activity.

As I surveyed the comfortable furnishings, well-stocked bookshelves, and oriental rugs, I wasn't even sure what room I was in. I assumed it was a living room but it could have been a library, family room, sitting room, or whatever else kind of room rich people have. I couldn't remember feeling so disoriented.

Edith went on, "So I hope you don't mind if an old lady gets carried away once in awhile. I won't bother you. I just would like us to have tea together occasionally. I thought maybe you'd be a little lonely too, being away from your family."

Before I realized what I was doing I went over to Edith's chair and hugged her tightly, then backed away, embarrassed. Edith stood up and returned the hug. Tears filled her eyes.

"You've made me feel very welcome," I mumbled, feeling teary myself. "I'm going to love it here, and I'll enjoy having tea with you, anytime."

Edith gave me a big smile. As if on cue, Charlotte came in with a tea tray holding delicate china cups and saucers, a large steaming teapot, and a plate of oatmeal cookies. Sugar, cream, and sliced lemon completed the array. We set about arranging napkins and filling plates and cups, while Charlotte stood by.

"If you give me the key to your luggage, I'll be glad to unpack for you," Charlotte advised.

I reached into my handbag and handed the keys to her. The tea had a soothing effect and I felt myself loosen up. The smell of pot roast wafted in from wherever the kitchen was, and I silently thanked Edith for planning this meal for me. I was starved. We sipped our tea and ate cookies in silence, both of us recovering from the awkwardness of our earlier get-acquainted moments.

Edith broke the quiet. "You'd probably like to see your room and rest some before dinner."

I'd already put my cup down and leaned back against the soft chair cushion. I was definitely ready. As we proceeded towards the imposing staircase, Edith stopped. "Let me give you a quick tour of the downstairs first. You're free to make yourself comfortable anywhere down here."

I followed her as she led me through hallways and into various rooms. We had been in the living room after all, but there was also a library, sun room, breakfast room, dining room, and a kitchen straight out of "Architectural Digest". Charlotte busied herself making a salad, and looked up long enough to tell me my clothes were hung and my bags put away.

Heading upstairs I saw many more doors but Edith didn't offer to open them. We walked to the end of the hall instead, where she proudly swept open the door to my room. Once again I stood with my mouth open. The room was L-shaped, with a queen-size bed, night tables, and a dresser at one end, and a sitting area with a sofa, bookshelves, and a coffee table at the other. Everything down to the last accessory was coordinated in soft pastels, very feminine. Through French doors I could see a large balcony overlooking the back yard. To my left was a lovely bathroom with separate vanity. The bedroom and bath were about the size of my apartment in Michigan.

"This is beautiful Edith," I told her. "I'll be more than comfortable here."

Edith patted my arm. "Dinner's in an hour. Rest up and I'll see you then." She closed the door behind her.

I walked out onto the balcony and viewed the yard. It had an abundance of flowers, shrubs, and trees, into which various size patios were tucked away. Lounging and dining furniture completed the picture. I drank in the perfumed air and profound silence and realized I was about to become very spoiled.

It was 5:30 pm. I still had my toiletries to set

out. Charlotte had not touched them. Maybe she thought I had strange potions and didn't want me to be further embarrassed. She'd already witnessed my open-mouth routine earlier.

I quickly organized the few items then sank into the sofa, collecting my thoughts. This was Friday. Mary Cappo expected me to call her Monday morning. That left me all weekend to get oriented. Good. I closed my eyes and dozed. When I awoke it was almost 6:30 pm. I was still on Michigan time and the nap refreshed me.

I washed my face and ran a comb through my hair, put on some lipstick, and went downstairs. I followed the good food smells toward the kitchen but as I passed the library I noticed a table set for two near the fireplace. Edith was fussing with the napkins and water goblets, placing them just so.

"There you are", she exclaimed. "I was afraid you were going to stay upstairs."

"I fell asleep. I hope I didn't keep you waiting too long." It was only 6:35.

"No, no. I knew you were tired. Sleep late tomorrow. You'll become adjusted to the new time in a couple of days."

The meal was delicious and I was ravenous. Edith clearly delighted in my enthusiastic response to everything offered. The warmth from the fire and my full stomach mellowed me. Charlotte cleared our plates and brought in apple pie and coffee. Edith and I chatted over dessert and I found myself telling her my life story, a condensed version. She was so easy to talk to, listening intently to everything I said. When she asked why a sweet person like me wasn't married, I went a little pale, and she immediately apologized for being so intrusive. She wasn't of course. Ladies of her generation expected women to be married by my age. I was used to the question. Mom and Aunt Martha had asked it at least every six months.

Thoughts of David grew in my mind. "I came close once, but it didn't work out," I answered, breaking the uncomfortable silence.

"Don't you worry, you have lots of time, you're still young," Edith backtracked now, making my single status seem perfectly normal. She deftly segued into a more practical subject. "Charlotte has emptied shelves for you in the refrigerator and freezer. I knew you'd want your own food favorites. Tomorrow I'll show you where you can shop and pick up some things you might need."

"Thank you," I stifled a yawn.

"This has been a long day for you," Edith added.

"You won't hurt my feelings if you go on upstairs."

"I think I will," I responded, as another yawn overtook me.

"Now, tomorrow there'll be coffee on the sideboard, juice and fruit in the refrigerator, and Charlotte will make you eggs or hot cereal if you'd like," Edith informed me.

"Edith," I felt a little uncomfortable, but went on, "I didn't expect any meals with my room rental, just kitchen privileges. This home, my room, everything, it's already beyond my expectations. I can't impose on you further."

She reached for my hand. "How much can you eat? Charlotte shops for an army. Half the time we throw food away. It's up to you though. If you're in a rush in the morning, feel free to help yourself. Otherwise, you can make your own meals. Oh, by the way," she added, sensing my concern, "there's no extra charge. Your monthly rental is more than enough to cover any meals you have. So that's that!" The subject was dismissed.

We said good night. As I went upstairs I pondered my good fortune. Edith was a warm person with the aura of old money. Charlotte had been with her for 30 years, I'd learned at the dinner table, and they had a protectiveness toward each other. Edith was lonely, it was clear. She had spoken wistfully about her children, now scattered and too busy to visit very often. She had her charity groups and bridge club, but at night when the doors were locked, Edith was alone in a houseful of memories. I sensed I'd be doing her a favor by taking an occasional meal with her. I decided I would do it. I needed someone too.

I prepared for bed. Charlotte had put everything away in an orderly fashion, and left my nightgown and slippers near the vanity where I would see them. As I turned back the covers I noted the soft printed sheets and fluffy pillows. A down comforter rested at the foot of the bed for the cool California nights.

I lay in bed and reviewed the day. So much had happened in 24 hours. I needed another day at least to come down. I was grateful for the upcoming weekend before I faced the realities of the working world.

I drifted into sleep and dreams. In my dream I was the mistress of Edith's beautiful hacienda, graciously pouring tea for David and his parents. David's mother kept hugging me and telling David how lucky he was to have found me. Suddenly she was hugging me too hard and I could barely breathe. Her face close to mine slowly contorted into that of a gargoyle, frightening me. Now she screamed I would never be good enough for David. No, no, no she kept yelling.

I awoke with a start. For a moment I thought I was in my bed back home. The full moon shining through the French doors illuminated my new surroundings, and brought me to the present. The dream left me unsettled. Will the old memories ever be gone?

The bedside clock ticked to the rhythm of my heartbeat. It was 2:30 am. I thought of David and our hopes that were not to be realized. Sadness overtook me. After six years I should be over him but almost anything could remind me of that wonderful senior year when we were together. Instantly time collapsed and old feelings surfaced. Shake it off I told myself. He's probably a successful attorney back in New York, with a proper wife and children, and definitely not thinking about me.

I tossed for a while and then fell into a deep sleep. David visited me in my dreams again. We were walking in the law quad on the Michigan campus, holding hands and laughing. He bent to kiss me and as I returned the kiss, he slowly faded away. I called his name but he never came back. People walking by pointed at me and chanted, "There's no

David," over and over.

This time when I awoke it was 8 am and the sun was streaming into my room. Thank you God for this new day I silently prayed. I wasn't a religious person, but I believed in God. I also believed that no matter how bad things seem, there's always a new day to start over. I was looking forward to this new day.

I stretched, then sat up in bed, plumping my pillows behind me. I surveyed the room and wondered to whom it once belonged. Maybe it was always a guest room. I lifted the telephone receiver on the night table, heard a dial tone, and replaced it on its cradle. Edith had told me last night at dinner that she had the phone activated in my name because she just knew I'd want to make some private calls right away. It was ready. I hadn't called Mom yet. She needed to know I'd arrived safely. It would be past 11 am at home.

I tried Aunt Martha's number but got her message machine. Probably both were out shopping. They're not too worried I surmised. I left a brief message and my new phone number.

I lay back again feeling lazy, my head buzzing with all I wanted to accomplish, when I heard a light rap on the door. I jumped out of bed, searched for my robe, and opened the door to find Edith there with a tray containing orange juice and coffee.

"I know I told you breakfast would be down-stairs, but I heard you stirring and thought you might like a waker-upper in your room on your first morning here," Edith smiled as she placed the tray on the coffee table. "Enjoy the morning, and take your time." She started to leave.

"Thank you Edith," I murmured, once again struck by her thoughtfulness. "Won't you sit with me for a few minutes?"

Edith hesitated, then sat at one end of the sofa. "Just for a minute."

I joined her and poured some juice from the de-canter. It tasted delicious and made me realize how hungry I was. A basket of warm bran muffins nestled against the coffee carafe.

"Charlotte baked them this morning. You must have at least one or she will be hurt," Edith feigned a sorrowful look.

"You're spoiling me shamelessly," I laughed, reaching for a muffin. I was starting to sound like a broken record.

"Did you sleep well last night," Edith queried.

"Yes, like a log." I spared her my fitful dreams.

"This was my daughter Sari's room. I hope you

like it." Edith looked at me expectantly.

"It's perfect. I thought maybe it was the guest room," I added.

"I guess it is now. I was going to put you in the "official" guest room but this room has such a pretty view of the gardens. It's quieter at the end of the hall too."

I wondered how much noise Edith and Charlotte could possibly make, but I appreciated the consideration. I was on my second muffin and cup of coffee.

"Maybe you'd like some cereal or eggs?" Edith asked.

"This is fine. I'm not a big breakfast eater. I think I could live forever on these muffins." I swallowed the last moist bite.

"Charlotte puts everything healthy in them, oats, raisins. I've never been able to duplicate them." Edith stood then. "I'll leave you alone. When you're ready to go out let me know and I'll point you in the direction of the market. There are some specialty shops nearby too."

I straightened the breakfast tray, showered and dressed. It was 10 am. I stepped onto the balcony and breathed the fragrant air. I sat down on a lounge chair, mentally planning my day. Take a walk around the neighborhood, buy some groceries, check the bus lines. My new office was within walking distance but I thought I might do some exploring. What better way than riding a bus around town with the locals, even though I was now a "local" too.

Suddenly I had the urge to call Carol. I went in, found her card, and dialed. She answered on the first ring, with an eagerness in her voice that said she was waiting for a special call.

"Hi, it's Linda," I spoke into the receiver.

There was a slight hesitation. I wasn't the one she was expecting. She recovered quickly and gave me a cheery hello. "Are you safe and sound at Mrs. Carter's?"

"Yes. She's made me feel so at home. My accommodations are great. I'm kind of on a high right now. Reality should set in when I start work next week." I rambled a bit, feeling a little discomforted by the shaky start. "I trust you made it home safely." I said this perfunctorily and was immediately sorry when I remembered the limo pick-up.

"Oh, yes, no problem." Carol made no mention of her means of transportation.

"Well, I wanted to give you my phone number. Maybe we could meet for lunch some time." I realized my lack of a car would limit my mobility. I'll worry about the logistics later I thought.

"I'd love to get together. Wait, let me find a pencil." After some rustling, Carol was back. She took down my number, we made some small talk, and said good-bye.

There's something going on with that woman, I mused. She sure doesn't owe me an explanation though. I looked forward to hearing from her and wondered when it would be.

I brought the breakfast tray downstairs, complimented Charlotte on her scrumptious muffins, and obtained a list of stores and directions from Edith. I grabbed an apple, at Edith's insistence, and put it in my tote.

The day was lovely. Yesterday's overcast skies had given way to bright sunshine. I loved to walk and as I picked up speed, I felt invigorated. The neighborhood was serene. An occasional lawn mower heard from behind discreet walls and hedges provided the only sign of life.

Within 20 minutes I was in a quaint shopping village. Tanned and toned women in shorts pushed strollers or sat at outdoor tables sipping coffee. I became acutely aware of my pale skin and comfortable, but not trendy, clothes. I wondered if there were special laws here on how to look in public and hoped there was a grace period for newcomers.

I selected a few staples at the market, and browsed in the candle shop next door. The smell of lavender filled the air, reminding me of my grandmother's home. I purchased two large candles, bubble bath, and some lavender sachet. I envisioned myself soaking in the large bathtub tonight, with the fragrance of lavender around me.

I'd worked up a thirst by now and a lemonade sounded good. I bought a frosty glass and sat outside drinking slowly and observing the scene. I remembered the apple and ate that. Luxury cars drove in and out of the palm-studded parking lot, depositing smart looking men and women doing their Saturday shopping. If I stay much longer I'll be charged rent I thought, and gathered my things.

The walk back seemed shorter for some reason. I let myself into Edith's house with the key she provided and put my groceries away in the kitchen. The shelves that had been cleared for my use were barely filled by my meager purchases. No one was around.

I went up to my room, wondering if Mom had tried to call. I set out my candles and tucked the sachet into my dresser drawers. It was 3 pm. I hadn't eaten lunch but the lemonade and apple satisfied me. What I really needed was a nap. My restless night and the time change had me yawning. I lay down on the sofa, pulled the quilt over me, and instantly fell asleep.

The incessant ringing of the telephone roused me. I stumbled to the bedside table and groped for the receiver. I cleared my throat and answered, "Hello."

"Linda?" Mom's voice was questioning.

"Hi Mom," my voice still gravelly.

"You sound different." Already California was changing me.

"I was taking a nap. The phone woke me."

"I'm sorry. I'm never going to get this time difference straight. Is everything OK?" There was a slight edge to Mom's voice.

"Yes. Couldn't be better," I assured her. My voice had returned to clarity.

We chatted for a while. Mom wanted a play by play description of everything that happened since we parted. I told her about Carol and Edith and my great new home, careful to keep it all light. Mom was a born worrier, probably praying for my soul as I rambled on.

After we hung up I went downstairs, made myself a sandwich, and visited with Edith. At 9 pm drowsiness overtook me. I excused myself and went to my room. Too tired to luxuriate in the bath I planned earlier, I washed my face and fell into bed. I slept a sound and dreamless sleep for the next nine hours.

Chapter Three

I awoke to sunlight and chirping birds. I stretched, marveling at the difference a good night's sleep makes, and thought about how to spend my last day before rejoining the working world. It was almost 7 am and I felt no rush to get started. I fluffed up my pillow and made myself comfortable. I must have dozed because the telephone startled me awake, and as I reached to answer it I saw it was 8:30.

"Hi Linda," Carol's voice responded to my sleepy hello. "You know if you were in Michigan it would be 11:30 now. Don't tell me I woke you?"

"Yes, no, well sort of. I was awake earlier but I guess I fell back asleep." I sounded apologetic and felt lazy

"Hey, enjoy the relaxation. The alarm clock will be ringing soon enough." Carol's tone was light and happy. "I don't have anything special planned today.

Maybe you'd like me to pick you up and show you around. I'd love to do it."

Carol's tempting offer took me by surprise but I was hesitant to accept. I had no plans but I was certain that the distance between Laguna Hills and Los Angeles was pretty far. It would seem like an imposition.

"Linda, are you there?"

"I'm sorry. I was thinking that it's a long way for you to come here. The offer sounds great though. I wondered what I'd do with myself today."

"I'm used to driving all over. Besides, it's such a gorgeous day it will be a pleasure," Carol enthused.

'OK, give me a chance to get dressed and have some breakfast and you're on."

We agreed to an 11 am pick-up. I gave Carol Edith's address and she assured me she'd find it in her Thomas Guide. I hung up and flew out of bed, suddenly energized by this turn of events. I laid out my prettiest slacks and shirt, with matching sandals that were a last minute purchase back home.

The shower water was invigorating. I let it run over me until my skin tingled. I dressed carefully, glad I'd splurged on the sandals. I made the bed, took a last look at myself in the mirror, and went downstairs. I was ravenous.

Edith was in the backyard and Charlotte was nowhere to be seen. Probably her day off. I called a hello to Edith and began making an omelet and toast.

"Something's eating my petunias," Edith declared as she came in the kitchen door. "Half my plants are gone."

Edith's yard was so lush with flowers it didn't seem that a few petunias would be missed.

"Your yard is gorgeous. You must work in it all the time to keep it that way," I commented as I stirred the eggs.

"Oh I just dabble now and then. My knees aren't what they used to be. My gardener comes twice a week and does most of the work. Did you sleep well?"

"Like a rock. Carol, the lady I met on the plane, called me this morning. She'll be here in an hour to take me sightseeing."

"Good. I'll be puttering in the back. Call me when she arrives so I can meet her." Edith went back out the way she came in.

I lingered over my coffee, looking forward to the day. I thumbed through the Los Angeles Times as I sipped, impressed with the activities one could engage in on a Sunday afternoon. When the doorbell rang it was only 10:45 am. Edith was still in the yard so I answered it, surprised to see Carol so early.

"I hope you don't mind that I'm early but I made such good time," Carol greeted. "I could have driven around for fifteen minutes but decided to come on up."

Carol looked understated and lovely in tan shorts and t-shirt, red sandals, and a red and tan print scarf around her neck. Suddenly my outfit didn't seem quite as attractive.

"You look like a California girl already," Carol went on.

"Come in," I welcomed, my spirits lifted by what I took as a compliment. "I just need to clean my breakfast dishes. Edith wants to meet you too."

Carol followed me through the hallway to the kitchen, oohing and aahing as we went. Edith came in and I made introductions. While they chatted I tidied up. When I finished they were laughing, having discovered Carol's mother and Edith had served at the same charity events over the years. Further confirmation that Carol wasn't a stranger to the privileged life. Edith wished us a pleasant day and we left.

"What a nice lady," Carol said as we walked through the courtyard. "And what a gorgeous house. Some of her antiques are museum quality."

I nodded in agreement even though my knowledge of antiques was almost non-existent. Carol headed to a red convertible with the top down. I slid into the leather passenger seat as she took the wheel. If my friends could see me now, I thought. I watched Carol as she drove away, deftly maneuvering the gentle curves of the street, thinking how beautifully she fit the car. I felt like I was in an ad for "this is the car you drive when you've arrived." This was my third day in my new home. I didn't have to deal with the working world until tomorrow. Today I was ready to sit back and enjoy myself. With Carol leading the way I was sure I would.

We cruised Pacific Coast Highway, the wind blowing our hair, then stopped for lunch at a fish house on the water in Malibu. Our window table afforded a perfect view of sailboats bobbing among the waves. We watched as we peeled shrimp and drank wine. After coffee and scrumptious peach pie, we were on the road again.

"In the mood for some shopping?" Carol asked as we turned onto the highway.

"Sure." The sun, the wine, and the good food had mellowed me. I felt carefree and shopping easily fit my mood.

"You need to see Rodeo Drive. Every designer who counts is there," Carol added.

Well that's good news I laughed to myself.

Designer boutiques had not been on my shopping list before today.

We drove up Sunset and over to Wilshire Blvd. Pretty soon we reached Rodeo Drive where the shop windows with their fashionably dressed mannequins beckoned. Carol parked in a nearby garage and we window-shopped in earnest. Occasionally we went inside and tried on shoes or jackets, none of which I could afford. We were looking at Hermes silk scarves when Carol picked one up, held it against my shirt, and then tied it jauntily around my neck. It brightened my face and gave my outfit a whole new look.

"See, this is meant for you," Carol enthused as she fussed with it to make it just right.

I looked at the price tag. I had coats that cost less than this wispy piece of silk. Yet I had to admit that it really looked good, and I figured I could wear it with other outfits. In a moment of weakness, or maybe strength, I don't know which, I agreed. It was meant for me. I made the purchase. The saleslady removed the price tag and began to box the scarf when I took it from her.

"I'll wear it home." I experienced the same excitement I remembered as a little girl, wearing new shoes home from the store, while carrying the old ones in the box.

Carol was casually browsing through the dress racks, saw I was finished, and joined me. I had the scarf around my neck before we were out the door.

As we walked, people frequently turned to give Carol a second look. She was oblivious to it. I wondered what it felt like to be as pretty as she was and not notice. All the shopping had made me tired and hungry, even though we'd finished lunch barely three hours earlier. Carol must have been hungry too. She suggested we stop again.

"You read my mind. I don't know where my appetite's coming from," I responded.

"Shopping can do that. I know a good Italian restaurant in Brentwood. We're not far. Is Italian OK?"

"Yes. A big salad and some pasta sounds good."

We drove in silence through the city streets. Soon we were in Brentwood and Carol pulled into a parking lot next to an ivy-covered building that appeared to be an old home. Bougainvillea bloomed profusely on trellises that surrounded a covered porch half-filled with diners.

"Good!" We're early enough to eat outside, if that suits you," Carol exclaimed.

"Fine with me."

We were seated at a corner table with a lovely view

of the garden and its bubbling fountain. As I studied the menu I felt relaxed and peaceful. I wanted to do something nice for Carol, but didn't know what. We ordered and sat for a while, enjoying the view.

"Linda, I think you'd like doing what I do," Carol said unexpectedly.

"Work for Probation? What makes you say that?" Her comment puzzled me.

Carol sipped her iced tea and looked past me for a few seconds before answering. "Today you spoke about your former students in such a caring way. You mentioned how rewarding it was to have a family conference and see a breakthrough in learning. I know you wanted a change but I'm afraid being a copy editor won't give you the same challenges."

"I'm not so sure. This whole move has been a challenge. It wouldn't bother me if editing seemed quiet by comparison. At least for a while."

"What happens when 'a while' passes?" Carol persisted.

"It may not. There are growth opportunities. It's a new publishing branch and I should be able to move ahead as it expands."

"Orange County is heading for a real hiring frenzy in the next few months. They need good people. People with backgrounds like yours."

"I know very little about law enforcement," I countered.

"You'll be trained in what you need to know about that. But you know people, and how to work with them. It's much harder to train for that, though heaven knows, the department tries."

"I don't know Carol. I'd feel like I was letting down Grenville Publishing. I owe it to them and myself to give the job a chance."

The waiter brought our salads and a basket of hot bread. Conversation halted while we enjoyed the food. I thought about Carol's comments. It was flattering to me that she thought I could meet Probation's standards, but my chances of pursuing such a job were pretty remote. I had no car and Orange County was at least 40 miles away. Besides, I was looking forward to being with a publishing company and wanted to give it my best shot.

"Linda, I hope you don't think that I see your new job as ....," Carol was grasping for the least offensive word, "boring or ....whatever."

"Hey, it's OK. I appreciate your interest and I'm flattered too." I smiled as I said it and Carol relaxed.

"It's just that I've been thinking a lot about my own job lately, some conflicts to resolve, and I've made a tough decision. I plan to act on it soon."

Carol's voice trailed off.

My fork stopped in mid-air. I looked at her quizzically. "You're not leaving your job are you?"

"No, not at all." Carol brightened. "Oh how did I get on this subject. We were having such fun and I turned into a heavy. I don't know why I even made that last statement. Forget it and let's concentrate on which decadent dessert we're going to have."

"We haven't had our entrée yet and you're on the dessert menu," I laughed. Almost on cue our plates of pasta arrived. The sunlight peeking through the trellis and the candles flickering on each table cast lovely shadows on the porch walls. We spent the next hour finishing our pasta, sharing a tiramisu, and lingering over espresso. Our conversation remained light and cheery.

Carol dropped me off at Edith's shortly after 8:30 pm. I thanked her for the wonderful day and she wished me luck on my first day at work. Carol promised to call by mid-week to see how I was doing. I stood waving as her car faded in the distance, and felt a shiver. I shook it off and went up the walk.

Edith was in the library when I came in. A pot of tea sat before her with several cups and saucers. A cookie tray sat next to the teapot. Several missing

cookies left a gaping space in what had been an art-
ful arrangement. Edith waved for me to join her.

"Did you have some company?" I asked as I
poured myself a cup of tea.

"My son Conner came by for a few minutes.
He's here on business. I didn't even know until
he showed up at the door full of apologies for not
calling." The telling of it seemed to make her sad.
"Then after all that he could barely stay. I wanted
you to meet him."

"That would have been nice."

"Next time, he said. But who knows when that
will be. How was your day?" brighter now.

"Almost perfect," I enthused. I told Edith about
our sightseeing, shopping, and meals. Edith admired
my scarf and we chatted for the next few minutes.
Then I excused myself to turn in. I wanted to be fresh
for my first day on the job. I also wanted to luxuriate
in the tub bath I'd promised myself yesterday.

I soaked in the lavender suds until my skin
looked wrinkled and white. I settled into bed totally
relaxed, eager to start my week and be part of the
mainstream again. The alarm was set for 7:00 am. I
turned out the light and had the last peaceful night I
would know for quite a while.

Chapter Four

"Good morning, Grenville Publishing." Barbara Nelson's voice was bright at 8:30 am.

"Good morning yourself. It's Linda, Linda Davenport."

"Well, well, you made it. Welcome to California! Are you settled in?"

"Pretty much. I can't thank you enough for finding Edith Carter for me. She's a wonderful lady, and her house ...... I'm at a loss for words," I trailed off.

"You'll be the envy of your friends. You're lucky I already have a house. I was tempted to move in with Edith." Barbara laughed, then turned serious. "Mary left a message for you. She wants you to come in by 10 am to sign your employment papers. She left the packet with me. She would handle this herself except she and Mr. Thompson are in a meeting with some people from our parent company. Mary thought it might last all morning."

"Fine. I just need some directions to the office."

Barbara gave me the streets I needed to follow and estimated it would be a 20-minute walk. I was already dressed but hadn't eaten breakfast. I had plenty of time to take care of that and read the paper too.

Edith was in the breakfast room with her pot of tea. Charlotte, back from her day off, was fussing with something that looked like lamb chops. I poured myself some orange juice and coffee and sat down with Edith.

"My you look nice. Ready for your new job?" she asked.

"I hope so. I feel ready." I sipped my juice.

"Charlotte made me an omelet but I could only eat half. How about having the other half with one of her famous muffins?" Edith was determined to feed me.

"You twisted my arm." In no time Charlotte popped the omelet into the microwave, took a muffin from the warming oven, and prepared a plate for me. While I ate Edith chatted about her children and their busy lives. When I asked her about her weekday routine she quickly responded.

"Oh, I'm busy enough. I play Bridge two or three days, volunteer at the library book store, have lunch with friends, crochet," Edith stopped.

"Sounds boring, doesn't it?"

"No Edith, it sounds pleasurable and at your age you've earned it," I said emphatically.

"That's what my kids say. But they still wish I'd sell the house and move to something smaller."

Charlotte glanced up from her work and made a not so subtle grimace.

Edith went on, "This house still has my family's presence everywhere. I never feel alone, even though I might get lonely. I just have to look around and I'm filled with love. A new place would be empty. Oh my goodness, listen to me, getting maudlin. Well, my heart is here and I can't help it. Having Charlotte is a blessing too."

I was sorry I brought the subject up. I didn't want Edith to be sad. I glanced at my watch. It was 9:30. I cleared my breakfast dishes and put them in the dishwasher, grabbed my purse and said good-bye. Edith and Charlotte wished me a good day and I was off.

The directions were easy to follow. I had on comfortable walking shoes and savored the exercise. My high heels were in my tote, to be put on before I entered the office. I rounded the last corner and there, looming before me, was the twenty story building that housed Grady, Inc., and at least a hundred other companies. It was 9:55. Barbara had the walking time right to the minute. I changed my shoes and headed for the elevators. Grenville Publishing was on the fifth floor.

The doors opened to a quiet lobby. I passed through an arch and more double doors, and was face to face with Barbara. She was 40ish, plump, and altogether pleasant looking. The rare person whose voice matched her face. We shook hands and went to a small office near the reception area. It was nicely furnished but didn't look like anyone worked in it. Barbara, the mindreader, noted my expression and volunteered that this office was used for interviews and wasn't assigned to anyone. She motioned for me to sit at the desk while she took a seat in the chair opposite.

Barbara spread the contents of the packet on the desk, identified each document, and showed me where I needed to sign. She left me alone to review everything and promised she would be back shortly to answer any questions. For the next few minutes I read and signed. The paperwork reflected what I had been told earlier about salary and benefits. No surprises. I was well satisfied. I arranged the papers in a neat stack and sat back, waiting for Barbara.

The upper half of the office wall facing the corridor was glass. I looked out and saw no one. The few desks within sight were empty. It was 10:30 am. Where was everyone? A flurry of activity suddenly erupted as double doors flew open and several men and women hurried out of a conference room. I recognized Mary Cappo, who looked flushed and not at all the in-control person I remembered. Barbara met her mid way. They conversed for a minute then simultaneously looked in my direction. Both proceeded into the office where I waited.

Mary greeted me warmly. "Linda, I'm so sorry I wasn't here to orient you. Mr. Grady called an all-staff meeting this morning. He doesn't call them very often, but when he does, they take precedence over everything else. We're on a short break now so I'll need to go back in soon. I don't know when we'll be finished."

"I understand. Barbara's given me the paperwork. It's all signed."

Mary glanced towards the conference room. People were starting to return. "I need to get moving. Barbara, would you give Linda her copies and show her around the office? Also, pull together the latest drafts on the "Blue Moon" series and have Linda look at them. Hopefully I'll be out by noon."

Barbara picked up the papers, and we all followed Mary out of the office and watched her disappear into the conference room. In minutes the double doors were shut and once again, silence. Barbara went to her desk, riffled through the papers and began tearing off sheets, stapling them together, and then handing them to me. She placed the remaining documents in a folder bearing my name and secured the folder in a file cabinet behind her desk. Next to the cabinet was a large door with the name "Harold Thompson, Managing Editor" on it. I wondered which one of the conference room group he was.

"Would you like some coffee before the grand tour?" Barbara asked.

"No thanks. I'm ready as is." I was feeling restless. There was a tone to the office that made me uncomfortable. Although the environment was unfamiliar, something didn't seem right. Even Barbara seemed a little on edge.

We went up and down the halls. Barbara efficiently identified offices and who occupied them. I learned that Grenville Publishing was less than a year old and still suffering growing pains. This bit of news didn't increase my comfort level. Barbara noted, however, that even Grady, Inc. had a rocky first year but was now amazingly successful. It didn't help.

We finished with a swing by the rest rooms and lounge, and ended up back at the office I had used to sign my papers. I sat down while Barbara retrieved the drafts Mary wanted me to read. They turned out to be numerous. I'd be occupied for at least an hour.

I read through "Blue Moon", captivated by the clever story line and how each small book in the series built on the previous one to become an increasing challenge to the young reader. I was on the last book when the conference room doors opened, disgorging the Grenville staff. People with red faces hurried to desks and phones. I searched for Mary but didn't see her. She was the last to leave, along with a tall, heavy-set man. They were both clutching files and looked exhausted. They headed towards me.

"Linda, I'd like you to meet Harold Thompson," Mary's voice had a reedy quality.

I extended my hand to meet his. "So nice to finally meet you Mr. Thompson."

"My pleasure," he replied, "and please, call me Harold. This is not the way I hoped your first day would go. I trust Barbara has started your orientation."

"Yes, she's been a great help." I didn't mention that I still didn't know where my office would be. That seemed like an important part of my orientation.

Harold and Mary shuffled their feet, then Harold

excused himself to make some phone calls. Before he left he suggested that Mary and I might want to have lunch together. Mary nodded. So did I. Saying she needed five minutes to drop off her files and make a call, she hurried off. I watched the office scene. Staff who weren't on the telephone were huddled in twos and threes, whispering and gesturing. I could have been invisible for the all the notice I received from them.

Mary returned still looking a little frantic. "We're done meeting until 3 pm today. Let's have a long lunch and I'll fill you in."

I had been puzzled by the morning's activity but wasn't sure getting filled in would make me feel much better. When I was teaching, and meetings like this were called, it usually meant programs were being cancelled and someone would be getting a lay-off notice. I was the new kid on the block here. My future didn't seem too secure at the moment.

We walked to a nearby restaurant and took a table in an alcove near the back. We both ordered chef salads and iced tea, then made small talk for a few minutes. How was my flight, were my accommodations satisfactory, hasn't the weather been beautiful.....? I was ready to grab Mary by the lapels of her tailored suit and scream, "fill me in, already" when she actually did.

"I'm not sure where to begin," Mary faltered. "As I told you when we first met, Grenville is a new subsidiary of Grady, Inc. We've had a slow but steady expansion. Mr. Grady himself thinks we're a great addition to his company. But he's a businessman, first and foremost. Last Friday he told Harold that he had some announcements to make and called this morning's meeting. His announcements were quite a surprise." She stopped and sipped her tea. The salads had arrived but remained untouched. I sat in rapt attention.

Mary went on, "Have you heard of Wainwright Publishing?"

I nodded. They were based in New York and grew larger each year by acquiring smaller companies that showed promise.

"Wainwright wants to buy Grenville and merge it with one of their companies. They think the merger will be beneficial to both and have offered Grady, Inc. an obscene amount of money to do it." Mary sighed and leaned back in her chair, relieved that the news was out. She watched my face intently, looking for a reaction.

I sat immobile, waiting for more. After a short staring contest I realized Mary wasn't going to give up any additional information until I made some comment first.

"From the expressions on everyone's faces earlier, the sale looks like a done deal. What's supposed to happen at 3 pm?" This was enough to restart Mary.

"Well, it's not exactly a done deal. Maybe 90%. Mr. Grady had some loose ends he wanted to tie up. He thought that would be done by three o'clock. We'll then learn what the future holds for Grenville, and its staff." Mary hesitantly added the last part.

I looked down at my salad, slowly getting warm. Little beads of oil were forming on the slivers of cheese. My appetite had left ten minutes ago. I was sure the answer to my next question wouldn't help bring it back.

"I haven't officially started with Grenville. Where will I fit into all this?" I tried to be upbeat, but sounded pleading instead.

Mary empathized with my position. Hers wasn't too solid right now either, she was quick to say.

"I wish I could be more specific," she continued. "I can tell you that Mr. Grady is fair, so whatever happens, he'll do the best he possibly can for everyone. Try not to worry about it. Let's have our lunch. Afterward you can go on home. There really won't be anything for you to do at the office under the circumstances. Be back at 9 am tomorrow and we'll have a game plan." With that she picked up her fork and poked around in her salad.

The end of discussion had been signaled. I made a feeble attempt to eat, mostly because Mary was doing such a good job pretending she was ravenous. We ate and spoke of lighter things, but tension hung between us. I felt for Mary. She seemed to be a genuinely sincere person who must be feeling a little guilty having encouraged me to come here, then this. She carried the burden of both our futures.

"Mary, whatever happens, I needed a jolt in my life. Well, maybe not this much of a jolt." Levity wasn't working. "I'm still glad I'm here. I want you to know that."

"Thank you," Mary murmured, her eyes welling. She went back to her salad in earnest.

We finished our lunch in silence. Mary insisted on paying the bill. We said our goodbyes at the corner and I watched her hurry off to find out what changes were about to take place.

The afternoon stretched before me. I wasn't ready to go home so I headed toward the village shops I visited Saturday. I strolled in and out of stores, occasionally catching my reflection in a mirror. What a sad sack! Brighten up. At least wait until tomorrow to decide whether you should be sad. I wanted to talk to Carol but figured she'd be at work. She'd have something to say about this, probably insist I try her line of work for sure.

When I reached home Edith was in the kitchen. She heard me and called for me to come and tell her about my first day. She didn't seem surprised I was back before 5 pm.

I filled her in. Charlotte chopped vegetables at the sink but didn't miss a word.

"Oh my dear," Edith twisted her hanky. "That wasn't what I expected."

"Me neither. Edith, you should have seen the place. People running to phones, huddling with each other. Worry on everyone's faces."

"Why don't you join me for dinner? Charlotte's making some lovely lamb chops and as usual made too many. You don't want to eat alone tonight."

"Thanks. I will. I'll go and freshen up and come down at 6. Is that OK?"

"Fine," Edith responded. She seemed happy that she didn't have to talk me into dinner this time.

I took off my suit and pulled on slacks and a sweater. It's probably too early to call Carol but I can leave a message on her machine, I reasoned. I so badly wanted to confide in her. As I expected, her machine answered. I left a brief message for her to call me tonight, hung up, and went out on the balcony. I lay on the chaise, trying to compose my thoughts and be optimistic about tomorrow, but my gut told me otherwise. I decided not to work myself up over something I had no control over. Tomorrow will come soon enough. At least I'll know then what I have to face.

Dinner was pleasant. Edith chattered about her children, her garden, her beach house that she never used, everything but my dilemma. I'd grown very fond of her in my few short days and knew Id miss her if I had to leave. After what seemed like a respectful time, I excused myself for an early bed.

I climbed the stairs, dreading tomorrow, yet hoping it would come quickly so I could make plans. Not knowing was the worst.

I read for a while then turned out the light. As sleepy as I was, I couldn't seem to settle down. When I finally did, I tossed and turned, waking almost every hour. I wondered why Carol hadn't called me. Tomorrow I'll have lots more to tell her I thought as I drifted off again.

Chapter Five

"We're so sorry." It was said in unison. I sat across from Harold Thompson, his huge desk between us. Mary Cappo fidgeted next to me. They gave a nervous laugh at their unplanned duet, while I digested the message I'd just been given. I probably set the record for the shortest career at Grenville Publishing, less than 24 hours.

"Please understand," Harold cleared his throat, "if we had had any idea this was going to happen, we would not have lured you from Detroit."

I silently laughed at his choice of words. Almost anyone could have "lured" me. They just happened to be first with some very good bait.

Grenville was no more, swallowed up by Wainwright Publishing. Harold and Mary were going to New York for the transition. Several Grenville staff members were being absorbed by other divisions of Grady, Inc. The rest were being let go. I fell into the last group. Mary had said Mr. Grady was fair. He turned out to be hugely generous too, or motivated by guilt, because he gave me three months' salary and plane fare back to Detroit.

"We do regret this Linda," Mary declared, taking my hand in hers. "This would have been a great working relationship."

Strangely enough I was not upset. I had felt worse yesterday. The severance pay, plus my healthy bank account, would hold me while I looked for something else. I would have to decline the plane ticket to Detroit. Returning under these circumstances was not a scene I wanted to be in. Mom would fight the urge to say "I told you so" but would lose the battle before I unpacked my suitcases.

No, I'll stay here. Grenville brought me here. I can thank them for that. As I organized my thoughts, I realized we had been sitting in uncomfortable silence. Mary still had hold of my hand.

"I think it would have been a great working relationship, too. I'm sorry we'll never find out," I responded. Mary relaxed her grip. "But I'm here now and I plan to make a life for myself in California. Thank you for having the confidence in me to offer me a job in the first place. I'm sure something will turn up."

Harold stood up. Mary followed. There really wasn't anything else to say. We all wished each other good luck, and it was over.

It was only 10:30 am. I could go back to Edith's and look at the job ads in today's Los Angeles Times, but I had all afternoon for that. Instead I stopped at a nearby Starbucks for coffee and a roll, and watched the passing scene. People hurrying in all directions, each seeming to have a sense of purpose. Here I sat, three thousand miles from what had been my home, and jobless to boot. If this turned out to be a dream, I wouldn't be surprised. I sipped my coffee and made a plan. Polish my resume and scour the ads for something challenging. I could write and had good analytical ability. There would be something for me in this job market.

Energized, I walked home. Edith was out. I was relieved since I didn't feel ready to be buried in sympathy just yet. I decided to call Carol again. I knew I'd hear her message machine but if I told her how urgent it was to call me, she'd do so, especially since she hadn't called back yesterday.

Instead of the machine, a male voice came on.

"I must have the wrong number," I mumbled. "I was trying to reach Carol Alder."

"This is her home," he responded. "Who is this?"

"Linda Davenport, a recent friend of Carol's. Is she home today, by chance?"

"No, she had an accident yesterday. I'm her brother Gregory," his voice broke. "It's serious."

"Serious.........how serious?" I gasped, my legs turning to jelly. Please let her be OK I prayed.

"Her car went off the road and into a steep ravine. She was heading east on the Ortega Highway, going pretty fast I guess from the looks of her car. She's on life support." Gregory fell silent.

I sank to the floor. Tears rolled down my cheeks. I couldn't believe what I was hearing.

"We just spent all day Sunday together. This can't be happening. Can I stay in touch with you?"

I heard muffled sobs. "Yes, call me here. Thank you for your concern."

After we hung up I sat motionless for what seemed like hours. Sounds emanated from downstairs. Suddenly I wanted to talk to Edith, cry on her shoulder. I was ready for all the comfort she could give. I went down.

Edith took one look at me and dropped her embroidery.

"What's wrong?" she cried as she headed towards me.

The words tumbled out between the tears. All

the tension and pent up feeling from the last two days bubbled up and spewed out like an unwatched pot of water left boiling too long.

"You lost your job and your friend is dying. Oh you poor dear!" Edith exclaimed as she held my hands.

I'd never said dying. I was sure of that. But we both knew what life support meant, and when Edith used the word the reality of Carol's accident unleashed another flood of tears. Edith's eyes were wet as she held me with such patience and loving care, until my emotions were spent. We sat on the sofa in silence. The sun was setting and the living room grew dark. Still no one moved.

Charlotte, who had kept a discreet distance, now tentatively entered the room with a tea tray. Edith seemed to enjoy a pot of tea for any occasion and this one was a doozy. Charlotte pressed a wall switch and soft lights went on. She busily arranged the cups and small sandwiches so they were within our reach, and left the room.

I dabbed my eyes with what was left of a shredded tissue. We both sat up straight, stretched at the same time, and laughed at the synchronicity of it. Laughing felt good after all the tears and infused me with some energy. Edith poured two steaming cups of tea and I gratefully accepted the cup she offered. I took a sandwich too. It was past dinnertime and I was a little hungry. Edith had probably missed dinner too from the way she munched on her sandwich.

"The job part wasn't as devastating as I thought it would be. I mean I was disappointed, but I had last night to think about options. In fact, when I came home today I felt pretty good. I decided to stay here and look for something else." I paused to take another sandwich. "I can update my resume and see what happens. I was given a generous severance pay, and that along with my savings, will see me through for a good while."

Edith listened intently. She seemed relieved I was able to speak again.

"But then I called Carol......," I had to stop to catch my breath and keep my composure. "Everything just fell apart. That sweet person, and her brother's just torn up."

"Do you know what happened?" Edith asked hesitantly.

I realized that I had only told her there'd been an auto accident and nothing about the circumstances. I didn't know much more myself but volunteered what Gregory had said.

"The Ortega Highway, that treacherous road,"

Edith said, shaking her head.

"You know it?"

"Oh, yes. It's a winding two lane road that connects Orange County with Riverside County, about 28 miles of blind curves and steep drop-offs that cut through the Cleveland National Forest. The Ortega is the only real connector between south Orange County and the city of Lake Elsinore at the other end. It's really a beautiful, scenic drive. Unfortunately people drive it too fast and take chances passing on blind curves. The Ortega is called 'blood alley' for good reason. Accidents there are usually fatal."

I sucked in my breath. The possibility of Carol dying was unthinkable to me.

Edith continued. "Do you have any idea why she was on the Ortega?"

"No. Maybe her brother does. He said her damaged car look like she'd been going fast. That puzzles me because on Sunday she impressed me as an extremely cautious driver."

"Linda, we'll just pray for a good outcome. In the meantime rest up. You'll be fresher tomorrow. When you call Carol's brother you'll probably hear good news too." Edith's voice was more hopeful than the look on her face.

I trudged up the stairs to my room, ran a hot

bath, and soaked for an hour. Last Friday I arrived here, this was only Tuesday, yet in four days I'd had more upheaval than the last four years.

I toweled off, wanting to call Gregory, but decided to wait until morning. Chances are he was at the hospital anyway. I went to bed, anxious for, and yet dreading, tomorrow. Please God, I prayed, don't let Carol suffer. I slept fitfully, dreaming crazy dreams I couldn't remember in the morning.

The telephone at Carol's rang several times. It was 11 am and I could wait no longer to talk to Gregory. The machine must be off I thought as I was about to hang up. Then I heard his hoarse voice answering.

"This is Linda Davenport. I hate to trouble you but I wanted to inquire about Carol."

"Linda……. Carol died last night," then silence.

"I'm so sorry," I answered feebly. "Is there anything I can do?" My voice sounded like it was coming from somewhere else.

"No. There won't be a service. Carol wanted to be cremated. When our parents died we decided then that we didn't want any prolonged grieving if something happened to one of us. I never thought we'd be dealing with it so soon." Gregory gave a deep sigh.

"Please take my number. If there's anything at all I can do, ever, please call me."

I could hear him fumbling for something and then he took down my number, thanked me, and hung up. I placed the receiver on its stand, sunk to the floor, and sobbed uncontrollably. Why, why, why? No answers came, nor could there be any that made sense. Eventually I composed myself and went downstairs to tell Edith the bad news.

Chapter Six

I needed a car. A week had gone by since I lost both my job and my friend and the only way I could handle the despair was through activity. The resumes I'd sent out resulted in responses from companies all over Los Angeles and the bus service was inadequate for travelling efficiently between interviews.

As I scanned the car ads, circling those that had appeal, the ring of my phone startled me. I was more surprised to hear Gregory Alder on the line.

"Linda, I hope you don't mind me calling. I was wondering if we could talk?"

"Talk? I'd be glad to. I've been worrying about you all week. How have you been?"

"Taking it a day at a time I guess. That's what everyone tells me to do. What I want to talk about I'd rather do in person. Can I pick you up, take you to dinner, soon?"

"Sure, if you'd like. When?"

"Is tonight OK? I can be at your house by 7 pm." There was extreme urgency in his voice.

I gave him the address and directions, then hung up, thoroughly puzzled by this turn of events. I couldn't imagine what he wanted to say that couldn't be said on the telephone. I went back to the car ads but couldn't keep my mind on them. It was 2 pm. A brisk walk would help my pent-up energy I decided, then maybe I'd be able to concentrate on my car search.

The bell rang at exactly 7 pm. I had envisioned Gregory Alder to be the male counterpart of Carol. Instead, a husky, brunet man, about my height, greeted me. My expression must have given me away. As Gregory extended his hand he said, "I know, you were expecting a Carol look-alike."

I laughed, slightly embarrassed. "I guess I was, but I do see a resemblance."

He had the same sweetness in his face that made Carol so endearing, but with a more masculine slant. His eyes seemed to hold the same sincerity, now shadowed by sadness. No wonder, losing his sister so tragically.

"Please come in," I offered as I stepped aside from the doorway.

Gregory was dressed casually in slacks and an open shirt. I was glad I was not overdressed in my blouse, skirt, and sandals. I had tied on the scarf I'd bought with Carol, which now had sentimental value to me.

"Thank you for seeing me on such short notice. You must be wondering what this is all about. I assure you I won't be wasting your time."

"I am puzzled, I confess, but I'm glad for the chance to meet you. I'm only sorry it has to be this way."

"We probably would have met eventually. Carol spoke to me about meeting you on the plane and how much she liked you. She thought it was the beginning of a long friendship." Gregory's voice cracked.

I was relieved to see Edith come in. Introductions were made and we engaged in small talk for a while. Edith kept everything light with her chatter so by the time we left the mood had softened.

Gregory settled me in the car, then took the driver's side. As he pulled away his next words increased my already heightened curiosity.

"I know a nice place in Santa Monica where

we can have a secluded table. I often take clients there when I want to talk privately. I made 7:30 reservations."

"Fine," I responded.

We drove in silence the few miles to Santa Monica while I wondered why we had to sit where we could speak privately. I glanced at Gregory. His jaw was set and he concentrated on the road ahead, deftly maneuvering in and out of traffic. I wanted to say something, but somehow his resolute manner did not invite conversation. He's taken the lead so far, I guess he can continue.

We pulled up to valet parking and soon were being shown to our table. The restaurant appeared as though it had once been someone's house, with several rooms of various sizes. We were seated in a little alcove that looked out to gardens and the ocean beyond. Under other circumstances I would have enjoyed the surroundings immensely. Tonight I was too tense.

"Do you like wine?" Gregory asked while he studied the wine list. "I was thinking of ordering a bottle of Chardonnay. They have one here from the Napa Valley that is excellent."

"Yes, I enjoy it, and I've heard so much about California wines I'd love to try what you suggest."

Gregory ordered wine and some appetizers and then gazed out the window until they were brought to the table. After the customary tasting and pouring, he waved off the waiter and turned to me.

"Linda, I apologize for keeping you in suspense. I wouldn't blame you if you left. I hope when you hear what I have to say you'll understand why I've been so mysterious."

"You did have me wondering what I was getting into."

"I know, I know. Here's the thing. I've been trying to recreate Carol's last few days. The day she had the accident she didn't go into her office until 10 am. She stayed behind closed doors until she left at 1 pm, signing out to the field. According to her secretary, this was unusual, as Carol rarely kept her door shut, and never left the office without giving her a specific destination where she could be reached. When her secretary asked her where she'd be, Carol jokingly answered 'it's a secret' and would call in for messages.

"Linda, you spent the day before with her. Did she say or do anything unusual? It seems you're the last one who had any real conversation with her." Gregory sat back and took a sip of his wine. He looked weary.

So this was it. A grieving brother wanted to account for his sister's last hours.

"You know I just met Carol. I don't know enough about her personality to recognize when she's not herself. She seemed pretty happy to me," I offered lamely.

"Since Carol's death I've been torn up. I admit it. But my mind is perfectly clear on this. Carol wasn't the same person these last few months. We were always close, could talk about anything. Then there started to be areas that were off limits. Her demeanor changed. She used to bubble about her job but started to become cynical.

"I sensed she was seeing someone, but she wouldn't talk about it. I used to know as much about her dates as she did. I last spoke to her after she arrived home from Detroit. I had wanted to pick her up at the airport but she said she'd take the shuttle, not wanting to trouble me."

My mind suddenly flashed to the limousine and the pant leg I glimpsed when Carol stepped in. It was no shuttle she had entered. I realized Gregory was leading up to something and it was more than a grieving brother's concern.

He continued, "So I called her at home that night to ask about her trip. She had visited an old friend but I think that it was an excuse to get away from whatever had changed her these last months."

"How did she seem on the phone?"

"A little brighter, but tired. She told me all about you. Then she said something strange." He paused and searched my face, probably wondering if I believed any of this. "She said I'd soon be seeing the old Carol again but she might have a few bruises. Then she laughed and said she had to hang up but she'd call me in a few days. I never talked to her again."

Gregory's face was tense. He crumpled the napkin on his lap.

"So you see," he went on, "you spent the last day with her and I'm desperate to gain any insight into what she planned to do."

"She did say something now that I think of it." I had recalled our restaurant conversation about her job and how intense she became. "Carol suggested I might prefer working in probation for the variety and challenges. Then she apologized for appearing to demean my publishing job. Kind of funny now since I don't even have a job. Anyway, she mentioned that she'd been thinking a lot about her own job and she was going to make a tough decision. When I tried to pursue it with her she laughed it off and changed the subject, said she didn't want to turn our nice day into a 'heavy', or something like that."

"See, there was something brewing. Please, can you think of anything else, anything at all?" Gregory pleaded.

I wondered if I should mention the airport limo. He would know Carol had lied to him and I didn't want to diminish her in his eyes. Or maybe it would just show she changed her mind at the last minute and accepted another offer. I'd let him decide.

"I did see her get into a black limousine at the airport. There appeared to be a man in the back seat but I saw only his pant leg." I watched Gregory's face but his tense expression didn't change. "I don't know if that means anything. I thought I should mention it."

"It just adds to the mystery surrounding Carol. Maybe the man she was seeing picked her up. I always had the feeling whoever it was was influential or married, or had something to hide. The relationship didn't seem to make her happy and I couldn't get her to talk about it." Gregory sat back and sipped his wine. "I feel like I let her down."

"How? It was obvious to me that she loved you very much from the way she spoke. Besides, she was an adult and had her own life. Maybe she knew you wouldn't agree with what she was doing. Whatever it was." I wanted my words to ease Gregory's mind but I knew so little.

"I'm sorry to put this burden on you. Why don't we order dinner?" Gregory signaled the waiter, who brought our dinner menus.

My head reeled, and all the dinner items looked the same. "Would you order for me? You've been here and know what's good."

"If you like jumbo shrimp, you'll love theirs" Gregory suggested.

I nodded and he proceeded to order shrimp for both of us. We sat quietly but there was sadness between us. After a few minutes Gregory leaned forward, almost whispering.

"I let Carol down because I couldn't save her life. I should have been more persistent with her, tried to help her even when she resisted."

"It was an accident. What could anyone have done?" I countered.

"No Linda. That's what I've been trying to lead up to. What happened to Carol was no accident."

"What are you saying?"

"I'm saying that somebody caused Carol's car to go off the road. Probably lured her there."

"That's quite a leap." Shivers ran up my neck.

"Why do you think this?"

"Carol was a very safe driver. After our parents were killed she became even more cautious. She never drove fast or took any chances. She called herself the 'little old lady from Pasadena' when she was behind the wheel."

"Safe drivers have accidents. Edith told me how treacherous the Ortega Highway is. She may have misjudged a curve in the road."

"No, I'll never believe that. Her car was estimated to be going over 80 miles per hour when it went over the side. She would have to be forced to go that fast. And she hated the Ortega, had a true fear of it. There was no reason I know of for her to be on it. She once told me if she was ever transferred to the boys camp Probation operated near Lake Elsinore she'd quit before she'd drive 23 miles on the Ortega to reach it." Gregory shook his head. "No, it wasn't an accident."

I was speechless. It was a relief when the waiter brought our dinners, although my appetite had slowly waned listening to Gregory. I picked at the succulent shrimp and wished I could have eaten them under different circumstances. Gregory also toyed with his food and finally requested "to go" boxes for us.

"I sure know how to ruin an evening, don't I?" he said.

"No, you're upset and concerned about your sister's death. I'm flattered you'd share your thoughts with me. I only wish I could be more helpful."

"You have been. Please don't think I'm strange. I won't rest until I figure out what truly happened to Carol. Who caused her accident, and why."

"Have you talked to the police?"

Gregory looked defeated. "The Orange County Sheriff has jurisdiction where Carol's car went off the road. As far as they're concerned it was an accident. They won't even listen to me."

"Isn't it their job to listen? Didn't you tell them what you told me?"

"I tried to. The first officer on the scene, Jim Randall, listened to me initially. He thought there should be longer skid marks. It looked like Carol braked for only about ten yards before she went over. He believed if she were losing control she would have sensed it sooner, put on the brakes sooner. Then when I went to see him a few days later he was too busy to see me. I finally reached him by phone and he curtly told me the investigation was closed. It was an accident. That was it."

Gregory's grief and frustration hung in the air

like mist. Impulsively I took his hands in mine. The gesture embarrassed him.

"Don't torture yourself," I consoled. "You need to accept that it was an accident. Honor Carol's memory but go on with your life." His hands relaxed as I continued to hold them.

"Linda, I know you mean well but there are too many unanswered questions. And those numbers. They mean something."

"What numbers?"

"I guess I forgot to mention them. Carol had an old chest she used for saving things that were special to her. Scrapbooks, items from our parents, that kind of stuff. I went through it after she died and at the bottom in a sealed envelope was a list of numbers, each in a series of five beginning with the letter A, six rows in all. Next to each series was a set of initials. Six different sets. Everything was in Carol's writing and done on Probation letterhead."

"Carol hid them?"

"It looks that way. The chest was always locked and she kept the key in a place only I knew about. She wouldn't have put them there if she didn't fear what they represented, or what she could do with them."

"She never mentioned them to you?"

"No, and I've wracked my brain trying to figure out what they mean. I'm sure they're connected in some way to Carol's death." Gregory dropped his hands from mine and leaned back.

We sat silently while our after dinner coffee turned cold. I wanted to ease the tension of the moment but decided to stay quiet and let what I heard settle in.

Eventually Gregory asked the waiter to bring the bill. He paid and we left the restaurant. It was a relief to walk out into the cool night and we headed to the car without further conversation.

On the way home Gregory apologized for the tone of the evening, and suggested getting together again under better circumstances. As he parked in front of Edith's he became serious again.

"Carol, I confided in you and you were so gracious to hear me out. The truth is, I don't know whom to trust. You're probably the only one who knew Linda that I don't suspect. The sheriff shot me down, pardon the pun. I'm sure someone got to him. Right now I have walls all around me but some way, somehow, I'll break them down. I owe it to Linda."

"If I can help you, I will." I heard myself saying. I don't know what I thought I could do but Gregory was so caught up in his misery I wanted to offer some support.

"Thanks Linda. I may request that help sooner than you think." He groped in his pocket and found his business card. Pulling a pen from the inside of his coat, he wrote his home phone number on the back. "Don't hesitate to call me, no matter what," he said as he handed it to me.

We walked to the door and said good night. I waited until Gregory drove off before I shut the door behind me. I climbed the stairs to my room pondering the evening's events, trying to sort out what was true and what was an overwrought brother's imagination. No answer came to me.

Chapter Seven

The day after my dinner with Gregory, a package came in the mail from Carol. Goosebumps rose all over me when I saw her handwritten note, dated the day of her accident.

Linda,

I know I'm presumptuous. You can toss this if you want to (hope you don't though). Look it over. You'd fit in great here. Talk to you soon. Will have lots to tell you.

Your friend,
Carol

Inside were flyers describing various probation programs, a job application, and the open period dates for hiring probation officers. The envelope, postmarked only two days ago, must have taken a long time to reach the mail room from Carol's office.

I was still trying to make sense of everything Gregory had to say. Now Carol's note made me feel as though she wasn't gone after all. With just a few words, her vibrancy came through. Sadly though, she was gone. Maybe even murdered. It was just too bizarre. Yet when I thought about yesterday's conversation I had to admit that Gregory didn't seem like someone prone to exaggeration. Carol had described him as a solid person she could always count on. She had spoken about his choice of law practice – wills and estate planning. Nothing glamorous about that. But that was Gregory, a serious and helpful person to a fault. Carol's words.

If Gregory's theory was correct, then the truth was somewhere to be found. I had to agree the circumstances seemed suspicious and Gregory's hands were tied. If he presented his ideas to Carol's co-workers they'd either think he was crazy or, if they knew he was right, they might cover up the truth. This could put him in danger himself. He was right when he said he didn't know whom he could trust. But he could trust me, and I needed a job. Probation seemed as challenging as anything else I was exploring. Maybe I should look into it.

I still had to resolve the car problem, especially

if I was considering Orange County employment. Before Gregory called yesterday I had circled some ads that looked good. Just as I was about to call the first one, my phone rang. I answered and heard the now familiar voice of an apologetic Gregory.

"Linda, I feel terrible about last night. You must have been relieved to come home."

"Well, it was a night to remember. But don't feel bad. I've been thinking about what you said and I'm not willing to just dismiss it."

"That makes me feel better. I'd feel a lot better if you'd give me another chance to take you out for lunch or dinner. I owe you a more pleasant day."

"You don't owe me anything, but you could do me a big favor."

"Name it."

"I need to buy a car. I could sure use some help with it."

"Just say when. I could free up some time this afternoon if that works for you. Say 3 pm?"

"OK. That will give me time to make a few calls. Thanks."

I hung up the phone without mentioning the package from Carol. Plenty of time later.

By the time Gregory arrived I had lined up three car purchase possibilities. The owners lived nearby and all said they'd be home. As we left the house Edith met us on her way in. I hadn't seen her since last night when I introduced her to Gregory. She looked surprised to see us together again.

"We're going car shopping. Gregory is going to help me. You know, the 'male' point of view," I offered in passing.

Edith laughed and wished us luck.

"Where to first?" Gregory asked as he started the car.

"How about Santa Monica. There's a '95 Thunderbird there just waiting for me." I read the address to him and we headed in that direction.

The first stop was fruitful. The Thunderbird was in good condition and the lady who owned it produced all the maintenance records. Gregory and I took turns driving it and agreed it would be a reliable car for me. No need to look further. I settled the purchase particulars with the owner, who said she'd have her daughter deliver the car to me tomorrow. I gave her Edith's address and we left. I felt pleased. My world was about to expand beyond the current bus routes.

As we settled in Gregory's car I told him about the package from Carol. He seemed a bit taken aback and remained quiet for awhile. When I couldn't take the silence any more I blurted that I might consider Probation as a career move. This jolted Gregory into a reaction.

"Right now I have such negative feelings about that department I'm afraid I can't say anything encouraging." Gregory looked straight ahead as he spoke.

"Carol didn't even know I'd be unemployed when she sent the material. But now that I am I have to admit that the work seems interesting. I've been thinking about what you said, about Carol's accident, and if I worked there maybe I'd hear something, gain some insight that could ease your mind. Then, there's no guarantee I'll be hired either. It was just a thought." I was feeling a little foolish.

"We have some time Linda. Do you want to take a ride to Orange County?"

We had already turned onto the 405 freeway. "Sure. I may change my mind just seeing the place."

"I doubt it. It's a great place to live and work. We'll drive around. I'll show you Probation's administrative office on Main Street in Santa Ana. First I want to show you something else."

We passed the Los Angeles airport. I had only recently landed there but it seemed like a lifetime ago. I relaxed and watched the various cities pass by, occasionally glancing at Gregory who kept his full concentration on the road. I didn't know much about him. Carol had spoken of him with the highest regard, using words like steady and dependable. The death of their parents had probably brought them closer together than they otherwise might have been. He'd certainly assumed an almost parental role with Carol.

This was only our second time together, both times under strained circumstances, although today was a little lighter than yesterday. I mused as to what Gregory would be like in a normal social situation. Somehow I felt he wouldn't be much different, even if Carol were alive. She'd never mentioned whether he was married but I guessed not. He'd made no mention of a wife. If he had one she certainly would have come up in conversation.

We had passed Long Beach. Shortly after I saw a sign announcing our entrance into Orange County. Gregory broke his silence.

"Oh Linda, heads up, start checking out the scenery. You're in conservative Orange County now." He took on the mock tone of a tour guide as he continued.

"We're now passing some vacant fields which

will no doubt become a housing development soon. Coming up on your left is South Coast Plaza, one of the premier shopping centers in the country. Great restaurants, too. Across the street are the Performing Arts Center and the South Coast Repertory Theater. Angelenos who say we have no culture must have never seen their wonderful presentations.

My head turned back and forth following Gregory's directions. He seemed to be having fun with his travelogue and I was glad for the change in mood.

"Pay attention to this next sight Linda, the Orange County Airport coming up on your right. John Wayne Airport as it's officially known. Don't laugh. Why shouldn't we name an airport after a movie star, even one more associated with horses than airplanes. Only problem here is that planes can't take off or land after 11 pm or before 7 am. The affluent folks in the surrounding area don't want their sleep disturbed."

"You're kidding aren't you?" I asked.

"Not at all. Right now there's quite a controversy here in the county over the use of a closed Marine base. Those around here, and in North County, want it to be converted to an international airport. It would take a load off John Wayne. The rest of South and Central county folks are against it, not wanting the noise and traffic an international airport would bring. The Board of Supervisors is 3-2 in favor of the airport, but a recent vote countywide showed that over 60% of the citizens are not. The Courts are trying to sort out whose argument will prevail."

"Not such a quiet little county after all," I added.

"You've got that right. Now I'll be quiet while you enjoy the view of the Irvine Spectrum to our left and the many homes in the surrounding hills." Gregory resumed his concentration on the road. Even tour guides need their rest.

The 405 merged into the 5 freeway as we continued south through Irvine, Mission Viejo, and Laguna Niguel. We were in San Juan Capistrano when I saw the Ortega Highway exit. My body tensed as the car turned off. Gregory was taking me to the accident site. I looked over but he said nothing. His hands clenched on the wheel said it all. Turning left on Ortega we drove for a mile past shopping centers and residential tracts. Gradually the road wound through a more rural setting of ranches and open spaces.

"I guess I know where you're taking me," I said, as much a question as a statement.

"I hope you don't mind Linda. I did sneak this in. But I think when you see where Carol's car went over you'll get a better feel of my view on her death."

As we drove on, twisting and turning, the two-lane road gave way to a dense forest of pine and oak trees. Rolling hills and an occasional deer came into view. In some spots a sheer wall of rock loomed to our right and a steep drop off fell to our left. We were in the Cleveland National Forest, and I marveled at its beauty and danger. I could understand why Carol wouldn't want to drive on this road. I'd lost count of the blind curves.

The car slowed down. We were on a section of road with a slight turn out on the left. Gregory made a U turn onto it and parked. Through the car window I could see a canyon and wide open spaces. Gregory stepped out of the car and I followed. The silence enveloped us, broken only by a chirping bird or the rustle of an animal in the bushes.

Gregory walked to the edge of the drop off. His head bowed and his eyes closed. I stood next to him, looking down at the yawning chasm, shuddering at the thought of Carol's last moments here.

"This is it Linda. Her car went straight down, over 200 feet."

"How was she found? She couldn't have been

visible from the road."

"A passing driver saw a wisp of smoke rising and stopped to investigate. When he saw the car up-ended he called 911."

"Did you ever talk to him?"

"Yes. I hoped he could tell me what happened but he wasn't much help. He was heading to Orange County from Lake Elsinore, thought the brush was on fire, and discovered the accident. He tried to reach Carol but saw that she was unconscious, held in by her seat belt. He was afraid to touch the car for fear of causing it to roll further down. So he called 911 and waited."

"Did he see ...."

"That's the first thing I asked him, if any car passed him or if there was anything suspicious about the scene. He didn't see any cars, or anything else for that matter, but admitted he wasn't really look-ing. When the sheriff arrived he gave his statement and left. The deputy took his name and number. That's how I found him.

I looked back at the road and tried to imagine Carol's car coming along then going over the side. This wasn't a blind curve, it was a fairly open stretch. Did she become distracted, lose control, try to correct and go off the side? She was supposed to be traveling fast. Nothing made sense.

Gregory walked over to the pavement and pointed with his toe where the skid marks, no longer visible, had started. He repeated how Carol had only braked for a few feet. Surely not the sign of a cautious driver.

"She was forced over the side. I know it. It's as if Carol is <u>telling</u> me," Gregory emphasized. "Enough. Let's go."

We returned to the car and started back the way we came. I had no words of comfort to offer and was grateful when Gregory changed the subject entirely. Soon we were on the 5 freeway headed north, with Gregory promising me an authentic Mexican dinner in Santa Ana. I enjoyed the ride and tried to shake off the sadness I felt having seen where Carol met her end.

Gregory turned off the freeway at Fourth Street in Santa Ana. Within minutes I thought I was in Mexico. Colorful shops and restaurants lined the street and families strolled with their children. Vendors sold fruit ices from pushcarts. The air was festive.

"This was a downtrodden area years ago but some enterprising businessmen, with the help of the city, refurbished it. Now it's a popular spot for Hispanics as well as others living nearby," Gregory explained as he pulled into a parking space. "Mama Rosa's has the best Mexican food this side of the border. Hope you're hungry."

We were in front of a café with outdoor tables covered in bright red cloths and protected by a latticework cover. Chili peppers and stalks of corn hung from the top. We went inside where the decorations were similar. Behind the counter a heavyset woman, her black hair in a bun, shaped tortillas and placed them on a grill, alternately shaping new ones and flipping the grilled ones. When they were just right, she piled them in a basket. The smell was heavenly. I was hungry and ready to try almost anything on the menu.

"Hola Rosa," Gregory called.

"Senor Gregory, como estas?" Rosa answered, smiling broadly as she turned and saw Gregory. "Tiene una novia hoy."

"No, no, una amiga solamente," Gregory blushed.

"Si, si, lo siento," Rosa continued with her tortillas.

My high school Spanish helped me slightly in realizing Mama Rosa thought I was Gregory's sweetheart, which he quickly corrected.

"I guess you come here a lot."

"When I go to court in Santa Ana I like to stop

here for lunch, sometimes dinner. You're the first lady I've brought here. Mama Rosa thinks I'm way too old to be single."

Not married, and probably a workaholic. And now obsessed with the loss of his sister. Poor Gregory.

We sat inside, by a window. A waiter, who also knew Gregory, brought chips and salsa to our table. Soon we were feasting on albondigas soup, enchiladas, rice, and beans. A delicious flan and cinnamon flavored coffee added an excellent finishing touch. Music from street guitarists wafted in from outside.

"This surely tops the few Mexican dinners I had in Detroit," I told Gregory. He sipped his coffee and watched while I cleaned the last morsel from my dessert plate.

Mama Rosa kept a discreet distance as we ate but now came to our table and spoke to me in halting English.

"You enjoy the comida, pretty lady?" She cast a sly look at Gregory.

"Immensely – con mucho gusto – the best," I laughed, stumbling over my words.

"You bring her otra vez – OK?" this time to Gregory.

"OK Mama Rosa, una promesa."

We relaxed and enjoyed the increasingly louder street music. A couple on the patio, holding hands, were being serenaded by a trio of musicians. The meal and the music had taken the sad edge from the afternoon. The tension had disappeared from Gregory's face, making me feel better as well.

"I told you when we started out I'd show you Probation's headquarters. We're close. Are you interested?" Gregory pushed his cup and saucer back and laid his napkin on the table.

This was the first mention of probation since Gregory had shared his views earlier. "Yes," I answered, "since we're close."

We were a few blocks from Main Street. Once we turned north on Main traditional office buildings replaced the fiesta atmosphere. Between 9th and 10th Streets a low slung white building reposed, identified by a small sign as the Probation Department. Gregory turned the corner at 10th and circled behind the building where an employee parking lot still held a few cars. It was almost 7:30 pm. He parked along the curb.

"Are you serious about applying here?"

"It's worth a try. The work seems challenging and I've always had some fascination for law enforcement."

"I didn't mean to discourage you. It's a good

field. Maybe just some of the wrong people in it. At least that's what I think now. They need good people like you..........and Carol."

"Thanks. I think I'd be an asset. I'm looking into lots of things now. I can afford to be choosy for a while. I don't want to change jobs every six months. If I can move into something worthwhile and grow with it, I'll be happy.

As we sat and talked, a few people exited the building, briefcases in tow, and went to their cars. I badly wanted to be part of the working world again. Tomorrow I'd have my car. One more step towards mobility. I'll pursue this job in earnest and maybe I'll learn something about Carol that will put Gregory's mind at ease. I wasn't convinced Carol had met foul play, but couldn't say she hadn't either.

The drive home was quiet. No travelogue this time. I rested my head on the back of the seat and closed my eyes. Soon we were in front of Edith's house, saying good night. I told Gregory I'd keep him apprised of my job hunt at Probation and watched him walk to his car. Edith was in the living room when I came in. It was time to fill her in.

Chapter Eight

"Oh my, oh my," gasped Edith, sinking into the oversized sofa and clasping her hands. "Poor Carol. Oh, I can't believe someone would purposely hurt her. And you're going to get hired at Probation and be a sleuth?"

I laughed at the mental picture of me in a trench-coat, skulking around corners.

"No Edith, not exactly. I need a job, they have openings, and if I'm hired, I might see or hear something. Mostly, I'd like to find out that Carol's death was an accident so Gregory can have some peace, on that issue at least. I think I'd like the work too."

"You'd be good," Edith assured me, "but driving to Orange County from here every day – what a commute!"

"Now that I have a car, or will tomorrow, I can have more flexibility in my job choices. I'm not crazy about having a long drive though."

"I'd hate to see you move. I so love having you here."

Edith spoke what I'd been thinking and didn't want to say. Eventually I'd have to relocate to Orange County if I ended up working there.

"This is so premature. Right now I'm not going anywhere. If I do get hired, well....I'll cross that bridge when I come to it."

"You're right. We're jumping way ahead." Edith unfolded herself from the sofa, and took her cup and saucer to the kitchen.

I felt tired, drained really, and just wanted to lay on my bed and sort through the jumbled thoughts buzzing in my head like so many disoriented bees. I excused myself and went upstairs, drew a hot bath, and soaked.

I luxuriated in the sweetly scented water, my head resting on the back of the tub, and thought of Mom. We'd developed a routine of phoning each other on weekends when the rates were cheaper. I'd kept our chats light and cheery, and spoke in vague generalities when she asked how my job was going. I hadn't the heart to tell her I was jobless. She'd worry so. Besides that, I didn't want to hear how she always knew coming to California was such a foolish idea, now borne out by my present circumstances. Once I'm employed again I'll manage to make the segue from one job to another seem plausible.

Mom cried when I told her about Carol. I believed her death was an accident when I did so. I didn't tell her later about Gregory's suspicions. What was the point in making her feel worse.

I closed my eyes and dozed a little, until my too-relaxed head jerked forward, awakening me. Thoughts of David floated unbidden into my mind as they often did when my guard was down.

I was back in Michigan at a student rally. The crowd was dispersing when he bumped into me, causing my books to drop. He apologized and stooped to retrieve them. When he handed them to me our eyes met and my knees almost buckled. I was too practical to believe in love at first sight, but that moment almost changed my mind. His deep blue eyes seemed to pierce right through mine and I stood fixated.

"Hi, I'm David Wyndham, and if you'll let me buy you a coke, I'd feel much better about crashing into you." His gaze never wavered.

I was already late for my study group yet I heard myself saying, "sure, my afternoon is free."

"And just who am I going to have a coke with?"

"Linda Davenport, I'm sorry."

"Don't be sorry. This is my lucky day. Is Rudy's OK?"

Rudy's was a favorite hangout of the frat boys. I'd never been inside.

"Fine. Doesn't the buyer usually have the choice?" It sounded stupid and I immediately regretted saying it, but David seemed oblivious.

I fell into stride beside him and wondered what I'd done right to have this beautiful man show an interest in me. Beautiful he was. Blonde wavy hair, a little too long, that clung to the nape of his neck in ringlets, sapphire eyes, and a smile that seemed back-lit. He must be extremely athletic I thought, as I tried to keep up with his gait. He slowed down when he noticed I was taking an extra hop every few steps.

Rudy's wasn't very crowded but everyone there seemed to know David. I felt at once privileged to be with him and also out of place. We took a corner table, ordered cokes and french fries, and for an hour traded bits and pieces of ourselves. David was in his last year of law school and planned to practice criminal law in New York, his home. He was impressed that I was on a scholarship. He spoke of vacations on Cape Cod at his parents' summer home and a planned trip to Europe after he graduated. I'd never been out of Michigan.

When David paid the bill I was sure I'd never see him again, but knew I'd never forget the afternoon. As we walked out to go our separate ways I was dumbfounded when he asked if he could take me on a real date some time. Either he was not done being amused by my simple life or he was genuinely interested in me. I was willing to find out. I gave him my dorm phone number and he jogged away, promising to call me soon.

I had met several nice young men in the past three and a half years. Some called as they promised, some didn't. I never really cared either way. They were pleasant pastimes. That was all. With David I cared a lot. So much so that I felt physically ill at the thought that I'd never hear from him. I didn't wait long.

Two nights later, reading in my room, I was called to the hall telephone. Dashing to answer, there was David on the other end. Was I free Friday night, he wanted to know.

Thus began a courtship that had me floating above ground for the next few months. David was smart, funny, a gentleman, and crazy about me. Words couldn't describe how I felt about him.

It was Spring. Two months before graduation for both of us. I was deeply in love with David and was sure he felt the same about me, but neither of us had expressed it. We talked around it in so many ways. David told me how he'd love to show me New York and implied we could have a great life there. I hinted that I really wanted to leave Michigan someday and always thought of New York as exciting. When David told me his parents were coming for a weekend in May, and he couldn't wait for them to meet the lady in his future, my heart almost burst.

As the weekend approached my anxiety grew. I wanted David's parents to like me so badly it was all I could think about. I even splurged on a new dress and shoes for our first meeting, and still worried about what they'd think. David treated my concern lightly, assuring me his parents would love me as much as he did.

Mr. and Mrs. Forrest Taylor Wyndham were the most striking couple I had ever seen. Both were at least six feet tall and towered over me. But it wasn't only their height. Their regal bearing, and expensive, impeccably tailored clothes screamed money and power. I felt like Cinderella at the ball, sure they would recognize my new on-sale outfit as the bargain it was, and judge me inferior.

David had composure enough for both of us and clearly reveled in this special moment, the people he loved most coming together. Forrest and Elise, they insisted on being called, were gracious and made polite small talk as we seated ourselves in the private dining room of the Michigan Club. They were Michigan alumni and commented about the changes since their last campus visit, amid reminiscing about their student days.

I was edgy and tense, as though I were waiting for lab results that I knew wouldn't be good. As much as I wanted the Wyndhams' approval, I was sure my best self was not coming through.

We ordered dinner and Forrest selected the appropriate wine with the expertise of a vintner. Soon the polite chatter was replaced by more serious conversation, directed at me. Their questions felt like a job interview, only the stakes were higher. I was being interviewed as to my suitability for their son David's life. My answers were honest, but not what they hoped to hear.

Looking back on that pivotal night, I've tried to define the precise moment when I knew David would slip away. Was it Elise's hard-to-conceal disappointment that I was not related to the Palm Beach Davenports, or that my dad had only been an accountant, or the realization that I could not have afforded U.of M. without my scholarship? David, who started the evening bubbly and enthusiastic, became increasingly quiet as he cast helpless glances at me.

Soon Elise was regaling David with her plans for an elaborate graduation party for him on the Cape, before he flew off for his month in Europe. She made sure he knew that all his former crushes would be there, having returned from their private Eastern colleges. Then Forrest enlightened me regarding his plans for David to join his law firm in Manhattan, where he'd be so busy for the next two years he'd barely have time for a social life.

On the other hand, my graduation celebration would probably be a dinner prepared by Mom, with my relatives and close friends in attendance, followed by a short trip to Mackinac Island. Then a year of student teaching before my credential was finalized.

The writing was on the wall and I saw it clearly. David and I might have deluded ourselves that our different worlds could come together, but the cold light of reality shining on them, courtesy of Forrest and Elise, told a different story.

The Wyndhams were snobs. How they ever reared someone as sweet as David, was beyond me.

We parted politely, with the Wyndhams wishing me luck on my future endeavors. The proverbial kiss-off. They were polite snobs at least.

David walked me to my dorm, my hand resting lightly in his. His palm was damp, the first sign I'd ever seen of nervousness in him. I thought about the evening and wanted it to be a bad dream. I wanted David to take me in his arms and tell me to ignore his parents, I was his no matter what. But it wasn't a dream and David gave me only a light kiss good-night. After that evening our time together was strained. David found excuses to be busy and soon we were seeing less and less of each other.

The night before graduation David and I had planned a quiet dinner together. We had made reservations weeks ago at our favorite off-campus restaurant, but since his parents' visit I fully expected David to find a reason to cancel. To his credit, he didn't. Yet when he picked me up, his hollow eyes and weak demeanor told me more than I wanted to know.

We had never really spoken much about the night with his parents but all it meant hung between us, clearly taking its toll. David was a shadow of the happy, full-of-life man I met months ago. He had been so anxious for me to meet his parents. Was he as shocked as I was to see their blatant snobbery? David was too fine a person to have knowingly put me in such an awkward position. I could only assume he was grappling with that disappointment, as well as the sad turn our relationship had now taken.

David told me how beautiful I looked as he held the car door for me. Tears welled in my eyes and I couldn't answer. He settled into the driver's seat and we traveled the few miles silently. Once seated in the restaurant, the conversation I dreaded began to unfold.

"I love you Linda. You're the sincerest, most honest person I've ever known. You can't even imagine how wonderful you are. And you're head and shoulders above any girl I've ever dated or thought I had a crush on." The last in obvious reference to his mother's remarks.

I sat across from David yet felt strangely detached, as though I were floating above, watching two nice people have a serious discussion.

He went on, "I deeply regret how my parents acted. It was a side of them I never expected. It pains me to talk about it now."

"David, I've been heartbroken. I love you more than I ever thought I could love someone and I want only the best for you. What does all this mean?" My voice cracked as I tried to keep from crying.

"It means that right now my parents expect me to spend at least the next two years establishing myself in my dad's law firm, as soon as I pass the New York bar exam of course. They made it clear if I do <u>anything</u> else........."

"Like getting married?"

David blanched, but went on, "........then I'll forfeit the opportunity they're giving me and will be on my own." There, he'd said it.

"You could do well anywhere." I offered lamely.

"You don't understand Linda. I owe my parents this much, and two years isn't that long. You'll be getting established in teaching anyway. We'll write to each other. I'll pretend you're there with me and one day you will be." He spoke as though he actually believed it.

I didn't know a heart could hurt so much. This was good-bye and I knew it, but I wasn't sure David did. He'd said I was honest. He was about to get a full dose of my honesty.

"David, I have no illusions. The truth is I'm not what your parents want for you. I don't have the right parents, didn't go to the right prep schools, don't move in the right circles. I don't even get credit for attending U.of M. because I had to earn a scholarship to do it. They can't help it. It's the world they live in and it's not mine. They want you to love someone with their social standing. When you marry it will be a merger of society equals."

"Two years, Linda, that's all. Don't read more into this."

Somewhere within me strength replaced the tears that threatened to burst forth. "David, I think you should read what's clearly written. After two years it will be some other obligation. Your parents will never accept me, and all the letter writing and promises won't change anything. You either take a stand now, and I'll be at your side every step of the way, or we both know it's over. And believe me, I don't want it to be over."

It came out like an ultimatum. The last thing I wanted. Before David had a chance to answer I blurted out words to soften the harshness.

"You're the best thing that ever happened to me, and I've dreamed of nothing more than a life with you. The truth is we both have families we love and we can't hope to have a happy future by alienating them." My words seemed hollow. I knew the alienation was one-sided. My parents would have adored David and welcomed him with open arms.

"Oh Linda, sweet, considerate, to a fault. Don't you know I can't have a happy life without you and it's tearing me up, because I can't go against my parents. Not now at least."

"Would you at least admit we wouldn't be having this discussion if I was Muffy What's-her-name from the Hamptons?"

David hung his head without a word but his silence spoke volumes. There was no use in pursuing this and I didn't want my last memories of David to be sadder than they already were. I put on a game face and dropped the subject.

The rest of our meal was spent in polite conversation, interspersed with large gaps of awkward silence. When David brought me back to the dorm, and hugged me tightly as he said goodnight, I felt my heart shattering with the sure knowledge we were over. We held each other for a long time, neither of us wanting to break the mood. Did David really believe this was temporary or was he trying to let me down easy? Only time would tell.

I watched David walk to his car. He turned and waved as he opened the driver's door, then was in and gone. I stood staring at the space his car had occupied, tears I'd held back now rolling down my cheeks. And that was the last I saw or heard from David Wyndham. So much for promises.

Chapter Nine

Books and papers were strewn across my bed. For the last week I had been studying for the written test I would be taking at Probation headquarters. My application had been accepted and the test was the first step in a long selection process, standardized through the State Board of Corrections. I was able to obtain past copies to acquaint myself with the types of questions that would be asked. Much of it was common sense, but some of the questions required knowledge of California law. I had devised my own crash course based on the Penal Code and Welfare and Institutions Code, and was feeling confident.

I loved having a car and was becoming used to driving the streets of Los Angeles. When I passed my road test for my California driver's license, Edith planned a little celebration dinner. Charlotte outdid herself with a scrumptious chocolate cake. I wondered if there would be a celebration if Probation hired me. I'd better pass the written test first.

I barely slept the night before the exam, scheduled for 8 am. I had mapped out my route to 909 N. Main Street, Santa Ana, and left the house at 6 am to allow plenty of time. I didn't go anywhere without my Thomas Guide, now becoming dog-eared from constant use. The page for downtown Santa Ana was open on the seat next to me. It was Saturday and traffic was light. As I left the 5 freeway at Main Street and headed south, it was only 7 am. I navigated the quiet streets of Santa Ana and soon reached Probation Administration. The parking lot was nearly empty. I eased my car into a space on the end and wondered what to do for the next hour, when I spotted a coffee shop across the street. A cup of coffee and a roll sounded good.

The smell of bacon wafted out as I opened the door. I sat at a table by the window and watched the parking lot slowly fill with cars. Sipping my coffee, I was glad I arrived early. It gave me a chance to compose myself. Strangely though I wasn't too nervous. If I don't pass the test, it means I wasn't meant to have the job, I rationalized. Others had come in for coffee but no one started a conversation or made eye contact. Everyone, including me, drifted out about 7:45 am and walked toward the glass double doors of the Probation department, now open and being monitored by a young man checking each person's picture identification and their test admittance card.

Soon we were settled in a basement classroom. A large elderly lady, Sarah Perkins, described the next three hours. We would have a multiple choice test, graded by the State, and some essay questions, graded by Orange County Probation. If we didn't receive a passing score, we would not go further in the competition. She wished us good luck then took a seat at the desk.

I finished the multiple choice in less than two hours. Most I felt I knew, the ones I didn't I gave my best guess. I turned to the essays, five questions about hypothetical situations and how they should be handled. My common sense kicked in and I answered each as thoroughly as I could. When I finished I checked everything over, turned in my tests, and headed to the parking lot.

Several others, so silent before, were now chattering about how they did, looking for assurance from one another. It would be two weeks before we learned the results. I wasn't going to fret about it. The last few weeks had been surreal so any outcome wouldn't surprise me.

As I drove off my growling stomach told me some food would be nice. I remembered Mama Rosa's and proceeded south on Main to Fourth Street and turned left. I wasn't exactly sure of the location but as the crowds of shoppers grew more dense and the smell of churros filled my nostrils, I knew I was close. Then I saw the familiar patio and the sign overhead proclaiming the best food this side of Mexico. As I slowed down a car exited a parking space right in front, and I slipped into it. I wondered if Mama Rosa was there, and if she'd recognize me without Gregory.

The place was packed with families but I was able to find a small table in the corner of the patio. I ordered their lunch special and iced tea, and relaxed into my chair surveying the scene. Parents and children speaking in Spanish and English provided a gentle hum of background noise.

My lunch was delivered piping hot and I dug in, hungrier than I thought. I finished quickly and sat back sipping my tea and feeling peaceful. I could have lingered indefinitely but people were waiting to be seated, so I paid my bill and left. I never did see Mama Rosa.

It was 12:30 pm. I didn't want to go home just yet. In fact I felt like shopping. I needed some new clothes anad this seemed as good a day as any to buy some. I had heard about South Coast Plaza and knew I wasn't too far away. Thumbing through the Thomas Guide, I saw that I only needed to go south on Bristol and I'd be there. I drove west on Fourth Street past Main, Broadway, and Flower. Soon I saw Bristol, turned left, and in a few miles South Coast Plaza came into view.

From the look of the ample parking lot, I wasn't the only one who decided to shop today. After circling several times I was about to give up when I saw a car pull out near me and I took the vacant space. I entered Nordstrom's and began perusing the racks of dresses and sport clothes. I had taken to walking each morning and my daily exposure to the perpetual sunshine had given my skin a nice bronze glow. I'd even noticed some blond highlights in my hair. As I held the brightly colored clothes to my face I saw how they flattered me. I purchased a flowered print skirt, two coordinating blouses, and a bright red slack outfit.

When I left Nordstrom's and entered the mall, I was feeling energized by my purchases. My wardrobe had always leaned toward darker, conservative colors. My new clothes definitely needed new shoes. As I strolled past one designer shop after another it seemed that Rodeo Drive had been recreated here. That made me think of Carol and a wave of sadness washed over me. I had not spoken to Gregory since the day he took me to the accident site. I decided to call him when I returned home. No longer in the mood to shop, the shoes would have to wait. I left and drove home.

Gregory answered on the first ring and sounded happy to hear from me. He apologized for not calling but work had been overwhelming. He congratulated me on passing the Probation application process and was sure I did well on the written test. We chatted a few more minutes then hung up. I felt better after talking to Gregory. He came across cheerier than before. And he never mentioned Carol.

While I waited for the test results I followd up on other job possibilities, but after the interviews I didn't feel any excitement about the positions. More and more I thought about Probation as a viable career and when two weeks passed I began to run to the mailbox each day looking for my letter. As I trudged back from the mailbox empty handed the third day in a row, I could hear my telephone ringing. I ran up the stairs and answered with a breathless hello.

"Is this Linda Davenport?" a vaguely familiar voice queried.

"Yes."

"This is Sarah Perkins from Orange County Probation. Congratulations, you passed your written test. I want to schedule you for your oral board and fingerprinting."

The breath I'd been holding now came out. "Wonderful," I responded. "When are you scheduling?"

"Next week. That's why we're calling everyone. We hope to start a new class in six weeks. How does next Tuesday at 10 am sound?"

"Fine. Is there anything I need to bring?"

"Just your birth certificate and driver's license. The information for the oral board will be given to you after you arrive. Report to our main office as before. The receptionist will direct you."

I ran down and told Edith, who expressed her happiness for me, even though there was a tinge of sadness in her voice. We'd grown close over the last weeks and we both knew a job in Orange County would eventually require a move.

I had no other interviews scheduled the rest of the week. My brief shopping spree had piqued my interest in sprucing up my wardrobe, especially after the compliments I received from Edith and Charlotte on my selections. I needed a haircut too. My normally shoulder length hair was now down my back and I'd been gathering it in a pony tail for convenience. The was not the professional look I wanted to project. Edith wore a stylish short cut that flattered her. I called her hairdresser, who was able to fit me in the same day as he'd had a cancellation.

The salon was humming when I entered. All around ladies were in various stages of manicures, pedicures, cuts, and colorings. Emil greeted me warmly and said a few nice words about Charlotte as he assessed my hair. He settled me in his chair and began manipulating my hair with his fingers, fluffing it, pulling it back, piling it up, then letting it fall.

"You have nice hair, thick, healthy. I have some ideas that will show it well and still be easy to keep up." Emil looked at me expectantly.

"I'm ready for something new. But I'm warning you, I'm all thumbs, so it has to be easy for me to do at home."

"OK, let's go."

He suggested a layered cut, ending just below my ears and tapered at the neck, a soft part on the left and soft bangs. He also suggested adding some blond highlights to the few already there. While he talked he arranged my hair around my ears to simulate the look of the finished cut. I liked it and gave him my approval. Two hours later I hardly recognized myself. My hair framed my face in such a flattering way I wondered what took me so long to make the change. As Emil was blowing it out he demonstrated the technique I should use at home. It looked easy enough.

Edith pretended she didn't know who was coming through the door, thinking some movie star had lost her way. Charlotte nodded her approval from the kitchen as she peeled potatoes. Later we had dinner together and my new look was the center of conversation. Tomorrow I'd head for the department stores to round out my wardrobe, and buy those new shoes I promised myself.

Chapter Ten

I was glad my oral board was scheduled for 10 am. The traffic into Orange County was definitely heavier on Tuesday, although I missed the worst of it by leaving at 8:30 am

The receptionist told me to have a seat and someone would be along to take me to the test area. In no time the now familiar voice and face of Sarah Perkins beckoned me. As she pushed the key code buttons on the hallway entry door she summarized what to expect.

"You'll have 45 minutes to study the questions for your oral presentation. The actual presentation won't be timed but it usually takes about 30 minutes. After you're finished, I'll take you to Personnel for fingerprinting and some other paperwork."

We'd arrived at a small office – my study area. The study materials and a clock were already on the desk. I seated myself. Sarah wished me luck and closed the door behind her. At least I wasn't locked in.

I perused the sheets of paper. There were three scenarios, each dealing with a hypothetical situation a probation officer might encounter. I would address the board members as though they were the probationer in each matter, outlining my course of action and the reasons behind it. My knowledge of the law and probation procedures was to be the foundation for my actions, along with the specific needs of the probationer.

I had done role playing as a teacher. Now I needed to construct my presentation in a way that balanced law enforcement and social work, met the probationer's needs, complied with court orders, and made sense. Wow!

I pored over each hypothetical, made notes, and outlined my responses. I barely looked at the time so was startled to hear a slight tap on the door, followed by Sarah telling me that time was up. I gathered my papers, smoothed out my skirt, and once again followed Sarah down the hall to a conference room. She introduced me to the three-member panel, all supervising probation officers, waited until I was seated, then took a seat in the corner.

For each scenario a different panel member took

on the probationer role. None of them accepted their probation plan without some argument. I listened, but stayed firm with my recommendations, each time reinforcing my concern for their successful completion of probation. When I finished I felt drained but hoped it didn't show.

The board then gave me the chance to tell something about myself and why I'd make a good probation officer. I spent about five minutes on this, looking for some slight sign of approval, but they were well trained in revealing nothing. I was thanked for my participation and Sarah escorted me to yet another office where I would be fingerprinted and fill out more papers. By the time I left the building it was past lunchtime but I wasn't very hungry.

"Yoo hoo, how do you think you did?" A ruddy faced woman about thirty with uncontrollable red hair approached me as I walked to my car. Upon my quizzical look she continued, "I saw you go into the oral board as I was leaving."

"It's hard to say. I think I said what they wanted to hear, but I couldn't read their faces," I answered.

"Me too. This is my second time around. I competed last year but made the "B" list, the kiss of death. This time I knew a little more what to expect. Hope it pays off." She ran a hand through her hair, made some straightening motions with no improvement, and sighed. "Would you like to grab a sandwich some where and commiserate? By the way, I'm Jan Sussex."

"Sure. I'm Linda Davenport. Where to?"

"There's a coffee shop near the courthouse a few blocks away. We can walk, or ride in my car."

"Let's walk if you don't mind. I'd like to burn off some tension."

As we started down Main Street I could tell walking wasn't Jan's favorite pastime. She was huffing and puffing after the second block and probably sorry she suggested it.

"I'm so out of shape," Jan said between deep breaths. "Maybe if I did this more often I wouldn't be."

We crossed the street at Civic Center Drive, went another two blocks and came to the Courthouse Café. When we were shown to our table on the patio, Jan gratefully plopped into her chair. After looking over the menu we both settled on club sandwiches and iced tea. It was pleasant sitting quietly in the shade, watching office workers go in and out of the surrounding buildings. Then Jan asked about me and what had brought me to Probation.

Soon I had told her about coming to California, losing my job before it even started, then looking into other opportunities. I didn't mention meeting Carol. When Jan probed further as to what led me to Probation, I told her about my experiences in Michigan with probation officers, my interest in working with people, and my desire for a challenge. This seemed to satisfy her.

"What about you, Jan?" I asked between bites of my sandwich.

"I have a degree in Criminology, even thought I wanted to be a police officer, then learned more about Probation and liked the balance between law enforcement and social work. I applied last year, passed the written exam, but choked at the oral board. I was really awful."

"Do you have a better feeling this time?"

"Yes. For the last six months I practiced in front of the mirror, answering every hypothetical question I could make up. I even had my parents and roommate pretend to be the panel. If I don't make it this time it's my own fault." Jan ran a hand through her hair in the same manner I witnessed earlier, with the same results. "This hair of mine has a mind of its own," she laughed, and I began laughing too.

I raised my glass. "Let's toast to our mutual success."

"I'll drink to that." We both laughed some more.

While I waited for the test results I busied my-self with daily walks and an occasional interview. I hadn't received any job offers but I wasn't concerned. None of the positions had excited me too much. I was scanning the ads less and less and beginning to realize if Probation didn't come through I'd have to come up with a new plan.

I'd fallen into the habit of picking up the mail when I returned from walking. Most of it was for Edith. I received an occasional letter from Junie, who regaled me with the exploits of her two girls, "growing like weeds", or a "sorry your abilities don't match our needs at this time" letter from one of my interviews. I wasn't prepared for the letter with the Probation address on the return portion of the envelope. I was fully expecting another phone call like last time and took the letter as a bad sign.

I sat down on a bench in Edith's courtyard and turned the envelope over in my hands. It was thin but then a rejection letter doesn't take up much space. The sound of the bubbling fountain was so relaxing that I closed my eyes for a few minutes, trying to prolong reading the contents, but finally couldn't wait any longer. I slowly tore open the envelope, unfolded the single sheet and read that Probation was pleased to offer me the position of Deputy Probation Office I, starting October 1, class #72.

My heart thumped in my chest like a tom-tom beating out the good news. I read the rest in a haze; the salary particulars, the fact that the class would be three months in duration, and finally, that I needed to contact Sarah Perkins with my acceptance.

I raced into the house and almost collided with Edith who was carrying a basket of fresh cut flowers in from her garden.

"I got the job," I cried as I hugged her and almost knocked her over.

"Careful, or you won't make it in one piece," Edith answered as she straightened herself out and picked a few stray flowers from the floor.

"I'm so sorry, but I didn't realize how much I really wanted this until now. Oh, Edith, I'm employed again, and in something I can really grow in. You're happy for me, aren't you?"

"Of course dear. It's what you want and maybe you'll learn what really happened to that poor Carol."

Carol. Yes, that would definitely be on my agenda. For now I wanted to bask in the good news, and later call Gregory. I handed Edith her mail and went to my room to call Sarah. I reached her on the first ring. She scheduled me for a county physical and psychological exam, the last step in the hiring process, and congratulated me on making it into the class of 18. I wondered if Jan Sussex had made it but figured it was inappropriate to ask. Sarah promised to send me the directions for the exam and the training center which would be my home for the next three months, and said good-bye.

I lay on my bed, absorbing it all. When I called Mom this weekend I'd tell her about my career change. She'd be thoroughly puzzled that I'd leave a nice publishing job to work with dangerous criminals. I could hear her now. I was too happy at the moment to worry about it though.

Gregory was another matter. He'd no doubt be pleased for me but my news would dredge up sad memories. I decided to call him and get it over with. Just leave a message on his machine. Quick and easy. He surprised me by answering.

"Hello." His voice sounded raspy.

"Gregory, it's Linda. Are you ill?"

"Allergies or a bad cold. I'm not sure which, but I can't stop sneezing. Luckily I didn't have to be in court today, so I stayed home. How are you?"

"Good. I wanted to let you know I got the

Probation job. I found out today and I start October 1. I'm really excited."

"Congratulations. When I feel better we'll have to celebrate," followed by several sneezes.

"OK, I'll hold you to it. Rest up and I'll talk to you soon."

It was a relief to hang up without any discussion of Carol. I went to the desk, pulled out some paper, and began to make a list of all I needed to do the next two weeks. As I jotted down items I realized with a little sadness that I would need to add apartment hunting in Orange County. Maybe not in the next two weeks, but in the near future. A daily commute from Edith's house to Santa Ana would be too exhausting.

That night dinner was a quickly put-together celebration of my new job. Edith brought up the long drive. She recalled the time it took to reach their house in Laguna Beach before the area became heavily populated and brought more traffic.

"The kids just loved spending summers at the beach. We were only a block from the ocean. By the time we came home in September they'd be brown as tree bark. Now they have no time to even bring the grandchildren." Edith's eyes misted. "The last time I drove to Laguna it seemed to take twice as long. I suppose I should sell the house but it would be like giving up precious memories. My husband always said I was too sentimental. I guess I am."

"Have you ever rented it?" I asked between bites of juicy chicken. "I hear beach rentals are pretty desirable."

"We did for a while but I didn't like the constant turnover. Luckily for me my husband handled all that. After he died I didn't have the energy or desire to keep it up. I could have hired a property manager but I didn't want to be bothered. The house has been closed for the past year. I should drive down and see it. Maybe you could go with me?" Edith tentatively posed the question.

"Of course."

We finished our dinner and lingered over steaming cups of espresso. It was the first time I'd seen Edith depart from tea, and she seemed to be enjoying the change. I watched her savor each drop as she sat deep in thought. Suddenly she put down her cup and saucer and sat upright.

"I've got an idea. I know it's just a matter of time before you've had it with the freeways and you'll want to move closer to your job. The beach house has been empty too long and it would be perfect for you. Not too big, and lots closer to Santa Ana than you are now. What do you think?"

"Edith, although it sounds fantastic, beach rentals are expensive. I couldn't afford it."

"I'll charge you what you pay here. It would be worth it to me just to have you there. I've never been comfortable leaving the place empty. If I can't have you here I'll at least have you in Laguna. Just take a look at it," Edith pleaded.

"You're hard to say no to. When can we drive down there?"

A very relieved appearing Edith thought for a moment then suggested Saturday. It was settled.

Edith insisted on driving. She knew the route and wanted her Jaguar to benefit from the open road. "It's had too much city driving," she explained.

It was fine with me. I luxuriated in the feel of the leather seats as I watched the passing scenery along the 5 freeway, now becoming familiar to me. Edith oohed and aahed at the changes as we entered Orange County. When she turned onto Laguna Canyon Road the landscape slowly changed to a more rural one. We wound along the two lane, tree lined road until we approached the village area. Homes dotted the surrounding hillsides and quaint shops bustled with customers.

Edith pointed out favorite haunts and lamented the disappearance of others. Soon we were on

Pacific Coast Highway and after a few turns onto residential streets, pulled in front of a white wood Cape Cod style cottage, tucked between two more modern homes. The yard was well maintained and flowers bloomed abundantly in planter boxes and flower beds.

"I see the lawn service I'm paying for is doing an excellent job," Edith commented.

"It's lovely," I murmured, taking it all in. This cottage was as cozy and small as Edith's Los Angeles home was grand. I couldn't imagine the Carter family having enough room.

"It's bigger than it looks from the outside," Edith said as if in answer to my thoughts. "Besides, as soon as the kids had breakfast they were at the beach. I'd pack a picnic lunch and could hardly drag them in by dinnertime. They had such fun."

The street we were on sloped down to the beach a block away. Today it was overcast. Only a few people could be seen on the sand. Beyond, the white caps gently swaying over the dark water looked like undulating mountaintops. I loved the place already and hadn't even been inside.

I followed Edith up the walkway. She fumbled with her key, working the lock until it opened. The door swung back to reveal a small foyer opening into a living room on the left, a kitchen/dining area to the right, and a center hallway that led towards the back. The floors were hardwood with colorful area rugs here and there. The furniture appeared to be comfortable. Overstuffed sofas and chairs in a canvas-type material with throw pillows in chintz and denim made the living room inviting. A beautiful oak bookcase filled with books and family photos lined one wall. A large oak coffee table sat between the two sofas, which faced each other before a white brick fireplace. Edith gazed at the photographs while I surveyed the kitchen with its white wood cabinets and stainless steel appliances. A round wooden table with ladder back chairs fit perfectly in the dining alcove where a bay window looked out to the trees and flowers in the front yard.

Edith headed toward the bedrooms and I followed. There were only three. One large, the master, opened to the right of the hallway, two smaller ones opened to the left. Edith darted to the bed in the master bedroom and began fluffing up the small pillows placed casually against the larger ones, then laughed at herself for doing it.

"Old habits die hard, I guess. I never liked limp looking pillows."

A pristine blue and white tile bathroom had

a large window that looked out to the small back yard. The colors complemented the blue and yellow color scheme of the master bedroom. The two smaller bedrooms were joined in the middle by a second bathroom. Each bedroom had a door that led into the bathroom. I imagined the Carter children fighting over the use of this shared room and Edith refereeing.

"What do you think?" Edith asked expectantly. "Wouldn't it fit you just fine?"

"I can see myself now curled up on that cozy bed with a good book. Are you sure you're OK with my staying here?"

"Absolutely. Who better?"

"It's a deal then. I can't believe my good fortune once again. You're just too kind."

Edith seemed pleased with my acceptance and continued to poke and prod into the closets and cupboards, satisfying herself that all was in order.

As we drove back to Los Angeles Edith regaled me with the family's summertime experiences in Laguna. The recollection seemed to bring her much pleasure.

"Once I move in, I want you to come and spend time with me, as often as you want. You can show me around your favorite places, and we can find new ones."

"Maybe I will. The change would be good for me," Edith responded enthusiastically.

I leaned my head against the seat and closed my eyes, thinking of Oct. 1. Next week I would be taking the physical and psychological exams. After that I'd be biding my time until I started work. Edith and I hadn't discussed how soon I would move to Laguna. I was in no rush and decided I'd wait until after I began training. I could handle the long commute for a while, and I wanted to have someone to talk to when I came home each day, full of all the new things I'd be learning. Edith had already seen me through as many crises in a few months as I had experienced in most of my life, and she had a great calming influence. No, I wasn't eager to leave the comfort of her home and her companionship just yet.

Chapter Eleven

I looked around at my fellow trainees, scrub-shined and dressed in their professional best, physically and psychologically certified to deal with troubled humanity. I had arrived early and found my desk set among rows in the large training room, my name neatly printed on a large white place card identifying it as mine. The rows were in alphabetical order and as I worked my way to my desk I was happy to see one in the back with a name card for Jan Sussex. She hadn't arrived yet but I looked forward to seeing a familiar face.

Each desk was equipped with a computer, telephone, various directories and manuals, writing pads, pencils, and pens. As I fingered the items I watched more of my classmates enter, look around tentatively, then make their way to their designated spot. A table was set up along one wall with coffee and doughnuts. A large banner above it proclaimed "Welcome BPOC #72", signifying our Basic Probation Officer Core Class. After people had settled at their desks they ambled over to the table, helped themselves to coffee, and chatted among themselves.

As the clock edged towards 8 am our trainers began drifting in. When Sarah Perkins entered there was a murmur of hellos and nods of recognition. She must have processed all of us from the looks of it. We returned to our desks, coffee cups and half-eaten doughnuts in hand. The room began to quiet down when Jan Sussex blew into it, purse and unruly hair flying behind her. She stopped and surveyed the scene, then walked toward her desk with a furtive glance at the clock. She seemed relieved that she was early by two minutes. When she spotted me she stopped and gave me a hug, then hurried to settle herself. Our first training day was beginning.

The morning was spent on staff introductions, goals and objectives, and our mission statement – to protect the community and rehabilitate offenders. Training Director Ronald Larimer welcomed us, introduced the three supervisors who would be guiding us through our program, and gave a brief overview of what to expect. During our three months in class we would learn about the major aspects of probation work, adult and juvenile, and have hands-on experience also, including visits to jails, institutions, and courts.

As he was finishing his opening remarks, a tall attractive lady entered quietly and stood behind him. Ronald looked around, smiled, and ushered her forward.

"Ladies and gentlemen, I'd like to introduce Karen Foster, our Chief Probation Officer. She has some words of welcome for you."

"I do," she answered. "Welcome and congratulations to all of you for making it through the sometimes daunting selection process. To repeat a well-worn saying – many are called but few are chosen. You can be proud you've made it this far, and I hope today is the beginning of a challenging and rewarding career for you."

Karen continued on in a poised and confident manner, telling us that she had started with Probation 25 years ago as a deputy probation officer, rose through the ranks, and became CPO three years ago. She described the changes in crime and clientele over the years, and how the department had changed with the times. She proudly announced how Orange County Probation is highly respected throughout the state and considered one of the top probation departments.   Many former Orange County staff had become CPOs in other counties, attesting to the good reputation the department enjoys. Her pride in her work and the department seemed to be shared by the training staff, who nodded and smiled as she talked.

Heather Caplan sat to my left and seemed mesmerized by Karen, muttering "wow" under her breath more than once. I thought Karen was impressive too, and elegant in her trim dark suit and heels. After she concluded her remarks we were dismissed for lunch.

Everyone stretched and looked around, trying to decide whom to invite to lunch or where to go. Heather took off her horn-rimmed glasses, rubbed her eyes, looked straight at me and asked if I wanted to eat lunch with her. At the same moment Jan appeared at my desk asking the same question. Heather and Jan made introductions and we headed to the coffee shop across the street.

"I'm so glad to see you Jan," I said as we walked out. "When I received my letter I was hoping you made it too."

"When I got my letter I couldn't stop smiling. My family was so relieved they wouldn't have to rehearse with me any more. Everyone was happy."

Jan laughed and tossed her hair back.

"I guess you two already know each other," Heather piped in.

Jan filled her in on our meeting after the oral board. Heather volunteered that she'd passed the first time around and didn't know if she'd try again if she hadn't.

"I'm glad I did. Otherwise I wouldn't be here with you lovely people now." With that Jan put her arms around both of us, ending the discussion.

We sat at an outdoor table at Nick's Café, peering inside through the large window. The décor was definitely '50s, a long counter with chrome stools, chrome and formica tables, and chairs upholstered in vinyl. Policemen and lawyer-types filled the inside. Some sat outside as well. The waitresses seemed to know everyone. When ours approached she immediately sized us up as the new kids on the block.

"Welcome to your first day of training," she greeted, handing us menus.

"Are we that obvious?" Heather asked.

"Yes, but don't worry, in no time at all you'll be among the regulars. But since you're first timers, let me warn you, our sandwiches and salads are huge. Unless you want to gain weight along with your knowledge, split an order. I'll let you decide and be back in a few minutes."

We watched plates being served at other tables. Our waitress hadn't exaggerated. When she returned we ordered a club sandwich split three ways and a chopped vegetable salad to share.

"What did you think of the morning?" Jan asked us.

Heather thought a while. "Pretty much what I expected. Lots of introductions and propaganda. I mean the propaganda part in the nicest way, of course."

"Yeah, I know what you mean. The pride seems genuine though. And we'll all reach our own conclusions about the department when we have more experience," Jan countered.

I thought of Carol. She had echoed the same pride after several years, yet just before her death something deeply troubled her, and it seemed work related.

"Hey, earth to Linda, are you going to weigh in on this?" Jan's voice brought me back to the moment.

"Sorry. I was daydreaming I guess. What's the question?" Heather and Jan laughed and repeated it almost simultaneously.

"I thought the morning was great. What about that Karen Foster! What a role model," I answered.

"Thin, too. I bet she doesn't eat here," added Jan, as she eyed the plates of food that had arrived. Our sandwich had already been cut into thirds, each section a meal of its own. We began dividing the salad into the three empty bowls our waitress brought. Once we had our portions set, had eaten a few bites and nodded our approval, we resumed our analysis of the morning's session.

"It seemed like everyone was a little uptight," observed Heather.

"Who, the trainees or the trainers?" Jan responded, chuckling at her joke.

"The trainees, of course." Heather looked surprised that Jan could take her statement any other way. "I guess that's to be expected when we're trying to make a good impression."

Evidently Heather included herself among the uptight ones. I wondered if she was as smart as she was serious. We finished our lunch, washing it down with huge glasses of iced tea, paid, and started back. We were to resume at 1 pm and had been advised earlier that promptness was expected.

When we settled at our desks, the mood of the room had changed significantly. The class members, strangers hours earlier, were now laughing and chatting among themselves. When the three training supervisors entered shortly before 1 pm, the room quieted down almost immediately.

Charlie Cunningham, gray and about 60 years old, addressed us, noting that we all looked relaxed and well fed, and ready for the afternoon. He explained that each supervisor would be responsible for six trainees, even though all three would be available for help from anyone who needed it. He then advised as to who would be supervising whom. Jan and I both had Martin Krause, a fortiesh balding man with a perpetual smile on his face. Heather was to be supervised by Barbara Sanders, who had long black hair and appeared to be in her late forties. When he finished the assignments, he turned the class over to Barbara.

"I want to explain to you how cases come to the department, in case any of you think we solicit them." She paused for the slight murmur of laughter that ensued, then went on. "Adults and juveniles come into our system differently. Not all adults who commit crimes receive probation. It is up to the discretion of the sentencing judge. Not all crimes qualify for probation either. One of our obligations is to prepare pre-sentencing reports to the court on all defendants referred to us, to address the issues pertinent to each case, and make a recommendation to the court to aid the judge in his decision. If probation is granted, then we supervise the defendant also, unless it's summary probation. But we'll discuss that later on."

Barbara looked around, decided she wasn't losing us, then continued. "Juveniles, on the other hand, begin their 'experience' with us by first being referred to us by the police, schools, or parents, before they go to court. Once referred, they go through our intake process, either custody or non-custody, then on to investigation, then supervision. When it comes to minors, we're one-stop shopping." Another murmur of laughter.

Barbara spent another half hour discussing details of the juvenile referral process, then told us that after a short break we'd have an opportunity to look over some case files to become familiar with their set-up.

"Oh," she added, "I neglected to tell you that all cases coming to us are assigned a number, preceded by either A for adult or J for juvenile. This number remains the same for each probationer no matter how long his or her history with us. Now stretch and get some coffee, and be back in 15 minutes."

Everyone began to move toward the door while I sat contemplating what I just heard. Carol had kept a list of six numbers, each preceded by an A. Now I realized they must have been case numbers, but what was their significance? They had been hidden away too. Were they a protection for her in case she was in danger?

"Hey daydreamer, are you going to take a break?" Jan looked down at me. "This stuff isn't all <u>that</u> fascinating."

"Sorry. My mind was wandering. Let's go."

I didn't want any coffee, so I walked outside for a few minutes. The warm sunlight felt good on my arms. Jan and Heather were in a lively discussion with two other trainees about where they'd like to be assigned once training was finished. I stood on the sidelines looking interested but in reality I couldn't get Carol out of my mind. I pictured her, not so many years ago, going through the same training, building her career, then in a flash, gone. I still wanted to believe her death was accidental but nagging doubts surfaced from time to time. The case number revelation this afternoon had me wavering again.

When we returned to class there were three case files on each of our desks. I had one A file and two J files. Barbara stepped to the podium, coffee cup in hand, and asked us to pick up a J file and open it.

She described each of the court papers on the inner cover, then walked us through the file, page by page, explaining the meaning and particular placement of each document. Slowly a picture emerged of the juvenile probationer I had before me. When I came to the pre-sentencing report prepared by the probation officer after the minor's first referral, I found the social history thorough and the recommendation well supported by the facts in the case. I could see how helpful this would be to a sentencing judge.

Barbara answered questions as she continued to take us through the remaining files on our desks. When we studied the A files, she pointed out the differences in the court papers between adult and juvenile, as well as the differences among the five adult courts throughout the county.

"We've tried to have consistent documents in each court, but each justice center, as their jurisdictions are called, insists on doing their business their way," she explained. "If you receive an adult assignment, it won't be long before you'll know the court from which a document originated just by the looks of it."

At 4:30 pm we had finished with the files before us. It had been a productive first day and I felt as though I couldn't absorb one more thing. Barbara no doubt sensed we were all on overload and told us we'd done enough for the day and could leave early. She wished us a cheery good-bye among the din of desk chairs being pushed back and feet shuffling toward the door.

I sat for a while as the room emptied. I hadn't spoken to Gregory since I let him know I'd been hired at Probation and I was anxious to tell him about the A numbers. We'd learned in class today that we could access basic case file information on our computer, although only the paper files would have complete information on a case. However, we were to have a legitimate reason for doing so, related to specific casework we were doing. I certainly had no legitimate reason to look up the numbers Carol had hidden and I didn't want to take any chances that would jeopardize my job. I decided not to bring it up to Gregory just yet.

That night Edith was all ears as I described my day. I realized that anything to do with crime held a certain fascination for people and Edith was no exception. I had just about finished my recitation of the day's events as we were finishing dessert, when the doorbell rang. We all jumped.

"Who could that be?" exclaimed Edith. "Charlotte, please answer it and don't forget to look through the security window first."

"Yes, yes," Charlotte mumbled as she headed for the door. She'd heard the admonishment a hundred times.

Soon Charlotte was approaching us with a vase of beautiful peach colored roses, their buds just beginning to open. When she ceremoniously handed them to me I thought she was mistaken until I read the card.

"With best of luck to you for a long and fulfilling probation career. Sincerely, Gregory." It was so unexpected and touching. I wondered how he knew today was my first day. I guess I must have told him but didn't remember doing it.

"What a nice young man," Edith enthused. "Those roses will light up your room."

"Let's keep them down here for all of us to enjoy," I said. "They're too beautiful to be in my room all day when no one's there." With that I placed the flowers on the coffee table in the living room, while Edith and Charlotte nodded in agreement.

Later that evening I called Gregory to thank him. We hadn't spoken in weeks and I was looking forward to catching up with him. He answered quickly, sounding tired, but happy to hear from me.

"Gregory, the roses are gorgeous. They were a

perfect ending to an exciting first day on the job," I enthused.

"I'm glad you like them. Carol always loved peach roses, and, well. . . . you sort of remind me of her. . . . in a way," he stumbled. "Not in looks so much, but how you seem so genuine. It's a not a quality I see often."

"Thank you. You couldn't have paid me a nicer compliment."

We chatted for a while about our recent activities. He had been working sixty hour weeks trying to keep up with a heavy workload. Not much time for social life, but he hoped to do some hiking near Yosemite when he could take a few days. Since Gregory had mentioned Carol I decided to tell him about the A files I'd learned of today.

"I hope this doesn't upset you, but today we were taught how cases come into the system, and the permanent numbers they're assigned. The numbers you said Carol had kept on a piece of paper hidden away I now believe referred to adult case files."

Long silence, then, "I suspected something like that. And the initials after each number probably belonged to the person whose file it was."

"That's what I was thinking. I have no way of checking the files though. We were lectured at length today about confidentiality, and need to know basis for obtaining case information. It was made clear that we couldn't use our investigative techniques for personal reasons. We even had to sign a statement that we understood this and would abide by it."

"I know Linda. Don't worry about it. I'll give you the numbers when I see you and maybe you'll come across them in the course of your work. But, please, don't do anything foolish, and always be careful. I feel like I've laid a burden on you and I shouldn't have."

"I'll be careful." I didn't want to end the call on an ominous note, so I changed the subject. "Edith offered me her house in Laguna Beach. I guess she knew the commute would eventually get to me. I'm not sure when I'll move though. I'll miss the family atmosphere and her sweet concern, but the drive is sure a long one."

"That was really nice of her and you're right about the commute. Is the house empty?"

"It's been empty since her husband died. It was their vacation home when their kids were younger. Later her husband handled rentals when they no longer felt like using it. Edith didn't want the head-ache of renting the house herself or dealing with a property manager when her husband passed on so no one occupies it now. She seemed happy that it would finally be used. She may come and spend some time with me too. I hope she does. I'm very fond of her."

"Things seem to be falling into place Linda. I'm glad. Let's have dinner some time soon. When I can get away from the office before 8 pm that is."

"You've got a deal." We said good-bye and when I hung up the phone I thought that this must be what it's like to have an older brother, without the sibling rivalry.

I turned in for the night with pleasant thoughts engulfing me as I drifted off to sleep.

Chapter Twelve

We were starting the fourth week of training and I was amazed at how much I'd already learned, and how much more was still to come. Each day was filled with lectures from various division directors acquainting us with their service, the flow of paperwork, and how all the pieces fit together. I had never seen so many printed forms, rules, and regulations, even in my years of teaching. Probation was definitely a bureaucracy that ran on paper.

Each director reported to one of three chief deputy probation officers, who in turn reported to the chief probation officer. We were described as a "flat" organization in that there were not that many levels of management, unlike Los Angeles County Probation, which had managers tripping over each other. Too many layers were considered inefficient. We were extremely efficient by that standard.

We had also visited all the area offices and had guided walk-throughs of each. We had yet to go to the courts or institutions but that was about to change. This was the week we were to go on the road in earnest.

The mood of the classroom had changed considerably from the first few days, when everyone was uptight and on their best behavior. We were more relaxed now and there was a definite camaraderie among the trainees. Although everyone got along well, small groups of friends had formed within the larger one. Heather, Jan, and I seemed to be a great balance for each other. Heather was deadly serious, Jan saw a joke or a laugh in almost everything, and I fell somewhere in between. In spite of our different styles, our supervisors seemed to think we were progressing satisfactorily.

Most of the class was in their late twenties to early forties, except Esther Cramer, who looked to be in her fifties. Esther had been a counselor at juvenile hall for years, then a supervising counselor for a few more years, when she decided to compete for the DPO class. She made it on the first try. The knowledge gained through her many years with the department served her well in the class. She freely joked about her "senior" status, often referring to herself as "grandma". Sometimes Esther joined us for lunch and would regale us with her juvenile hall experiences. Now as we were about to embark on the juvenile supervision portion of our training, her little stories took on new importance.

Martin Krause led the session this morning. Martin was a great training supervisor, supportive and knowledgeable. He stressed how important it was to take our work seriously, because we had the power to make decisions that affected people's lives. But he cautioned us not to take ourselves too seriously, lest we get caught up in our own authority. There is no "black and white" in this work he'd say, only shades of gray. Our job was to select the best shade of gray for each case. Once we had our own small training caseload, we would do case staffings, and he predicted that we'd see how each of us would pick different shades, and yet be able to support our choices.

As Martin took the podium shortly after 8 am, chatter subsided. Everyone settled at their desks, coffee cups in hand and manuals open to the day's agenda.

"Today we'll visit Juvenile Court and sit in on some detention hearings," Martin began. "As you'll remember, when a minor is taken into custody and placed in juvenile hall, he or she cannot be held longer than 72 business hours without a detention hearing. This hearing determines whether the minor should be detained further or released pending his next court appearance. There is no bail in juvenile proceedings. The judge determines release or detention on the severity of the crime, past history, and family support, among other factors."

Martin went on, "After lunch, we'll tour juvenile hall, the administration building, intake and release areas, and the living units. We should have time as well to visit the school and look at some of the educational programs, which are fully accredited by the way, so kids incarcerated here don't fall behind in their community school once they're released. If there are no questions, let's go."

Everyone rose and worked their way towards the door. By now we knew the drill for field trips. It took four cars to haul 18 trainees and three supervisors from one site to another. Usually the three supervisors drove and one trainee volunteered on a rotating basis. Today Esther was the designated trainee/driver, so Heather, Jan, and I followed her out to the parking lot, and piled into her minivan, along with George Grosky, a trainee almost as serious as Heather.

"I won't need directions for this gig," Esther

chuckled as she made a turn on Grand Avenue and headed for the 5 freeway. "I remember when juvenile court and Probation's main office were all housed in that five story yellow building across the courtyard from the current Juvenile Justice Center. Things were so much simpler then. No x-ray machines either."

Sarah maneuvered the van onto the freeway and shortly we were exiting at Chapman Avenue. We parked in the garage on City Drive and proceeded to the courthouse entrance to wait for the rest of the class.

The eight story courthouse was impressive, lots of stone and marble. It sat to the right of a large cobblestone courtyard, juvenile hall sat at a right angle to the courthouse, while the Manchester Office building (the yellow building Esther had mentioned) sat directly across from the courthouse, at a right angle to juvenile hall. The three buildings formed a U-shape, surrounding the courtyard on three sides. At various benches attorneys conferred with parents of the minors they represented. People with briefcases walked in and out of the buildings, while others sipped coffee at patio tables.

When the last of our group arrived we filed into the courthouse, each placing our handbags, or whatever was being carried, on the airport type scanner.

Once everything was retrieved, Martin gathered us in the lobby for a briefing.

"This courthouse, the 'Betty Lou Lamoreaux Juvenile Justice Center' was opened a few years ago. It was named after a now retired juvenile court judge who fought long and hard for a larger courthouse, something this fast growing county needed badly." Martin waved his right arm upwards. "The second and third floors have a balcony configuration which gives this lobby a grand feeling. The district attorney, public defender, and social services have their offices here.

"This morning we'll be going into Judge Prescott's courtroom on the sixth floor. Juvenile court hearings are not open to the public so you'll only see parents, relatives, or guardians along with attorneys and probation staff. He'll take the bench shortly so let's go."

We took the elevator up, and followed Martin and the other supervisors, Barbara and Charlie, into the courtroom. No sooner were we settled in the back rows when the bailiff asked everyone to stand and Judge Prescott entered.

I liked the order of the courtroom. It appeared to be one of the last places where courteous behavior was required and practiced. Judge Prescott seemed as though he wouldn't put up with any breach of proper conduct either. After we all sat down again, he shuffled through some papers, spoke to his clerk, then called the first case. Since these were detention hearings, each of the minors was in custody in a nearby holding cell. The first boy was brought in by the bailiff from a side door. He looked embarrassed when he saw his parents and hung his head as he sat at a table next to his attorney. His parents fidgeted and looked at their watches. They seemed familiar, and annoyed, with the process.

Judge Prescott read the charges from the petition, one count of 459 of the penal code (burglary) and one count of 148 of the penal code (resisting arrest). The boy, already on probation for previous crimes, sat silently while the district attorney provided the judge with reasons for his continued detention. Then the boy's probation officer stood and concurred with the recommendation. The defense attorney made a plea for release but he didn't sound like he was convinced of his own arguments. The judge pondered it all then ruled for further detention and set a pre-trial date a month away. After advising the parents they could have an after-court visit with their son at juvenile hall, the boy was led out and his parents left the courtroom.

A parade of similar cases continued for the next two hours. Some minors had only one parent present, some had none. About half of the juveniles were released until their next hearing. They were mostly first offenders or had sufficient home support to guarantee no further problems pending their return to court.

Martin signaled to us to leave and we exited the courtroom while Judge Prescott conferred with an attorney between cases. In the hallway everyone murmured their reaction to the morning, with all agreeing on the professional manner of the judge and the general solemnity of the proceedings.

"Let's take a lunch break and meet in front of juvenile hall at 1 pm. Houston will give us a tour," Martin advised. Houston Sellers was one of two co-directors at juvenile hall, an operation too big for one director's management. We had met Houston early on when various department heads had addressed our class. He struck me as headed for a heart attack with his ruddy complexion and intense manner. I guess overseeing several hundred incarcerated juveniles could take its toll over time. Houston had been there for five years.

Esther suggested we walk across the street to the Block, a fairly new shopping center with several restaurants. George declined. He brought his usual apple and protein bar and said he'd eat on one of the benches and then take a walk. Jan, Heather, and I thought going across the street was fine and headed off, Esther in the lead.

We agreed on a Mexican restaurant that had patio tables, ordered off the lunch special menu, and sat back to soak up the sun and reflect on the court proceedings. Jan had humorous comments about the attorneys, parents, almost everyone who passed before us. Heather on the other hand, saw high drama in each case and had assumed equally dramatic backgrounds for each family.

"You two are a pair," chuckled Esther. "You'll need a little humor to get you through some of the tough cases, but you'll soon find most people volunteer for the mess they're in, and sympathy won't get you far. Deal with the facts and help the probationers do the same."

As Jan and Heather thought over these words of wisdom, our food arrived and attention was diverted to eating. We people watched and spoke of lighter subjects until it was time to go back to juvenile hall.

We were a prompt group. By 1 pm everyone was assembled by the front entrance. Martin ushered us to the reception desk where we showed our identification and were given a red visitor's badge to wear. We were then buzzed through a door that we entered only after walking through a metal detector. Houston was waiting for us in the inner lobby, along with Leticia Gable, the other director. She was tiny, blond, relaxed, and friendly; a marked contrast to Houston, who looked redder than I remembered him and in bad need of a vacation.

Houston pointed out the administrative offices that surrounded us where the directors, assistant directors, and support staff worked. We were then taken through another locked door and down a long corridor that led past offices for the duty officers and towards living units at one end and the intake and holding area at the other. Esther nodded and said hello to various staff as we passed, clearly enjoying her role as DPO in training.

Leticia gave a running commentary on the larger and more secure facility this was compared to the original juvenile hall this building replaced as part of the new Juvenile Justice Center complex. When we reached the control station we gathered again to get a briefing on the rest of our tour. The control station consisted of a bank of computers and television monitors along with buttons that opened various locked doors. It was manned at all times by deputized probation counselors. After Leticia finished explaining this important hub of the system, her pager buzzed and she had to excuse herself. Houston took over with the seriousness to which we were all becoming accustomed.

"We'll be visiting the intake and holding area first, with a stop at the medical unit. When minors are brought in by the police, this is where they are first processed." Houston must have given this talk a hundred times. "If they are under the influence they are kept in a special holding room where they can be observed constantly and receive any medical attention needed. Once cleared through Intake, they are assigned to a living unit based on age, size, and seriousness of offense."

We followed Houston and soon were in the intake area where several boys and one girl were in various stages of being processed. It must have been a busy morning. We met the staff on duty and were walked through a typical intake. Afterwards, we spent some time at the medical unit where the nurse on duty explained her role. Then we trailed Houston to a boys' living unit.

We entered another locked door where twenty boys resided. Doors and tables were painted in bright blues and reds. Here their meals were eaten and school was held. Boys left the unit only for exercise. Along the wall were individual cells where the boys slept. Houston explained that in this particular unit all the boys had received several months in custody and were awaiting openings in a ranch or camp. Most of them, due to their age, would be going to Rolling Oaks Forestry Camp near Lake Elsinore.

Martin interjected, "Tomorrow we'll be touring there."

I felt goosebumps. We'd be traveling the Ortega highway, passing where Carol met her end. Could Carol have been on her way to Rolling Oaks? It didn't make sense since she didn't work with juveniles, but what other reason put her on that road? I snapped back to attention when I heard Houston's voice.

"……..that was a terrible tragedy. I never really knew Carol but she had a great reputation. She could have been the chief one day. Well, on to happier subjects, like incarcerated kids."

Everyone laughed at the absurdity, but on the scale of tragedies, death trumped incarceration for most people. No more was said about Carol and we finished our juvenile hall visit by late afternoon.

As we drove with Esther back to our cars, Jan asked her if she had known Carol Alder.

"Not really. I saw her a few times when she still worked juvenile supervision. She'd come see kids who were in the hall. She seemed pretty professional, and everyone who knew her seemed to like her." Esther turned the corner and the training center came into view. As she pulled up to let us out, she added in a low conspiratorial tone, "I heard she was on her way to Rolling Oaks to meet with the Grand Jury foreman, but no one knows why, and now it's too late."

I had to bite my tongue to keep from asking her how she knew, but Jan, always inquisitive, did it for me.

"Well, a neighbor of mine is on the Grand Jury, and they were at Rolling Oaks the day Carol had the accident, doing their annual inspection. She heard that someone from Probation had called and spoke to the foreman that morning. She, the caller, wanted to confirm the Grand Jury's visit to Rolling Oaks and asked if she could have some private time with the foreman before they left. He apparently agreed, but never got the name of the caller, only that she was a female."

"So how do they know it was, uh Carol, was that her name?" I felt myself blushing at the pretense.

"Because no one from Probation showed up at Rolling Oaks, and Carol was headed in that direction when she had her accident. You put two and two together....," Esther shrugged her shoulders.

We climbed out amid shouts of "good-bye" and "see you tomorrow" and went to our cars. As I drove home I mulled over the day's events. What I'd heard about Carol's possible intentions the day she died finally provided a plausible reason for her to be traveling the Ortega highway. I was starting to hate even saying the name of that road, so beautiful and yet so treacherous.

While I snaked along in bumper to bumper traffic on the 5 freeway, I had plenty of time to think and what I was coming up with didn't ease my mind. What I knew about grand juries didn't jibe with my thoughts about Carol. Grand juries were independent watchdogs that monitored government functions and investigated criminal wrongdoing. If Carol wanted to meet with the foreman she must have had something to report. I remembered how she alluded to making some changes in her life. She'd said something similar to Gregory.

As I replayed that day it occurred to me that Carol would have brought documents to support whatever she wanted to tell the Grand Jury foreman. Maybe the A numbers she had hidden were connected somehow. Gregory made no mention of finding a briefcase in her car, only her purse. It all seemed so odd yet I was beginning to believe that Carol meeting with foul play was a possibility. Keeping my eyes and ears open and my mouth shut would be my motto for now.

I had transitioned from the 5 to the 405 freeway, still moving slowly towards my exit, and had been on the road over an hour. I came to another realization, one I had been putting off. The commute was wearing me out. At least three hours on the road each day were two hours too many. Since my visit to Edith's beach house she had occasionally reminded me of her offer, quickly following the reminder with assurances that I could stay with her as long as I wanted. She just wanted me to know her offer still stood. It was about time I made plans to move.

At dinner that night we had our usual chat about the day's training. Edith seemed to find vicarious excitement through my work, although I avoided any mention of Carol and what I'd learned. After Charlotte had cleared the dishes, we lingered over coffee. I decided I couldn't wait any longer to mention my decision. I had mentally rehearsed my words, hoping she'd realize necessity was prompting me, and that I'd miss her immensely.

"Edith, as I sat in traffic tonight I concluded that it's time for me to bite the bullet and move to your house in Laguna. I'm going to miss you and your warm home, and Charlotte's cooking, and everything. But if I keep spending so much time on the road I'm not going to be fit to do my job."

"I know. I've been wondering when you'd 'hit the wall'. Isn't that what runners do?" Edith wasn't sure about her analogy. "Anyway I'm surprised, but glad, you held out as long as you did. Let me know when and I can have the utilities turned on."

"Is this weekend too soon? Maybe you could come down with me for a while. A little vacation for you."

"That's a thought. I could renew acquaintances with the neighbors, if any of the old ones are still left." Edith's face brightened at the prospect.

I let out a sigh. This came out better than I thought. I was glad Edith accepted my suggestion to stay with me in Laguna for a few days. I guess we both wanted to ease into the transition.

"I'll start packing my clothes and things later this week. I think my car will hold everything."

"If not, I can take some in mine. I'll be following you there," Edith added. "Let's see, I'll have some keys made for you, call the utility companies, what else?" She tapped her fingers on the table as she thought.

"Thanks Edith. I've said it before but I don't know what I'd do without you." I was truly grateful.

"I guess we're family for each other, and if a person could choose their family, I'd easily choose you," Edith chuckled.

"Likewise."

I excused myself from our impromptu love fest and went upstairs to take a look at my closet. Since my shopping spree several weeks ago I hadn't added anything new to my wardrobe. Between Edith and me, one trip was all I'd need to make.

Charlie Cunningham was the trainer in charge today. He gave us some background on Rolling Oaks, a 128-bed correctional institution for boys ages 16 – 18, set amid sixty acres in the Cleveland National Forest. This was our day to tour the facility, and it would be an all day affair, given the distance and the size of the grounds.

"The land belongs to the United States Forest Service. At one time the buildings that now comprise Rolling Oaks were part of a forest conservation camp. In the late sixties the county was granted a twenty year use permit for the grand sum of $1.00.

Thus they acquired the grounds and structures for a boys camp to be operated by the Probation Department. The permit keeps getting renewed every twenty years. You could say Probation and the Forest Service have a symbiotic relationship.

"I was once a counselor there, so I'm looking forward to revisiting the place, checking out the improvements." Charlie rocked back on his heels, arms folded across his chest. He seemed to be the elder statesman of the group, and through the years had managed to work almost every probation assignment. I wondered what he knew about Carol.

Charlie continued on about the various programs offered to the boys, then decided we should see for ourselves and said we should leave.

Ironically it was my turn to drive one of the cars in the trainee caravan. I had no desire to be on the Ortega highway, much less drive it myself, but I didn't let on. Charlie handed out a sheet of directions to the drivers.

"Remember, as soon as you've driven about 22 miles on the Ortega, you'll see a family campground and general store on your right. The road leading to Rolling Oaks is about a mile beyond that, on your left. A sign at the intersection bears the camp's name. Once you turn on the entrance road, you'll travel over a two mile stretch, ascending about 3500 feet until you reach the gate. I'll be in the lead car and will tell them through the intercom that we're here." Charlie paused, then added, "they have a great cook, so be ready for a good lunch."

I could hear Jan licking her lips behind me. She was always on a diet, until her next meal.

We gathered our belongings and worked our way to the parking garage. My T-Bird comfortably seated only four, so it was the usual group, Jan, Heather, and Esther, who accompanied me. By the time we entered the 5 freeway going south it was 9 am and traffic was much lighter. Heather sat next to me with the directions in her hand, dutifully looking at every exit so as not to miss ours.

"We have a little way to go Heather," informed Esther from the back seat, "we're still in Santa Ana. You don't have to start watching until we pass Laguna Niguel."

Heather relaxed slightly, silently nodding in agreement. I suppressed a smile.

It was a beautiful, sunny day, about 70 degrees. The kind of day I was becoming accustomed to here. In Michigan it would probably be brisk but still not too cold yet. Mom didn't mention the weather much in our telephone conversations. Besides, everything was relative. What passes for a good day in Michigan would most likely bring complaints in southern California. I was glad that I'd be driving in good conditions, hopeful it would reduce my anxiety.

"Guys, this weekend I'll be moving to Laguna Beach. No more long, long drive to and from work."

"Lucky you," Jan said. "I love going down there but couldn't even afford one of their tiny fixer-uppers. Maybe some day."

"Maybe if you got about six room mates to share the cost," added Esther jokingly.

"That would be swell. I have enough trouble with the one room mate I have," Jan declared.

"How so?" from Heather.

"Oh, little things. We're just two different personalities and it's taken us a year to realize. She's good with her share of the rent though, and she doesn't keep late hours. I'm probably not the easiest person to live with either." Jan ended the subject and no one else pursued it, or my pending move.

We reached Laguna Niguel and Heather once again sat at attention, staring at exit signs. When she announced Ortega coming up I felt a churning in my stomach. I took a deep breath and told myself it was only a road, I'd be fine, but I couldn't deny the emotion that was wrapped up in it for me. I eased to the right of the freeway to make the exit, then turned left on the Ortega, glancing at my speedometer to note the mileage so I'd know when I had gone 22 miles.

As we passed gas stations and small shopping centers I was brought back to the day that Gregory had taken me here. I never thought that on my next trip I'd be the one driving. I recalled that soon the stores and residential streets would give way to open spaces and a woodsy setting. Within minutes we rounded a curve, and just like Dorothy in the "Wizard of Oz" when she opened the door, we entered a different environment. Rolling hills and farms in the distance provided a serene vista but as we continued along the now two-lane roadway, dense oaks and shrubs rose to block our view.

My passengers were quiet as they took in the scenery and I silently prayed that Jan or Heather wouldn't start questioning Esther about Carol's accident. Once it got started they'd get into details I didn't want to hear.

The road was truly a beautiful drive. Very few cars passed in the opposite direction. Charlie's car was ahead of us but I'd lost sight of him on the many curves. I remembered Edith saying how reckless drivers would pass on blind curves and I took each one cautiously hoping I wouldn't meet one head-on.

Heather's cry of "oh, look over there" broke the solitude. She had spotted a deer by the side of the road, half hidden by the brush. We all managed a quick glimpse as we drove by. City girls captivated by the country.

Esther was the one who brought up Carol. We were approaching the Riverside county line and had passed many steep drop-offs along the way. Esther casually commented that we must be near the tragic site where Carol Alder died. Heather and Jan craned their necks to look to the left. I kept my eyes straight ahead. Driving safely was a good excuse not to look

"Is this exactly it?" Heather asked.

"I'm not sure," Esther answered. "Somewhere around here. I heard her parents died in an accident too, several years ago."

"So sad," Jan said. "Was she married?"

"No, no husband, no kids, just a brother she was close to. I think he took it pretty hard."

"He must be afraid to get in a car, given the family history," concluded Jan.

I looked at my speedometer and saw we'd traveled about 20 miles. "OK Heather, start watching for the campground and store. It should be coming up on the right pretty soon." I was glad to change the subject.

Shortly the campground came into view. It was the first sign of people we'd seen in miles. We were back in civilization, such as it was. Within minutes we reached Long Canyon Road, the entrance road to Rolling Oaks. I could see Charlie's car parked on the side of Long Canyon, waiting for the rest of the group. I made my turn and fell in behind the other cars following Charlie. When he saw we were all together he started the climb to the top.

If I thought the Ortega twisted and turned, it paled in comparison to Long Canyon Road. I wasn't prepared for the same turns and drop-offs which were accentuated by the steepness of the two mile climb. I hugged the inside of my lane as I slowly ascended, keeping my eyes on the road ahead and Barbara's car in front of mine. As we rounded curves a beautiful and silent valley spread out to our right. My passengers were thoroughly enjoying the view, their heads turned to the windows. I could catch only occasional glimpses when the road turned and afforded me a straight on vista.

The hills were brown and full of boulders. Even the large oaks growing in abundance had a dryness to them. Scrubby bushes dotted the peaks and valleys of the terrain. A small bobcat scooted across the grass on the shoulder and took refuge in some nearby oleander bushes. Overall the effect was peaceful, almost surreal, rather than drab.

As we neared the top the road forked to the left. A sign denoted the entrance to the hotshot camp, a compound of mobile homes that housed the forest service firefighters assigned to keep watch over the area. We continued straight ahead until the road dead-ended, then made a left to the gated entrance of Rolling Oaks. Charlie, in the lead car, was already at the intercom announcing our arrival. Shortly the gates swung open and we proceeded into the camp. Low, brown, barracks-like buildings were surrounded by dense trees and bushes. Groups of boys wearing tan shirts, pants, and heavy workshoes, accompanied by adults in a similar outfit, walked in various directions.

Esther decided to give us a preview of what we'd probably hear soon enough when she announced that half the boys in camp went to school all day while the other half were on work crews. This alternated Monday through Thursday. On Friday everyone went to school half a day.

"Who thought of that?" wondered Heather.

"Don't know for sure. It's been that way since

the camp opened," Esther responded. "I think it has to do with the fact that the grounds are so vast, and the boys maintain it all, buildings too, it wouldn't make sense to have them suit up in work clothes and go out and just get started when it would be time to come back for school."

"What about Friday, then?" persisted Heather.

"Friday isn't a regular work crew day. The boys wash the camp vehicles, there are seven in all, and do other chores that keep them near the dormitories. Well, here we are. Get ready for the 'good ole boys'." Esther chuckled.

We had reached the parking lot. I sat for a minute looking at the surroundings. We were directly in front of the administration building. Narrow roads led off the parking lot in different directions.

Jan exited the car first and over her shoulder asked Esther who the "good ole boys" were.

"The guys with the cowboy boots, the shitkickers. When they're not living here in staff quarters they're living out in the wide open spaces with their guns and their motorcycles."

Esther went no further with her explanation. Everyone in class was now gathered in the parking lot, stretching and gawking, and commenting on the quiet surrounding us. Charlie started to say something, then stopped. We all followed his gaze to the long porch connecting the two front entrances of the U-shaped administration building. Sauntering along the porch and down the walkway to greet us had to be Eldon Crowley, the camp director. Charlie had told us a little bit about him this morning, that he'd been the only director the camp had had, and was responsible for most of the camp's program.

Watching him walk toward us I had the feeling that this was a man out of his time. Not because of his age, which had to be mid sixties, but because probation had changed so much in the last thirty years, and time seemed to have stood still here. Charlie had mentioned that Eldon was the only director who had never rotated from his assignment. He tactfully avoided mentioning that Eldon probably wasn't capable of handling any other assignment.

Esther whispered close to my ear, "Here's the biggest 'good ole boy' now."

"Welcome class #72. I see we have the usual bunch of good lookin' women," Eldon greeted.

I detected a slight wince on the supervisors' faces. We were in the age of heightened sensitivity to anything remotely resembling sexual harassment and the slightest remark could result in a lawsuit. Staff had been trained endlessly on all the nuances but the training apparently hadn't seeped in to Eldon's head.

"Remind me to tell you about my extra help experiences here," Esther muttered under her breath.

Eldon had positioned himself by the flagpole which stood on the grassy area between the two center walkways leading to the administration building. His arms were crossed over his chest as he scanned the group.

"This morning," he began, "I'll introduce you to my assistant director and six supervising probation counselors, as well as office support staff. The duty officer will describe our programs, then we'll head to the kitchen and meet our cooks. After lunch you'll get a tour of our shops, visit a dormitory, and see some of the work crews in action. We'll finish at the school where the principal will tell you about a student's typical day. Let's get started."

We followed Eldon into the administration building, through the entrance door on the right of the porch, and entered into a large living room. There was a wall of windows at the far end that looked out to the tree shrouded campgrounds. To the right of the windows was a wall with doorways leading into offices. The wall to the left was intersected by a long hallway that connected this side of the building to the other side. Offices opened on either side of this hallway. A short, stocky man came out of the corner office and was introduced as SPC Hector Garduno, the current duty officer.

The class was now seated informally on the sofas, chairs, and floor. Hector described his duties, which for the day shift of 6 am to 2 pm consisted of dispatching the work crews, visiting work sites, and trouble shooting problems as they arose. As if on cue, his two-way radio called and after some discussion, Hector excused himself to look into a situation at the school.

By that time the other supervisors and assistant director had settled among us and each in turn spoke briefly about their duties. Four supervisors supervised one dorm each, and the other two split day and evening shift duty officer responsibilities. Just as Jan started mumbling about the lunch they promised us, Eldon announced it was time to "trek to the kitchen for some good grub." What a way with words, that Eldon.

We walked outside, past the school, and up a hill to an old wooden building with a large front porch. Wonderful smells wafted through the screen door. It was a beautiful November day, sunny, cool, and crisp. The fresh air and the cooking aroma made me reminisce about my childhood and summers spent at my grandmother's farm in northern Michigan.

Her farmhouse was a larger version of the building where we now stood in front.

We walked single file through the door and past brimming pots of potatoes and vegetables, trays of fresh baked rolls, and apple pies. When we had moved through to the dining room, Eldon introduced us to Maggie Ferguson, the head cook.

"Hope you like swiss steak, mashed potatoes, and gravy," she said by way of welcome.

Our growling stomachs groaned approval. We were seated at tables set up for us at one side of the room. Boys began filing in from a back door, the early lunch work crew we were told. They each took a tray and began selecting their lunch, cafeteria style, then sat at tables on the other side of the room. We got up and did the same, returning to our seats with loaded trays of wonderful food.

The boys spoke quietly among themselves and eyed us between bites. As for us, we were busy buttering rolls, and savoring mouthfuls of meat, potatoes, and vegetables.

"It's almost worth being a juvenile delinquent to have meals like this every day," Jan offered, rolling her eyes and patting her stomach.

"Oh Jan, really!" Heather answered, picking at her plate. "This is good, but if you ate like this every day you'd be fat."

"You mean fatter, don't you?" laughed Jan.

"Esther, when was it you worked here?" I asked.

"When I first started working at Probation, I was extra help. That's an hourly, no benefits, classification where you're used at will to fill in shifts at one of the institutions. Although I was assigned to juvenile hall, I'd sometimes get called to work a shift here. Back then there were very few females working as counselors at the camp. I took the shifts because I needed the money, but I felt like I earned every cent putting up with the lechers up here, led by Eldon, the grandest of them all."

Esther had our attention. Even Jan put down her fork.

She went on. "I was never what you'd call a 'babe', even in my younger years. But I was thinner and curvier, and not gray, and I swear some of these guys would whistle at anything female that drew breath." Esther thought for a while, then continued. "You probably noticed Eldon didn't even acknowledge me. But he remembers me all right. I actually had the nerve to complain to him about some of his dirty-mouthed staff. Of course he laughed it off, said I had no sense of humor, and if I was going to be so uptight, maybe I shouldn't come up here anymore."

"What did you do then?" Heather was bug-eyed.

"At first, nothing. After all, I'd gone to the director and he made me feel like it was my problem. Eventually I had to tell my supervisor at juvenile hall because I kept refusing to take shifts at Rolling Oaks, and he needed to know why."

"Did he do anything?" from Jan.

"He said he'd report it to his director, who's since retired. I never heard any more and I never took any more shifts at Rolling Oaks. Later I spoke to other female extra help counselors who had similar experiences. I think very little has changed. They're a world of their own up here."

"Remember the sexual harassment training we had?" Heather added. "There's an obligation to report these things to Personnel and they'll be investigated. And there could be disciplinary action. That's what the Personnel Director said."

"Probably in the rest of the department, but up here it's swept under the rug. Until Eldon goes anyway. He sets the tone." Esther pushed her empty plate away. "You sure can't beat the food though."

That was something we all agreed on. I had just had my last bite of apple pie and felt like I needed a nap. Instead we were about to gather up for a tour of the camp.

Back outside the fresh air invigorated me and once we were on our way around the camp I got my second wind. We made the rounds of the auto repair, paint, and construction shops. Boys were busily involved with projects in each. We went through one of the four dormitory buildings, housing thirty-two boys each, four to a room in bunk beds. Each building had sixteen boys on each side, four bedrooms, and a living room, connected to the mirror-image other side by a long bathroom with toilets, sinks, and showers.

As we walked through the campgrounds work crews were busy raking leaves, sweeping, painting, or hammering. Lastly, we visited the school, where the principal was waiting to tell us about their individualized curriculum and goal to prepare each boy for high school graduation. We looked at the classrooms with their computers, the art projects, and books. It was impressive, but as we left, Esther muttered again about how the teachers preferred showing movies to teaching, and that most of the kids couldn't read beyond a third grade level.

As I drove down the hill I felt as though I was leaving a completely self-contained world of problem teenagers and questionable staff. We were silent for most of the ride, everyone probably mulling over their impressions of the day. As we moved farther from the camp and closer to the city I relaxed, especially when no one mentioned Carol as we passed the accident site. Soon I was turning north on the freeway, easing into the growing traffic. We were back in the city's hustle-bustle and far from a mountain top camp removed from it.

Chapter Thirteen

"Whew, that's the last one." I sank into a living room chair and eyed the box I just put down. Edith was on the sofa, feet up, shoes off. "I can't believe we're finally done."

"It's a good thing you're not a clothes horse like my daughter or we'd have needed a U-Haul." Edith rubbed her right foot at the arch, then leaned back against the sofa cushions.

"You helped me so much. All I have to do is unpack this last box and I'll be just about settled in."

Edith's Laguna home was furnished and had a fully equipped kitchen. Putting clothes in the closet and arranging my meager personal belongings was all I had to do. Edith had brought enough clothes and toiletries of her own for a stay of several days and she had already put them in one of the bedrooms. I was happy that Edith would be with me for a while to ease the transition. Charlotte was pleased to be able to have a few days off to visit her sister in Ventura.

It was 5 pm and we hadn't eaten since breakfast. Edith had the foresight to pack some staples for the kitchen but there was nothing to make dinner, and neither of us felt like it anyway.

"There's a nice little coffee shop a few blocks from here. What do you say we get a bite to eat and then stop at the grocery store and do some stocking up," Edith sat up and stretched as she said it.

"I think you read my mind. I'll just wash my hands and be ready."

We freshened up and headed out to Edith's car. She drove the streets with the familiarity I hoped to soon acquire. We turned on Pacific Coast Highway and went a short distance before Edith pulled into the parking lot of "The Corner Cottage."

"This place has been here for over thirty years. The food is simple, but good," Edith informed me as we got out of the car.

"Same owners all this time?"

"I think one of the sons owns it, or manages it, now. It's still in the family anyway."

"We were greeted by a teenaged hostess who sat us at a corner booth. French windows were opened outward and groups of potted ferns were placed on wicker plant stands against one of the walls. The place had the feel and look of someone's old home converted to a restaurant.

A waitress took our order and brought us large glasses of iced tea. We sat back and sipped. I could feel the energy draining out of me and figured Edith must be in worse shape. Surprisingly, she seemed energized and was chatting on about how nice it felt to be back here and seeing familiar places.

We had both ordered the Saturday night special, pot roast and mashed potatoes, and dug into the piping hot dishes as soon as they arrived.

"This was a great choice," I said between mouthfuls.

"The restaurant or the pot roast?" Edith queried.

"Both. They could give Charlotte some competition."

"If Charlotte heard that you'd never get one of her homemade muffins again. She thinks she's the only one who can feed me properly."

"I think I put on a few pounds with her good cooking, which would make my mother happy. She always thought I was too thin."

"How is you mom?" Edith asked.

"She seems fine. She and my Aunt Martha get

along better as widows than they did when their husbands were alive. I guess necessity makes people more tolerant of each other. Anyway, they keep busy. Mom and I talk about once a week and she's always got some story to tell about where they visited or who they saw."

"Do you think she'll every visit you?"

"She's never flown, too afraid. I've talked to her about coming out here in the winter, especially now that I'll have the extra room, but she said it would make her too nervous. I don't want to push it. She already thinks I've become too fearless since moving here."

"How so?"

"Working for Probation, mainly. She doesn't know the publishing job went under. I didn't have the heart to tell her I became jobless within my first week here. I knew she'd worry so. Now she thinks I gave up a great publishing job to associate with criminals."

"Couldn't you tell her now what really happened, since you're employed and all. She wouldn't worry after the fact, would she?" Edith pondered the thought.

"No, but I'd just as soon leave it alone. Mom will get used to my work. I tell her about my training and how professional it is. She's coming around."

A busboy cleared our plates and the waitress followed with two chocolate sundaes, the finale of the dinner special.

As Edith plopped the cherry into her mouth and used the spoon to catch the chocolate sauce dribbling down her dish, she asked me how I felt about my new career, now that several weeks had passed.

Even though I'd kept Edith up to date on my daily training, it was practically a dinner ritual, she probably wasn't sure if I was in it for the long haul. I thought a while before I answered. Was this really the career for me or a rebound thing? I had been busy learning and assumed Probation was for me. My level of interest and excitement were pretty much the same as my first day of class. That seemed like a good indicator. Only time would tell, but for whatever reasons, I believed I made the right move.

"I don't think there are any accidents in life," I philosophized. "Meeting Carol, losing the job that brought me here, receiving the Probation job application," my voice trailed as I thought of how I received it after Carol's death. "Everything has led me to a place I really enjoy, that challenges me, and gives me hope for a fulfilling future. I'd have to say I feel good about my new career and that it'll be a lasting one."

"Good," Edith patted my hand. "You'll make a wonderful probation officer. Now let's stop at the market and pick up some breakfast things, and get home. I'm exhausted after this big meal."

It had only been a week since I moved to Laguna Beach but already I was feeling more relaxed. My commute to and from work had gone from three hours daily to about an hour. In the morning I used the extra time to walk on the beach, enjoying the invigorating ocean breeze, and breathing in the fresh air. The air here was so much cleaner than in Los Angeles, even Edith had to admit she'd miss it when she returned home. She didn't seem eager to do it any time soon though. Many of her old neighbors were still here and she'd spent the last week getting re-acquainted.

As for me, I felt blessed with the fact I could live in such a peaceful place at a fraction of what it would cost on the open market. I had to take some ribbing at work though. Jan half-seriously asked if Edith would consider adopting her. Heather told her it could only happen if Edith didn't have to meet her first. Eventually the joking got old and we returned to the more sedate business of juvenile crime.

NO STONE UNTURNED

We were winding down the juvenile portion of our training. Our last efforts before we launched into adult probation were to try to clear some warrant cases. When we entered class one morning, each of us found several J-files on our desks. Barbara Sanders was at the podium waiting for us to settle down with our coffee cups. When the chatter ceased, she began.

"You each have six juvenile files that have gone to warrant. Warrants of arrest have been issued either because a minor failed to show up for a court hearing, or ran away from home or an institutional commitment. Once the court orders an arrest warrant, only the court can clear it, and this is accomplished by bringing the minor before the judge. Warrants are usually discovered when a minor is arrested on a new offense and the arresting office does a warrant search."

Barbara paused, took a sip of coffee, and went on. "We don't have the manpower to actively work these cases, that is, go out and search the neighborhood where these kids might be. Therefore, the files are banked, and when a minor turns up on a new charge, his case is reactivated. But," and she grinned, "when we have a training class, we allow ourselves the luxury of trying to clear a few cases using the trainees' efforts. It's a good experience for you and occasionally we actually find a few kids, usually sitting at home, the parents hiding them out."

Barbara waited for questions. There were none, so she continued. "For the next three days you will investigate the cases in front of you. Make calls, go to their homes, whatever you have time for. Should you encounter one of these kids, do not attempt to bring him or her in. Contact the local police or sheriff and ask for assistance. Document the case file and move on."

After a few "what if" questions, Barbara released us to our task, saying she'd be in her office down the hall if we needed her.

I looked at the files before me, all stamped "Warrant" in large letters. I picked up the first one to find it belonged to a sixteen year-old girl. She had run away from the Santa Ana Youth Home after only two days of a three-month commitment. She had two drug arrests, the last one also involved a stolen car. The probation report indicated her parents lived in Orange, had tried to help her through counseling, but were at their wit's end. The probation officer's memo to the court, requesting the arrest warrant, advised that after her runaway she broke into her parents' house, took some clothes and jewelry, and hadn't been seen since. That was four months ago.

I called the home phone number listed in the file. After several rings a high pitched female voice answered.

"Is this Mrs. Richard, Mrs. Selma Richard?" I clarified as I looked at the face sheet of the probation report.

"Yes."

"This is Linda Davenport, a probation officer in Orange County." I could hear Mrs. Richard suck in her breath. "I'm following up on your daughter Wanda's probation case. As you know there has been a warrant for her arrest since she left the Santa Ana Youth Home without authorization, burglarized your house, and fled....."

"Have you found her?" Mrs. Richard broke in anxiously.

"No, Mrs. Richard, I'm sorry to say we haven't. I was checking to see if you might have heard from her, a phone call, letter, anything that might suggest her whereabouts."

"No, nothing." Mrs. Richard was sobbing softly. "I don't know if she's alive or dead. How can a child worry her parents so? If she hadn't gotten into drugs I know she'd be here today. We're a good, church-going family. I don't know what went wrong." She sobbed loudly now, then blew her nose.

"I didn't mean to upset you. She must at least be staying out of further trouble or the arrest warrant would have been discovered." It was a lame try to cheer her. "Please let us know if you hear anything at all, even from her friends."

"What is your number?"

"It's 555-471-6131. Ask for Linda Davenport. Otherwise you can call our general number, 555-471-3000 and ask for the juvenile warrant officer. Thank you for your time."

We hung up and I made some notes in the file. Mrs. Richard didn't sound like someone harboring her daughter. I put the case file aside, one down and five to go.

The next file was twice as thick. The owner, Miguel Gonzales, was seventeen, and a gang member, with a list of increasingly serious criminal offenses to his credit. His last one, an assault on a police officer while being arrested for being drunk and disorderly had earned him six months at Rolling Oaks. He had been there two months when he ran way. As I perused the camp's special incident reports, I noticed the date of his disappearance, June 19, the same day Carol had had her fatal accident. I felt a shiver. Anyone escaping from Rolling Oaks would have to travel on the Ortega Highway eventually. Could he have seen anything?

I read the reports carefully. The night counselor in Miguel's dorm had noticed that his bunk was empty when he made his last check, about 5:30 am. The window near his bunk was open and the screen was out. His pajamas were on the floor and his work clothes and shoes for the next day were missing. The duty officer was notified and a search of the grounds was initiated, with no luck. The sheriff was called, who also searched the campgrounds and the road leading to Rolling Oaks, took a report and left. An arrest warrant was issued the next day.

I thought about my visit to Rolling Oaks and the dense forest that surrounded it. No kid would have the nerve to run through those woods at night, with snakes, bobcats, and mountain lions roaming free. Even if he did, he'd still end up on the Ortega Highway. If he went left he'd head to Lake Elsinore, right towards Orange County.

Miguel had lived in Santa Ana, with his mother and several siblings. His father had been killed in a drive-by shooting three years ago; the bullets intended for Miguel's older brother Santo. Mrs. Gonzales didn't seem to have the energy to control her children. The boys had turned to gang life, and the girls had gangster boyfriends. It struck me that Miguel would have nothing to lose by returning home. Mrs. Gonzales would probably not turn him in. Chances are that's where he was.

My only field trips had been with the class to the courts, institutions, and other area offices. I decided it was time to make my first home call and this was a great case to do it. I checked the address in my Thomas Guide. The Gonzales home was near First Street and Harbor, a heavy gang area. I had my cell phone if I needed to call for help. I'd drive by the house and if it looked OK, I'd go to the door. Otherwise, I'd continue on.

As I gathered my belongings, a few of my class-mates were doing the same. A home call was better than a phone call any day. A picture could replace a thousand words, to paraphrase an old saying.

I drove south on Grand to First and made a right turn. As I crossed Broadway I looked at the view north and south. The stately palms and well-kept older homes and businesses reflected a pride of own-ership that soon disappeared as I neared Harbor.

Graffiti and weeds sprouted side by side. Dirt front yards outnumbered grass two to one. I looked for Peony Street and thought I'd gone too far when the faded street sign, turned sideways, appeared. I turned left and followed the numbers until I came to 641, a small one story stucco, once white, but now badly in need of paint. A shutter on the front window teetered on one nail and the screen door was full of holes. The street was amazingly quiet. Some front yards sported cars up on blocks, but there was no sign of anyone working on them. I felt safe enough to venture to the door.

The door bell was hanging out of its socket, so I knocked on the metal part of the screen door. No response. I knocked again and thought I heard the sounds of movement and low voices inside. I stepped back in time to see someone looking out the front window and then pull back as my gaze and his briefly met. Within a few seconds the door opened slightly and a short, heavy, dark haired woman peeked around and stared at me. She had not been the one in the window.

"Mrs. Gonzales?" I asked.

"Si, jes," she answered.

"I'm Linda Davenport from Probation. May I come in and talk to you about Miguel?" She looked around nervously. "I won't be long," I added.

"OK, come in," Mrs. Gonzales acquiesced, and pushed open the screen door so I could squeeze through.

Once inside the door I quickly surveyed the

scene. I stood in a small living room, kitchen straight ahead, and a hallway to the left that presumably led to bedrooms and a bath. I heard a door shut, which seemed to make Mrs. Gonzales more nervous.

"Do you have company?" I asked, trying to sound casual.

"No, no, just mi hijo, my son, Santo," she replied a little edgily.

Mrs. Gonzales had not asked me if we'd found Miguel, making me think she probably knew where he was. We both stood awkwardly in the middle of her small living room. I wasn't sure if she lacked social graces or just wanted me out fast.

"It might be easier to talk if we sat down," I offered.

"Jes, jes, sit down," she answered, taking a seat in a dilapidated easy chair while motioning me towards the equally dilapidated sofa across from her.

I opened my field book and pulled my pen from my purse to take notes. Mrs. Gonzales sat on the edge of her chair, hands twisting in her lap, casting occasional glances toward the hallway. My visit was definitely making her uneasy.

"Mrs. Gonzales, it has been five months since Miguel ran away from Rolling Oaks. Has he tried to make contact with you or other family members?"

"No, no, I don't see him," she answered quickly. "Nobody see him."

"Where do you think he might be hiding all this time?" I was sure she was lying and she didn't seem too comfortable doing it.

"I don't know. He don't come or call. Don't know." Mrs. Gonzales gazed into her lap.

"Do you understand there's an arrest warrant out for him? If he is stopped by the police for any new offense they'll discover it and bring him in. If he turns himself in before something like that happens, it will be much easier for him."

Mrs. Gonzales lifted her head and I could see tears forming in her eyes. "I tell him that but he don't listen," she gasped as she realized her slip.

"When did you tell him?"

"I tell him before he has all these troubles, but now I don't see him." Mrs. Gonzales made a feeble effort to cover her earlier statement. Just then a door opened and slammed shut, and a bare-chested, tattooed, burly young man I took to be Santo came into the living room and sat down next to me. I thought Mrs. Gonzales would faint.

"My mother don't understand English too good. She gets mixed up. Maybe I can answer your questions." He stared into my eyes as he spoke. Not exactly threatening, but there was a message in his look.

His mother understood well enough and he knew it. I closed my field book and put my pen away.

"Thanks for the offer but I'm finished. Here's my card Mrs. Gonzales. If you hear anything at all, please call me." I stood and handed my card to her, ignoring her son and his tough-guy act. "Thank you for your time."

I let myself out the front door and as I walked towards my car I could hear a tirade in Spanish coming from Santo. Poor Mrs. Gonzales.

I threw my field book onto the passenger seat and sat behind the wheel of my car pondering my first home call. A picture is definitely worth a thousand words. Oh yes. I would not have been able to observe the dynamics of the household in a phone or office call. I grabbed my field book again and made some notes while my impressions were fresh. When I glanced up I could see a face peering from around the tattered drape in the front window, and quickly pull away as I looked back. I made my notes rapidly and drove off, retracing in reverse my route back to the office.

Chapter Fourteen

I bustled around the dining room, putting last minute touches to the table setting. Gregory Alder was coming to dinner and I was looking forward to seeing him again. We had occasionally spoken on the telephone, but had not seen each other since I started training almost two months ago. When I called to give him my new address and phone number, I insisted he let me cook a meal for him. He accepted without hesitation. Now I was hoping the roast chicken and vegetables finishing in the oven would be as good as when my mother made it.

Edith was still with me but declined my invitation to join us. She and some local friends with whom she had become reacquainted had tickets to the Laguna Playhouse. Her parting words were that she wouldn't be back until late, and she emphasized *late*. I think she secretly thought a romance was brewing. I chuckled to myself at that thought. I felt more sisterly towards Gregory than anything else, and that was fine with me. Hearts don't get broken that way.

The doorbell rang exactly at seven. Gregory greeted me with a bouquet of flowers and two bottles of wine.

"I brought red and white since I didn't know what you were preparing," he explained as he saw my puzzled look. I hadn't expected anything so his overflowing arms took me by surprise.

"You are too generous," I answered, and took the flowers while he put the wine bottles on the kitchen counter.

"It smells good in here. This is a real treat. Thanks for having me."

"I hope it tastes good. I haven't done much cooking since I've been here."

"So I'm an experiment then?" he laughed.

"I guess so, but remember, we'll both be eating the same thing."

I took two wine glasses from the cupboard and let Gregory do the honors. Since chicken was the entrée, he chose the white, a Chardonnay from Napa Valley. While he poured I carried a tray of cheese and crackers into the living room, pulled two easy chairs to the coffee table, and motioned Gregory to sit down.

"What's new with you?" we said in unison, then laughed at our common train of thought.

"You first," he offered.

"Well, we finally finished our juvenile training. We start adult work on Monday."

"That should be a bit more challenging. Adults have had longer to work the system."

"True. But it will be nice to speak on an adult level to a probationer, instead of trying to make sure I'm not further ruining some messed-up kid's psyche by telling him to be responsible."

"Getting jaded already, my, my!" Gregory chided as he reached for another cracker and piece of cheese.

"Is that how I sounded? Sorry. I just hear that adult work is more direct. No parents or school-teachers to deal with. Fewer bleeding hearts." I thought of Miguel's mother, certain she was harboring him, but still presenting a frightened roadblock to his discovery. I hadn't mentioned this visit to Gregory, since I feared it would lead to a discussion of Carol's last day and Miguel's escape coinciding. I wasn't sure where Gregory was in his grieving process and I didn't want to open a healing wound.

"What about you? Still working twelve hour days in the much cleaner business of wills and estates?" I was eager to change the subject.

"Touche," he answered. "It hasn't been all work and no play though. I took a few days recently and went to Puerto Vallarta, laid on the beach, and ate too much good Mexican food."

"You surprise me, but good for you. That explains your nice tan."

"I needed to get away, regroup I guess. I sold Carol's condo and most of the furniture. I gave her clothes and other things to charities and kept some family items for myself. It was a painful process."

"It must have been. I would have helped but you never mentioned it to me whenever we spoke."

"No, it was something I needed to do by myself. Bring closure, as they say, but I don't think closure really takes place. Maybe numbness is a better word." Gregory paused and sipped his wine. I remained silent, unsure what to say.

"Secretly I hoped I'd find something in Carol's place that would confirm or dispel my belief that her death was no accident. But there was nothing new, just the list of A numbers. I meant to bring them to you, but I left without them. I'm sorry. Maybe you'll be able to figure out who they belong to some day, when I can remember to give them to you." Gregory set down his glass and leaned back, annoyed with himself.

"Don't worry about it. Maybe my foray into the adult world will give me some insight into those mysterious numbers. I'll do whatever I can legally to at least identify them." I almost brought up Miguel's warrant case but thought better of it. A seventeen year old boy would have no connection to an auto accident. Besides, Gregory's face had taken on a solemn look. Why raise his hopes unnecessarily.

"I'd better put those beautiful flowers in water and check on the dinner too while I'm at it."

"Need any help?" Gregory asked.

"I'll holler if I do. Relax and enjoy your wine. It's delicious by the way."

Eventually I would have the A numbers in my possession and I felt a responsibility to pursue Gregory's obsession, a responsibility I didn't want but felt obligated to meet. I thought of Carol, her young life snuffed out, her mysterious comments to both Gregory and me about making changes, her ill fated trip to Rolling Oaks to meet with the Grand Jury foreman, if that's what her reason for being on the Ortega turned out to be.

I pulled the roasting pan from the oven and

lifted the lid. Juices were bubbling and the vegetables and chicken had browned nicely. I covered the roaster and put it back in the oven, lowering the heat to keep it warm. All I had to do was add dressing to the already mixed salad, and find a vase for the flowers.

The small pantry yielded vases in several sizes. I selected a cranberry colored bowl-shaped glass which looked like it would go well with the predominantly pink and white carnations and proceeded to arrange them in it. I then finished the salad, put the chicken and trimmings into serving dishes and called Gregory to the table.

"Did I mention how lovely this place is?" Gregory commented as he took his place. "It's so warm and relaxing. It looks like you."

"I wish I could take credit. Most of this is Edith's. A few of my personal things are around but not much. I traveled light when I moved to California. But I do love this place. It suits me and Edith has no objections if I want to make my own changes. So far I'm satisfied to be here and leave things as they are."

Gregory helped himself to large portions of everything and ate heartily, full of praise on the tastiness and beautiful presentation. Always the gentleman.

"You're making me feel like Martha Stewart," I replied awkwardly. I was never good at accepting compliments, but was secretly pleased at how well the meal turned out.

We spent the next two hours leisurely eating and talking, with no more mention of Carol. We lingered over coffee and dessert, a rich vanilla ice cream topped with brandied cherries. Gregory declined my offer of an after dinner drink but stayed to help me clean the table.

"I have an early morning golf game. I'd better get going or I won't be able to get up by seven," Gregory explained. It was going on eleven.

"Why would someone who gets up early every day for work not want to sleep in on Sunday?" I teased.

"We golfers are a strange lot. What can I say. It's part of my rebellion against 'all work and no play'. Do something recreational at least once a week."

"Have a good time. I'm happy you're taking time for yourself." We walked towards the door.

"This was the nicest evening I've had in a long time. I'd cook for you but I don't want to ruin our friendship. But I know some great restaurants. I'll call you. Thanks again." Gregory gave me a light kiss on the cheek – brotherly. I watched from the door until he drove away, waving from the car window.

I put the leftover food in containers and was finishing the kitchen clean up when Edith returned. She was all bubbly about the play she'd seen and anxious to hear about my evening, somewhat disappointed that Gregory had already left.

"We had a great time," I assured her. "It was a peaceful evening for both of us. Something we each needed. By the way, the dinner came out delicious, and there are plenty of leftovers if you're hungry."

"I couldn't eat a bite. We treated ourselves to huge sundaes at the ice cream parlor on Forest Avenue after the play. I'll probably still be full at breakfast. Sit down and talk to me. I've got some thoughts about next week."

Next week was Thanksgiving. I was looking forward to the long four-day weekend and wishing that Edith would stay another week so we could have Thanksgiving together. I hadn't mentioned anything to her, but hoped she would think the same. I sat down on the sofa. Edith had settled into an armchair.

"Charlotte wants to stay at her sister's until after Thanksgiving. She called me yesterday full of tales about the fun they're having. She'll come back to

Los Angeles on the Monday after. I have no reason to hurry home so I was thinking, why don't I prepare an old fashioned Thanksgiving dinner here. You can invite that nice Gregory and any friends from work that you'd like. It'll be our last get-together before I leave you on your own." Edith looked at me questioningly, seeking a reaction.

"You read my mind. I wanted us to have Thanksgiving together but I didn't want to interfere with any plans you might have made. This is such a family holiday, and you're my family here. I don't know if Gregory or my friends at work have plans but I'll check. This is so sweet of you Edith."

"Good, it's all settled then. I love all the good food and good smells that go with the holiday. Now you young lady, start extending those invitations." Edith sat back against the chair cushions, anticipating the shopping and preparation of the next few days.

"I'll get on it first thing tomorrow." I headed for my bedroom, excited about the promise of next week with its new training and the ushering in of the holiday season.

It was too early to call Gregory, he'd still be on

the golf course. I knew Esther was having her family over on Thanksgiving, she'd talked about it for the last two weeks. That left Heather and Jan for now. There were others in the training class who were friendly types but I didn't feel close enough to them to invite them for a traditional family holiday dinner.

Jan answered on the first ring, breathless as usual. "What are you late for now?" I laughed. "This is Linda in case you didn't guess."

"On my way to church. I have about a minute."

"Can you come to Thanksgiving dinner here at Chez Davenport and experience one of Edith's culinary masterpieces?"

"You lifesaver! You've got a deal. My parents are going to my aunt's in Riverside and I couldn't face dinner with my geek cousins. My roommate's going to her boyfriend's parents. I thought I'd be eating a lonely burger at McDonald's but you came to the rescue. Got to go. Thanks a million."

"There's appreciation I thought as I hung up. I dialed Heather, doubting I'd get another such enthusiastic response. I was right. Heather thanked me profusely but said she'd be with her parents, grandparents, etc. etc. Two down and one to go. I'd try

Gregory later in the afternoon. In the meantime, I'd settle in with a book. I felt like being lazy and an overstuffed chair by the fireplace was a perfect place to do it.

I had dozed off, my book in my lap. When I awoke it was almost four. I still had to call Gregory and thought he'd probably be home by now. I stretched and headed for the phone. Gregory answered.

"I was about to call you and thank you for a great evening last night," Gregory responded, not expecting to hear from me.

"I had a good time too. The flowers look even more beautiful today now that some of the buds are opening. The reason I called, Edith wants to prepare Thanksgiving dinner here. She's returning to Los Angeles on Monday, sort of a holiday dinner and farewell rolled into one. We'd love to have you join us if you don't have other plans."

"Actually I don't. I had toyed with the idea of going to Catalina for the long weekend but the weather's been cool and I thought I'd just enjoy the quiet time at home. So no plans and I eagerly accept your invitation."

"Perfect. Jan Sussex from my training class is coming too. But I have to ask a favor of you."

"Sure."

"The story of Carol's accident has spread to the training class." I tried to choose my words carefully. "I've never mentioned meeting Carol or knowing her brother. I thought I'd have a better chance of finding something out if no one knew I had any connection. Even though I didn't expect you to bring Carol up, Jan might, she's quite a talker. If she does I'll change the subject but…."

"I understand. What about Edith?"

"I'll mention it to her too. Sorry for the intrigue." I felt a little foolish.

"No. You're right. Mum's the word. Can I bring anything?"

"Edith will have it covered. Just bring a good appetite. Two pm. See you then."

I hung up, pleased at the prospect of my favorite people all together for a great holiday meal. But little doubts nagged at me too. Jan would want to know how I met Gregory. I'd never talked about him at work and to suddenly spring this eligible bachelor on her on Thanksgiving would be to open a can of worms. I redialed Gregory.

"You're not canceling are you?" Gregory laughed when he heard my voice.

"No. I just realized that in addition to not

mentioning you're Carol's brother, we have to come up with a plausible way we know each other. I'm sorry. I'm not good at lying. Already I'm finding one lie leads to another." Silence from Gregory. "Are you there? I won't blame you if you decide this is just too much."

"I'm here. Just thinking. You know I do estate planning. If it comes up, we can say we met through Edith when I came to her house to finalize a trust, or something like that."

"That would make sense. I'll let Edith know. Thanks. See you Thursday." I felt relieved as I hung up but still had to clue Edith in. I heard her puttering in the kitchen and went in to see her.

After I finished laying out the scenario the twinkle I saw in Edith's eyes told me that not only could I count on her, but she also loved the subterfuge.

"Of course. From now on, Gregory will be my attorney. In fact, maybe I'll have him look over some of my papers. We don't want anything to interfere with what you do at work, about Carol that is."

"Edith, you're a gem. I'm sorry to have to complicate things so. But I know Jan. She's so inquisitive. Better to have our ducks in a row before the questions start."

"Don't worry. Our ducks will be lined up and

ready." Edith chuckled as she poured cornbread batter into a baking pan and put the pan in the oven.

As I walked into the classroom Monday morning I heard a yoo hoo and turned to see Jan coming up behind me.

"Aren't you early? It's not one minute to eight yet." I couldn't resist teasing the perpetually late Jan.

"I'm trying to do better, and what do I get." Jan had a downcast look.

"So you want me to congratulate you for doing what everyone else does?"

"Well this time, anyway. You have no idea what it took. My hairdryer conked out, I couldn't find my car keys, but here I am, with time to spare. Yes, congratulations are in order. But skip it, I want to know what I can bring Thursday and who else will be there."

Questions already. I was glad I'd thought ahead.

"I asked Heather but she's going to be with her family. It's just you, me, Edith, and Edith's attorney friend."

"Male or female?"

"Male."

"Single?" Jan's eye's brightened.

"Jan, this isn't a meeting of Orange County Singles, it's a Thanksgiving dinner. But, yes, he's single."

"Probably Edith's age, huh?"

I acted as nonchalant as I could muster, "I think he's mid-thirties or so. Should I ask him to bring his resume?"

"No. I'll get it out of him when we meet." I made a face and Jan laughed. "Just kidding. I'll be on my best ladylike behavior."

We were at our desks now, opening our manuals to the day's agenda. I was about to threaten Jan with something awful if she didn't behave Thursday when our trainer for the day, Charlie Cunningham, took the podium. Instead I gave her my most threatening "you'd better!" look.

Charlie had kept a low profile during most of our juvenile training. He had held various positions throughout the department in his long career but from remarks he had made, clearly liked adult work the most. He was about to launch us into this final phase of training and appeared eager to start.

"Today, and for the remainder of your training, you'll learn what happens to juveniles when they grow up and commit crimes. Many of our adult offenders started their criminal careers as minors and unfortunately never rehabilitated, but the majority of adult probationers are new to the system. As you were told your first day, not all adults who commit crimes are referred to probation, unlike the juvenile system where probation is the first stop after an arrest and before court.

"Most adults can commit crimes, be convicted and sentenced, and never be referred to the Probation department. However, the California Penal Code requires that all cases with a possible prison sentence have a pre-sentence report prepared by probation. So any defendant who may face state prison is referred to us to investigate the matter and complete a report for the judge recommending for or against probation. Remember, our job is only to recommend the defendant's suitability for probation, based on specific criteria you'll learn. If we recommend a denial, the judge will then impose the appropriate sentence. Some crimes, by law, are not eligible for probation, and that must be addressed, but the judge can refer the cases anyway. What the judge orders, we do."

I thought of Carol, supervising officers who did pre-sentence reports. She seemed to enjoy the work. My thoughts were interrupted by a question from George.

"Why would a case be referred if the crime made it ineligible for probation?"

"Good question. Our pre-sentence report is the only document that presents the facts of the crime, statements of defendant, victims, and interested parties, a family and criminal history, and an evaluation and recommendation in one stand-alone report. The judges find this helpful in determining what sentence range is appropriate. Sometimes they'll even grant probation, although technically they shouldn't."

The power of judges.

Charlie went on. "Since the pre-sentence report can have a great influence on the outcome of a case, the officers assigned to Adult Investigation must be thorough in their investigative techniques and clear and objective in their report preparation. The only area of the report that allows for subjectivity is the evaluation, but even then the evaluation must be supported by the foregoing facts. The department sends its best investigators and writers to this assignment.

Score another one for Carol. The department must have had great confidence in her to make her a supervisor of these talented officers.

"Once a defendant is placed on probation," Charlie intoned, "he's then supervised by a probation officer in a similar way as juveniles, without the school counselor or protective parents running interference. Before we get into the actual investigation and report writing, I want to acquaint you with a typical day in adult court. Shortly we'll head over to Dept. 5 in the Superior Court. Judge Carlos Higuera presides in this courtroom and handles the criminal arraignment calendar and probation violations.

"Stella Graham is the probation officer assigned to his court and if you are designated for adult work, you'll come to know her well. She's been in this courtroom for fifteen years and worked for many judges. She has only the highest praise for Judge Higuera, as does most everyone in the system and the community as well. He's fair and even-handed but takes no nonsense, and he comes down hard on repeat offenders."

I could envision supervising the same adult for twenty years. Juveniles grow out of their child status when they reach eighteen, adulthood goes on forever. But then, if someone was on probation for twenty years it meant he was re-offending and he'd probably earn a prison sentence eventually, which would take him off probation. As I adjusted my reasoning, Charlie continued.

"We'll observe Judge Higuera while he hears

arraignments, then he's agreed to meet with us in his chambers and answer any questions. He always enjoys chatting with the new DPO class. Let's get going. Check the board to see who drives the carpool. We'll gather behind the building and you can follow me to the courthouse. When you park in the visitors garage, make sure you bring in the parking stub so it can be validated by one of the clerks in the RPO office."

"RPO?" someone called out.

"Resident Probation Officer," Charlie answered. "Sorry. I'm so used to it the initials come out automatically. Our DPOs, because they are residents in the court, are called RPOs. Judges are pretty fussy about who we send, too. We had a young man in South Court in Laguna Niguel who didn't leave the position until he retired. The presiding judge there had no qualms about telephoning the CPO if she even thought we might transfer him."

We gathered our things and filed out. I enjoyed getting out of the classroom and was glad we only had about a month to go. I was anxious to start working in a real assignment, even though I had no idea what one I'd want. It was Heather's turn to drive. Her little Mazda barely held Esther, Jan, and me but we piled in anyway. We'd become used to traveling as a group.

"Today I really feel like a trainee," Esther muttered, dejection in her voice.

"Because?" from Jan.

"All the juvenile stuff had familiarity to it after all my years in institutions. Working with adults is a whole different ball game. I don't know if I'm up to it."

"Sure you are," Heather answered her. "They're just bigger kids."

We all laughed. More because Heather rarely joked than the actual humor of her statement.

Heather had maneuvered her car near the supervisors and proceeded to follow Charlie as he turned on Grand Avenue towards First Street. Charlie drove slowly, keeping the four-car caravan in sight. We turned left on First and continued through Santa Ana, eyeing the street vendors, laundromats, and tortilla factories. First Street was run down compared to Fourth Street with its Mexican village ambience. While the feeling on Fourth was festive, the feeling here was dismal. Pregnant women pushing strollers with one or two more children at their side seemed to comprise the majority of shoppers. They looked poor and tired. I thought of my one and only home visit so far, and how Mrs.Gonzales looked the way these women did, beaten down by poverty and too many children.

"Do you think those kids out there will be on someone's caseload some day?" Jan asked.

"Some will, no doubt," Esther said with the confidence borne of working years in the juvenile system. "At least seventy-five percent of our institutional kids are Hispanic. So many of their parents are from Mexico and unskilled, and work two or three jobs at low wages just to make ends meet. The kids have little supervision and are easy prey for gangs."

We were approaching Flower Street. Charlie signaled for a right turn. Everyone followed to Civic Center Drive, circled around and into the parking lot behind the court house, took a parking ticket from the machine and found a spot. It was almost 9:30 am. We walked through the back entrance and gathered around Charlie in the hallway.

"Court is already in session. We'll go into Dept. 5 quietly and take seats in the back row. Judge Higuera usually takes recess around 10:30 or so. He'll signal to us to come into his chambers then." Charlie turned and we followed him up the escalator to the second level and into the courtroom.

We walked into the middle of what appeared to be Judge Higuera berating a female defendant for appearing in his courtroom in a sheer and revealing low cut dress. Her embarrassed attorney stood at her side while the judge spoke about courtroom decorum, warning the woman that her next appearance required more modest dress or he would send her home without hearing her case. She had apparently plead not guilty to her charges but instead of setting a pre-trial date, the judge continued the matter for a week, no doubt to see if his words had any effect.

"Next case," Judge Higuera called.

A tall, heavyset man stood up from the district attorney's table. "Bruce Carson for the people, your honor."

A young woman sitting at the defense attorney's table got up and walked over to a caged area to the right of the judge's bench, and asked a prisoner inside to step forward. He did.

"Margo Oroski from the public defender's office, representing Hector Zamora, your honor."

Judge Higuera nodded. "Mr. Zamora, you're charged with two counts of burglary, a felony, in violation of Section 459 of the California Penal Code. How do you plead?"

"My client pleads 'not guilty', your honor." Mr. Zamora stood behind the screen in his orange jail

jumpsuit. An older woman and a younger pregnant one in the second row didn't take their eyes
off of him, as they dabbed away tears. Mother and
wife, so it seemed. Hector had enough sense to look
ashamed.

"Pre-trial set for two weeks from today. Dept. 22.
You will remain in custody pending this hearing."

"Thank you, your honor," said Ms. Oroski.
She returned to her seat at the table and Hector
went back to his. The two ladies were now quietly
sobbing. Ms. Oroski looked over her shoulder at
them for a long time. Her silent message worked.
The two women gathered their purses and left the
courtroom.

Several more cases were disposed of in quick order. Charlie whispered to us that no one could move
a calendar more efficiently than Judge Higuera. We
had been given a copy of the day's calendar to follow
and of the hundred cases scheduled, thirty one had
already been heard. A recess was called at 10:45.
The judge ceremoniously rose, waved to Charlie to
follow, and we all proceeded through the back door
and into the judge's chambers. Stella Graham joined
us.

Judge Higuera was impressive; tall, dark haired
with silver at the temples. He carried himself with

dignity as he warmly welcomed us and took a seat behind his large walnut desk. His chambers were impressive too. His desk was placed near the middle of the rectangular shaped room. A high and wide window was directly behind. The light coming through cast a glowing backdrop making the judge seem illuminated. Two brown leather sofas with end tables were placed in an L-shaped configuration at the far end, and three leather chairs were arranged directly in front of the desk. Potted plants, lamps, and family photos gave the room a warmth that belied the serious nature of the business conducted in it.

We took seats wherever we could fit, some slouching on the arms of the sofa, some on the floor. I noticed the walls were covered with many awards and framed certificates which honored the judge's philanthropic work. When Charlie commented on the charitable work Judge Higuera performed, especially with an orphanage in Mexico, the judge seemed embarrassed and shrugged if off as "just giving back."

"Let's hear about you folks. When do you graduate and get turned loose on crime?" He chuckled at his joke, which broke the polite tension everyone seemed to feel walking in.

Charlie brought him up to date on our training progress, with our last five weeks devoted to adult probation. The best for last, he concluded.

"You're not biased, are you Charlie?" Judge Higuera countered. They obviously knew each other well as shown by the friendly glances and casual banter.

"Just a little." Charlie admitted, but it wasn't news to anyone. "Some of these trainees will probably be assigned to adult work. Why don't you and Stella give them an idea of how best to work with you so their cases run smoothly for them and for the court."

"Sure." Judge Higuera leaned back in his chair and clasped his hands behind his head. "Stella, you could practically take the bench by now. Why don't you tell them what a curmudgeon I am and how they can avoid my wrath."

Stella laughed out loud. "Your wrath, wow, this will be hard. The truth is, and I'd say this even if the judge were not here, you won't find a fairer or firmer judge in the county, or one who is more receptive to probation's input. But do your homework. If one of your probationers is in here on a probation violation that you've filed, a technical one, not a new law violation, have your supporting documentation together, because you can be sure your probationer will have an attorney ready to make a liar out of you.

"Since my position here is to represent you in court, please provide me with what I need to speak up on your behalf. If something new comes up at the last minute, call me here in the courtroom. Good communication between us will result in the judge having the information he needs to render a judgment." Stella looked toward Judge Higuera, who nodded in agreement.

"Probation has a great representative in Stella," the judge stated. "We're able to complete a lengthy calendar every day due in large part to her efforts. And I look forward to working with whomever of you get anointed for adult assignments." With that he looked at the clock and stood up. "I need to get back on the bench if we're going to do that calendar clearing I spoke about. Thanks for coming. See you Charlie," he added as he donned his robe. He and Charlie shook hands. Stella ushered us out into the hallway and headed back to the courtroom.

We stopped by the RPO office to have our parking stubs validated. Charlie introduced us to the clerical support staff there and had us peruse a few files going to and from court. This department doesn't do much without paperwork accompanying it I thought, as I looked through the thick files that documented the criminal and personal lives of the owners.

After a while Charlie got our attention. "We'll go back to the office now, take a lunch break, and be back at our desks at 1 pm. This afternoon we'll go over the elements of a pre-sentence report and review a few actual reports. On Tuesday you'll each be assigned a current case to investigate and prepare your very own report."

There was a collective sucking-in of breath. Charlie laughed and commented that that sound always followed his announcement but not to worry. Our investigative techniques would be closely supervised and he promised our final report would make the department proud. With that we filed out to the garage and our cars and went back to the office.

Jan wanted to go across the street to Nick's for lunch. Heather wanted to go shopping, and Esther had brought a sandwich and planned to stay in and read. So it was Jan and I who ate together, splitting one of Nick's huge "health" salads.

Between bites Jan found breath enough to comment on Judge Higuera's looks and demeanor. "He's one classy man. How old do you think he is?" she queried.

"It's hard to say. I was trying to see the date on

one of his degrees to give me an idea but I was too far away. He's probably in his late fifties, don't you think?"

"Probably. A well-preserved late fifties. I didn't see any wife-type pictures. But there were lots of pictures of a young woman who resembled him. His daughter, maybe?"

"Could be. Come to think of it, I heard Esther say his daughter is on the Santa Ana City Council. That probably explains some of those award presentation pictures where the judge is smiling happily in the background."

Jan scooped up the last of her salad and dunked her bread in the remnants of dressing. "There were pictures of the judge receiving awards too."

"Esther said he does a lot of charity work, especially with an orphanage in Mexico, near Ensenada, I think." I remembered Esther speaking about Judge Higuera almost with reverence. "No wonder he's well thought of. A real renaissance man."

"Listen to us. We sound like schoolgirls with a crush. To change the subject, what can I bring Thursday. I'd like to help out."

"I'll check with Edith but I doubt she'll want anything. This meal is her swan song for now. She seemed pretty excited about the chance to cook a holiday dinner and she's probably planning to do all the family favorites."

"I'm salivating already and I just finished lunch," Jan laughed.

We paid our bill and walked back to the office. The remaining weeks of training loomed in my mind. With our focus on adult work I realized I could access adult records without raising suspicion. I would need to get the A numbers from Gregory first and then wait for the right time to go into the computer. I felt like an aging Nancy Drew. Shaking it off, I said, "Let's go and learn all about how to do a pre-sentence report. Ready, Jan?"

The smell of baking and the clatter of pans greeted me as I walked in the door. From the look of the kitchen countertops Edith had been a busy lady.

"Hi, how was your day?" Edith asked. She had traces of flour in her hair.

"Busy, and it looks like yours was too." I eyed the cooling loaves of banana bread and bowls of cut-up fruits and vegetables.

"Just a few preparations for Thursday," Edith answered with a wave of her hand. "I guess I never get used to cooking for less than five. Besides, I love Thanksgiving leftovers."

"Jan wanted to know what she could bring but I'm guessing you've got it covered."

"How sweet. Just tell her to bring her appetite. I'll take care of the rest." Edith returned to the sink where she'd been rinsing baking utensils.

I chuckled to myself. Jan's appetite went with her wherever she did.

"So what did you learn today?" Edith asked over her shoulder. She loved to hear daily progress reports about my training.

I poured myself a cup of coffee and leaned against the counter, slowly sipping the rich brew. "We started adult work and spent the morning in Judge Higuera's courtroom and chambers getting an introduction to the court scene. He's quite a person!"

Edith stopped her wiping and stood looking thoughtful for a minute. "Carlos Higuera?" she asked.

"Yes, do you know him?"

"I know of him," Edith replied. "He lives in this area. His daughter used to play at the beach with my kids, although she was quite a bit younger."

"Did you ever meet him?" I continued.

"Yes, once or twice at picnics, or some such

group event. His wife was very active in organizing community activities. She died several years ago, cancer I think. I wasn't coming down here that often then and I lost track."

"It seems like he does community stuff too, if the pictures in his chambers are any example."

"I do recall he was involved in one cause or another. I heard that his daughter, Tina I think her name is, is carrying on the family tradition. She's on the Santa Ana City Council and may run for congress."

"Just the one child?" I was starting to feel a little nosy.

"Yes. Seems his wife had a hard time just having one, lots of health problems. They sure doted on Tina, though. She looked pretty spoiled to me." Edith poured herself a cup of coffee and sat on a stool facing me. "Oh, dear, what a gossip I sound like. Forgive me. Tina's probably a lovely young lady now."

"Edith, you're such a sweetheart. I'm the one who's been playing twenty questions."

"You must be starved," she said, changing the subject. "I made a nice tuna casserole. It's just finishing up in the oven. Why don't you get comfortable and then we can eat and you can tell me about the rest of your day."

"Sounds good." I rinsed my coffee cup and went to my bedroom to change. I could see Judge Higuera's chambers, and the many pictures, and couldn't recall seeing any that looked like his wife was in them. You'd think as a widower he would want a reminder of her. Maybe it was too painful for him. No doubt about it, adult probation was going to be very interesting.

Chapter Fifteen

Edith basted the turkey while I arranged pickles and olives on a relish tray. It would be two hours before Jan and Gregory arrived, but the wonderful aromas of turkey, dressing, and pumpkin pie had me hungry already. The dinner table looked so festive it could have been in a magazine. Edith made a centerpiece of gold and rust-colored chrysanthemums, dried leaves, and greenery from the garden, and had found a white tablecloth with pilgrims parading around the border in the same colors. Her gold-edged china and crystal tied it all together, making the whole thing look like a work of art.

"I think we're just about done," Edith said with satisfaction. She stood with her hands on her hips admiring the table and the countertop full of covered dishes and breads.

"There are only four of us Edith. Who's going

to eat all this food?"

"Your nice friends can take home some leftovers. Maybe I'll take some home for Charlotte and me when I leave Sunday." Edith looked wistful. "I'll miss you, honey."

"Me too. Let's not talk about it now. We still have four days. I'm going to take a shower and get ready for our guests."

As the time drew nearer, I realized I was on needles and pins thinking of Jan and Gregory meeting. I knew Edith and Gregory would be careful, but I wasn't sure if Jan would connect Gregory's last name with Carol. Alder wasn't exactly a common name. I let the shower run over me and concentrated on pleasant thoughts.

We were about to toast Edith for the second time. The first was when we all sat down to a table that fairly groaned with delicious food. The second was after dessert when our stomachs were now doing the groaning. Gregory, who had done a masterful job of carving the succulent turkey, raised his glass and intoned, "To the lady who missed her calling as a chef and party-giver extraordinaire. Cheers!"

Edith basked in the genuine appreciation shown

her, raising her glass with a shy smile, her cheeks slightly flushed. "I always loved cooking for my family, even though I have Charlotte now. This brings back wonderful memories."

"Well I never had a family dinner this perfect," Jan claimed. Leave it to her to keep the mood from getting too sentimental. "Either the stuffing was too dry, or the cranberry sauce too runny. Can I come back here every holiday?"

"I'll bet that you're a good cook," Gregory chimed in before anyone could answer.

"Why, just because I look like I love to eat?" Jan laughed. "Wait, don't answer that. But yes, I do like to experiment in the kitchen. I might even experiment on you if you let me."

"I'll get my appointment book before you change your mind," Gregory responded. They both laughed as Edith and I watched their friendly banter.

I never counted on Jan and Gregory hitting it off in such an amazing way. They had arrived simultaneously, and had made first name introductions at the front door. By the time I came into the living room a few minutes later they were chatting like old friends. Jan looked especially nice in a floral print dress and fitted jacket. She'd even managed to tame her hair into a flattering style, pulled back from her face, but falling softly around her shoulders.

I joined Edith in helping to arrange the flowers Gregory had brought. A box of See's chocolates sat on the counter, a gift from Jan. When Edith and I carried in the tray of drinks and hors d'ouevres, Jan was in the midst of telling Gregory about our training experiences. Her usual animated style was more so today. She had Gregory's full attention.

"I feel sorry for the criminals who have to report to you. You'll be relentless." Gregory put his hands in a prayer position in mock seriousness.

Jan turned to Edith, thanking her for inviting her, while she accepted a glass of wine and an olive and cream cheese appetizer.

"I love hearing your training tales. Somehow yours sound more exciting than Linda's. Aren't you in the same class?" Edith questioned.

Jan let out a hearty laugh. "Yes. I think I just pull out more drama. Linda's the practical one. And you should see Heather. Now there's a lady who could use an occasional laugh to lighten up." She then launched into a description of Heather Caplan, our most serious trainee. We were doubled over in laughter at her anecdotes.

I watched Gregory, clearly captivated by Jan. Who'd have thought! The lively conversation continued throughout dinner and by the time we had finished toasting Edith, there was no mistaking that Jan and Gregory were very much attracted to each other. We lingered over coffee. When Edith placed a plate of after-dinner mints on the table, Jan was quick to echo our sentiments.

"If I put one of those in my mouth it would pop back out. It couldn't get past the pumpkin pie still waiting to go down."

"Well you two will have to take doggie bags home," Edith offered. "Linda and I will never be able to eat all these leftovers before I leave Sunday night."

The reminder of Edith leaving gave me a twinge. I would surely miss her. At the same time I looked forward to being on my own in California for the first time since I arrived. Edith said she'd come down for visits. I would hold her to it.

Edith began to clear the table. I started to help amidst her protest that I visit with my friends. From the looks of my two friends, they didn't need me in the conversation. I continued carrying dishes to the kitchen until the only ones left on the table were the coffee cups in front of Jan and Gregory.

I rinsed dishes while Edith loaded them into the dishwasher. As she took a serving platter from my hands, she glanced over her shoulder, then leaned toward me and whispered, "I think we've made a match. What do you think?"

"The same thing you do." We smiled and continued working.

Edith had filled two plastic containers with turkey and trimmings, and two smaller ones with slices of pie. She bagged one of each for Jan and Gregory, who gratefully accepted the offering.

At eight o'clock our guests departed. Gregory offered to walk Jan to her car, probably to get her phone number if he hadn't already obtained it earlier. Edith hugged them both as they left. When the door was shut behind them I resisted the urge to peek out the front window. The shutters were closed and I was sure they'd see me if I opened the slats even a little.

Edith and I sank into the sofas and started laughing. "I think you'll have a hard time keeping Gregory's last name a secret now," Edith chuckled. "Those two will be seeing lots more of each other."

"I'll cross that bridge when I come to it. Let's finish the table and then I'm turning in. All this eating and matchmaking has worn me out."

As tired as I was I couldn't fall asleep. Visions of Jan and Gregory floated through my head. I had never seen Gregory so relaxed or Jan with such a glow. Her hair could never be trusted to stay in place, but during the evening as it fell loose from the comb that held it back, small ringlets framed her face in the most attractive way.

Suddenly I thought of David and our first meeting and how when I returned to the dorm and looked in the mirror I almost didn't recognize myself. My eyes were bright, my cheeks flushed, and the whole effect was totally flattering. I hope Jan and Gregory have a better outcome than I did with David I thought as I finally drifted off to sleep.

The long weekend went too fast. Friday Edith and I lazed around, ate turkey leftovers and speculated on Jan and Gregory. I had expected a telephone call from Jan but the phone was silent. Edith and I took a long walk on the beach at sunset, taking in the beauty of the peaceful scene.

"I'll miss this," Edith sighed. "I'm going to have to come back often."

"I hope so. It'll seem funny to be here alone, not having your wise counsel when I need it the most."

Saturday Edith began packing her clothes for her return home Sunday. Charlotte would probably get there first and have a nice dinner prepared, a reunion of sorts. While Edith rummaged around, I decided to call Gregory. He had not given me the A numbers that Carol had hidden away. There really hadn't been the opportunity but now that I was on the adult side of my training I wanted to have them in case I got the chance to legitimately look them up.

Gregory's answer machine picked up after four rings. As I gave my name, I heard Gregory's "hello."

"You are home after all," I chuckled.

"Yes, I'm resting." He sounded tired.

"Didn't you have the day off yesterday?"

"I did, but last night Jan and I went to a movie and on a whim decided to go dancing afterward. She's got more energy than three people. Right now my legs are begging for mercy."

I never thought of Jan as a bundle of energy but maybe the dance floor brought it out. They sure didn't waste time getting together.

"You and Jan really hit it off." I didn't know what else to say.

"She's a sweet person and so much fun. I haven't had that in my life for a while."

"Does she know your last name?"

"Yes, we did exchange those. It didn't seem to

register and I didn't mention my sister."

At some point it will have to come out if they keep seeing each other I thought. I pushed it out of my mind and told Gregory the reason for my call. He excused himself and went to retrieve the numbers. He gave them to me one by one and I repeated each, including the initials, to make certain I'd written them correctly.

"I may come across one of these files in the course of my work. I'll be prepared now."

We spoke a while longer then hung up. I looked at the list of numbers, then tucked them in my purse, wondering where they'd lead me.

Chapter Sixteen

When I returned from work Monday night it seemed strange to unlock the door on an empty house. No cooking smells or cheery hello greeted me. I had barely shut the door behind me when the phone rang. A hello from Edith after all. She let me know she was home and settled, glad to see Charlotte and catch up on the last few weeks. We chatted for a while then said goodbye with promises to keep in touch.

I changed into jeans and a sweater then poked around in the refrigerator for something quick to prepare. There was still plenty of turkey but I couldn't face another turkey sandwich. Instead I put on a pot of coffee, scrambled some eggs, and made toast. I found a bran muffin and heated that. It would be dessert.

I sat at the counter and ate, thinking about the

day. I hadn't spoken to Jan since Thanksgiving and had expected her to be bubbling with news of her evening, maybe even the weekend, with Gregory, but she was subdued. She was already at her desk when I arrived in class, looking over the day's agenda. She glanced up, waved, and went back to her reading. I sat down at my desk, said hello to Heather who had been staring at me, and turned to the papers in front of me. I had the feeling Heather had been filled in and was probably bursting with the knowledge, but she was too straight-arrow to say anything to me.

Barbara Sanders was our instructor today. Last week we had each received an adult case to investigate. Most of us had not gone beyond a perusal of the case file and some appointment setting. After the four-day weekend we needed some review before getting back into it.

Barbara went around the room, asking each of us to summarize what we'd done so far. We had all been assigned misdemeanor cases. Most of the defendants were first offenders, their offenses ranging from bad checks to shoplifting. No one was in custody.

"I'm pleased to hear how you're progressing," Barbara said after listening to our reports. "Remember, before you interview the defendant,

read the arrest and crime reports carefully, and talk
to the victim, and any other interested parties. You'll
be much better prepared for the sob story the defendant will try and lay on you. Also, run DMV, local,
and state record checks. Your defendant may be
new here, but could have a record in another state,
such as the state in which he was born. Take good
notes during your interviews. They will be the basis
for you pre-sentence report and you want the information you've gathered to be able to support your
recommendation.

"Charlie and I will be available the rest of the
morning for any questions or problems that come
up."

My case seemed fairly simple. A woman named
Sally Niznik had stuffed a blouse and sweater into
a large shopping bag she was carrying and left the
department store without paying. A security guard
had been watching her and apprehended her outside
the store. She said she had put them there for safe-
keeping while she shopped and forgot they were still
in her bag when she left.

When Sally appeared in court she pleaded nolo
contendre or "no contest", which we learned is not
an admission of guilt but has the same effect as a
guilty plea for sentencing purposes.

I looked over at Jan. She was going back and forth between an open penal code and her case file, completely engrossed in her work. I'd never seen her quite this dedicated. It definitely kept her from making eye contact with me.

The room was buzzing with phone conversations and paper shuffling. I went back to my file, working diligently until lunchtime. I decided to corner Jan then.

As the class began to trickle out the door around noon I looked over at her. She was fidgeting with her purse but still at her desk. I grabbed my purse, went over to her and in my sweetest voice asked, "Where to?"

"Wherever," Jan answered, still avoiding my gaze.

I secretly hoped Heather would have other plans so I could talk to Jan. She had made no move to join us and waved us off when we walked toward her desk, pointing to the sack lunch she had. So far so good.

"Do you want a salad across the street or Mexican food in Santa Ana?"

Jan shrugged. "Across the street's fine."

We walked over to Nick's, crowded as usual, but found a small table inside. We sat, ordered, and sipped our drinks. Finally I couldn't wait for the strangely silent Jan to speak up.

"Jan, what's the matter? You haven't said two words to me all morning. Didn't you like the turkey?" I didn't meant to say it like that but it broke the ice.

When Jan stopped her nervous laughing she answered. "You know I loved the turkey and everything else. That's the problem. I'm embarrassed."

"Embarrassed?" I was incredulous. "What on earth for?"

"I flirted too much with Gregory, and he flirted back, and now we've gone out a couple times, and oh......"

"Oh what?"

"I was thinking maybe you liked him and I stole him, or something like that. Like I was too forward and beat you to him." Jan was genuinely dismayed.

"I hardly know Gregory. He's a nice guy but not really my type. I had no designs on him, believe me. I'm happy you two hit it off." I meant it but felt guilty about the "hardly knowing" part. He was really my friend, not Edith's attorney, as Jan had been told. I doubted that Gregory had said anything yet but if the relationship continued to develop the truth would come out.

"Are you sure?" Jan's eyes were intense. "I'd feel so much better if I could believe that."

"I'm sure. In fact Edith and I were talking about your budding romance after you left Thursday night. If your relationship goes somewhere it would be great. Now relax, eat your lunch, and tell me what you and Gregory have been up to."

Jan dug into her salad with apparent relief and between bites regaled me with their weekend of long phone conversations and dates at the movies and dinner.

"Gregory is such a sincerely nice person and amazingly he's interested in me too. I feel so comfortable with him, like I don't have to be thinner or prettier or anything but me. I don't know how long this will last but I'm going to enjoy the ride."

I wanted so badly to tell Jan about Carol, and how I really knew Gregory, but I was already in too far with the subterfuge. 'What a tangled web we weave…….' went through my head.

"Maybe it will be a permanent ride."

"Time will tell," Jan mused, happily restored to her old self.

The week went quickly. We were each assigned

a second case to investigate before we'd finished our first one. Charlie said to get used to it because adult investigation assignments were a juggling act of court deadlines, interviews, and report writing. Being organized helped. I enjoyed making the various law enforcement contacts, even the defendant interviews. Sometimes it was daunting, thinking of the authority I had over other people's lives. All the more reason to do a thorough job.

Charlie wished us a happy weekend on Friday and told us we'd have a break on Monday from our investigative work. We would be visiting a new drug program in Santa Ana and attending the dedication ceremonies. It sounded like an important event and I was beginning to enjoy anything that took me out into the community. I looked forward to a quiet weekend of reading, lolling on the beach, maybe shopping. I hadn't bought any new clothes since the shopping spree I went on while living at Edith's. I'd been rotating my new outfits with suits I had worn as a teacher. A couple of new dresses wouldn't hurt my budget.

I arrived in class early Monday, well rested from my lazy weekend, and feeling spiffy in a new navy and red print dress with a matching short, fitted jacket. I even splurged on a pair of red pumps to complete the outfit. When a wolf-whistle from laid-back George Grosky greeted me I knew my money had been well spent.

Martin took the podium to orient us to the morning ahead. The Safe Haven residential drug treatment program for adults, based in New York, had opened a branch in Santa Ana, with a capacity for twenty-five men and women. Residents would be there by court commitment for a minimum of a year, with outpatient follow-up for another year. The program was to be housed in a building previously used by the Probation department as a school for delinquent boys. The school had closed years ago, paving the way for lengthy negotiations between the city of Santa Ana and the founders and benefactors of Safe Haven in New York, who had wanted to expand their successful program to the West Coast. When all the agreements were completed, the building was refurbished for an adult clientele with separate bedroom wings for men and women and a common living room and kitchen area in the center. Staff offices were arranged around a large reception area at the main entrance.

The first residents had moved in this week,

brought over from jail after being ordered by the court to participate in this program that offered the hope of recovery for even the most serious drug abusers.

"If you are assigned to Adult Supervision, you may have some of these residents on your caseload. As their probation officer, you will work closely with the staff at Safe Haven. Failure in the program is a probation violation, but I'm jumping ahead." Martin took a breath. "Today you'll just get to enjoy the hoop-la surrounding a major event for Santa Ana. The mayor will be there, the city council, the head honchos from New York, lots of speeches, but good refreshments, I hear."

Everyone laughed. Martin could always put the personal touch on any situation.

We gathered our belongings and left the office. Safe Haven was only three blocks away so we walked, our parade of probation trainees soon joining the crowd that had gathered on the grounds in front of the platform set up near the entrance.

Safe Haven was a one-story building spread out among mature trees and expansive lawns. The stucco exterior sported a fresh coat of white paint, setting off the red tile roof to advantage. If one didn't know better, the place could be taken for a small hotel.

Dignitaries were assembling on the platform, looking over notes, conferring among themselves. On the lawn in front, folding chairs were lined up in rows, most of them filled. Barbara and Charlie had gone on ahead and garnered seats for the class which they were now busy guarding politely, fending off spectators who tried to sit down. When we arrived a look of relief came over their faces. We took our seats where a program had been placed on each. I gave it a quick glance and was about to read it more thoroughly when something achingly familiar distracted me.

I heard him before I saw him. Someone was thanking him for coming in place of his parents, offering regrets on his father's illness. I was immobile. My head wouldn't turn and I'm sure if someone talked to me I would have been mute. Then I heard David's voice, unmistakable from the voice I remembered, the one that ran through my head unbidden through the years.

"My dad would have so enjoyed being here today. He's doing much better but his cardiologist wouldn't allow him to travel. Of course my mother won't leave his side so you must settle for me." David still had the self-effacing quality that made him so special to me. But would a special person leave me the way he did?

I took a few deep breaths. My heart, which had seemed to stop, was beating again. Fortunately my classmates were so busy looking around they hadn't noticed the state I was in. Get yourself together, I willed. With any luck he'll never see you and this will soon be over.

The chairman of the Board of Supervisors was about to take the podium. I could hear the chairs sliding around on the platform as the other speakers sat down. I kept my eyes down, looking at the program in earnest. There in bold letters at the bottom were the names of Elise and Forrest Wyndham, major benefactors for both Safe Haven drug treatment centers. David was listed as the legal counsel for the centers. My mind raced as I began filling in the years. David's still under his dad's thumb and his father's cardiac problems prove he does have a heart after all. I guess I'll never get over that hurt. Suddenly the crowd became silent and the voice of Board Chairman Williams was welcoming the large turnout.

I looked up slowly, keeping my eyes on the podium. From the periphery of my vision I could see men and women sitting on each side. I didn't trust myself to scan the platform, not sure how I'd react once I saw David, especially if we should make eye contact.

Chairman Williams was effusive in his praise of this special event and all the people it had drawn. I focused on him completely.

"Before we meet the people who have made this happen, I want to welcome and introduce training class 72 of the Orange County Probation Department. Please stand and take a bow. You'll be an important part of Safe Haven's program." With that he gestured toward our rows, where our trainers beamed as they stood up, the class following suit. I wasn't counting on this. Staying invisible wasn't going to happen.

I stood, my eyes set on Chairman Williams. While we were being applauded, for what seemed like an eternity, I let my gaze drift a little, and there was David, looking at us. How many times I had dreamed of seeing him again, how it would be, but reality is much harsher than romantic fantasies. He looked more mature, but not older. His hair was cut shorter but it still managed to escape into a curl here and there. His dark gray suit, gray shirt, and deep blue tie made his blue eyes sparkle the way I remembered. I felt a lump in my throat, fixated on David's face, remembering our good times.

We started to sit down when David saw me. I couldn't turn away. He stared at me in a puzzled state of recognition. When we last spoke, I was planning to be a school teacher in Michigan. A probation office in California is quite a leap. Whatever circumstances he was trying to reconcile in his mind, he knew it was me. Our eyes locked and his face seemed to drain of color. He mouthed "Linda?" to me and I nodded. I finally looked away. By now Chairman Williams was beginning the program of speakers. I sat back and watched as various city officials spoke about how happy they were to have such a successful drug program here, and how each played a small role in bringing this about. I could hardly concentrate, occasionally looking at David, who was still staring at me.

When councilwoman Tina Higuera was introduced I was jarred from my thoughts. Jan nudged me, reminding me that she was Judge Higuera's daughter. The lady with political ambitions. Tina was small, dark and pretty. Her shiny black hair was pulled back at her neck with a red ribbon that matched her red dress. She was bright-eyed and confident with high cheekbones suggesting an Indian heritage. She spoke with the authority of one who was comfortable in the public eye.

"Words can't express the excitement I feel today, seeing our two years of hard work culminating in the opening of Safe Haven here in Santa Ana. All of you know what a well-respected and successful program Safe Haven has been in New York. When they decided to open a West Coast branch many cities vied for the chance to be their home. Santa Ana feels honored to have been chosen and to be able to provide a first class drug rehabilitation program for the citizens of Orange County.

"I'd like to introduce someone whose help has been invaluable in tying up all the loose ends such an endeavor creates, our legal counsel and son of the Forrest Wyndhams, David Wyndham." Tina waited for David to join her at the podium, shook hands, and then retreated to her seat.

David glanced at the crowd, composed himself, and began by thanking Tina for the nice comments, then launched into what was probably a fine speech but my buzzing head couldn't take it in. Another nudge from Jan, "What a babe!" I nodded. He was definitely a babe.

"………as counsel and as my parents' representative, I will spend as much time here as needed to aid the management and staff of Safe Haven in the smooth start-up and operation of the West Coast branch. Now I invite you to join us inside the lobby for informal tours of the facility and a buffet lunch."

David gestured toward the building as everyone clapped. When the applause subsided people started moving toward Safe Haven's entrance where guides were stationed ready to provide tours.

Jan and Heather jumped up, and I followed, not wanting to be caught alone with David, should he try to reach me. Charlie and Barbara were at the end of the row, ushering everyone toward the building. Martin went on ahead, no doubt hungry for the buffet lunch. I stayed within the center of the group and kept my eyes on the approaching facility. I didn't dare turn around and face David.

Soon we were in the lobby and our class dispersed, some wanting to take a tour, others wanting to eat. I wanted only to disappear. As I looked around trying to decide what to do I realized that as hard as it would be to talk to David, I'd feel worse if he didn't seek me out at all. Then the touch of a hand on my elbow brought me out of my thoughts and into David's gaze. This is it. Be strong. You weren't the bad guy here.

We looked at each other for a long time. Finally I held my hand out to shake David's hand and in a voice I hoped was under control said, "Hello David. What a surprise for both of us."

He took my hand and covered it with his other hand, in a warm grip that sent little currents of excitement through my body.

"Linda, you look more beautiful than I imagined you would."

"You took time to imagine me?" I responded, immediately regretting my words.

"I deserved that, and more, I know." David looked around. Jan had just noticed us and stood looking astonished, with her fork midway to her mouth. Heather had filled her plate and joined Jan, following her gaze in our direction. We were attracting an audience.

"We can't talk here Linda, and there's so much I want to say."

"Your silence all these years told me plenty. Anything else is probably best left unsaid."

"A lot of things have happened, to you too, it looks like. We should at least catch up. Would you be willing to meet me after work today? There's a nice coffee shop on Tenth Street and Main. Please?"

The pleading in his eyes made me melt. Against my better judgment I agreed.

"I'm off at five. I should be able to be there by

5:30. Is that okay?" I queried.

"Fine. I'll be there." David's face brightened. "Goodbye 'til tonight."

I rejoined my friends who stared at me with a look of confusion and anticipation.

"An old friend from college days. Didn't expect to see him here," I tossed off as nonchalantly as I could muster.

"That babe is a friend of yours?" Jan seemed incredulous.

"We had a few classes together. No big deal." They weren't going to get anything out of me yet. "Now what's good at the buffet table? I'm starved"

By the time we returned to the office I was actually looking forward to meeting David. The initial shock of seeing him had been replaced by a steely resolve to treat him as I would any other friend I had not seen for a while. For too long I had harbored resentment over the treatment I had received from David's parents, feeling diminished in their eyes. But I had much to be proud of. My head would be held high when I met David tonight.

I went through some case files, making notes for tomorrow. It was nearing five o'clock and I didn't feel like starting anything this late. I cleared my desk and went to the restroom to freshen up. I ran a comb through my hair, trying to accentuate the blond highlights here and there. I reapplied lipstick, which matched the red in my dress. Looking good! I felt confident and hoped I'd survive our meeting with my confidence still in tact when it was over.

The traffic was heavy as I drove through the Santa Ana streets. I turned on Main and neared Tenth shortly before 5:30. I parked in the lot behind the coffee shop, checked myself in the mirror and went in.

David was already there, seated in a booth towards the back. He stood when he saw me approach, gave me a tentative hug that weakened my knees, and then we both sat down. I took the seat opposite him. We both stared at each other until the waiter came to take our order. Then David finally spoke.

"I was afraid you wouldn't show up. I'm so glad you did."

"You know me, always reliable." I sounded too casual. I had no idea where this meeting was going and I was too afraid to let down my guard for fear I'd blubber all over the table.

"Yes, I know you. I've yet to meet anyone like you." David looked into my eyes as he said it.

The honesty that David always admired in me

came to the surface. "Oh, please, David, I still remember my last glimpse of you driving away from my dorm, after you promised you'd write, and two years would go by fast, and...and....nothing, nothing for all these years. If you hadn't seen me by chance, we'd still be apart. What is the point of all this?"

David was taken aback by my switch in tone. "You're not the only one who was hurt. You may not believe it but I suffered too."

"Really? Everything was in your hands David, not mine. You made your choice and it didn't include me. Pretending otherwise insults my intelligence. The proof is in the pudding, as my dad used to say." Anger and sadness washed over me.

The waiter brought our coffee and some scones. While he placed everything on the table I talked myself into staying neutral and calm. Just an old friend, remember.

"I guess from your perspective it was pretty cold the way I left, and then not hearing from me, what else could you think. But if you'll hear me out maybe you'll feel differently. Even if you walk away and I never see you again, I'll be eternally grateful for this opportunity to set things straight. You deserve to know the truth." He sat with his eyes downcast, probably wondering what verbal barrage I'd throw at him next.

I put some jam on a scone. "Okay, I'd like to hear the truth." I put a little too much emphasis on the "truth" and felt ashamed. I didn't want to be unkind. I smiled at him, "Tell me."

David sipped his coffee and began. "After graduation I returned to New York. I declined the European trip much to my parents' surprise. I wanted to start studying for the bar exam so I could begin working for my dad that much sooner and complete my two years. Besides I would have thought of nothing but you in Europe. My plan was to take you there after we were married and enjoy it together."

I shifted in the wooden booth. This was going to be hard to hear.

"I passed the bar on my first try. So many times those first few months I started to write to you. I missed you so and tried to pour out my heart in letters, but they all sounded like legal briefs when I read them over. I'd tear them up and start again. But months went by before I knew it. I was kept so busy at my dad's firm that I'd come home exhausted, too tired to even make a phone call.

"I knew what my parents were doing. But by then I didn't care. I was fulfilling my obligation. I talked about you every chance I could. I was determined my parents would love you like I did. I think they were even coming around. Then my dad had a massive heart attack. My big strong dad, who'd never had an unhealthy day, just keeled over at the office. He almost died.

"Our family went into a tailspin. My mother couldn't handle it. Suddenly I was in charge of everything. Luckily my dad's strong constitution brought him through but the episode left permanent damage to his heart. His recuperation was slow. It was months before he could return to work on a limited basis." David paused for a drink of his coffee and took a scone.

"They're good," I said as I brushed the crumbs from my lap. David had just told me about a major family crisis and I was recommending the scones. It seemed insensitive. So far I had managed to say the wrong thing every time I opened my mouth. I made an attempt at recovery.

"I'm sorry to hear such bad news about your dad. He's fortunate he had you there."

"It turns out that way. My dad was always such a hard driving person. He had a difficult time emotionally accepting his limitations. He started working more hours than he should have and had a minor set back last year. He's on stronger medication now and is coming along well. I think he finally got the message that if he doesn't slow down he'll stop for good. My mom's at his side, watching him like a hawk."

"That's good news David." My words sounded hollow. I had a hard time feeling too sorry for Forrest Wyndham, but I was beginning to feel some sympathy for David. It must have been quite a time.

"Anyway, the point of all this, to answer your earlier question, is that once we got through the first crisis, almost three years had gone by. For a while I had no sense of time, only the need to get through each day, dealing with my mother's fear, my dad's illness, and the abundance of work on my shoulders at the law firm.

"When my head was finally above water I realized I'd let you slip out of my hands. I figured that you'd probably forgotten me, maybe were even married. Pride, stupidity, you name it, kept me from writing or calling. I was sure you'd gone on with your life and any contact from me this late would only be upsetting. Looking back I'd do it much differently. I'm older, sadder, and wiser, and as the saying goes, hindsight is 20/20. I hope you can forgive me." David drained his coffee cup and leaned back, finally taking a bite of the scone.

"You should have called. I would have been waiting. But as each year went by you became a more distant, sweet, sad memory."

"Seeing you today was like an answer to my prayers that some day I'd have a second chance. At first I thought I was dreaming, that I'd blink and you'd be gone. In my thoughts you were teaching school in Michigan. Then you appear before me in California, training to be a probation officer no less. You want to tell me about your last few years?"

"I guess we both had a shock today." I spent the next few minutes filling David in on my teaching, coming here for a publishing job, ending up at the Probation Department. I left out any reference to Carol and her accident. I let David think I was drawn to Probation by a newspaper ad that intrigued me. When I finished, David was shaking his head.

"Who would have thought we'd both end up on the West Coast," David sighed.

"I ended up here, but aren't you just visiting?" I questioned.

"Yes, for now. I'll be coming back and forth as a legal consultant for Safe Haven. It's the intention of their Board of Directors to open a facility in San Diego once this one's worked out the kinks. I'll be involved there too. Between the two programs, and maybe a third in Los Angeles, I'll be here quite a bit."

"What about your dad, his needing your help and all?"

"Things have settled down for him. His office staff has been beefed up and after his last scare my dad definitely follows his doctor's advice. I don't need to be there full time."

Silence hung between us then like something palpable. The thought of David in the same city with me made me thrilled and frightened at the same time. The old feelings had quickly surfaced, scaring me. I couldn't risk another heartbreak. When the waiter brought our bill, I decided to leave.

"Thanks David. I appreciate your explanation and truly regret what you experienced with your dad. I can forgive you, but it's hard to forget. Anyway, we're older now, and different. The years have probably changed both of us in ways we don't even realize. It was wonderful seeing you again though, and knowing you're well."

We were both standing now. I held my hand out to him. David took it and held it between both of his.

"Could we get to know each other again?" After

what seemed like minutes, David let go of my hand and fumbled in his pocket, came up with a business card and handed it to me. "I'll leave it up to you. Unless you have someone in your life, that is," he added as an afterthought, his eyes searching mine."

"No I don't," I answered as I took the card.

He seemed relieved. "Your best chance of reaching me is my cell phone. Maybe we could have dinner some night. I won't press you."

We walked to the parking lot together. David waited until I drove out of the lot before he got into his car. We had said a cordial goodbye but I'd made no promise to call. As I drove home I turned my radio to the loudest music I could find, anything that would drown out the thoughts roaring through my head.

Chapter Seventeen

I went through the rest of the week in a blur. The classwork was completed somehow, but I couldn't say how. At night I brooded. I must have handled David's card a hundred times, and almost picked up the phone at least a third of those times. True to his word, David never tried to reach me. He could have found my work number easily. He didn't have my home number. I guess it was up to me.

When Friday arrived I wasn't looking forward to the weekend by myself. Jan and Gregory planned a trip to Yucaipa on Saturday to pick apples and buy some fresh cider. Jan invited me to join them to get me out of my mopey mood, but I declined. I would have felt like a fifth wheel. Besides, watching their budding affection for each other would have pained me further under the circumstances. I guess I wanted a shoulder to cry on.

Friday night I called Edith and asked if she'd like some weekend company. She was glad to hear from me and insisted I come Saturday morning and spend the night. Music to my ears. I went to sleep that night thankful for a place to turn. Edith could always put things in balance.

When I neared Edith's familiar courtyard I could see her handyman putting up Christmas lights along the second story balcony. Edith was out the door before my car was parked.

"You look tired honey, working too hard?" After a long hug, Edith appraised me at arm's length.

"Not too hard. I must look terrible." I grabbed my overnight bag and walked towards the door. The smell of cinnamon wafted in from the kitchen. I hoped Charlotte was baking her scrumptious rolls. Inside the entry I stopped to take in the familiar scene. Charlotte bustled in to greet me.

"I have hazelnut coffee or hot cocoa, and some cinnamon rolls just out of the oven." Charlotte grinned in satisfaction. No event passed without food to accompany it.

"You two sure know how to make a girl feel welcome." My eyes were starting to brim. One more nice gesture and I'd be a sloppy heap. Edith sensed my fragile demeanor and took hold of the situation.

"Charlotte, why don't you fix a nice tray with everything on it and bring it into the library. I'll help Linda unpack her things and we'll be right down." With that she hoisted my bag and headed up the stairs. I dutifully followed behind.

Once in my old room Edith set the bag aside and put a hand on each of my shoulders. "Do you want to talk? Because you look like you lost your best friend."

"No Edith, I found him again. But it's just as bad." I sat down on the bed. Warm tears started down my cheeks as I began to tell Edith about seeing David again.

"That sounds like good news to me. Two people who cared about each other coming back together."

"There's so much more. We never broke up. It's just that he never called me again. I wasn't what his parents had in mind and they put pressure on him. I was heartbroken for so long and then when I thought I'd healed I saw him again. All the old feelings flooded back." I stopped to blow my nose.

"Did he explain himself?" Edith questioned.

"Yes, and I guess I understand but I'm afraid to be vulnerable again." I went on to tell Edith what

David had told me about his dad's illness and all his obligations, his apologies and wish for us to get to know each other again.

"Sounds like he still has feelings for you. Don't you think you owe each other the chance to see where those feelings might lead?"

"But what about him not calling me, or fighting for me? I don't know if I can trust him to be the man I need him to be."

Edith thought for a while and then answered slowly. "People don't often do the things we expect them to do. It doesn't make them bad or unworthy of a second chance. A young man like your David, fresh out of college, with a powerful father who expected a return on his educational investment, would probably have a hard time doing anything other than what he did. He surely suffered too. Now circumstances have brought you together again. I don't believe in coincidences. The time wasn't right for you before, maybe it is now. This is something you'll need to play out or you'll always regret it."

I looked at Edith. She was right. I was in turmoil because that was what I wanted to do but was afraid of the consequences. There are no guarantees, but what David and I had once was worth resurrecting if it meant anything in the first place.

I wiped my eyes. "Thank you. You've put into perspective what has been jumbled in my head all week. Now we'd better get to those rolls and coffee or Charlotte will feel neglected."

"You'll call him?" Edith asked expectantly.

"When I get home tomorrow night. I'm not even sure he's still here in California, but I've got his cell phone number, so I'll be able to reach him."

"Good." Edith grabbed my hand and together we headed for the library where I enjoyed the most luscious rolls Charlotte had ever baked.

Driving home Sunday afternoon I was full of anticipation for the week ahead. Spending time with Edith was just what I needed. She caught me up on her family's activities and I filled her in on work and Jan and Gregory's romance. We laughed over silly things and when I left, I had an invitation to spend Christmas with her. Mom would be disappointed I wasn't flying to Detroit but it would be impossible to do so just when our class was finishing up and preparing for graduation.

When I walked in the front door of my house at six o'clock it was dark and quiet. I switched on the hall light and went towards the bedroom carrying my overnight case. As I entered the room the phone message light was flashing. I set the bag on a chair, turned on the bedside lamp, and hit the message button. Two messages, one from Mom and the other from Jan, hoping I was feeling better. Disappointment welled up that neither had been from David, that he hadn't somehow tried to learn my home number. He said he wouldn't press me. So far he'd kept his word.

I unpacked, changed, and made myself an omelet. I'd put David's card on the counter earlier and eyed it as I sipped some hot tea. He had an array of numbers; his New York office, the Santa Ana Safe Haven office, and his cell phone. At this time of night the cell phone made the most sense. I dialed the number and listened to the rings, then a message machine came on. At the beep I identified myself, said that I'd like to hear from him, and gave him my home number. When I hung up my hands were shaking. I put the card in my purse and then cleared my dinner dishes. When I went to bed I fell asleep wondering how long it would take for my call to be returned.

When I arrived at class on Monday, Jan was seated in my desk chair telling Heather all about her weekend. She gave me a wary eye as I approached but seemed relieved that I wasn't in the funk in which she last saw me. A small bag of apples was next to my desk, fruits of her mountain trip with Gregory. We chatted for a while longer, agreed to have lunch, and then settled in for "clean-up" day. That's what Charlie had called it when we left on Friday. No lectures on Monday, just a day to finish investigations, put files in order, in other words, "clean-up".

I had two sentencing reports to finish and some telephone calls to make. We were on our last assignment before graduation and I was glad we were almost finished. Our thoughts were now turning to where we'd be assigned. I put David out of my mind as I fished in my purse for a tissue for my runny nose. I came up with not only a tissue but a piece of paper with the six A numbers on it. I'd forgotten they were there and looking at them now reminded me I still hadn't checked on them. Since we were working adult cases this would be the best opportunity to do that without arousing suspicion.

By mid morning I finished dictating one report. The other wouldn't take long, and the phone calls could wait until afternoon. The A numbers seemed to stare back at me, waiting to tell their story. I switched my computer to the records screen, entered my officer number, and the first A number on the list, A43271 with the initials S.G. after it. Up popped a brief history of Santo Gonzales and his criminal convictions. The case was closed and the file checked out to officer 2849. The last remark on the screen: File currently lost.

The next five A numbers provided almost identical information. Closed cases, all checked out to 2849, all currently lost. While I puzzled over the commonality, I scrolled to a new screen that identified probation officers by their number. Ed Gerber was the owner of 2849. The directory showed him to be a supervisor in adult investigation. I wanted so badly to look at those files but how could I call and ask for even one without some reason that made sense. I was already over the line.

I tried to busy myself with my own work but the nagging voice in my head seemed to be Carol's. It wasn't just coincidence that the six A numbers represented such similar cases. All Santa Ana residents with a history of assaultive behavior and drug use, and all cases closed and checked out to the same person. And now lost, but maybe not. The heck with it. I was calling Ed.

Ed Gerber picked up on the first ring. In my

most innocent voice I explained I was a trainee doing adult cases and I thought he might have some files that could be helpful in my current investigation of a Santa Ana drug seller. The files might contain information about associates that could give me a better picture of the defendant. I didn't mention that the files were shown as lost. The records section could have failed to update the screen.

"What are the A numbers?" Ed asked.

I breathed a relieved sigh. So far so good. "The first one is A43271, Santo Gonzales, the second ...."

"Those files," he interrupted, "I never had them. They were checked out to a former supervisor, Carol Alder, who I'm sorry to say died tragically in an auto accident last year. I supervise her old unit and inherited the same officer number."

Hearing Carol's name my mind raced. No files were found with her.

"Are you there?" Ed questioned.

"I'm sorry. Yes. I wasn't prepared for that piece of news."

"Sorry to bum you out. It was quite a shock here. Anyway, the files were apparently checked out by Carol, the morning of her accident, but no one has ever found them. I have her old office and they're not here."

"Thanks. I'm sorry to heave bothered you."

"No bother. Good luck on your training."

I hung up, trying to digest the information I'd just learned. On Carol's last day of life, she checked out these six files, files important enough to keep their numbers written on a separate piece of paper hidden away. She then left the office without telling anyone where she was going. But Esther thought she was on her way to meet with the Grand Jury foreman while he was at Rolling Oaks. Why? For the first time since Gregory posed his theory to me about Carol's death not being accidental, I believed he was right.

I looked again at the names attached to the A numbers. Santo Gonzales, Gilbert Silva, Bartolo.... wait, Santo Gonzales? Wasn't he the older brother of Miguel, one of the juvenile warrant cases I worked? In fact he was the one who tried to intimidate me when Mrs. Gonzales gave herself away about Miguel. The coincidence of all this was getting spooky.

"Ready for lunch?" Jan was at the side of my desk. How long had she been there?

"Sure." I answered, folding the list of numbers and tucking them into my purse. Thankfully Jan didn't seem to notice. "What are you in the mood for?"

"Just a salad. I'm trying to lose weight." Every

Monday Jan started a diet, which usually fell apart by Thursday.

"Right, I forgot, it's Monday," I laughed.

We went across the street and took one of the sidewalk tables. Jan bubbled about her weekend with Gregory while we waited for our order. I wondered if he'd told her about Carol yet but Jan didn't seem like she was holding any secret information. I planned to call Gregory tonight to tell him what I learned.

While I listened to Jan I thought of David. I wanted to share my news too but held back. Maybe David was sorry he left me his card, and I might not hear from him after all. I stayed silent, thinking I was beginning to be a repository of secrets. I wasn't crazy about the role.

The rest of the afternoon I buried myself in work. By the end of the day I was tired but I'd finished my second report, all my phone calls, and had even mentally prepared myself for tomorrow's meeting with Martin to receive my performance evaluation. I was anxious to be home and take care of my other business.

I headed straight for my bedroom to see if I had any phone messages. None. I dropped my purse on the bed and kicked off my shoes, trying not to be disappointed. I changed into slacks and a t-shirt, all the while staring at the phone, willing it to ring. And it did. I jumped slightly at the sound, then composed myself and answered.

"Linda, it's David."

I sank onto my bed, goosebumps all over my arms.

"Hi David. It's good to hear your voice."

"Yours too. I almost gave up on you calling me. I haven't stopped thinking of you since I saw you."

My heart fluttered at his words. What a silly game we've both been playing, yet part of me still wanted to protect myself from further hurt.

"Me too. I just needed some time to think about what to do. I realized I'd never feel right if I didn't give us another chance." I paused and wondered if David could hear my heart thumping through the phone.

"Thanks Linda. I wanted it to be your decision. I won't let you down. Anyway, I'm back in New York now and I'll be here through the Christmas holiday. I've got a flight back to Orange County on January 4th and plan to spend two or three weeks with Safe Haven staff. Can I call you as soon as I get in?"

"Yes, that would be great. By then I'll have graduated and be in my new assignment. I can bore you with all the details."

"You could never bore me Linda."

My body was jelly now. I gathered my composure and calmly replied, "We'll see."

"Linda........ my parents said to say 'hello'," David's voice faltered a bit.

I stiffened at this unexpected turn. Were they holding out an olive branch?

"Hello to them too," I mustered.

"Linda?"

"Yes?"

"I can't wait to see you."

"Me either."

"Good-bye for now."

"Good-bye." I hung up the phone, dazed and happy. David and me. I wanted to close my eyes and not open them until January 4th. My rumbling stomach told me to face reality and eat something.

I went to the kitchen and put together a salad, opened a can of tuna and dumped it on top, and poured a diet Coke. Gregory replaced David in my thoughts as I tried to think of how to tell him what I learned about the A numbers. They had a connection, that was apparent. Carol knew just what it was too. Maybe it cost her her life. I shivered at the thought.

I browsed the newspaper while I ate. The local

edition of the Los Angeles Times was full of murder or accident stories. The latest in the drug/gang wars was duly reported. As I scanned recent events I stopped on the name Luis Hebron. His name was on one of the A files that was lost. He was now apparently in a group of men contacted by the police for "suspicious behavior" in a known drug trafficking area. All were released when a search of their persons found no contraband. I tried to recall what the computer screen said about Luis but couldn't. Only that his case was closed. If he doesn't clean up his act it will be open again soon.

I cleared my dishes and tidied up the kitchen. I was beginning to love this little Laguna cottage, so generously provided by Edith. She was a blessing in so many ways.

I used the phone in the living room to call Gregory. He answered on the first ring, probably expecting it to be Jan. We made small talk for a few minutes, then I dived in with my A file news. I went through how I checked the computer records and contacted the supervisor who now has Carol's unit. When I finished Gregory was silent for so long I thought we'd been disconnected.

"Gregory?"

"I'm here. Sorry. I'm just going over in my mind

what you told me. Carol checked out all six files on the morning of her accident, and now they're lost?" He sounded incredulous. "Where could they be?" They weren't in her car. Her purse was, but nothing else."

"Wouldn't she have had a briefcase?" I questioned.

"Yes, she had one. If she had files then she would have put them in it. So that's missing too I guess."

"Could it have been thrown from the car when she crashed?" I winced when I said it. Gregory was probably reliving the whole scene as we spoke.

"All the windows were up in her car when it was found. They were shattered in the crash but none of them had an opening big enough for a briefcase to fly through."

"Gregory, there's something else I learned."

"What?" he replied, his tone frozen.

"I think Carol was heading to Rolling Oaks to see someone on the Grand Jury, maybe the foreman."

"That would explain her being on the Ortega. When did you learn this?"

"A few weeks ago," I answered sheepishly. "Carol's name came up when our class was about to tour Rolling Oaks. It seems one of my class-mates has a neighbor on the Grand Jury and they were scheduled to do their annual inspection the day

Carol had her accident. She, the neighbor, heard that an unidentified female had called the foreman and wanted some private time with him at Rolling Oaks, but never showed. I guess I should have told you sooner. I'm sorry."

"Don't be sorry. I know you were trying to spare my feelings." Gregory's voice was weak.

"It seemed like idle speculation at the time. But now that I know about the files, the whole thing makes more sense." I took a deep breath. "Gregory, I think you're right that Carol's death wasn't accidental. She knew something about someone and was about to report it...."

".......and someone stopped her." Gregory completed the sentence. "Be careful Linda. I mean it. And thank you for what you've done."

"I made you feel sad is what I've done."

"I've been sad, but now I no longer feel crazy."

We laughed at that, then talked for a while longer before hanging up. I made a promise to myself to do what I could to put this mystery to rest.

Chapter Eighteen

"Training seems to have been a breeze for you." Martin looked at me over his reading glasses as he perused my file.

"It didn't always seem that way some days," I responded, appreciating the compliment.

"You did have some tough cases for a trainee, but you handled them well."

"I felt like I was always asking you or one of the other supervisors endless questions."

"That's how you learn. Your questions were good ones, by the way." Martin placed my file on his desk and looked at me. "So where would you like to be assigned?"

"Does my preference make a difference or will I just be sent where the department has the need?" I felt I knew Martin well enough to make the comment and was relieved when he laughed.

"A little of both, with the department's needs taking priority. You're learning faster than I thought."

"I like to write, so I wouldn't mind going to an investigation unit, but I'd prefer adult investigation. I worked with juveniles for years as a teacher so adult work would be a change for me." Martin pondered my answer, clueless that I had an ulterior motive for that assignment.

"Your writing skills are excellent and we can always use good investigators. No promises though. Assignments will be made by this Friday. Congratulations on your good work!"

By the time I left Martin's office it was 4 pm. Heather and Jan were discussing something when I reached my desk. Both of them seemed pleased.

"Well we know you're a superstar. Did Martin confirm it?" Jan giggled.

"Yes, of course. I may bypass being a deputy probation officer and go straight to supervisor. Martin's going to check with Ron Larimer." I kept a serious expression.

Jan's eyes widened at this unexpected news and her face became deadpan. I could no longer suppress my laughter.

"I've been had," she screeched as she pummeled my arm, embarrassed that she believed me for a second.

"What are you two so pleased about? Did you find out you made it through training?"

"Yes," Heather responded. "We wish we knew where we were going though."

"They're so cagey," Jan added, jerking her head toward the supervisors' offices. "They probably know exactly where we're going but want to make us suffer until Friday."

"You'll suffer a lot more once you get out in the real world of probation work." Esther had stopped by our desks and chimed in. "Enjoy these last few days."

"Killjoy," Jan sighed.

"I for one am anxious to join the 'real world of probation'. I'm as ready as I'll ever be." My response halted the direction of the conversation. Jan quickly added her desire to be "on the streets."

"You sound like a gunslinger, Jan," chuckled Esther. "As for me, they can put me anywhere but on the street. I've asked for juvenile intake and if I get assigned there it will suit me fine."

"You've been in institutions for years. Don't you want to get away from those kids?" Heather asked, wide-eyed.

"Not really. I'm comfortable with what I know. It's hard to teach an old dog new tricks, so they say." Esther shrugged her shoulders. "And I'm one old dog!"

"Go on," Jan gave her a shove. "I'm heading out. Anyone want to go for a drink or a hamburger?"

"Not tonight. I've got leftovers at home and I just want to soak in the tub." I didn't add what I was thinking….and dream about David.

Esther begged off too, but Heather accepted Jan's invitation. We all went off in our own direction.

Soaking in my tub that night I let my thoughts go, wanting to be enveloped in David as I was in the warm bath water, but Carol kept sneaking in. It was almost as if she was saying to me, you're on to something Linda, don't let go. In spite of the water's warmth I could feel goosebumps on my arms. I shivered and ran more hot water into the tub, sinking into it up to my chin. Soon I'd have my first assignment, my own office, and some autonomy. If there's something to find out, I'll find it.

When I entered the classroom on Friday there was a buzz among the trainees. Today assignments were to be made and the nervous chatter reflected everyone's anxiety. I had resigned myself to accepting whatever was chosen for me but kept my fingers crossed that it would be adult investigation.

At 8:05 Ron Larimer entered the room with a

stack of papers. The class instantly fell silent. Ron rarely came into the classroom, trusting his supervisors to properly guide us. Today was an important moment. This milestone could only be entrusted to the training director.

"Good morning, and congratulations on successfully reaching the end of your training." He cleared his throat and continued. "It seems like you were just welcomed in to the probation department. Now your heads are full of knowledge, and you're soon to be unleashed into the world of crime." He chuckled at his little joke and everyone else laughed politely.

"Alright, no more small talk. On to what you're waiting for, the assignments. Before I announce them, let me say that some of you will get what you want, others won't. This is due not only to available openings, but where we feel your skills are best suited. Remember, this is your first assignment. You will have many more in your probation career. If you don't receive what you asked for this time, you probably will in the future. OK, here goes, and please hold your groans or cheers until the end."

Ron began in alphabetical order, first the trainee's name, then the assignment, then the name of the new supervisor. As he made his way through the alphabet there was shuffling and sighing. When he reached Heather's name she sat frozen, then broke into a grin when he announced she would be assigned to juvenile investigation. Heather was a good writer and her natural curiosity and analytical skills made investigation a good fit for her.

Then came Esther, who looked like she'd been holding her breath since Ron took the podium. When he announced juvenile intake for her she let out a whoop, then covered her mouth in embarrassment. The whoop broke some of the tension and there was tittering throughout the room.

When Ron reached my name and I heard adult investigation, I was relieved and scared at the same time. And when he said Ed Gerber would be my supervisor, my stomach did a flip. This was Carol's old unit. When I'd meet with Ed I'd be in Carol's old office. Jan looked over and winked. She knew I wanted this assignment but of course didn't know why.

I hardly paid attention as Ron continued until I heard him announce that Jan was being assigned to adult investigation as well, only to a different unit. Promptness was not Jan's strong point and I wondered how she'd handle all those court deadlines. The look on her face was one of mild surprise, but not disappointment. She wanted to work with adults and this was a good place to start. I realized it would be nice having a close friend working along side me.

When Ron finished, the noise level in the room grew steadily as everyone talked among themselves about their new assignments. After a few minutes of this, Ron raised his arm to silence the group.

"Now that you know where you're going, let's talk about how we'll do it. For the next week, you'll report to your new supervisors and gradually begin assuming your workload. On Friday, you'll return here for some fine-tuning. Then when you come back after the Christmas holiday you'll report full time to your assignment. Graduation ceremonies are the following Friday. Any questions?

George Grosky wanted to know how long we'd have to remain in our assignment before we could be transferred. He clearly was not pleased to be heading for juvenile supervision.

"Usually two years, but that could change depending on the department's needs."

Ron may as well have said 200 years. George didn't seem encouraged.

"Why don't you folks take a coffee break, then come back and get ready to meet your new supervisors. They're coming over here about ten o'clock to meet you individually and orient you to their unit."

With that Ron left the podium.

"Nick's?" Esther asked.

"Let's go." Answered Jan.

Heather and I joined them. We found a table inside and ordered coffee. Jan ordered a Danish. She didn't mention her perpetual diet.

"Are we all happy? I know I am." Esther sat back in her chair looking satisfied.

"Me too," Heather agreed.

"Do you think I was given investigation to learn how to be on time?" Jan asked. "Although I have been getting better, you have to admit."

"Yes, you're tardier by much fewer minutes lately." Esther offered in concurrence.

"Jan, did you ever think that you and I would have the same assignment?" I looked at her pulling apart her Danish and buttering it.

"No, but I'll be glad to have you nearby. Maybe we can go to the jail together for interviews. Won't that be weird, walking in there, so important, some poor guy's future in our hands." Jan chewed on her roll.

"I'm glad I'll be working with juveniles. There's something about dealing with adults that's a little scary right now," Heather commented.

"Since you look like you're only about 18 it makes more sense. Don't take that as an insult. You'll be glad some day you don't look your age." This from Esther.

The conversation continued on, each of us speculating about how we'd fare in the "real world" of probation work. Up until now we'd been pretty well insulated by training supervisors hovering over us and the strength of our own group camaraderie.

"I think it's time to start back and meet our supervisors. I hope they have patience." Heather pushed her chair back and the rest of us followed.

When we returned to the classroom the training supervisors were laughing and talking with a group of men and women I assumed to be our new supervisors. Some I recognized from earlier field trips. I tried to place Ed Gerber from his telephone voice but couldn't. Everyone was looking at everyone else with anticipation.

Ron Larimer stepped to the podium once again and the room became quiet.

"I'll call each of your names, followed by the name of your supervisor. Please stand when your name is called and accompany your supervisor to one of the empty offices down the hall for a get-acquainted meeting."

The roll call began and one by one trainees and supervisors paired off and left the classroom. When my name was called I stood and Ed Gerber stepped

forward with a big smile and a handshake. His pleasant appearance was welcoming. He wasn't much
taller than I was, about 5'7" I guessed, with a thick
head of black hair tinged with gray. His handshake
had been firm and he made nice eye contact. So far
I was pleased.

We found an empty office. Instead of taking a
seat behind the desk, Ed sat next to me in one of the
client chairs in front of the desk.

"Welcome to adult investigation Linda. I've
heard very nice things about you."

"I'm glad of that. This was my first choice so
I'm pretty happy right now."

"Sometimes the workload can be quite heavy.
The officers get frustrated by the constant court
deadlines. But you'll start off with half the usual
cases so you can take the time you need to adjust to
the work flow, interviews, background checks, re-
schedules, etc. etc."

"Now I'm getting nervous," I laughed. "You
mean everything doesn't always go smoothly?"

"I like your sense of humor. It helps to have
one in this business. We're setting up an office for
you which will be ready when you start next week.
I'll walk you through our intake process on Monday,
introduce you to our assignment clerk who strives to

dole out the new cases evenly, and have her explain the point system."

"I'm looking forward to starting." I wondered if Ed remembered my phone call to him. So far it didn't seem like it.

"Do you have any questions?"

"I'll probably think of a hundred by next week but right now, no."

"I want to see you do well. I have an open door policy, and you're allowed at least a hundred questions each day." Ed chuckled at his joke, then surprised me. "By the way, did you ever find those files you called me about?" He did remember.

I hoped I was casual when I responded even through I could feel my cheeks flush. "No, I gave up. I had to finish my investigation without the extra information I wanted. Deadlines, you know."

"Yup, have to meet those deadlines. It's funny about lost files though. They have a way of turning up eventually. Usually when you least expect them."

Ed stood up, shook my hand again, and said he'd see me Monday at 8 o'clock. I walked back to the classroom and went to my desk. Jan hadn't returned yet but Heather and Esther were trading comments about their first impression of their new bosses. Esther seemed to have something to say about all the supervisors, information she had gleaned through the years from others. She looked up when I sat down.

"How'd it go?"

"Really well. I like Ed Gerber. He seems relaxed and open. Someone I can learn from."

"That's pretty much the scoop on him. You lucked out." Esther put her seal of approval on my assignment.

Just then Jan returned, flushed and smiling. She plopped down next to us and sighed. "My supervisor isn't much older than me. She must be on the fast track around here."

"Plus she's cute and speaks Spanish," Esther added, "and very, very, competent. Started out as a counselor in juvenile hall eight years ago and hasn't stopped moving up."

"You're a regular oral history," Jan concluded. "Is there anyone's bio you don't know?"

"Let me think," Esther furrowed her brow and stroked her chin in feigned deep thought. "I guess not."

"Well, Ms. Ortiz seems happy to have me. I don't want her to change her opinion. I'll even set my alarm an extra half-hour early. I'll get there before everyone...." Jan stopped and started laughing.

"You're getting carried away," Heather cautioned as the rest of us nodded agreement.

"Next Friday, when we all come back for 'fine tuning'," Jan did a perfect imitation of Ron's voice, "let's go out for a nice Christmas lunch and compare notes on our first week."

"Great!" Esther agreed. "I was thinking we could do a little gift exchange too. You know, pull names out of a hat with a $20 limit, or whatever."

Jan started scribbling names, dumped a box of paper clips onto the desk, and placed the folded pieces of paper into the empty box. We drew names and hid them away, smiling at the thought of the new experiences the next week would bring and how much we would have to tell each other next Friday.

Chapter Nineteen

"I want to come to your graduation," Edith exclaimed as she finished her mince pie. "I'm so proud of you."

Edith's Christmas dinner was even more sumptuous than her Thanksgiving spread, if that was possible. At her prompting, I had given her an almost day by day account of the past two weeks until I thought she and the other guests would keel over in boredom. But Edith couldn't seem to get enough.

"It would be an honor to have you there," I answered. "You'd be my only 'family'."

"That settles it. I'll come down, and maybe stay a day or two." Edith was all smiles.

I was surrounded by Edith and her three children, Conner, Harold, and Sari, who had all managed to take some time from their busy lives to spend Christmas with their mother. Edith fairly glowed.

It was the first time in years that they had visited at the same time. This was my first meeting with them and their spouses. No grandchildren yet. A point which Edith commented on occasionally with a wistful look.

Edith's children were as warm and friendly as she. I briefly fantasized on what it would be like to grow up in such a loving atmosphere. Not that I hadn't, but as an only child our house was pretty quiet. I always loved the rough and tumble that went on at my friends' houses where brothers and sisters were present. Of course my friends often said they envied me with no brothers or sisters to pick on me. I guess the grass is always greener, as they say.

"Linda, we're so glad mom found you," Sari enthused. "We feel so much better knowing she's got someone close she's so fond of. We always worried about her in this big house alone."

"Oh please, I have Charlotte," Edith claimed, "and this house has so many warm memories. I'm never alone. But you're right about Linda. She's put a spring in my step."

"Alright, you have me blushing, but I have to say I don't know how I would have made it here alone without Edith's loving concern, and Charlotte's baking."

"Everyone laughed as Edith added, "But you don't look like you've gained weight."

"No, but it was getting close. I moved to Laguna just in time."

The mention of Laguna Beach started everyone reminiscing about childhood fun at the beach. When I glanced at the dining room clock it was after seven. As much as I hated to break away, I had to drive back home. Tomorrow was a work day.

Amid good-byes and hugs, and packed with Christmas leftovers that would keep me for a week, I told Edith as I left that I'd see her Thursday night.

Driving home I thought about my new assignment and how different it seemed having my own office and being part of a unit of experienced investigators. Graduation was four days away. I'd no longer be a trainee and would have my official badge. By the time David arrived I'd be on my way to handling a full load of cases.

True to his word, my new supervisor, Ed Gerber, eased me into the investigation routine. Recapping my last two weeks for Edith reminded me of how much I'd learned under Ed's tutelage. We had visited Judge Higuera's courtroom again, spending two mornings listening to arraignments and probation violation hearings. The attorneys showed great respect for the judge, who was a commanding presence. It was fascinating to watch how well he moved the calendar along from the bench.

Stella Graham, the judge's court officer from Probation, sat at a desk just inside the railing that separated the court personnel from the spectators. After each case, the attorney and his client would go to her desk to confer with her and receive paperwork. Some defendants were in custody behind a caged area to the right of the judge's bench. Their attorneys spoke to her alone and would then bring paperwork to the caged area for their client to take back to the jail.

Ed also made sure I met the case assignment clerk, the clerical supervisor, and everyone in my unit. Charlene Little, a long time investigator, was designated as my mentor, someone to go to for routine questions or information on whom to contact in a particular type of case. I soon learned that everyone developed their own rolodex of reliable contacts they'd built up over the years. I'd soon be building mine. In the meantime it sure saved time to be able to ask a co-worker for help.

Charlene was a bundle of energy, pretty, trim, and athletic looking. She had been in investigation for ten years and didn't want to be assigned anywhere else. Ed had said she was so highly praised by the attorneys and judges that the department didn't dare move her. She seemed to thrive on deadlines and had never filed a case late. Few could say that.

Once Ed had oriented me to the flow of work he turned me over to Charlene, promising to check on me, and encouraging me to seek him out whenever necessary. So far Ed and I had only one meeting in his office, which was so sparsely furnished and plain I could hardly imagine Carol inhabiting it. No doubt she had dressed it up with her personal style.

Supervisors' offices were larger than the offices of the probation officers they supervised. Their walls met the ceiling too, unlike those of the probation officers, which stopped about a foot from the ceiling on three sides. Conversations meant to be private could usually be overheard if voices were too loud. I made a mental note to be sure and keep mine down.

So far I hadn't scheduled any interviews. Three misdemeanor cases had been assigned to me but their court dates were six weeks away so I didn't feel rushed. Charlene showed me the procedure she followed when first receiving a case, demonstrating by pulling out a log sheet with various headings.

"This job is all about deadlines," she laughed, "and once you get them all straight, the rest will fall in place."

She was right about that. First there was the defendant's court date. Then, depending on which court his case was to be heard, there was a filing deadline for that. The South Justice Center for example had mail deliveries from our office only twice a week, so that had to be figured in. The typists wanted our dictation no later than two days before the court delivery deadline, so the dictation date had to be backed up from that. If the case was a felony, add another nine days to the total.

I could see why a log was needed. In training, these computations had been figured for us before we received a case. I thought of Jan having to cope with the variety of deadlines when she could barely make it to work on time. At our Christmas lunch she had alluded to the deadlines 'making or breaking' her. Hopefully she had a mentor who would keep her on track.

I exited the 5 freeway at Laguna Canyon Road and wound through the tree-lined drive that served as the only access from the freeway into Laguna Beach. This roadway could sometimes be as dangerous as the Ortega when people drove too fast around its blind curves. Tonight there was little traffic and I could enjoy the peacefulness of this beautiful stretch of road before me. Through my open sunroof the stars twinkled down. I drove leisurely, taking in the sights and smells. Houses on hillsides seemed to be suspended in mid-air and the ocean breeze wafted through my car windows with a salty tang. I'd talked to Mom this morning and Detroit had already had its second snowstorm. How lucky I was to be here.

Soon the village was in view, as Laguna's downtown was referred to, where the beautiful Christmas decorations added to the considerable charm of the city. Edith would enjoy seeing this when she came Thursday. The streets were still fairly empty and in no time I was parked in the driveway of my house.

After putting my care packages from Edith in the refrigerator I proceeded to the bedroom with my overnight bag. The message machine was blinking so I pushed the "play" button and listened while I emptied my case. The first message was from Jan, hoping that I'd had a nice day at Edith's. She'd invited Gregory to have Christmas dinner with her family and she bubbled on as to how well it went. They were strangers a month ago, now……..well, they weren't strangers anymore.

The next message played and David's voice filled the room.

"Hi Linda, Merry Christmas. It's snowing here. I had a quiet day at home with my parents and assorted relatives but my heart was in California. Can't wait to see you on the fourth. I'll call you after I arrive. Well, Happy New Year, too. Sorry I missed you."

Just hearing his voice was a treat I hadn't expected and it warmed my heart. So he had a quiet day. I wondered what his New Year's eve would be like. I wouldn't fault home for not staying home but the thought of him on a date with someone was too painful to imagine. As for me, I talked Edith into staying through New Year's Day. Maybe we could have our own little party.

The final message was from Gregory, asking me to call him when I got in, no matter how late. He sounded serious and all the warm fuzziness I was feeling began to dissipate. I found Gregory's number and dialed. He answered on the first ring.

"It's Linda. Is everything OK?" I felt apprehensive.

"Yes, everything's great. By the way, Merry Christmas."

"Same to you." I didn't mention Jan's message in case he was trying to keep their dating low key. "So why the urgency?"

"I had the greatest day with Jan and her family. All the way home I kept thinking how wonderful she is and how fond I am of her. I'm pretty sure she feels the same way. I don't know where this is going but I can't keep Carol from her any longer."

"Have you told her?" I hesitated. Once Jan knew there was no way I could be left out of it.

"No, but we're at that stage in our relationship where family history has come up. Jan's so open I've already heard stories back to her great grandparents. Today at dinner her parents were full of anecdotes about relatives. Jan knows my parents were killed years ago, and that my only sibling died, and she's never pressed me for details. But I feel so dishonest. As we get closer, it's bound to come up. I have to tell her, Linda. I can trust her." Gregory sighed. I could feel the weight on his shoulders shifting to mine.

"When do you plan to do it?" I thought of all the subterfuge we'd engaged in and knew I'd be relieved when it was no longer necessary.

"I want to tell her with you present."

"Me?"

"Yes. You've been so good about protecting Carol's memory and you're in this position because I put you there. Jan thinks you're a true friend so I want her to understand how you became a part of this. I don't want her to feel let down when she learns the truth."

"It makes sense. What are you doing New Year's Eve?"

"My golf club's having a dinner dance. I'm taking Jan. What about you?"

"Edith will be here. She's coming down for my graduation. We'll probably have dinner here and watch the ball drop on television. Why don't you and Jan come over before your party or do you think it will cast a pall on the evening?"

"Maybe, but it's as good a time as any. And we'll have the rest of the evening to sort things out." Gregory's voice had lost the earlier tension.

"How's six o'clock? We can have some champagne and clear the air."

"Perfect. See you then. Thanks Linda. Knowing you, and now Jan, has helped me through the worst time in my life."

"My pleasure," I added lamely. "See you New Year's Eve."

The days leading up to graduation were busy as each of us settled into our new assignments, to be reunited for the last time at our graduation ceremony. Our offices contained the standard issue, a desk, computer, and chair, plus two side chairs for clients.

A filing cabinet completed the furniture allotment. Most DPOs personalized their offices with pictures and plants. I did the same.

The week before Christmas I browsed the unique shops in Laguna and found some framed pictures of seascapes and Laguna's coastline. At a local nursery I purchased a large potted ivy for my file cabinet and a smaller pothos for my desk, hoping they'd thrive in the artificial light in my office. Window offices were at a premium and it would be a while before one became available that I might have.

My purchases livened up my office and gave me something more pleasant to look at than bare walls. The plants looked great and showed no signs of dying after the first week. I started to receive more cases and even held my first interviews, so that by the day of graduation I felt less and less like a trainee and more like an investigator who's been around a while.

Edith arrived in Laguna the afternoon before graduation. She had such a warming presence. I was happy she'd be in the audience when I received my badge. When I told her of our New Year's Eve plans she rolled her eyes and acknowledged that Gregory was dong the right thing, even though getting through it would be awkward.

Edith settled her belongings in one of the

bedrooms and announced that she was treating me to dinner at the Hotel Laguna. She'd already made reservations in their ocean view dining room. It was to be a pre-graduation celebration.

We drove there in her car, the hotel valet parked it, and we walked through the long lobby to the dining room. The hotel itself sits on the corner of Pacific Coast Highway and Broadway, in the heart of downtown, and occupies the land all the way to the beach behind it. The dining room extends out over the sand, and its wall of windows facing the ocean gives the feeling of being on a ship. We were seated at a window table. The sun had started to set making the sky a paintbox of pink and purple over the gently rolling waves below.

Edith had a nostalgic look as she gazed at the view. "My husband and I came here so many times. This place used to be famous for prime rib but now they feature seafood. It's still one of my favorites no matter what's on the menu."

"You can't beat the scenery," I answered. "I think I could look at the ocean all day."

"It's always changing, isn't it," Edith added. "By the way, I recommend their crab cakes or shrimp scampi, always delicious."

"You can have both if you like. We have that as a

combo tonight." Our waiter had reached our table in time to hear Edith's comment and stood poised to take our order.

"Shall we make it two orders?" Edith asked.

"Yes," I nodded.

"And do you have that wonderful rice pilaf?" Edith queried.

"We do. Will that be two orders also?"

We both said yes and added a bottle of white zinfandel to our dinner. Edith insisted on a toast.

The waiter made a ceremony of uncorking the bottle and passing the cork to Edith to sniff. I've always thought the formalities surrounding wine were pretentious, swirling it, smelling it, sipping it before giving final approval. Watching Edith go through the motions so seriously made me want to chuckle. When the ritual was completed and our glasses were poured, Edith raised hers to mine in a lovely toast.

"To you and your new career, and your life in California, and your future with David, and ......"

"Edith can you make all those wishes on one glass?"

"That's why I ordered a bottle," she laughed, "......and a final toast, that your beautiful common sense will always guide you."

We clinked our glasses, getting a little misty-eyed.

Then our rolls and salad were served and hunger overtook nostalgia. When our entrees were brought they were as delicious as Edith had promised. We split a strawberry shortcake for dessert and sat sipping cappuccino long after the sun went down. Reluctantly we left, savoring the great evening as we headed to the car.

Once home we both turned in, exhausted and anticipating the next day.

The graduation ceremonies were held in the courtroom adjacent to the Main Street Administration building. The court was used occasionally for civil trials but today it was put to a happier use. The air was festive as family and friends of class #72 took their seats in the spectators section. The class itself was to be seated on chairs placed within the hearing area. A podium was set up in front of the judge's bench for the speeches by the Chief Probation Officer and the Training Director.

When the audience was seated, the class filed in from the entrance behind the bench and we took our designated seats. I surveyed the group, quickly spotting a row of redheads that could only be Jan's family. Next to them sat Gregory. That was a surprise. He hadn't mentioned coming to this. Maybe he was able to get away at the last minute.

Jan, dressed in a camel colored suit with a dark green blouse, looked beautiful. Her usual flyaway hair was tamed beneath a tortoise comb behind each ear. She and Gregory made fluttery hand gestures to each other. She was obviously not surprised at his presence. Edith beamed at me from the first row.

Ron Larimer took the podium and the room fell silent. The training supervisors flanked him on either side as he began his speech by congratulating us on our achievement, and summarizing for the audience what that achievement entailed. Listening to him I realized how much I had learned in the last three months and how proud I was to be associated with such a fine department, highly recognized throughout the state.

My eyes caught Gregory's, but they seemed far away. I guessed he was probably reminiscing about Carol, who not so long ago was having her own graduation. I turned my attention back to Ron who was now preparing to introduce Karen Foster, who would present us with our graduation certificates and badges.

Karen took the podium with enthusiastic applause from the class. She was well liked and approachable. Having come up through the ranks, she was respected for her knowledge and integrity. She also congratulated us and after a few more welcoming words, began to call out each of the graduates by name to approach the podium and receive their certificates and badges.

One by one we came forward, shook hands with Karen, Ron, and the training supervisors, and returned to our seats, officially deputy probation officers, with the paperwork and badge to prove it. I looked at my gold badge encased in black felt within a leather wallet-type case, number 637. I looked over at Jan who was fingering hers. She looked up and mouthed "go get'em girl" and smiled, flushed and happy. I thought of Carol and looked back at my badge and all it symbolized. I'll get'em Carol, I thought. This one's for you too.

After the ceremony everyone socialized over punch and cookies, provided by the cooks at the Santa Ana Youth Home, a probation operated treatment facility for younger boys and girls. Hugs, kisses, and congratulations flew all over the place. While Jan was busy with her family, Gregory whispered in my ear that all was set for he and Jan to come over New Year's Eve for a celebratory drink. She'd hear the rest later. I nodded in confirmation and turned to look for Edith. I was ready to go home, my newly earned status symbols in tow.

Chapter Twenty

Edith was quite adept in the kitchen. In her younger days she had hosted many parties and I began to suspect that Charlotte might have learned her own culinary skills from her. It was New Year's Eve morning and Edith was putting the finishing touches on a liver pate. She'd already made the dough for cheese balls, to be baked later, and was now pulling out the ingredients for rumaki.

"Edith, there's only going to be four of us tonight. Do you really think we'll need all this food?" I couldn't imagine much eating being done once Gregory started his story.

"We'll have leftovers then. Who wants to cook on New Year's Day." Edith was undeterred.

"I give up. Let me help at least."

"Just relax. I hardly get the chance to do this any more. It brings back pleasant memories."

"I left Edith to her preparations and went to set out the champagne glasses for our toast later on. I arranged serving plates on the dining room table, ready to hold Edith's specialties. I was feeling a little nervous about tonight, but relieved too. I didn't want Jan to think less of me and hoped she'd understand the reason behind the secrecy.

I stood back and looked at the table. A floral Christmas arrangement in the center and a few candles with sprigs of greenery around them completed the look. Jan and Gregory were coming at six. I had plenty of time to soak in the tub and prepare myself for an evening where the consequences could be good or bad.

Our guests arrived promptly at six. It was hard to reconcile the lovely Jan I saw at the door with the breathless, flyaway hair person I met after the written probation officer test. Tonight she wore a simple black dress that slimmed her in all the right places. Her hair was pulled back and fell in soft curls to her shoulders. A silver necklace and earrings with a light blue stone completed her elegant look. Gregory beamed at her.

Edith and I had dressed in our party best, which

for me was black silk slacks and a pink chiffon top. Edith wore a long cream colored skirt embroidered with red flowers around the hem and a red knit long sleeved, v-neck sweater. After hugs and happy New Year wishes we settled in the living room. I helped Edith carry out her array of appetizers to oohs and aahs from Jan and Gregory. Champagne was poured and toasted and several passes were made at the hors d'ouevres. The polite chitchat began to wane and then Gregory took over.

"On this special night, and the beginning of a new year, there's something I need to say."

My heart did a flip-flop. Here it comes. Edith leaned forward expectantly in her chair. Only Jan sat oblivious to what would happen next.

Gregory turned toward Jan. "Jan, I have always considered myself an honest person."

"Unusual for a lawyer, too," Jan laughingly nodded. Then she took in our serious faces and a look of puzzlement crossed hers.

"I haven't been completely honest with you," Gregory forged ahead.

Jan was beginning to look frightened but made an attempt to cover it. "Don't tell me you're going to confess to a wife hidden away somewhere?" Not smiling now.

"No," Gregory replied, "but I have, I should say had, a sister."

"You told me about her, killed in an auto accident, wasn't she?" Jan was trying to adjust to this shift in mood.

"Yes, she was, but I left out a significant part of the story. Tonight I want to tell you everything, and because I pulled Linda into this, unwillingly I might add, I wanted her here too."

Jan had the look of someone who had been lured into a trap. I was tempted to say something but wasn't sure what so I kept quiet. Gregory could row this boat by himself.

"My sister Carol worked for the probation department. Linda met her on the airplane flying out to California. Carol was returning from a vacation in Michigan. It wasn't until after Carol's death, and my suspicions about it, that I met Linda."

"You mean you aren't Edith's attorney? And what do you mean 'suspicion'?"

"Let me finish and I'll answer any questions you have." Gregory went through the details of the accident, meeting me and sharing his doubts about how Carol died, and how I ended up seeking employment at Probation through Carol's suggestion. He explained the need for secrecy because he didn't know whom he could trust. I could picture him arguing a case in court, calm, methodical.

As she listened Jan visibly relaxed. A murdered sister is tragic but a secret wife would have been impossible.

"So, that's it," Gregory sighed. "I want you to know that anything Linda might have held back, or said, was done to honor my request for privacy. And now that you've heard it all, I know I can trust you to do the same."

"You can," Jan confirmed, taking Gregory's hand. "What a burden you've had. Now I can share it with you too."

A look of relief flooded Gregory's face. He'd put himself out on a limb for Jan and she hadn't let him down.

"How about some more champagne," Edith offered as she jumped up to retrieve the bottle cooling in the ice bucket.

We all toasted again, this time to a happier new year. As we unwound from the previous tension Jan recalled how Carol's name had come up when our class went to Rolling Oaks, and how hard it must have been for me to stay silent.

"I guess I didn't pay that much attention to her last name or I might have connected the dots or at least wondered at the similarity," Jan mused.

"I'm so relieved you know, I can't put it into words." Gregory sat back, content.

"Me too," I agreed. "The day we visited Rolling Oaks, passing the accident site," I shuddered at the memory, "and later when Esther mentioned her neighbor being on the Grand Jury and maybe Carol was on her way to see them, it started to make sense to me, that Carol's death might not be accidental."

"Do you think she was on to something?" Jan's eyes seemed to double in size at the prospect.

"I do, and then there are the six A numbers she had hidden, all gang members, and all their files conveniently lost," I added.

Gregory had not mentioned the A numbers. Jan now looked at him questioningly.

"In my anxiety to tell you everything I overlooked the numbers. I found them in Carol's effects after her death. She had kept them in a locked box that was meant for valuables as well as privacy. I passed them on to Linda, who checked them out."

"You did that? Weren't you afraid of getting into trouble?" Jan queried.

"Yes, but we were working adult cases and I had computer access. The investigation I was doing had gang affiliations so I stretched it a bit to use as an excuse to check the six A numbers. They were all Santa Ana gang members with closed cases and all their files, which had been checked out to Carol, were now lost."

"Goodness! That's got to be more than coincidence. Maybe Carol was taking them to the Grand Jury meeting." Jan was becoming a part of our sleuthing team.

"No files, or briefcase, were found at the accident scene. Where are they?" Gregory chimed in. Blank faces peered back at him. "We're at a standstill for now," he concluded.

Thus ended our discussion on the revelations of the evening. Gregory looked at his watch and said they'd have to leave or they'd miss dinner at the country club. As we hugged and kissed good-bye, Jan whispered in my ear, "mum's the word." With this assurance that the new knowledge was safe with her, Gregory and Jan left to celebrate the rest of New Year's Eve.

"That went well, don't you think?" Edith asked as she closed the front door.

"I think so. I feel better now that true confessions are over."

"How about some more champagne?" Edith started to refill my glass before I could answer.

"If you want me to be awake to watch the ball drop, you'd better pour me coffee instead," I demurred.

"This is your first New Year's Eve in California. You'll stay awake."

With that we toasted again, feasted on the remaining hors d'ouevres, laughed and talked, and managed to stay awake to see the new year in together.

The next week at work had a whole new feel to it. No more trainee. That was now last year. Cases were flowing to me on a more regular basis although I was still below the full quota of more experienced officers. Thanks to Charlene, I had organized my appointment and dictation schedules so I wouldn't be rushed. I was enjoying the work, and the pace, and now that January was here, I was looking forward to seeing David again. He hadn't called me since Christmas but that was OK. He'd be here on the fourth, just days away.

I didn't see Jan at all the first day back after the holiday. Then on Wednesday morning we met on the way to the typing pool. She gave me a wink, but no mention of Carol. We chatted about her New Year's Eve party, which in her estimation was perfect. Then we headed off in different directions after planning to meet for lunch.

I thought of David again. The one secret I still kept from Jan. I had passed him off as an old college friend. Not exactly untrue, but hardly the whole story. I still was unsure where David and I would end up. Time would tell and I'd deal with it then, as far as telling Jan went. She'd probably believe that it was a friendship that grew into love after our chance reunion at the Safe Haven dedication. In a way we were starting all over so if love were the result I wouldn't be far wrong.

I finished my business at the typing pool and returned to my office to find a new referral in my inbox. I'd already learned that the first thing to do was check the charges and court date so I could begin the logging process and make sure I allowed sufficient time to conduct the necessary interviews. I perused the referral slip and noted charges of drug sales, a Santa Ana case. The law-abiding citizens of that city must be sick of this criminal element I thought as I began logging dates.

Then a note at the bottom of the referral made me shiver. "File Lost – duplicate file being made." I looked at the A number and rummaged in my purse for the list of six A numbers that were beginning to be a heavy weight on me. A45998 – Luis Hebron, a match with A45998-LH. The case had been referred for a pre-trial report, which meant no plea or conviction had occurred yet. It was to be heard in Judge Higuera's courtroom.

I sat transfixed at the possibility of gaining some knowledge that would unlock the mystery of Carol's death. I knew that somehow those six lost cases had a connection but doubted that Luis Hebron would know that. The cases probably reflected something larger that was happening, but this was a gift dropped in my lap. I planned to make the most of it.

"Snap out of it, daydreamer, it's lunch time." Jan's voice jolted me from my mental scheming.

"How long have you been standing there?" I asked, embarrassed.

"Long enough to know you were in La-La land."

"I guess I was." I grabbed my purse and got up. I was glad Jan knew about Carol. Now I could tell her about my new case. "Let's go somewhere where we can talk."

"How about the Main Street Café down the block. They have booths," Jan suggested.

"Perfect."

We headed out and down the street. The café

was not crowded but I preferred a booth in the back where there was no chance of being overheard. Once we were seated and had ordered, Jan looked at me expectantly.

"I received a new case this morning. The defendant is one of the six lost case files. I matched the A number."

"How will you interview him and keep a straight face?" Jan queried.

"I'll have to work on it. It's a pre-trial case so he probably won't want to talk to me anyway, especially if he has an attorney. It's drug sales, Santa Ana, and Judge Higuera's courtroom , just like the others.

"Weren't we told that Judge Higuera is tough on those guys?"

"Yes, but for some reason these particular guys all have closed cases. Except for Mr. Hebron, who now has his reopened since he can't seem to stay out of trouble. As soon as I get back I'm going to run a current record check, review the arrest report, and start setting appointments." I settled back as our lunch arrived.

For a while we ate in silence. My head was buzzing. Jan seemed to be contemplating what she'd heard, chewing and staring into the distance.

"I was thinking about everything you and

Gregory told me the other night. He and I talked a little about it since. He's got me convinced her death wasn't an accident, yet it's hard to believe someone would want to kill her. I didn't know her, but from all I've heard, she wasn't the type to have enemies, especially such vicious ones."

"I know. That's how I felt at first. But I believe she had information that might have ruined someone so it was important enough to that person or persons to keep her quiet.

"Be careful Linda. I'll keep an ear out for anything that might mean something. Go slowly, OK?" Jan leaned forward with a pleading look.

"I will. Gregory said the same thing. Let's go back. I'm anxious to tackle this." I called for the check, we paid and left. All the way back to the office I felt an undercurrent of excitement. Soon I'd be facing one of the mysterious six, significant enough to have his A number hidden away by Carol.

Once at my desk I pulled the referral packet and looked at the court officer's notes. Stella had highlighted that the defendant was represented by Manuel Serrano, not the public defender's office. I was becoming familiar with the names of the private criminal attorneys and recalled that Manuel Serrano was well known and expensive. I flipped through the police report to find Mr. Hebron's occupation, seeing "garage mechanic" listed. No doubt his income was supplemented by drug funds. I didn't think a mechanic could afford Manuel Serrano.

I went about requesting record checks on Luis Hebron; DMV, FBI, Orange County Sheriff's Office. Once I received the District Attorney's file and the results of the record checks I'd have a much better picture. I didn't want to conduct any interviews before gaining this information. I didn't expect Hebron to be truthful. I needed facts if it might be necessary to confront him on any misrepresentations.

I tried to call Luis at home to set an appointment for the next week when I'd have my background information. A lady with limited English answered and said he wasn't home.

"May I have his work number?" I asked. "This is very important."

"He no work. I mean, he work sometime, but I don know where." She sounded flustered.

"Are you his mother?"

"Si, jes, I think he come home before seven. I not sure."

"Would you have him call me? I'll give you my name and number. Do you have a pencil and paper?"

"Jes, I find one." I could hear rustling by the phone as Luis's mother looked for something to write on. " I back."

I slowly spelled my name and repeated my number until I was sure she had it, then hung up wondering if he'd get the message, or even bother to return the call if he did. I put the court packet in the pending file and started to work on another case when Ed Gerber popped into the doorway.

"How's it going?" he asked as he slid into the chair opposite my desk. Ed was not an 'over-your-shoulder-every-minute' supervisor, which I appreciated. Still, he liked to touch base regularly with his officers.

"Not too bad. My latest case is an interesting one though." I reached around and pulled out the packet I had just filed and handed it to Ed. "Remember the missing case files I called you about when I was in training? Well, this is one of them."

He let out a low whistle. "No kidding!" Let me look at this.

As he thumbed through the packet I realized that we had never discussed anything about these cases beyond the fact that they were missing. Now that I had to do an investigation on one of them I could ask questions without raising any suspicion. I waited until Ed had reviewed the court information.

"I still need the D.A.'s file and the record checks. I'm a bit puzzled that a garage mechanic could retain Manuel Serrano, among other things.

"A garage mechanic, sure," Ed laughed. "Serrano won't even touch one of these cases without a $10,000 retainer."

"What do you know about any of them Ed?" I queried, hoping he'd give me a clue as to why Carol kept their numbers in secret.

"Not much really. By the time I came into this unit they were already lost. Carol Alder, the previous supervisor, had mentioned concerns to me about some cases seeming to get special treatment, but she didn't say which ones."

"Did you know her very well?"

"Only as a co-worker. We both supervised adult investigation units and would have coffee together occasionally. You know, commiserate on the state of crime, that kind of stuff. She was very professional, a hard worker, well liked. We were devastated when she had that tragic accident. I was reassigned to her unit afterwards to maintain some stability. Her staff was pretty torn up.

"When I tried to locate the missing files I learned that they had been checked out to her. Why do you think she'd want them?" I hoped I wasn't going too far. Ed's expression didn't suggest that I was.

"I wondered that myself but really don't have any idea. She was on the Ortega Highway too, with no reason in the world that I can think of to be there." He leaned back, eyes far away.

Evidently Ed hadn't heard the rumor that Carol was on her way to see the Grand Jury. I wasn't going to tell him. Then he'd start asking me questions. I wanted to learn from him, not the other way around. Apparently he wasn't going to be a fountain of knowledge.

Abruptly Ed stood and handed the packet to me. "Got a meeting. Keep me posted on this one." With that he left. I returned the packet to its file and went about the rest of my work.

Driving home that evening I wished it were still summer and light enough so I could take a walk on the beach. I felt restless after the day's events and anxious about David's arrival tomorrow. Too much anxiety to settle down but it was already dark so I didn't think it would be a good idea to be alone on the beach. If only I had a big dog to walk with me.

The streets of Laguna still reflected a few twinkles here and there from left over holiday decorations. I couldn't face going home to an empty house just yet so when I spied The Corner Cottage on my right I made a quick decision and turned onto the street adjacent to the restaurant. Someone pulled out of a parking space just in time for me to slip in. There were even some minutes left on the meter. Enough to take me to six o'clock, when I wouldn't need to feed it anymore.

I was seated at a booth near the back. The dinner crowd was just starting to trickle in and I watched as the booths began to fill up. The waitress took my order and returned with a diet coke and my dinner salad. I turned my attention to my food when a vaguely familiar voice made me look up. Being seated at the booth next to mine was Tina Higuera and two other women. Tina had been talking as they approached and continued her conversation as she slid into the booth. Her friends seemed to be paying serious attention.

I had seen Tina only once before when she was on the podium with David and that was from afar. She was now much closer, facing towards me, and I could see how pretty she was. Her long black hair was not tied back this time, but hung loosely in soft curls around her shoulders. Her dark eyes were bright and animated. With her creamy complexion she made quite a stunning appearance. Whatever she was telling her friends had them listening intently. Occasionally one of them would say something but their backs were to me and I couldn't hear them.

I went back to my salad when once again I jerked to attention as Tina carried on her conversation.

"........and David and I have been talking all week about the program. He'll be back tomorrow and I can't wait for his help on some of the issues we've had since Safe Haven opened."

Talking all week? My heart did a flip. Well, he is their legal consultant, I rationalized.

"I bet you can't wait for his help," one of Tina's friends teased. "He could help me anytime he wants." Both friends laughed.

"You two, this is just business," Tina stammered, blushing. "But I have to admit, if I have to work with someone on sticky issues, he'd be at the top of my list."

I went back to my salad, appetite gone. When my hamburger arrived I looked at it wondering if I should get a "to go" box. I decided to tackle it, appetite or not. I needed the energy. By now food had been delivered to Tina's table, so the conversation halted while they settled into eating.

I'd heard enough to add another layer of anxiety to my already growing load. I hated that it hurt me to hear Tina and David had been talking. They'd be talking a lot more once he arrived in California, and in person too. I looked over at Tina, head down, sipping some soup. I couldn't blame her if she set her cap for David. I wondered what he thought of her. This isn't getting me anywhere I reasoned. I finished my hamburger, paid, and left, giving one last glance at Tina on the way out. Her eyes briefly met mine with no sign of recognition and then went back to her meal.

I drove home wishing I'd never stopped for dinner.

When I arrived at the office the D.A.'s file on Luis Hebron was on my desk, volumes 1 and 2. The record check was in my in-box, all twelve pages of it. I read with amazement the number of arrests for drug use, sales, assaults, and burglary that Hebron's background check revealed. For these offenses he received various amounts of jail time and a suspended prison sentence. Until two years ago. Since then his charges were either dismissed in court or reduced to a lesser offense that resulted in a minimal punishment such as a fine or community service. Judge Higuera had heard these cases and meted out the dispositions. Where did he get his 'tough on crime' reputation if he did this?

The telephone rang and when I answered a female voice asked me to hold for Manuel Serrano. In a moment he was on the line.

"Miss Davenport, Manny Serrano here. I represent Luis Hebron. I understand you are doing his pre-trial report."

"Yes I am. I left a message with his mother yesterday. Did she call you?"

"Mr. Hebron called me. I'd like to set up an interview appointment for him. I'll accompany him, of course. Would next Tuesday at 2 pm be convenient?"

I looked at my calendar. It was blank for that time. I almost wanted to suggest another date to regain some control but chose not to play that game.

"That would be fine. I'll see you both then," I answered. I marked my calendar.

"Thank you Miss Davenport." Click.

I went back to the file. Carol had listed Hebron's A number in her group of six and she'd spoken to Ed about cases she thought received lenient treatment. This was obviously one of them. If only the other files would turn up. I was becoming more certain that Carol had the files with her on her way to Rolling Oaks. But where were they? I shook my head and put away Hebron's paperwork for now.

The rest of the day was routine and went quickly. I tried to push thoughts of David's return out of my mind but as the end of the workday neared it became impossible. I stayed at my desk until 5:30 doing busywork, then cleared away the papers and left.

Driving home Tina's happy face kept flashing through my head. Had she heard from David already? I could picture the two of them with their heads together puzzling over some program problem, her dark sensuous looks contrasting with his blond fairness. Poster children for fighting drug abuse. I almost laughed at my own thoughts. This isn't high school Linda. Grow up!

I could hear the telephone ringing as I opened the front door. I rushed to get it before the machine picked up and was greeted by Jan. Disappointed that it wasn't David, I managed my cheeriest hello.

"Where were you all day?" Jan queried. "I came by your office a couple of times but no sign of you."

"You must have come by when I stepped out for a minute. I was pretty much behind my desk all day. Sorry I missed you."

"Just wanted to catch up. I've got a bunch of new cases, nothing big, bad checks, shoplifting, that sort of stuff. How're you doing with your mysterious missing file case?"

"I heard from his attorney. They're both coming in next Tuesday."

"Whew! Wish I could be in on that interview."

"I sure hope something comes out of it. You know, something that will help me figure out why Carol kept that file number hidden away."

"He might be stupid, but his attorney won't be. I'll bet he hardly lets him talk." Jan sighed. "The bad guys seem to have the edge."

I had to agree. We chatted a while longer then hung up. I had grabbed the phone in the living room when I first came in. As soon as I hung up I dashed to the bedroom hoping the message light was blinking. I sank into the chair by my bed, wondering if David had arrived safely, assuming he'd call me as soon as he could.

I had never asked him what time his flight would arrive. Now I was sorry. At least I wouldn't be on such pins and needles if I knew he had a late flight. I sat for a while then concluded a hot bath would do me good.

I ran the water slowly, adding bath salts until

the tub was almost brimming. I lowered myself in and sank back, enjoying the scent of lavender and the heat of the water enveloping me. Gradually my muscles relaxed and so did I. When I emerged and toweled off I felt loose and sleepy. My anxiety about not hearing from David was gone, but I still wondered where he was.

It was only nine o'clock but I could hardly keep my eyes open. I turned back my bed and was about to sink into it when the phone rang. I let it ring twice before I answered with what I hoped was a calm hello.

"Linda, I hope it's not too late?" David's voice sounded tired.

"No, not at all," I answered, thinking that no time could ever be bad hearing from him. "How are you?"

"Fine. A little tired. I just arrived and I'm waiting for my rental car."

My heart leaped knowing he was calling me at his first opportunity. "It's so good to hear your voice. Where are you headed?"

"I'm staying at the Village Inn in Tustin. It's close to Santa Ana where my business will be. Can I take you to dinner tomorrow night?"

"Yes. Why don't I meet you since my office is in

Santa Ana too. Where would you like to go?" I was reluctant to give David my address just yet. And it did seem like a waste of time for me to go home and for him to drive all the way to Laguna.

"There's a nice Chinese restaurant on Main and Chapman. I remember you used to like Chinese food." Pause.

"I still do. I think I know the place but I've never eaten there."

"It's right on the northeast corner. It's called Mr. Foo's."

"I'll find it."

"How is six thirty?"

"Perfect. I'll see you then."

"OK. Goodbye until tomorrow."

I hung up in a happy delirium. The tiredness I felt earlier had left me. I wanted to dance around the room, sing, anything to burn off the energy now pumping through me. Instead I pulled the covers up and lay staring at the ceiling, thinking how wonderful everything was. What one phone call could do to change a mood! I lay there basking in warm feelings until sleep overtook me and brought me very pleasant dreams.

Chapter Twenty One

It was six twenty five as I reached Main and Chapman, Mr. Foo's clearly visible on the corner. I had left the office after five and stopped at Main Place to buy some new earrings, something in silver to complement my black and gray knit suit. I found the perfect pair, but now I had only minutes to find a parking space. Luckily the parking lot behind the restaurant had several. I slipped into one, did a hasty smoothing out of my hair, and walked toward the entrance.

The restaurant was dark as I entered and it took a moment for my eyes to become adjusted. Just as I began to make out faces I saw David walking toward me, arms open wide. He pulled me to him in a gentle bear hug as he greeted me hello.

I hugged him back and hoped he didn't sense my trembling.

"You're a sight for these tired eyes," David exclaimed as he held me at arm's length. "Let me look at you." He was all smiles.

I noticed that the crinkles around David's eyes were a little deeper, but they only gave more character to his face. We stood taking each other in for a minute, then hugged again.

"Have you been busy today?" I asked, as we followed the waiter to our table.

"Not too much. I spent most of the day laying the groundwork for the next week or so. Depending on how that goes. ....," his voice trailed off as we were seated and given menus. We ordered and sat back while the busboy brought hot tea and a bowl of crispy Chinese noodles.

"Well Linda, tell me about your job. How does it feel to be a probation officer?" David's clear blue eyes held mine. The same deep feeling that hit me when I first saw him years ago rose up in me again.

"I like it. I just graduated from training the end of December so it's all a bit new to me now. Did I tell you I was assigned to Adult Investigation?"

"No, what's that?"

"It's a unit that handles cases going to court for sentencing. We prepare the sentencing reports after interviewing the defendant, victims, witnesses, arresting officers, and anybody else interested in the case, and make a recommendation for or against probation based on our findings. It's the only report the judge has that pulls together all the facts of a case into one document. I actually requested this assignment."

"It sounds interesting. I bet you're good at it."

"I think I will be. It's still a little early to tell. Tell me what you're up to and how long you'll be here."

"Safe Haven is having the usual growing pains. I'll be spending most of my time with the Board members and staff trying to work out some of the glitches. The parent program in New York had similar problems when it started years ago. Now it's running smoothly. I hope to incorporate some of these ideas in Safe Haven here if the Board will agree."

I thought of Tina and doubted that she'd be in opposition to anything David would suggest.

"I'm sure they want things to go well," I assured him.

"I plan to be very hands-on, spending lots of time at Safe Haven, walking through the process from commitment to release."

"Isn't that more than a legal consultant is supposed to do?"

"Yes and no. From my point of view any part

of the program has the potential for legal problems. The more I understand about the operation, the better to avoid them."

"That makes sense."

Our appetizers arrived and we began filling our plates with egg rolls and pot stickers. Memories of dinners we shared in college came flooding back to me. We loved Chinese food because it was tasty, cheap, and filling.

"How many of these do you think we ate in Ann Arbor?" David asked between bites.

"Hundreds," I laughed.

We ate and reminisced about our college days. Both of us remembering the good times and carefully avoiding the bad. We managed to finish our sweet and sour chicken and chop suey. By the time our fortune cookies arrived we couldn't touch another morsel. We opened our cookies anyway to read the fortune. Mine said, "You are a person who makes wise decisions."

"Let's see, mine says, 'Don't let a new opportunity pass you by'," David read. Then he looked at me for a long time.

"Linda, sometimes I wish we were still back at U. of M. I'd do things so much differently."

"I guess hindsight is 20/20. It's too late to redo

anything. Let's just hope we do the right thing now." I still felt uncomfortable thinking about how we parted years ago. It didn't take much for the old hurt to surface and I wanted to keep it down.

"You could always put the right face on everything. I'm going to pay attention to my fortune. You know fortune cookies can't be wrong. Can I see you this week-end? We could go to the beach or take in a movie."

"That would be fun. Sure. You never did tell me how long you're staying."

"Three or four weeks, maybe more. It's hard to say. Depends on my progress. Once Safe Haven is going well, we'll be looking at sites in San Diego to expand there. I'll probably be in California more than New York."

Music to my ears. "Why don't you come to Laguna on Saturday, say about noon. I'll pack a pic-nic lunch and we can go to the beach. I live just a block away."

"Perfect." David's eyes lit up. "I'll need your address." He pulled a small notepad from his coat pocket and tore off a sheet.

My reluctance gone, I jotted down the number and street and told him the easiest way to get there. He folded the sheet and patted his heart with it be-fore he put it in his pocket.

We walked out of the restaurant into the cool evening. I wondered if it would be warm enough Saturday for lunch on the beach. I followed David into the parking lot when he stopped.

"Where's your car? I'll walk you to it." David questioned, looking around.

"Over there," I pointed and headed towards my Thunderbird. "Where's yours?"

"It seems to be next to yours," David laughed, and gestured towards a Buick convertible. "You don't think I've gone Hollywood with the convertible, do you?"

"As long as you don't wear dark glasses at night, too."

"I promise, only if it's sunny."

David took both my hands in his and we stood for a long time saying nothing. Then slowly he put his arms around me, hugging me gently and stroking my hair. I felt so safe and warm in his arms. I didn't want to move. He kissed me softly on the mouth, then again a little harder. My knees almost buckled from the excitement running through me. He didn't go any further.

"I won't push you Linda. I just couldn't help it." David stood back.

"You're not pushing. I feel the same way. But I

want to go slow. OK?"

"OK."

David waited while I got into my car. He waved as I drove away, mouthing "see you tomorrow."

It was one of those crisp, sunny days that make you glad you're alive. Not hot enough to go into the ocean, but warm enough to sit on the beach and watch the gently rippling water catch the sun on its surface, like a thousand tiny diamonds.

After I'd left David I stopped at the market to pick up provisions for our picnic. I knew my meager pantry wouldn't yield enough for a hearty lunch. Now we were relaxing in beach chairs I'd found stashed in the garage, with a blanket spread before us, laden with food and drink.

"You outdid yourself, Linda," David said as he reached for another cold shrimp.

"I went shopping and was carried away by the choices," I offered lamely as I realized we had enough food for several people.

"I'm not complaining. This is delicious. Especially the pumpkin bread." David was enjoying himself.

"I wish I could claim credit for that. Edith made some loaves at Thanksgiving and put two in my freezer. I pulled one out last night. You can take the rest with you if you'd like."

"I'd like. I have a little kitchenette where I'm staying. This will go good with coffee in the morning."

We lay back on our chairs, savoring the fresh air and sunshine, sipping wine, feeling lazy.

"I think I could stay like this forever, or at least the next few hours," I murmured sleepily. I waited for a response from David. When he remained silent I looked over to see that his eyes were shut, his wineglass starting to tip in his hand. I eased it from him and set it down on the sand between us. Poor David, he must be exhausted I thought, as I gazed at him sleeping contentedly, his lips slightly parted. I settled back and closed my eyes too. I was in such a dreamy state I felt suspended in time.

Being side by side with David on a warm, sunny beach, listening to the ocean's roar, had to be as close to paradise as I'd ever been. In the midst of this reverie, Carol popped into my mind, along with my upcoming interview of Luis Hebron. What a way to ruin a beautiful moment.

I hadn't told David about Carol. At the beginning it didn't seem right. The fewer who knew, the better. But if he was going to be in my life, he needed to hear it sooner than later. I'll tell him today, I decided. Having made the decision I must have drifted off myself. A slight tug on my arm woke me.

"Wake up sleepy head. Look at the sky." David pointed upward.

The sun was no longer visible and dark clouds were taking shape in the distance.

"Who's a sleepy head? When did you wake up?" I asked, punching his arm.

"A minute ago. I started getting cold. I guess that woke me. Otherwise I probably would have slept until tomorrow. I haven't felt this peaceful in ages."

"Me too. I guess it's over now. We'd better pack up before it rains." I pulled myself up hesitantly, sorry that the mood was broken.

We quickly packed the leftovers in the picnic basket, shook out the blanket and folded it, folded our chairs, and headed towards David's car. We were inside when light raindrops began to fall. David drove the short distance to my house, and once in the garage, helped me take everything in the house.

It was almost five o'clock and the sky was growing darker by the minute. "I'll make some coffee or tea, if you're not in a hurry," I offered.

"I'm not. Coffee sounds good."

I set about putting away the food from our picnic, leaving out the rest of the pumpkin bread for David. What was I thinking when I shopped. I'll have enough food until Spring. I put the coffee on and while it was perking I went and sat next to David in the living room.

We both looked through the bay window at the now steadily falling rain, our sides barely touching.

"How about a fire?" David suggested, eyeing the logs in the bin next to the fireplace.

"They're just for looks. It's a gas fireplace," I said as I got up and flipped the switch. Red and orange flames rose up around the realistic cement logs, giving the living room a lovely glow.

"Let's hear it for modern conveniences," David laughed.

I went to the kitchen and brought back two steaming mugs of coffee. David had plumped the pillows on the sofa, patting the spot on his right. I settled in beside him, handing him one of the mugs. He touched it to mine in a toast, our eyes holding for a long time.

We sipped our coffee and listened to the crackling of the fire and the splashing of the rain, now coming down hard against the windows.

"David, there's something I want to tell you," I

started hesitantly. I could feel him stiffen next to me.

"This isn't the big good-bye, is it?" David asked half jokingly.

"No," I responded quickly.

"Sorry, you sounded so serious. I guess I'm still insecure about us," he explained.

"It is serious, but for a different reason." I had his full attention. "When I first told you about how I came to work for the Probation department, I left something out. I've only shared this with two people, Edith and Jan Sussex, a good friend of mine. I want to tell you now because I want you in my life and I don't want any secrets. But it's in the strictest confidence. Agreed?"

"Agreed."

I told David how I met Carol on the plane, our brief but growing friendship, and her sudden death. Then, my meeting with Gregory, his fears about Carol, losing my job, and all that followed. David listened intently, with only an occasional 'wow' or 'really?'

"I was living with Edith at the time so I felt she needed to know. Then Gregory met Jan at Thanksgiving, they hit it off, and he didn't feel right keeping if from her. Now I'm telling you. The circle widens."

David leaned back against the cushions, digesting what he'd just heard.

"I don't know Linda, is all this safe?" He took my hand and held it tightly. "Look at what happened to Carol."

"Then you don't think it's an accident either?"

"Not the way you tell it. The missing files that just happen to have the numbers that Carol had hidden away? Something's not right."

"Did I mention that I'm interviewing one of the mysterious six next week?"

"I hope you won't let on that you suspect anything."

"Don't worry. This will just be a regular professional interview. No one at Probation, other than Jan, even knows I met Carol. I'm anxious about it though. He'll have his high powered attorney in tow."

"You'll be fine. You've got good instincts." David patted my arm. "Just one of the things that endears you to me."

David pulled me to him and I lay my head on his shoulder. We stayed that way for a long time, peaceful, listening to the rain as it continued to hammer at the windows.

"I love you Linda," David said softly.

"I love you too," I answered without reservation. "I thought I could go slow with you, but I can't. I love you so much, it's hopeless."

David gently turned me around to face him. "Not hopeless, hopeful. That's how I feel too. No other woman I've met can compare to you. All I think about is you." He kissed me on the mouth, soft, lingering, then deeper, more passionate. I responded with the same feelings. It felt wonderful not to hold back. I let my hands roam over David's body, as he explored mine.

"Stay the night David," I groaned as he kissed my neck.

"Are you sure?"

"I've never been more sure of anything," I answered as I led him from the couch to my bedroom.

I woke up early, the sun streaming through the half open shutters announcing that the rain was over. I slowly stretched as sweet memories of the previous night seeped into my thoughts. I turned to see David still sleeping soundly next to me. I wanted to touch his face but didn't want to wake him.

David and I had never made love before last night. We only went as far as heavy necking in college. The desire was there but we both had room mates and the thought of a motel was too sleazy for us. I wanted my first time to be special and David respected that. Last night could not have been more special. My body still tingled with the recollection.

I left the bed as quietly as possible and was immediately embarrassed by what I saw. In the heat of last night our clothes had been strewn everywhere. Now they lay where they fell, a guilty reminder of the power of passion. But there was no guilt involved. We loved each other and last night was the culmination of feelings that had built over too much time. I picked up David's clothes and hung them over a chair. Mine went into the hamper.

I took a shower and put on jeans and a sweatshirt. David was still asleep as I tiptoed from the room.

I dumped last night's coffee and put on a fresh pot, poured two glasses of orange juice, set the table and then peeked in on David, who was starting to stir. He was so beautiful to watch. As he began to wake up he had a disoriented look on his face. Then he focused on me and gave me a wide smile.

"I thought last night was a wonderful dream. I'm so glad it wasn't." David put his hands behind his head, propping himself up on the pillow. "I'd kiss you but I desperately need a toothbrush."

"I just happen to have everything you need in the

bathroom. Get dressed and come into the kitchen. I'm making breakfast."

"You're not kicking me out already are you?" David laughed.

"Hardly, just trying to nourish you. Get going, sleepy head." I tugged at the covers but he held them tight. I gave up and went back to the kitchen.

I could hear David finally moving around, then the sound of the shower running. Soon he appeared in the kitchen, his hair still damp, wearing his clothes from last night. He looked down at his wrinkled appearance and shrugged. We both laughed.

"Didn't your mother teach you to hang up your clothes when you took them off," I teased.

"My mother never taught me anything remotely connected to last night." David took my hands and kissed them, then sat down at the table. "This looks delicious."

We were both hungry and ate our eggs and bacon without saying much. I watched David put jelly on his toast. He had such strong hands but his movements were so gentle. I could eat him up with a spoon. Was I besotted or what. David leaned back in his chair, sipping coffee and looking satisfied.

"Did you have plans for today?" David's question took me by surprise.

"Nothing special. I brought home some dictation but it's not urgent. I was wishing you'd stay. It's so sunny and clear we could go back to the beach." I hoped I didn't sound desperate.

David's face fell. "I'm so sorry. I promised I'd spend the afternoon at Safe Haven. I've never been there on a Sunday. Tina thought I could benefit from seeing the visitors and observing the family dynamics. It helps to understand the stresses the patients are under."

"Sounds more like the work of a psychologist, not a lawyer." The mention of Tina's name chilled my warm feelings and I answered in a tone colder than I intended.

"Like I told you before Linda, the more I know about the program, the more prepared I'll be to handle any problems."

"Of course. Just my disappointment showing." I attempted to recover, not sure it was working.

"I'd much rather spend the day with you than a bunch of drug users in treatment and their dysfunctional families. But I signed on for it...." his voice trailed and he spread his hands.

"Tina, is that her name?" I feigned a memory lapse. "She seems quite involved too for a councilwoman."

"She was the major force in bringing Safe Haven to Santa Ana, so she has a strong desire to see it be successful and expand. Her reputation is probably riding on it. She wants to run for the California assembly so being behind a successful drug program will help her a lot."

She probably gets what she wants I thought. I hope David's not on her wish list. I remembered Edith saying she thought Tina had been spoiled by her parents. Now she was a young adult, bright, pretty, and with a well-respected judge for a father. The package couldn't be much better.

David pushed back from the table and began clearing dishes.

"You can leave those. I'll have plenty of time to do them. You probably want to go home and change, don't you, unless you're trying to start a new look."

"I guess you're right. I do look like I slept in these clothes."

I walked David to the door as though I had no care that he was leaving.

"Thanks for a beautiful time Linda." David held me in a bear hug that I sunk into. "The memories will carry me through this crummy afternoon. I'll call you tonight."

We kissed goodbye and I watched at the door until David's car turned the corner and was out of sight. I cleaned up the kitchen, made the bed, and took my briefcase into the living room. I pulled out a case file, my interview notes, and dictating machine. I began to dictate a pre-sentence report while Tina Higuera's pretty face and bright eyes danced before me almost as clearly as if she were in the room.

Chapter Twenty Two

My papers were assembled and I'd thoroughly reviewed the file on Luis Hebron, such as it was. His rap sheet was impressive for a criminal. Plenty of arrests for assaults, batteries, burglaries, and drugs, with many never making it to court. I had spoken briefly to the attorney prosecuting the case. He wasn't looking forward to going up against Manny Serrano. By the time it was over he would have everyone thinking Hebron was the victim. He likened it to the 'O.J.' defense.

The receptionist rang me at 2 pm to announce the arrival of defendant and attorney. I waited a few moments to compose myself, then went into the lobby to escort them back to my office. What a pair they made. They looked so much alike they could have passed for father and son. I introduced myself and they followed me back. Once seated across from me, I decided they looked more like the before and after of a makeover.

Luis was sloppily dressed in an ill fitting white shirt and a too short tie, probably borrowed from someone so he could look presentable. He needed a haircut, and from the look of his hands he might have actually been a garage mechanic. By contrast, Manny Serrano could have stepped from the pages of Gentlemen's Quarterly. Fiftiesh, with a full head of dark hair graying at the temples, he looked dapper in a charcoal gray pinstriped suit, light blue shirt, and perfectly knotted navy tie. His whole persona screamed money and custom tailoring, yet he had a slickness about him that made me think he could probably ooze oil if we shook hands too hard.

They sat there looking at me expectantly, Manny the professional, Luis the bored criminal, both sizing me up in their own way. I confirmed that Luis was here for a pre-trial investigation and that the charges against him were two counts of drug sales, specifically cocaine. If convicted there was the possibility of a prison sentence. Luis was mute. Manny tersely replied, "That's correct."

I started by gathering information for the face sheet of the report. Manny let Luis answer the questions pertaining to his address, employment, and family background. When I asked for a pay stub as proof of employment Luis squirmed and looked at Manny, who advised me one would be supplied at a later date. Sure. I finished the face sheet, put it aside, and pulled out a note pad to begin the interview. Manny leaned slightly forward.

"Miss Davenport, please be assured that my client wishes to cooperate fully, but on advice of counsel, he won't be answering any questions pertaining to the current charges, to which he's plead not guilty." He leaned back. His client, cooperating fully, was picking his teeth with the end of a matchbook cover.

"Alright then, let's discuss this." I pulled his rap sheet from the file, purposely letting the report unfold clumsily onto my desk to demonstrate the length of the printout.

Manny twitched slightly, but retained his composure. Luis was more visibly upset at seeing his criminal history in my hands.

"Hey, that's old stuff, and a bunch of lies, too," Luis shouted. "You already got me figured guilty, don't you?" His expression was grim.

I was beginning to love the righteous indignation of the accused.

"Your guilt or innocence will be for the court to

decide. This does show a pattern of criminal behavior over an extended period of time." I fingered the pages noisily on purpose.

Manny spoke up. "It's understandable that my client would be upset. He's not here to be judged on past behavior. I'm sure you have noted that many of these past charges were dismissed, as I'm confident the current ones will be." He patted Luis's leg reassuringly. Luis went back to his dental hygiene.

"Yes, I have noted that. Especially in the last two years. Why is that?" I looked straight at Manny, who reddened ever so slightly.

"Bad arrests, obviously. No case could be made. What else?" He shrugged his shoulders, then looked at his Rolex.

"Are you in a hurry, Mr. Serrano?"

"No, but I don't believe we have any more to discuss." Polite but annoyed.

"If we can't talk about the present charges, and you blanketly dismiss Mr. Hebron's prior criminal history as irrelevant, we probably don't have anything more to discuss. I will be talking to other parties involved in this case and will have my report filed with the court prior to the court date. Do you have any questions before we conclude?"

"None," replied Manny. Luis looked like he

might be trying to form one but Manny stood up abruptly signaling the end of further discussion.

"Thank you for your time, Miss Davenport." Manny held out his hand and we shook. Luis made no such polite gesture, instead leaving my office quickly, turning the wrong way in the hall.

"I'll walk you out to the lobby," I said, guiding Manny's arm in the right direction. Luis turned around and slouched along behind. When the elevator doors closed behind them I returned to my office.

I reread the arrest report. Luis had sold two grams of cocaine to two different undercover officers in the same evening. He was arrested after the second sale was completed. Pretty straightforward. No explanation as to why the police waited for the second buy to arrest him.

I picked up the phone and dialed the second officer's number. Surprisingly he answered. I identified myself, and commented on my good luck on reaching him so quickly.

"Catching up on paperwork," he replied. "But you can't be too lucky if you have to do a report on Luis Hebron."

"That's why I'm calling. I just finished interviewing him, if you could call it that, and he's like a puzzle where the pieces don't fit."

"Amen to that."

"He has a history with you?"

"Oh yeah, he and his buddies. We call them the "teflon six" because criminal charges never seem to stick."

"Six?" My heart skipped a beat, thinking of Carol's six A numbers.

"Yeah. We try to make life miserable for them but they can bob and weave with the best of them. Did Luis have his slick attorney with him?"

"He sure did. Since it's a pre-trial, he wouldn't let Luis say much. I was curious why you waited for the second sale to arrest him."

"For a stronger case. It's harder to yell entrapment when two separate sales go down the same night."

"I suspected that. Thanks for you help."

"Anytime. Good luck with the dirt bag."

I hung up, more perplexed than ever, and decided to write the most thorough report possible. Every charge in Luis's prior criminal history would be detailed in it. I'd include statements from both undercover officers and as many others as I could find who could speak to his criminality. Lastly, I'd deny probation, describing his lack of fitness, recommending that the prescribed sentence be imposed should he be found guilty. The pre-trial hearing was in three weeks. If Ed didn't object, I'd attend the hearing too. Some probation officers had done this on cases that had troubled them. This one definitely troubled me.

The time between the interview and the hearing passed quickly. Investigations surged after the holidays so I was constantly juggling deadlines as new cases rolled in. Sometimes I'd stay home for a day and dictate reports without the interruptions and distractions of the office. On those days I'd manage to cook a nice meal and David would join me in the evening. We spent our weekends together too although David would occasionally have to cut the time short to visit Safe Haven. It seems that Tina had a not so uncanny knack for identifying some crisis on a Saturday or Sunday that could only be handled by David.

The Hebron report had been filed a week before the hearing. Ed praised me on it and even offered to accompany me to court on the hearing date. When I told him that Luis had been referred to by the arresting officer as one of the "teflon six", he rolled his eyes, wondering if that meant the same six whose files Carol Alder had checked out the day she died. I was sure they were but feigned a casualness I didn't feel. No one at Probation except Jan knew that I'd met Carol and had more than a passing interest in these cases. Each bit of information I learned about them made me more convinced that Carol's death was no accident.

Ed and I arrived at Judge Higuera's courtroom shortly before 8:30 am, the time set for all of the hearings that morning. We would probably have to sit through a few other cases before Hebron's was heard.

We took a seat in the back. The courtroom was almost full with spectators and defendants not in custody. I scanned the room for Luis but didn't see him, although I saw Manny Serrano conferring with a bailiff near the front. Manny, too, scanned the room, probably wondering if his flaky client would show up.

In a matter of minutes the bailiff called the courtroom to order and Judge Higuera took the bench. Still no Luis. He called the first case, listened to arguments for and against dismissal, then set the matter for trial. The prosecuting attorney looked relieved. The defendant and his attorney were noticeably disappointed. We sat through several such cases.

Every time the courtroom door opened Manny turned around. Finally Luis sauntered in at 9:45 am. Manny had a look of ease mixed with anger at his client's flagrant disrespect for the court proceedings. Luis, wearing the same outfit he'd worn to my office, nodded to various familiar faces before he sat down next to Manny, who whispered something into his ear. Luis turned red. I guess he was capable of being embarrassed after all.

We sat through a couple more cases, each handled with crisp efficiency by Judge Higuera. The court probation officer, Stella Graham, was kept busy writing and handing out various papers to defendants or their attorneys, occasionally making a comment to the court about last minute information from the probation department. Judge Higuera looked so distinguished in his black robe that he could have been an ad for judicial professionalism.

"Will the parties in the Luis Hebron matter come forward," the judge intoned in his now familiar baritone.

Manny and Luis arose and stood before the bench. The prosecuting attorney joined them. Judge Higuera was reading what looked like my report while Luis fidgeted. When the judge looked up, Manny spoke.

"Manuel Serrano, representing Luis Hebron, your honor."

"Donald Phillips for the people."

"Your client has plead not guilty to both counts of drug sales." The judge returned to the report.

"Yes your honor."

"Are the officers who were party to the arrest present?" He continued turning pages.

I looked around the courtroom but no uniforms came forward. The officer I spoke to was eager to see Luis behind bars. Why wasn't he here?

The bailiff cleared his throat before he told the judge that no one from Santa Ana P.D. was in the courtroom. Judge Higuera looked annoyed. Manny had a slight look of satisfaction on his face.

"I'll continue the matter until l:30 this afternoon and I expect the arresting officers to be present." He pounded his gavel and called the next case.

The D.A. rushed out, no doubt to call the arresting officers. Ed and I looked at each other. Just then Manny and Luis walked by. Manny looked surprised to see me but nodded and kept going.

"Should we go for lunch and come back at 1:30?" Ed asked. "We've killed half a day already."

"Why not," I answered, gathering my purse.

We walked to a nearby sandwich shop, ordered at the counter, then found a seat outside at an umbrella table on the patio.

"What do you think of the police being a 'no

show'?" Ed queried between bites. "Didn't you talk to one of the arresting officers?"

"Yes. He definitely wanted Hebron put away. Even let two buys go down before the arrest for a more solid case."

"He'll probably be here this afternoon."

"I hope so. What will happen if he isn't?"

"Hebron most likely walks. The whole case hinges on the officers' testimony." Ed had polished off his cheeseburger and sat back with his coffee cup, looking around. "This is nice. I usually brown bag it but it feels good to go out."

"It does." I'd been bringing my lunch too most days. It was easier and saved money. Being out of the office was a nice change for me also.

We watched the passing scene for a while. When one o'clock approached we started back. The courtroom had started to fill up. I recognized some carry-overs from this morning. Manny and Luis were already at the front but I saw no sign of a Santa Ana police officer. Manny glanced over his shoulder frequently. His eyes held the intensity of someone willing something to happen, and he carried an assurance that he'd be successful.

At 1:30 Judge Higuera took the bench. After riffling through some papers, he called the Hebron case. The prosecuting attorney stood, as did Manny and Luis, and asked to approach the bench. Manny joined him. The prosecutor did most of the talking, which we were unable to hear, but from the body language it didn't look good for his side. Still no Santa Ana police in sight, probably the topic of their discussion. After a few minutes the parties returned to their places, the district attorney looking grim, Manny looking smug.

"In the matter of the people versus Luis Hebron, the case is dismissed in the interest of justice," Judge Higuera ordered, followed by a rap of the gavel.

Ed and I looked at each other in disbelief. One of the "teflon six" had done it again. Luis's initial re-action of slight confusion was quickly replaced with an air of cockiness. Manny was now into full-blown slick attorney mode. As they walked by us on their way out of the courtroom, Manny once again nod-ded to me. Luis gave no sign of recognition.

It was such a let down. Yet what just happened was in keeping with the recent history of Luis and his five cohorts.

Ed whispered, "Let's talk to Stella at the recess."

I nodded in agreement. We sat through some more cases, but I paid little attention to them. I was anxious to hear Stella's take on this. She had been Judge Higuera's court officer for years and should have insight we didn't have.

Finally a recess was called. Ed and I went to the front of the courtroom where Stella's desk sat. She looked up as we approached, greeting Ed like an old friend.

"Do you remember Linda from the training class?" Ed asked.

"You look familiar," she answered. "The last class, wasn't it?"

"It was. I'm in Ed's unit now. I wrote the Hebron report."

"Oh," Stella shook her head. Our visit was making sense to her now. "You did a great job. Very thorough. Not the outcome you wanted though."

"We were hoping you could help us understand what happened," Ed responded.

Stella shrugged. "The arresting officers didn't show. Why? Who knows? Without their statements under oath, there's no case. I know the D.A. tried to reach them. I wish I could tell you more. It's as simple as that."

"Does this happen often?" Ed questioned.

"Occasionally. It seems to occur more frequently with Manny Serrano's clients. I guess he's worth his high price. I don't know how those slugs he represents pay him though." Stella shook her head again and went back to the papers on her desk. Others were waiting to speak to her. "Anything else I can help you with?"

"No. Thanks anyway," Ed answered.

We drove back to the office in silence. I was determined to unravel this mystery of the "teflon six" but didn't know where to go next. Carol was definitely on to something about it and ended up dead. I didn't want to come to the same end. Everyone's warned me to be careful. What to do?

I rubbed the back of my neck to ease the stiffness and ward off the tension headache I felt coming on. Ed looked over in sympathy.

"Why don't you call the arresting officer you spoke to earlier. Maybe he can explain why he didn't show," Ed suggested.

"I thought of that," I answered, but in my mind I realized that whatever made him back off would not be something he'd share with me. I'd still try.

Once at my desk I pulled the Hebron file and found the officer's number. After a few rings the call switched to a secretary who advised me the officer was out for the rest of the week and did I want to leave a message. I left my name and number even though I felt certain I'd never hear from him.

I looked at my in-box. Two new referrals. I was carrying a full load of investigations now and had no time to dwell on Hebron's case. Besides, David was coming for dinner tonight and I wanted to leave early to stop at the supermarket. My ringing telephone startled me out of my deep thoughts. Expecting it to be a business call, I was surprised to hear David's voice.

"Linda, I'm sorry but I'll be a little late tonight." He sounded distant.

"How late?" I had asked him to over by 6:30.

"I'm not sure. Seven, seven thirty. Will this ruin dinner?" Now apologetic, still distant.

I was planning on meatloaf and mashed potatoes. Both could hold for an hour or more. I was more concerned for his reason, which he didn't give. "No, it'll work. At least I'll have an excuse if you don't like my cooking." I pretended a lightheartedness I didn't feel.

"Thanks Linda. I'll call if it's any later. Bye." It was so abrupt, not like David at all.

My head was now pounding. I so wanted to confide in David tonight about what happened in court and all the confusion I felt about being in the middle of something I never sought. But with David's tone I wasn't sure how receptive he'd be or if he'd even show up.

I found some aspirin in my purse and went out to the drinking fountain to take them. Once back in my office I pondered my relationship with David. Since the night he first stayed at my house, all the walls between us had come down. We declared our love for each other and the ensuing weeks brought us closer and closer together. I knew David would be returning to New York eventually but he hadn't brought it up. Safe Haven was growing satisfactorily. Soon David would be assisting in the development of a similar program in San Diego.

We talked about a future together. In my dreams I envisioned a life for us in California although David had never said he'd permanently leave New York.

When I first met David in college he seemed to be a happy-go-lucky guy. I now realized he was a more serious, conscientious guy. It seemed as though he carried the full burden of the success or failure of Safe Haven on his shoulders. And Tina. If only she'd buy a one-way ticket to Tahiti.

Last Sunday David and I were all set to hike in the canyon when his cell phone rang, and Tina was on the other end almost hysterical, according to David, wanting his advice on how to handle some program problem.

David didn't seem happy when I asked if she did this all week too or just when he was with me on the weekend. We went on our hike but David was so preoccupied I finally suggested that we cut the day short and he go take care of whatever it was that had Tina in turmoil. He seemed relieved that I had given him permission to go. Tonight was to be the first time I would be seeing him since then. So far it didn't look promising, but I still held out hope.

I browsed the supermarket, selecting some fresh fruit for a compote. David was health conscious and the fruit would make a nice dessert. If he canceled altogether I'd eat it for breakfast.

I arrived home in plenty of time to prepare dinner and set the table. While the meatloaf was baking I peeled potatoes, hoping the phone wouldn't ring. If David called again he'd either be too late for a decent dinner or canceling. And without his saying so, I'd know Tina was involved.

I finished in the kitchen and it was only 6:30 pm. I decided to change into something more comfortable and went into the bedroom. My heart jumped when I saw the message light blinking. I hadn't bothered to check when I came home. Now I didn't want to hear it, so sure it was David, but I couldn't ignore it either. I pushed the play button.

"Hi Linda, Gregory. It's been a while. Jan tells me the weary world of Probation hasn't beaten you yet. Give me a call so we can catch up. So long for now."

I let out the breath I'd been holding. So far David was still on. Gregory sounded good, upbeat. His relationship with Jan had done wonders for him. She too was an even sparklier version of herself. I had told Jan about David and me and I was sure she had shared the news with Gregory. He'd be too much of a gentleman to ask but his desire to "catch up" probably meant he was hoping I'd tell him myself.

I slipped into a sweater and slacks, and was brushing my hair when the doorbell rang. I quickly touched up my lipstick and ran to the door, where a tired but smiling David stood.

"Not as late as I thought I'd be," he said as he came in, kissing me lightly on the cheek.

"Good. I missed you." I pecked back on his cheek as he passed.

"Something smells good and I'm starved." David made exaggerated sniffing sounds as he peeked into the oven.

"Meatloaf. You've had it before." There was a testiness to my voice that I hadn't intended. David made no mention, just kept poking around the kitchen, lifting lids, and peering into pots.

"Looks like mashed potatoes too. My favorite."

"They seem to go well with meatloaf," my voice still edgy. Get a grip!

I busied myself in the kitchen with last minute preparations. David had settled into the living room sofa and made a pretense of reading the paper but looked like he was fighting sleep.

Suddenly I felt ashamed of myself, behaving like a jealous teenager. David had given me no reason to mistrust him. Whatever interest Tina might have in him I couldn't imagine him encouraging it. He was so wrapped up in the success of Safe Haven he probably thought all her frequent calls were as important as she made them out to be.

I sat down next to David and stroked his hair. His eyes were half shut and he relaxed his head onto my shoulder.

"I looked forward to this all day," David sighed. "I wish I wasn't so tired so I could be better company."

"Having you here in any condition is fine with me. Dinner will be ready in a few minutes. You can doze if you'd like and I'll call you when it's on the table."

When we sat down to eat, David seemed a little

fresher from his short nap. We had a leisurely meal and he listened intently as I told him about my day in court with Luis Hebron. He shook his head at the outcome.

"There's an Oscar Hebron at Safe Haven. They could be brothers," David mentioned. "Oscar doesn't seem to have any visitors besides his mother, so if they are related they can't be too close."

"I doubt that Luis would take the time to visit his brother anyway. He doesn't seem the concerned type."

"Especially if his brother was trying to rehabilitate himself. Might make him feel guilty." David helped himself to more mashed potatoes.

"I've never understood the appeal of mind altering drugs. Maybe it was my straight-laced upbringing but I've never been tempted to try that junk. Aside from it being illegal, I want to keep my mind and body clear."

"Linda, I see these users every day at Safe Haven, trying to stay clean yet I know they are wishing for one more hit of cocaine, heroin, whatever their downfall is. You can see it in their eyes, the way they talk. The success of the program isn't just how well they do while there, but how well they do outside with their old friends and temptations. I'll be amazed if ten per cent make it once they're home." David leaned back, dejected at the thought.

"Is that why you've seemed so worried lately, kind of here and not here?" I ventured into this territory cautiously. I couldn't resist the opportunity once he opened the door. The question aroused his attention.

"Somewhat. I didn't mean to burden you with my concerns. It's not just the residents, it's the staff. I'm not sure everyone's as dedicated as they need to be. Tina has taken it upon herself to oversee the staffing and . . . . . ." his voice trailed and he looked uncomfortable.

The ubiquitous Tina. "Isn't she a councilwoman? Or did she quit that job to run Safe Haven?" I kept my voice even. If David noticed my sarcasm he let it go.

"Sometimes I wonder myself. She spearheaded the campaign to open the program so she's pretty invested in it. I didn't expect it to be . . . . . . enough of my problems, I need to tell you something."

David reached across our empty plates and took both my hands in his. A shiver of dread went up my spine.

"I need to return to New York, meet with the directors of Safe Haven, and catch up with my parents. I'm not sure how long I'll be there."

I was so relieved that the news wasn't something

else that I smiled and relaxed.

"Looks like you're happy I'll be away," David said with a look of mock hurt.

"I'm never happy when you're away. It's just that you were so serious I wasn't sure what I was going to hear. Going to New York for a while is not as bad as . . . ."

". . . . . . .still gunshy? No Linda, not this time." David pulled me onto his lap and kissed me gently on both eyes, then my mouth, then harder. I kissed him back with the passion he could always arouse in me. Before I became too weak in the knees I stood and we both headed to my bedroom.

"For such a long trip, you need a proper send-off," I whispered as we fell onto my bed.

"Don't be too proper," David answered as he pulled off my sweater.

And we weren't.

Chapter Twenty Three

David had been gone for two days and the weekend looming before me would have been lonely if Gregory and Jan hadn't invited me for dinner. They wanted to try a new fish restaurant in Newport Beach and I offered to meet them there rather than have them drive to Laguna Beach to pick me up.

I worked my way through the Saturday night traffic on Pacific Coast Highway. At each stoplight I peered between the shops and restaurants to catch a view of the sailboats bobbing along the oceanfront. The beach life was so carefree. Once again I was thankful that Edith allowed me to rent her Laguna house.

I spotted the restaurant and made a turn into the parking lot adjacent, stopping for the valet to take my car. Gregory and Jan were already inside waiting to be seated.

Gregory greeted me warmly. It had been weeks since I last saw him. His demeanor was calm and he looked younger then I remembered. What love won't do! Jan and I hugged, commenting that it was nice to see each other away from work. Jan looked lovely in a blue pantsuit. Her unruly red hair was pulled back at the top with a sparkly blue barrette, the rest falling around her shoulders in soft curls. They made a handsome couple.

It was so nice to be with people with whom I could talk openly. While we enjoyed wine, appetizers, and delicious crab and shrimp entrees, I found myself talking about David, my frustration at the Hebron case, and the still elusive six files. Gregory seemed able to put the cases in perspective although he hadn't given up on the idea that they figured into Carol's death, which he still considered murder. I returned to talking about David, a much nicer subject.

"When are we going to meet this guy?" Gregory asked.

"I saw him once," Jan interjected, "at the Safe Haven dedication. Quite a doll I must say."

I blushed, remembering that day, passing David off as an old college friend. Not untrue, just not the complete story. I decided to leave it at that. It was easier than dredging up sadness from the past. Jan believed our reacquaintance had blossomed into love. The whole story would have been too personal.

"When David returns from New York I'll have you over for dinner. You'll like him."

"When will that be?" Jan looked up from the remains of her crab legs.

"I wish I knew. David said he wasn't sure. The head office of Safe Haven is in New York and David needed to meet with people there. He's seemed very preoccupied lately. Something's going on that he doesn't want to share with me. He says the Safe Haven program's going well but I wonder." I didn't mention Tina. I was still uncomfortable about her and not sure where she fit into any of this.

"He has a lot of responsibility," Gregory noted. "I remember all the hoop-la when Safe Haven was first proposed, then approved. Finally opening the program was a huge step, but it's the problems that come up during the first months of operation that even the best planning can't always foresee. He'll work them out. He doesn't want to trouble you."

"You're right. Anyway, he'll be back one of these days and I can't wait for you to meet each other."

"Anyone for dessert?" Our waiter proffered menus. After a brief perusal, we made selections, and enjoyed every last crumb.

"I'm sure my meal tonight covered my calorie requirements for tomorrow too," I declared as we left, "but I don't regret one bite."

"I second that," added Jan.

While we waited for our cars to be delivered we promised to do this again soon. As I drove home I felt a warm glow from the evening. The wine probably helped too. It would be such fun double dating with Jan and Gregory. David, please hurry back.

I slept late on Sunday morning. A nice luxury. I had a slight headache from the two glasses of wine from last night. I stretched in bed, contemplating my low tolerance for alcohol. Not a bad thing I decided.

I showered and put on jeans and a t-shirt. The day was sunny. Maybe a jog on the beach later, then some grocery shopping. Such excitement!

The Sunday Times was on my front walkway. I retrieved it and breathed in the fresh air and heady scent of star jasmine. Definitely a walk on the beach today. I separated the pages of want ads and threw them in the trash, and headed back in for breakfast.

The coffee was done brewing so I poured myself

a cup while I sorted the paper by sections It usually took me most of the week to read the Sunday paper. Today I'd probably finish most of it. I glanced at the headlines on the front page then turned to the local section. The usual weekend murders and car accidents. A name caught my eye and sent a shiver though me. I read with amazement.

Santo Gonzales, 22, was fatally shot early Saturday during a suspected drug deal in Santa Ana. He was found lying in an alley near Fourth and Flower at 2 am and was pronounced dead at the scene. Patrons of a nearby bar reportedly heard loud arguing, then what sounded like two gunshots. They caught a glimpse of a dark, late model sedan driving away, but could not read the license number. Anyone with any information on the assailant or assailants is asked to call the Santa Ana Police Department.

The article went on to state that Santo was a known gang member and part of a group often dubbed the "teflon six" because their arrests never seemed to end in convictions. I shivered again. Santo was Miguel Gonzales's brother. Miguel was the runaway from Rolling Oaks whose house I visited while in training. I could picture vividly Mrs. Gonzales in her living room, Santo nearby intimidating her. Now he was gone. Killed like her husband. Poor lady. What a sad life.

I put down the paper and made breakfast, although I didn't have much of an appetite. If David were here we would be spending the day together. I missed him so. As I buttered my toast I wondered what he was doing now in New York, where it would be early afternoon . I'd only heard from him once since he left. There was noise in the background and he couldn't talk long. I hoped whatever was troubling David before he left would be worked out by the time he returned.

Between the Gonzales family and David I was beginning to work myself into a melancholy mood. Enough of this pity party. I cleaned up the kitchen, grabbed my house keys, and jogged toward the beach.

The air was invigorating. The ocean smell penetrated my nostrils as I moved along at a rapid pace, clearing my head of jumbled thoughts. After twenty minutes I slowed down to a walk, taking my shoes off so the gentle waves could lap over my feet. It wasn't a hot day so the beach wasn't too crowded. I tired after a while and sat down on the sand in a rocky cove. I gazed at the water and let the peacefulness wash over me. I had been sitting there for a few minutes when I heard the laughter and chatter of young women approaching. I paid little notice until they flopped on the sand nearby. I was somewhat sheltered by the cove and doubted that they saw me. I went back to my reverie when their conversation snapped me to attention. I looked again and couldn't believe my eyes. There was Tina and her two friends. Edith had said Tina grew up in Laguna. Maybe she still lived here. This was the second time I'd seen her.

"Looks like you're enjoying your day off," a pretty blond speaking.

"Safe Haven's not nearly as interesting when David's not there," Tina answered, running her fingers through her hair. "But he calls me every day, the next best thing."

I felt like I'd been shot in the heart. Calls her every day? Calm down. There's a logical explanation.

"So what's happening with you two?" the blond again.

"Not enough. He follows me around like a little puppy, not that I'm complaining."

"Maybe he's working up his nerve to ask you out," offered the third woman.

"Whew, how long does it take," sighed Tina.

"One of these days I'm going to do it myself. See what he says."

"Lots of luck," her friends chortled in unison.

I wasn't surprised that Tina had set her cap for David but I couldn't imagine him following her around like a "puppy". He never talked about her in other than professional terms. Maybe it was wishful thinking on her part. I thought of all the times she called David with a program problem when it was probably only an excuse to talk to him. David, so concerned about Safe Haven's success, seemed oblivious to her ulterior motives.

God, I didn't need to hear this. Was David's recent preoccupation due to her? Maybe he was finding himself attracted to her and didn't know how to deal with it. I sat there until they left, then trudged home, my thoughts jumbled again for a different reason.

I immersed myself in work while David was gone and tried not to give in to doubts about David's love for me. Our last night together was too perfect to think he was interested in Tina. When David had called he told me how anxious he was to return but still had business to take care of before he could do so. I told him I missed him and kept it light, burying any urge to bring up Tina.

Crime must have been on the rise because our workload was heavier than usual. Jan and I barely had time to grab a quick lunch before we had to return to our desks. I even volunteered for overtime cases. The extra money was nice but mostly I wanted to keep busy, leaving no time to dwell on my future with David.

I was in the midst of looking over a new referral when interrupted by the telephone. I answered but heard only silence. I stated my name once more, ready to hang up if no one responded, when I heard a faint "hello".

"Hello," I answered, "who's calling?"

"Is this Mrs. Dabenpor, probation officer?" a faintly familiar accented voice questioned.

"It's Miss Davenport, yes, and you are?"

"Mrs. Gonzales. You come see me once, give me your card?"

My pulse quickened. The mother of Santo and Miguel. "Yes, I remember. I'm very sorry about Santo. I read about it in the paper. Can I help you with something?"

"Jes." She paused so long I thought she'd left, then she spoke again. "Miguel, he want to turn himself in. He so scared. We both scared."

"You have Miguel with you?"

"Si, jes, he home. He don go nowhere. He don want no more shooting, no trouble. He go back to that Oaks camp and be good. Please. What we do?

I thought quickly. If she had some way to bring him to my office I could arrange with the warrant unit to take him into custody. He'd have to go to juvenile hall until he had a court hearing, but if he hadn't committed any new offenses, he'd probably be returned to Rolling Oaks with some more time tacked on to his original sentence for running away.

"Mrs. Gonzales are you able to bring him to my office?"

"Jes, my brother, he has car, he say he'll help me."

"Can you come in tomorrow morning?"

"Jes. Tell me way to come. I be there with Miguel."

I gave her directions and had her read them back to me. We were set for 9 am tomorrow. I immediately called the supervisor of the warrant unit and told him what happened. He said he'd send two officers to my office by 9:30 and wanted me to take a statement from Miguel in the meantime. I hung up feeling excited and apprehensive both. I intended to take more than a statement about his runaway. I would see what he knew about Carol's accident, if anything.

I was at my desk before 8 am, having barely slept the night before. Dozing then waking, I finally gave up on sleep and lay in bed thinking of my meeting with Miguel. Too bad it took Santo's death to turn himself in. At least for now he'll be spared the same fate.

I showered and dressed, ate a quick breakfast and packed myself a lunch. As I drove up Pacific Coast Highway, I was invigorated by the salty smell of the ocean wafting in my open windows. By the time I reached my office my adrenaline was pumping like a freshly discovered oil well.

I busied myself at my desk, preparing for the interview. The only file on Miguel was with the warrant unit so I had to rely on my memory of my last review of it. Not too much of a problem since Miguel's runaway coincided with Carol's accident. The contents of his file seemed etched in my mind.

As nine o'clock approached I began to worry that Mrs. Gonzales might have changed her mind, or that Miguel ran away again. When the reception- ist phoned me to tell me my appointment was in the lobby I breathed a huge sigh of relief, composed myself, and went out to greet them.

Mrs. Gonzales looked as if she'd aged ten years since I saw her a few months ago. She sat at the edge of her seat, wringing a hanky. Next to her sat a skinny, disheveled dark haired boy with sad brown eyes I took to be Miguel. I greeted them and glanced around wondering where her brother was. As Mrs. Gonzales arose she noted my look and volunteered that her brother was waiting in the car. I guess he didn't want to see his nephew taken away in handcuffs.

We settled in my office. I shuffled papers on my desk passing time so that mother and son could relax a bit. Miguel had some of the bravado of Santo. I suspected that he tried to follow in his older brother's footsteps, the only role model he knew. Deep down he seemed like a scared kid who got a bad break where parents were concerned.

I explained to Mrs. Gonzales and Miguel that he would be taken to juvenile hall, and in a few days have a court hearing. The warrant would be recalled and the judge would decide whether he'd be returned to Rolling Oaks. Mrs. Gonzales twisted her hanky. Miguel hung his head.

Before we began the interview I read Miguel his Miranda rights. He said he understood them and wanted to talk to me.

"Tell me what happened the day you left Rolling Oaks," I asked him.

Miguel looked down at his shoes, then at his mother, then shrugged.

"Miguel, you need to explain to me why you ran away. The judge will need to know to make his decision and I'll see that he receives the information you give me. So, let's begin."

He shifted around for a while, then his mother nudged him. "Tell the lady, like you tell me," she admonished.

"I didn't like it there. We had to work all day cleaning the camp and it was hot, guys picked on me too." Miguel suddenly seemed energized.

I could imagine Miguel was an easy target for some of the big boys I'd seen there. He looked much younger than his 17 years.

"Didn't the counselors stop the guys from picking on you?"

"They always did it when no one was around. If I reported it then it would be worse for me later." Miguel sat back with a look of recollection crossing his face.

"Go on. What happened that made you leave?"

"I was thinking about it for a few days. Then that night after lights out somebody squirted soap on my head. The night counselor was on the other side of the dorm. I tried to wipe it off with my sheet and everyone was laughing. The counselor never even heard them.

"I was awake the rest of the night. When it was quiet and I could hear snoring, and the counselor had gone back to the other side again, I put on my clothes and climbed out the window. I hid in the bushes until the duty officer passed my dorm on his rounds and then ran down to the road."

"Weren't you frightened? There are many wild animals out there."

"A little. I stayed on the road and only once saw a deer. They don't scare me."

"Then what?" I made notes as I listened.

"I followed the two miler road down to the highway. It was almost daylight when I reached it."

"Weren't staff changing shifts about then? Didn't anyone see you?"

"When a car came along I hid in the bushes. No one saw me."

"OK Miguel, you've reached the Ortega. Where did you go next?"

"I turned right and kept following the road for hours until I was pretty far from the camp. Then I hitchhiked when I was near San Juan. A truck driver stopped and called my brother Santo and he picked me up near the freeway."

"The truck driver didn't wonder why you were out on the road all alone?"

"I told him I got lost camping with my cousins. I guess he believed me." Miguel sat back in his chair, satisfied that he was finished.

"Where have you been these last few months?" I was pretty sure I knew the answer.

Miguel squirmed and looked at his mother. Mrs. Gonzales's face grew red. Silence. I repeated the question.

"My house. I been at my house hiding," Miguel blurted out.

Mrs. Gonzales looked anguished. "I don like him hiding. I tell him 'turn himself in' but he don lissen, and my son, Santo," she crossed herself, "he say 'stay, don go back.' Miguel lissen to him. I very sorry I not tell the truth when you come to my house. Now Santo's killed. Miguel, he scared. I hope everythin come out all right."

"You did the right thing bringing him in Mrs. Gonzales." She gave me a weak smile but I sensed some relief on her face that she hadn't done everything wrong.

I glanced at my watch. It was almost 9:30 and

the warrant officers would be here soon. I had all the information I needed to advise the court on Miguel. I put down my pen and sat back. The next would be off the record for now.

"Miguel, while you were on the Ortega Highway, did you see anything unusual?"

The look on Miguel's face told me I'd struck a nerve.

"Like what?" He shifted nervously and looked at his mother, whose face once again took on a frightened look.

"Like a car accident."

Miguel started to sob. Then Mrs. Gonzales began weeping. I clasped my hands together to keep them from shaking.

"The poor lady," Miguel almost whispered. "I saw her car coming fast so I hid in the bushes so I wouldn't get caught. There was another car right behind. I heard screeching and then the first car came off the road and down the hill and landed on its side."

"And you were in the bushes the whole time?"

"Yes."

"What happened to the second car?"

"It stopped and someone got out but I couldn't see who it was. The person never went down the hill at all, just stood there, then went back into the car, turned around and left."

"You mean went back in the direction he or she came from?"

"Yes."

"What did you do then?"

"I went to the car and saw the lady. Her eyes were closed and I think she was dead. She had like a big purse and I thought there might be money in it so I opened the door and grabbed it but then I heard another car stop so I ran back in the bushes."

"With the 'purse'?"

"Yes. But there was no money in it. Just folders with papers."

My heart leapt. Carol's briefcase and the missing A files. "What did you do with it?"

"I left it in the bushes. I waited for a long time until the police left and the lady was taken away. Then I ran as fast as I could down the road. I told you the rest of it. Am I in more trouble?"

I didn't answer his question. Could he have helped the police?

"Did you see anything of the second car that could identify it?"

"No. I only heard it."

Before we went further my phone rang, the

receptionist letting me know the warrant officers were here. I asked her to send them to my office. In the few minutes it took them to come down the hall I wrapped things up with Miguel and his mother. There was no more discussion of the accident.

The warrant officers handcuffed Miguel, who was compliant. Mrs. Gonzales winced when the handcuffs clicked shut and quickly wiped a tear from her eye.

"Thank you Miss Davenpoor," she said as she followed her son and the officers out of my office. I provided the written statement taken from Miguel to one of the officers so he could prepare a report for the court, then shut the door behind them.

I sat at my desk and pondered the information I'd just received. Gregory's suspicions were correct. Carol's death wasn't an accident. But who would want her dead? The answer had to be in her briefcase, probably destroyed by now having been exposed to the elements these past months.

I chose not to include the accident information in my notes. It didn't add anything to Miguel's runaway status, which is what the court was concerned about. The sheriff's department had closed their investigation. Had they known there was a second car involved maybe they would have investigated further, but that could still be brought to their attention. How or when I wasn't sure. First we needed Carol's briefcase.

I went through the rest of my day on auto pilot, anxious to go home and clear my head. Finally at four o'clock I straightened my desk and left.

On my way home I stopped at the supermarket for a few items then headed home to put a light meal together. First, I checked my messages. None. I missed David terribly and was hoping for a call from him. He sounded so strained in our conversations but insisted it was only work pressures. OK, I believe you David, I said to myself, over and over.

I broiled a chicken breast and made a salad. While finishing a cup of tea I looked at the clock. Gregory should be home from work now. I went to the phone and dialed. He answered on the second ring.

"Gregory, this is Linda. I've got something to tell you."

Chapter Twenty Four

We parked in a secluded spot off the side of the road where the car wouldn't be easily spotted. Gregory and I sat silently for a while, contemplating what we were about to do, then left the car. Three days had passed since I filled Gregory in on Miguel's story. With some sadness, and yet relief at being vindicated, Gregory proposed we go as soon as possible to see if we could find Carol's briefcase. Whatever we did next hinged on the contents. We hoped they would be intact enough to read.

So here we were, early on a Saturday morning, flashlights in hand, slowly inching our way through the scrub brush and down the steep slope. Birds circled overhead as if to question our presence in their domain. An occasional unidentifiable animal sound startled us and made me wonder if we were being wise to take this on ourselves.

"Careful Linda," Gregory cautioned, as I stumbled over a ropy knot of dead branches in my path.

We were probably fifty feet down from the road and had no idea in which direction Miguel had hidden or how far he had descended before he hid. Since he'd been walking on the road and had to hide fast when he heard a car, we assumed he didn't go too far down. We decided to start our search where we were. The place where Carol's car landed was a bit farther down so we could always work our way down to it.

"Why don't you search to the left, I'll work towards the right," Gregory suggested.

We separated and slowly grew farther apart as we carefully picked through the dense growth looking for Carol's briefcase. When we each had ventured about two hundred yards in each direction, we turned and headed back towards each other, only a little farther downhill this time. After an hour with no results, we stopped to rest. Gregory sat on a large rock and stretched his legs. I sat cross-legged on the ground nearby.

"I should have asked Jan to come along. It would have helped us cover more ground," Gregory said.

"Does she even know we're here?" I asked.

"No, I didn't tell her. I'll see her tonight. Maybe

I'll have good news to report."

"We'd better get at it if we want to have good news." I stood up and dusted myself off. Gregory did the same.

Once again we followed our search pattern back and forth, probing, kicking, and separating dense and tangled growth, hoping to reveal the hidden briefcase. Nothing. We were now in the general area of where Carol's car had landed.

"If Miguel ran to her car and saw the briefcase, then ran when he heard another car stop, he wouldn't have had time to go too far to hide," I suggested. "Maybe we should concentrate just below and around the area where the car was."

"May as well," Gregory answered wearily.

We both headed lower down the hillside, separating into opposite directions, continuing our poking and prodding. Between bug bites and scratches from thorny bushes I was about ready to call it quits and sensed Gregory felt the same. If the briefcase was here it was certainly not evident.

Gregory stopped to wipe his forehead. "Maybe the animals have long since destroyed what we're looking for. I'm about to give up."

I was sitting on a tree stump, ready to agree with Gregory. I glanced over the vast expanse of brush, plants, and trees and thought of the needle in a haystack analogy. The sun was almost overhead, casting a rippling effect as it filtered through the tree branches and bounced off the scrub. Suddenly I thought I saw something gleam in the distance. I walked in the direction of the bright object but lost sight of it. I scanned the area to no avail.

A breeze rustled through the trees and as the sunlight came through, I spotted the gleam again. I kept my eyes on the spot and walked toward it, separating dead branches and tangled weeds as I went. As I came closer I fell on my knees and started clawing away at the growth. Gregory joined me and as we worked we slowly uncovered what appeared to be a briefcase. The gleam that had caught my eye was the brass clasp on the outside of the case.

"Finally. I can't believe it," Gregory uttered as we both feverishly dug to free the case from its hiding place. With a strong tug, Gregory pulled the case out from under a bush which had grown over it. Remarkably it appeared to be in good shape.

"It might have been hard to find but these bushes actually protected it," I volunteered.

"Let's see if what's in here was protected," Gregory answered as he pulled open the clasp and looked inside, spreading the opening wide.

There were six case files and what appeared to be a typed letter attached to one of them. Gregory pulled out the file with the letter. We both sat back in amazement at what we read. The letter was written by Carol and addressed to the Grand Jury foreman.

"I am a Supervising Probation Officer in Adult Investigation and would like to ask that you investigate several court actions. It seems that there are certain cases, I've brought six as an example, that receive extremely lenient dispositions when they appear in Judge Carlos Higuera's courtroom. I met with Judge Higuera several months ago to discuss these concerns and he explained them away as the vagaries of the justice system. However, since that time I have learned some things that make me believe these lenient dispositions are more than that.

My decision to come to you has been a difficult one, made all the more difficult because I have subsequently entered into a personal relationship with Judge Higuera, albeit one I plan to sever. I have found Judge Higuera to be a fine man, a widower deeply devoted to his daughter Tina, a Santa Ana councilwoman. They are well known for their philanthropic work across the Mexican border. Yet

I believe that somehow Judge Higuera is making wrong decisions, perhaps under duress.

I have reviewed these cases for commonality. All defendants live in Santa Ana. One of the cases I brought today, Edgar Morales, has a brother Gabriel who is a Santa Ana policeman. Is he using his influence so his brother and cohorts get off easily?

Lastly, while recently serving as officer of the day, I received a call from a lady who would not give her name. She said her drug infested Santa Ana neighborhood is unsafe yet her complaints to the police accomplish nothing. The neighborhood boys brag about how they have "friends inside" and can get all the drugs they want from Mexico. I believe there may be a common thread between this court and street drug activity.

I have not shared this with anyone at Probation. I wanted to bring it directly to you as a fair and impartial investigating body although I know I will have to answer for my actions when this all comes out. I did tell Judge Higuera a few days ago about the phone call and my belief that the Grand Jury should look into this. He seemed visibly nervous but did not try to change my mind.

I will make myself available to you today to answer any questions. Thank you for your time."

Sincerely,
Carol Alder

"Whew," Gregory let out his breath, as he slumped on the ground, the letter in his hand. "This explains a lot. Now what?"

I was still taking it all in. Carol's suspicions. Carol dating Judge Higuera. Was it his pant leg I saw when Carol was picked up by the limo? Probably. Maybe she told him on the way home of her plans to see the Grand Jury, thus setting in motion a tragedy that she couldn't foresee.

"Linda?" Gregory's voice was raised.

"I'm sorry. I was lost in thought with what we found. So much to process. What do we do with all this?"

"That's what I was wondering. First, let's get out of here and go somewhere where we can think."

"Let's go back to my place," I offered. "It's quiet. I'll make us some lunch and maybe we'll come up with a plan."

"Great tuna salad," Gregory praised as he helped himself to another sandwich. "Digging through weeds really works up an appetite."

I scooped some fresh fruit from a bowl and served some to Gregory. "I'll say. Just think, we could have walked away empty-handed. Maybe Carol's spirit was guiding us."

"I wouldn't be surprised," Gregory agreed. "Where we go next is critical. Someone went out of his or her way to stop Carol. Whoever it was would probably do the same to us."

"Who knew besides Judge Higuera? Somehow I can't imagine him killing Carol. There were other ways he could have stopped her if he wanted to."

"Maybe those cases were just the tip of the iceberg and Carol was on to something more than even she realized."

"We can't just sit on this. I should tell my supervisor what we found and let him take it up to our chief, but then he'll know I already knew Carol. Our previous conversations about her will be reevaluated against that. My credibility will be gone no matter how I explain it. Everything I do will be suspect. What a mess!"

"Linda, I can keep the files and initiate any action. That will keep you out of it. I have some thoughts on this."

"Tell me."

"Judge Higuera has to be involved, maybe unwittingly, but nevertheless involved. Starting with his courtroom, what would he have to gain by giving certain cases lenient treatment?"

"Nothing that I can imagine. In fact he's risking his reputation by doing it. I doubt that he needs money. If he is involved, it can't be for that."

"What if he was pressured by someone, to protect someone. A quid pro quo. Lenient treatment in trade for.........what?"

We sat silently for a few minutes, two hapless crime solvers, looking for clues. All I could come up with was Judge Higuera's devotion to Tina, but she seemed to be an upright citizen, even though a spoiled one. But what if she wasn't so upright? I could still see her on the beach, tossing her curls, her demeanor flirty even with her girlfriends. There seemed to be a wild side under the surface. She struck me as manipulative too, setting her cap for David, who so far seemed oblivious, but how long could that last?

"Gregory, the only thing that makes any sense

at all is that Judge Higuera was somehow making these decisions to protect Tina."

"The councilwoman? What would he have to protect her from?" Gregory's astonishment indicated he didn't think much of my idea.

"He adores Tina. His wife is gone and as far as I know she's his only family. I don't think she's the sweet person she appears to be but a father's love can be blind to that." I thought of my own dad and how, unlike my mother, he could overlook the dumb things I did growing up. He would give me a hug and a kiss and tell me that a hundred years from now it wouldn't matter to anyone. I guess that goes for almost anything but it always soothed me then.

"So what could adorable Tina have done to make her dad go soft on criminals?"

"Steal maybe?" Even that didn't sound right to me. If she was connected to these Santa Ana gang cases, it wouldn't be through theft. They're into drugs, and probably guns.

"I can't imagine her stealing," Gregory responded. "Maybe she's a hard core drug addict. She sure looks it." He laughed at his own sarcasm.

"You think you're funny, but maybe you're on to something. She doesn't have to be on heroin and have tracks on her arms to give her away. Maybe she snorts cocaine or takes speed. Maybe that's why her eyes are so bright."

"And there she is, spearheading a drug treatment program in Santa Ana. What a piece of news if that got out." Gregory chuckled, then put down his coffee cup and leaned back. "My God, that would be enough to have Judge Higuera allow himself to be pressured. All those cases were drug related. Linda, that could be it. Tina's a user and took one too many chances, got caught, dad gets pushed by......who? She stays out of trouble but so do his or her buddies."

I flashed on David and his dedication to making Safe Haven successful. What a blow it would be to have Tina bring embarrassment to the program with illegal behavior. David had been so preoccupied the weeks before he returned to New York. Even in our earlier conversations he sounded troubled, chalking it off as too much work. Does he suspect something about Tina but doesn't want to explore it for fear of the walls caving in?

"I was thinking of David and how this would affect him and Safe Haven. Whatever we do we have to be on firm ground." I began to clear the lunch dishes.

"What do we do next? We can't blatantly accuse Tina Higuera, councilwoman and judge's daughter, with just speculation. We need some proof. I'm an attorney, but I don't practice criminal law. I do know we could get ourselves in a pile of trouble jumping to conclusions."

"OK, let's look at what we know. Carol's letter mentioned a Santa Ana policeman, Gabriel Morales, whose brother Edgar was one of the criminal cases. Then there was the anonymous caller who said the gang kids had 'friends inside' and could get drugs from Mexico." I loaded the dishwasher and tried to compose my thoughts. "It's well known that Judge Higuera and Tina travel to Baja every two or three weeks to bring food and clothes to an orphanage. But what do they bring back?"

"I follow your logic Linda but it's a big leap from a judge being lenient on some cases to regularly transporting drugs into the United States."

"What if he didn't know he was doing it? A small package of, cocaine let's say, would be easy enough to hide but it would have tremendous street value. Every two or three weeks, a nice steady supply, unwittingly brought over the border by an upright judge and his equally upright daughter."

"Don't they use drug sniffing dogs at the border?" Gregory asked.

"Maybe if you're as well known as Judge Higuera you get passed through. Especially if you were seen earlier in the day bringing needed supplies to poor orphans."

"If the judge was caught with drugs at the border it would prove our theory, but it still wouldn't explain who took Carol's life," Gregory offered.

"It would be a start. In fact it's the only way I can think of to pursue this and not have our names involved."

We had moved to the living room and sat opposite each other, silent for a while.

"You're a good investigator Linda. Your powers of deduction are right on. We need to alert the border patrol and I think I know how we can do it."

"You do?" I sat upright.

"Yes. When Carol had her accident an officer from the Sheriff's Department responded to the scene. His name was Jim Randall. He seemed to think there was something unusual about the accident but when I tried to reach him some days later he wasn't available. I could tell him what we found and ask him to tip off the border patrol."

"How do you know he'll talk to you now?"

"Time has gone by. There's new information. Besides, if the judge's car is searched and nothing is found, no harm done. He'll think he was searched routinely and shouldn't suspect anything. Our names won't be much if he's clean, though."

"And if he's clean we're back to square one," I replied, liking the search plan.

"Then I guess you'll have to bring the files to your supervisor and hope he's understanding," Gregory added. "But let's go with our plan first before you start doing your mea culpas. Where's your phone book? I'll try to call Jim Randall now."

"I've got a county directory in my briefcase. I'll get that." I headed into the bedroom and brought out a small book, flipping through the pages until I landed on Orange County Sheriff's Office. "This looks like a good number to try," I said, handing the book to Gregory.

He went to the telephone and dialed. It was apparent from the one-sided conversation that Jim Randall was no longer there. Gregory hung up and turned to me.

"Would you believe Randall's now a private investigator with an office in Santa Ana? The watch commander didn't know the number but said it was in the phone book under Randall Investigations."

I went to the hall closet and retrieved the phone book. Gregory thumbed through it and quickly found the listing. He dialed and waited, then left a message on an answering machine.

"No one there now. I left my number rather than yours. He should remember me."

"Let's hope he calls you." I stifled a yawn and shifted positions.

"Alright, I get the hint. I'm tired too. I'll be on my way."

"You don't have to rush off, really."

"I wouldn't mind going home and taking a nap. I'm taking Jan out tonight and she loves to dance. I need some energy."

"Are you going to tell her what we found?"

"Not right away. I trust her completely but this should be between you and me for now."

"I agree. I never told her about my interview with Miguel Gonzales, at least the part where he told me about seeing the accident and finding the files."

Gregory and I walked toward the door. He thanked me for lunch and promised to call me as soon as he heard from Jim Randall. I would keep the files for now, hidden safely in my bedroom closet.

It was three o'clock. I contemplated a long walk on the beach but when another yawn came over me I decided a nap sounded good to me too. I kicked off my shoes, grabbed an afghan, and curled up on the couch where I quickly fell asleep.

❧❖❧

The ringing telephone woke me from a dream where I was on the beach with the case files. A wind came up and began scattering papers over the sand. As I frantically tried to gather them they seemed to sprout wings and fly away. Just as I realized I could never reach them I was awakened by the phone. I answered groggily, thankful it was only a dream.

"Hi Linda. Are you feeling OK? Your voice sounds hoarse." It was David.

I cleared my throat, trying to rise out of my stupor. The sound of David's voice was so sweet to my ears. I willed myself to be fully awake.

"I'm fine," I answered. "You caught me taking a nap. How are you? I miss you so much."

"I miss you too, in fact too much to stay here any longer. I'll be finishing up some loose ends and I'll be back in a few days."

"That's great because I've almost forgotten what you look like." How could I say that. I remembered every little crease on his face.

"That's no good. Luckily I remember you very well, your big brown eyes, silky hair, soft lips……"

"Stop. I'll never sleep tonight."

"OK, but on a serious note, I've still got some

things about Safe Haven that need resolution but I can do only so much here. I'm worried though that the resolution might not be pleasant. I'll have to take that chance."

"This sounds mysterious."

"I can't share any more right now. I promise to be more forthcoming when I see you."

"Which will be?"

"By next Wednesday. I'll be in by dinnertime. Maybe we could go to the Laguna Hotel for dinner and watch the sun set over the ocean."

"You've got a date. I'll make reservations for seven. Will that give you enough time?"

"Plenty. See you then. I love you."

"I love you too. Come back safely."

After we hung up I thought about what Gregory and I had accomplished today, our suspicions about Tina, and what it would mean to Safe Haven and David if they proved to be true. David had alluded to continuing problems. Neither of us had shared our secrets. As I mulled this over the phone rang again. This time it was Gregory.

"I didn't wake you did I?"

"No, David did that earlier. In fact, aren't you supposed to be sleeping?"

"I was, then I received a call from Jim Randall."

"Did he remember you?"

"He sure did. I brought him up to date on everything. Funny thing is he was always suspicious about Carol's accident too but was told by his supervisors that it was accidental, they were closing the books. Anyway, he knows some of the border patrol agents who work on the Tijuana border. He's going to talk to them, find out what they know about Judge Higuera, and then let me know. He has to go to San Diego Monday on a case he's working. He'll do it then."

"This is fantastic. Do you think he'll persuade them to search the judge's car the next time he comes through?"

"Probably. Especially if he alerts them. They can't afford to ignore a warning like that." Gregory sounded pleased.

"So we just sit back and wait until you hear further?"

"Right. I'll let you know as soon as I know something."

"Thanks Gregory. You're a good man. Have fun tonight." We hung up.

I sank back on the couch feeling elated and apprehensive at the same time. I was wide-awake and restless with no particular plans for the rest of the weekend. I hadn't seen Edith for a while and wondered if she'd mind having an overnight guest. I hated calling at the last minute but she could always say no. I dialed her number and she answered with a cheery hello.

"You little stranger. How've you been?" Edith seemed happy to hear from me.

"Working too hard, and lonely. I thought about driving up and spending the night with you, if you don't have plans and don't mind company."

"No to both. You're always welcome. I'm afraid I've already had an early dinner but Charlotte can put something together for you if you're hungry."

"Don't bother. I'll grab something quick on the way. I should be there by seven thirty or eight."

"Drive carefully. See you soon."

I straightened the living room, packed some clothes and toiletries in an overnight bag and by six o'clock I was driving north on Pacific Coast Highway, windows down, listening to a golden oldies station, and wondering what the next week would bring.

Chapter Twenty Five

It was fairly slow for Monday. No new referrals all day and that was fine with me. Some of the judges had started summer vacations, which accounted for the diminished court activity. Maybe crime was taking a vacation too.

The brief weekend trip to Edith's was just what I needed. We gabbed for hours, catching each other up on our lives. I felt a little dishonest not sharing the news of our find off the Ortega, but Gregory and I had promised each other it would be between us for now and I didn't intend to break that promise. Charlotte filled me with her scrumptious cooking and sent me home with enough leftovers to keep me in meals for the next week. A care package for the working girl, she called it. When I unlocked my door Sunday night I felt pampered and rested.

Now I was occupied by thoughts of David, who

I'd see in two days, and the outcome of Jim Randall's visit to San Diego and the border patrol. Waiting was worse than anything.

I busied myself shuffling papers and preparing for two interviews tomorrow. I dictated a report and sent it to the typing pool. By the end of the day I was as organized as I'd ever been. Charlene would have been proud. Just before I was about to leave Jan popped her head in the door.

"Hey twinkle toes, I heard you went dancing Saturday night," I greeted, and immediately regretted my loose lips. She would know I talked to Gregory, and wonder why.

"How'd you find out?" Jan asked, sounding puzzled.

"I called Gregory Saturday but he was just leaving to go out with you. Wanted to say hello. We didn't get to talk. He probably didn't think it was anything to mention." I lied, I hoped convincingly.

"Of course. I keep forgetting you're old buddies. We had fun. But I came in to tell you that I spoke to Heather today and she wants to have a reunion lunch with you, Esther and me, some time next week. So check your calendar and tell me what looks good."

Relieved, I flipped calendar pages. "Tuesday or

Wednesday would be fine."

"They're OK for me too. I'll call Heather and let you know." Jan disappeared as quickly as she came.

I heaved a sigh, hating the subterfuge and wondering when all our suspicions would be laid to rest. I was dying to call Gregory but I knew if he had any news he'd call me. I grabbed my purse, locked my office, and left.

I took the long way home along Pacific Coast Highway, enjoying the ocean sights and smells. On the spur of the moment I stopped at the Fish Shanty, a little hole in the wall restaurant between Corona del Mar and Laguna Beach, and treated myself to the best fish and chips on the coast. By the time I reached home, full and tired, I was ready for an early night.

By Tuesday afternoon I was getting pretty anxious. I had finished my two interviews and organized all my notes. Still no new referrals, which gave me extra time to work on the cases I already had, and to think too much about David, and when I'd hear from Gregory. Surely Jim Randall must have called him by now with some news. If I didn't hear something before tomorrow night I'd be a basket case when I met David.

Jan came in to confirm our lunch date for next Wednesday, which seemed to be the best day for everyone. She suggested Mama Rosa's. Apparently Gregory had introduced her to the restaurant too. We chatted for a while. She seemed happy for me when I told her David would be back tomorrow. After she left I decided to call it a day myself. It was four thirty and I'd worked through lunch because my first interview went longer than I'd anticipated. Some defendants won't talk at all, others won't shut up. You never know what you'll get, but I'll take the talkers any time.

I went straight home and dashed to my answering machine, relieved to see a blinking light, hoping it was Gregory. It was.

"Linda, Gregory. I tried you at the office but you'd just left. Call me at home after seven. I won't be there until then. Talk to you later."

It was just five thirty. Seven o'clock seemed like an eternity from now. I changed clothes and heated some of the leftovers Charlotte had given me, eating slowly and watching the hands on the kitchen clock. When I finished, I cleaned up. Still only six thirty.

I went into the living room and lay down on the couch with a magazine. I must have dozed off because when I next checked the time it was seven thirty. I hurried to the phone and dialed Gregory, who answered immediately.

"It's Linda. What's happening? I've been on pins and needles all day."

"Good news so far. Jim Randall called me this afternoon. He spoke to the border patrol agents on duty yesterday afternoon. They all know Judge Higuera and his daughter Tina. In fact they seem to have royal status according to what Jim heard."

"How so?"

"They come down every two or three weeks, usually on a Saturday, with their car laden with clothes, food, and toys for a large orphanage just outside of Tijuana, called La Puerta Abierta. They return later the same day, auto empty, passing through the border with the inspection waived. When Jim told the agents of our suspicions he said they couldn't believe it.

"Does that mean they won't do a search?" I asked, disappointment welling up.

"No. They're willing to do a search, drug dog and all, just to prove us wrong. In fact it might be this weekend since they haven't seen the judge for over two weeks and figure he's due."

"That's great. But if they don't find anything we're back to square one."

"Probably. Let's hope that if we're right and the judge's car has been transporting something illegal that he won't miss bringing it this weekend. It'll be a long time before they search him again if they come up empty."

"More waiting then."

"Looks that way."

"David's coming back from New York tomorrow night. I think he's going to tell me something about Safe Haven, something he's concerned about. It's going to be difficult not to alert him to our suspicions about Tina and her dad.

"I know, but if you tell him, he may act differently around her without realizing it and it could make her more cautious."

"You're right Gregory. We can't do anything to blow this. I'll put on a game face. Thanks for all you've done. Take care."

"Bye Linda. I'll be in touch."

Well, we're in it now I thought as I hung up the phone. I was so keyed up I decided a run on the beach would help me unwind. I took my house key, put on a sweater, and slowly jogged toward the beach, picking up my pace as I neared the water.

The sun was starting to set and the sky was a beautiful palette of pink, blue, and purple. The crisp ocean air and the wind on my face energized me, and within minutes I felt loose and relaxed.

I followed the coastline for several minutes.

Other joggers passed me and waved. I should do this more often I realized, heading for a rock to sit and rest before starting back. I watched the sun slowly lower and thought about how my life had changed in less than a year, from boredom in Detroit to anything but boredom here in southern California. I would have never thought a year ago that I'd be reunited with David or be an amateur sleuth. I hoped I hadn't bitten off more than I could chew.

The sun was slipping below the water's edge, giving its last golden shimmer before disappearing. I started home, wanting to be there before dark. One more night and David's back. My heart leapt at the thought and I jogged home with nothing but that thought in mind.

I made a last minute check of my hair and make-up in the rear view mirror before turning my car over to the valet at the Laguna Hotel. I stepped out, straightened my skirt and looked around the parking lot. David usually rented a convertible but I didn't see one tonight. In fact the lot wasn't very full at all for such a popular place.

"I loved the Laguna Hotel, its charming façade, and casually elegant interiors. I especially loved the dining room that seemed to hang over the ocean. With its expansive walls of glass you could almost see the waves crashing under you. I'd asked for a window table when I made the reservations and looked forward to watching a beautiful sunset in David's company.

I walked the long hallway from the hotel's entry to the dining room at the far end. Only two window tables were occupied and David was nowhere in sight. The maitre'd asked if I wanted to be seated at our table while I waited but I decided to wait instead on the banquette at the dining room's entrance. I never liked being the first in a party to arrive, then sitting alone at the table for what seemed like endless minutes waiting for the rest.

At seven fifteen I began to wonder where David was. He had my cell phone number so he would have called me if he were delayed. As I fretted over the possibilities I saw him walking hurriedly down the hall toward me. I stood to greet him, weak-kneed as usual when I first saw him after an absence.

We embraced wordlessly for a while. David seemed a bit thinner, his face tired, but when he smiled his blue eyes crinkled and I still saw the college boy with whom I first fell in love.

"Long flight?" I asked.

"Yes. We were late leaving New York. We made

up a little time in the air but then I had to wait in a long line for my rental car, then fight the traffic here. Have I complained enough?"

"Poor baby, let me comfort you," I joked and patted his back. "I'm so glad you're here. I'll take you in any condition."

"Seeing you is the best medicine. Let's sit down." David took my hand and we were shown to our table.

We ordered wine and smoked salmon and while we sipped and nibbled we watched the white caps slowly rolling in, then recede out to sea again, only to gather strength and roll thick and foamy back toward us. David was anxious to hear what I'd been doing. I filled him in on my busy work schedule and impromptu visit to Edith. I felt dishonest not telling him of finding the missing case files. He knew how important they were to me.

"So there it is. Exciting isn't it?"

"You didn't mention Gregory. Haven't you seen him?" David asked casually as he put a piece of salmon on a cracker and popped it in his mouth.

I blanched, then composed myself. "We've spoken once or twice." Oh how I hated this. "He's been busy plus he and Jan are quite an item so any free time he has he spends with her. They're anxious to meet you by the way and I've promised that we'd all get together when you returned."

"I'd love to. Give me a week or so. I've got some tough days ahead of me."

"Can you tell me? You mentioned something on the phone."

"Let's order dinner first." David signaled the waiter.

After we placed our order David sat back in his chair gazing at the ocean and sunset drama playing outside the window. He looked so thoughtful, like he was searching for just the right words. He took another sip of wine, then put the glass down.

"Let's see, where do I start?" David began. "Before I left for New York you probably noticed how preoccupied I was."

"That I did," I responded, wondering what in the world was coming.

"You know how much it means to have Safe Haven develop into a successful program. Headquarters in New York expects it. Their plans to expand on the West Coast would be greatly affected if Safe Haven was less than the flagship they want it to be."

"But it is going well, isn't it?"

"Yes, but it could all fall apart if what I suspect, and plan to act on, takes place."

"Why would you do anything to jeopardize the program."

"I'm not the one jeopardizing it, Tina is."

"Tina?" My voice came out a little high and squeaky. "How?" I added in a more normal register.

"Linda, I'm telling you this in the utmost confidence. I trust you and I need to talk about this, get some guidance, before I make a mistake."

Dear God, I was starting to feel like a double agent. In what part of my brain would I hide this secret.

"I'm convinced Tina uses drugs," David continued. "At first when I saw her all bright-eyed and energetic I thought she was just one of those high energy people. But then sometimes at the end of the day her speech would be slurry, her eyelids half shut. Then one afternoon I saw her rummaging around in the nurse's office where the meds are kept, and shortly after she was peppy and climbing the walls. I started watching her more closely. I saw this pattern over and over."

"Do you think she was taking drugs from the nurse's station?" Now I knew Gregory and I were on the right track.

"Maybe. The count on some meds has been short

occasionally. What I really think is that she hides her stash in there. That office is off limits to anyone but medical personnel but Tina seems to have free rein to roam all over the place."

"She and her father are pretty much the do-gooders of Orange County and Mexico. Weren't her efforts instrumental in making Safe Haven happen in the first place?"

"Yes, that's what makes this so hard. If she were any employee she would be quietly dismissed. But she's Tina Higuera, councilwoman, with aspirations to run for the state assembly. Not to mention her jurist father."

"Have you told anyone about this besides me?"

"I confided in my dad, then we had a meeting with the director of Safe Haven in New York. The consensus was I should be as discreet as possible."

"How do you accuse someone discreetly of using drugs?"

"My idea is to talk to her about my observations, ask her to seek help, keep it as quiet as possible. Hopefully she'll cooperate and Safe Haven won't suffer."

"When do you plan to do this?" I kept my voice steady even though my heart was pounding.

"Tomorrow or Friday. The longer I wait, the

worse it gets. You have no idea Linda how this has weighed on me."

The waiter brought our meal, steaming hot clams for David, shrimp for me. It was a welcome break from our conversation, which was making me increasingly nervous. David wanted this to go away quietly. What would happen if he knew our plans? Our results would be anything but quiet. And if David spoke to Tina soon she may think twice about any trip to Mexico this weekend, if one was intended. Could I convince David to hold off on any discussion for a while without telling him the reason? And how would he react to that?

I toyed with my food, having lost my appetite during David's revelations. I'd made a promise to Gregory to keep our discovery of the files and our suspicions secret, at least until after the border patrol search. But David had similar suspicions. Couldn't we work together on this? I couldn't sit here any longer listening to David pour his heart out and not be honest with him. I'd make my peace with Gregory later. David needed to know the whole story.

"These clams are the best," David offered as he shucked another one. For the moment he seemed to have forgotten the Tina problem. "Don't you like your shrimp? You've barely touched them."

"I have other things on my mind. Something important I didn't tell you. I hope when I explain you'll understand why."

David put down his fork and stared at me. "What?"

I began with Miguel Gonzales turning himself in, telling about finding the files but leaving them in the bushes off the Ortega, and Gregory's and my successful search.

"Linda, that's good news. Did you turn them over to your supervisor?"

"No, there's more. In Carol's briefcase there was a letter she had written to the Grand Jury asking for their investigation of Judge Higuera's court practices. She implied that he might be being pressured to make lenient dispositions on certain cases. The case files were her examples. She never made it to Rolling Oaks, as you know.

"Here's the part you're not going to like." I proceeded to tell him of our suspicions that Judge Higuera was protecting Tina, that somehow she might be connected to these cases due to drug activity, and that we suspected their frequent trips to a Mexican orphanage were a good opportunity to bring back drugs. They were apparently never searched at the border due to the judge's good samaritan reputation. Now because of a contact Gregory made, they'd be searched this weekend if they go.

"So you see David, we're all on the same track, only ours is more far reaching."

Now it was David's turn to lose his appetite. He looked out the window, the waves crashing more heavily now, punctuating the depth of our discussion. Finally he looked at me.

"Let's see. You still have the files belonging to Probation, and you and Gregory hope to catch Tina and her dad smuggling drugs. Maybe it will happen this weekend. This could really damage Safe Haven's reputation, and you weren't going to tell me?" David's face was a mix of sadness and frustration.

"I knew how this could affect you and I told Gregory. But this goes beyond a drug program. It seems more certain than ever that Carol died because of what she knew and was about to reveal. Gregory was afraid that if you were given advance warning of the border search you might behave differently around Tina, inadvertently tip her off. The results of this search are the only hope we have right now. That's why I'm telling you, so you won't have that talk with Tina. Let this play out. If nothing is found in the car they will only think they've been routinely searched for once. Then you can proceed with Tina however you like." I ended on a pleading note. I could feel tears welling and reached for a tissue. "I'm so sorry David. You've worked so hard to make Safe Haven successful. Surely it can be salvaged if worse comes to worst."

David seemed to relax a little from the initial shock. What I couldn't bear was his disappointment in me, evident in his demeanor.

"What will you do with the files if nothing is found in the search, or even if something is? I don't think withholding them from the department is smart. Aren't you risking your job?"

"Probably. I'll cross that bridge when I come to it. But more than anything I want to make things right with you. I never dreamed our sleuthing would involve Safe Haven, but we can't turn back now. All I'm asking is that you give us this weekend. Will you?"

"Of course," David's eyes softened and he took my hands in his. His tender gesture made my welling tears spill over and I let them fall, not wanting to let go even long enough to dab my cheeks. Luckily there was no one sitting near us to witness the emotional scene.

"You're doing the right thing Linda. There's no script for this. What you're telling me only confirms my suspicions about Tina. Safe Haven might take a hit, but it will survive. The staff is first-rate, and Tina's contributions? Well, as a councilwoman she fought to bring this program here. A paradox it now seems. She'll have to live with the consequences of her choices."

"So you're not too angry with me?"

"No. It was a lot to take in at first, but strangely I feel relieved. It's out of my hands. No dreaded talk with Tina for now. Maybe never if your instincts are correct. What do you say we finish our dinner, order an outrageous dessert, and then take a walk on the beach."

"I'll agree if you promise to follow me back to my house and tuck me in." I smiled, for the first time in about an hour.

"Oh I can do much better than that," David winked.

We hurried through our meal both anticipating a much better ending to the day.

Thursday couldn't go by fast enough. I had lain awake until three in the morning worrying about how Gregory would react when he learned that David knew everything. I toyed with not telling him but my conscience wouldn't let me be that unfair. So while I grappled with my conscience trying to convince it otherwise, I realized the only right thing to do would be to tell Gregory as soon as possible. I finally fell asleep on that thought. Now I could hardly wait to talk to him but it wasn't a conversation that could be held while we were both at work.

We'd had a sudden influx of referrals after our lull so I was kept busy logging in new cases and reviewing D.A. files. I barely saw Ed. In fact I avoided him, so fearful he'd say something that would make me confess to him about the files. That would have to be resolved too. I couldn't keep them but the longer I did the more explaining I'd have to do. Later on that one. First Gregory.

I headed home shortly after five, making only a brief stop for some fresh fruit at the farmer's market on Forest Avenue. Once in the door I put the fruit away, changed clothes, and dialed Gregory's number. I almost hoped I'd get his machine so I could prolong the inevitable. When he answered I had to quickly compose my thoughts.

After some small talk, I jumped in. "David came back last night." I paused.

"Good! When am I going to meet him?" Gregory asked.

"Soon I hope. I told him I promised you and Jan we'd have dinner together when he came back. He's all for it. But there's something more urgent right now."

"Such as?"

"David confided in me that he suspects Tina of using drugs." I went on to tell of his plans to confront her.

"Wow, I guess we were on the right track but that could blow the car search out of the water." Gregory let out a low whistle.

"That's what I thought. So I had to tell David about finding the files and our plans. Otherwise he would not have understood when I asked him to hold off confronting Tina. I'm sorry Gregory. Under the circumstances David had to know."

"What a bind this has put you in. You did what you had to do. Isn't David worried about Safe Haven?"

"You bet. His plan was to talk to Tina discreetly, have her volunteer to go into treatment. A minimal impact on the program, which he says is well staffed and running smoothly. If the car search reveals what we think it will, it won't be so quiet. He thinks Safe Haven will survive the irony of one of its leading supporters being a drug user."

"Maybe even a seller."

"That would really be something. Anyway, David's on our side and he promised to behave normally around Tina and see what this upcoming search brings. If it produces nothing then he'll deal with Tina as he originally planned."

"These next few days are going to drag," Gregory sighed.

"Look how far we've come."

"You're right. Linda, I can't begin to thank you for what you've done. In all her life Carol never had a better friend than you and you were just getting to know her."

This unexpected compliment touched me and I could only think to utter a simple thank you. We hung up and I went to make myself something to eat. I brought a tray into the living room so that I could watch the evening news. All I wanted was the next few days to go by.

Chapter Twenty Six

The ringing telephone aroused me from a deep sleep. I groggily reached for it and glanced at the bedside clock. Eight-thirty. Who would call me this early on a Sunday morning.

I cleared my throat. "Hello," I answered in my best attempt to sound like someone who's been awake for a while.

"Have you seen the morning paper?" It was Gregory, excited and high pitched. He didn't wait for my answer. "The judge and Tina were found with several bundles of cocaine. They're both in custody at the border."

I jerked up, now fully awake but almost speechless. "It's in the paper?" was all I could muster.

"In the California section of the Times. Headline, 'Prominent Judge and Councilwoman Daughter are Weekend Drug Smugglers'."

"Gregory this is unbelievable! Our suspicions were right. Let me read the article and I'll call you back."

I leapt out of bed, put on my slippers, ran to the front door and retrieved my paper. I pulled it apart until I came to the California section. There on the front page was a picture of a startled looking Judge Higuera and a pouty Tina being led away by border patrol officers, the raised trunk lid of the judge's car visible in the background. I began to read.

"What began as a routine border patrol search resulted in the seizure of ten pounds of cocaine wrapped in two ounce bundles, street value estimated at several hundred thousand dollars. The bundles were hidden in the trunk, under the spare tire, of a car owned and driven by prominent Orange County Judge Carlos Higuera. He and his daughter Tina, a Santa Ana councilwoman, were returning to California from one of their regular trips to an orphanage where they brought food and clothing.

Judge Higuera appeared stunned at the finding and denied any knowledge of how the drugs came to be there. He was heard to say 'Tina, do you know about this?' Tina Higuera has made no comment. The judge and his daughter were held overnight and will be released to their attorney on Sunday to be returned to Orange County where federal authorities will begin proceedings."

I sank back on the sofa. I could picture the office tomorrow, buzzing with this shocking news. And David, my God, has he read this yet? What a Pandora's box we opened.

I called Gregory who answered quickly. "I guess I'm almost as stunned as the judge," I said by way of hello.

"I know Linda. It's what we suspected and hoped to find but now that it's happened the fallout is going to be tremendous."

"We have to strategize don't we? The sooner the better. Can you come over here later?"

"Sure. How's one o'clock?"

"Good. See you then."

Next I called David. When he answered I could tell by his voice that he knew what had happened.

"David, I'm so sorry for what this will do to you."

"Don't worry Linda. I'll spend today at Safe Haven with the staff fending off reporters. What about you?"

"Gregory's coming over this afternoon. We have to come up with a plan before tomorrow. Probation and the courthouse will be on its ears with this news. We know there's more to this than just the drugs. I can't go in to work unprepared."

"You'll work things out. I'll call you tonight. We can compare notes on how we shored up the dam. Love you."

"Love you too." I hung up, exhausted already but facing a full and important day ahead of me.

I ate a quick breakfast, showered and dressed, and then went to my closet where the files had been hidden. I had never really gone through them. Today I would, praying that their secrets would speak to me.

After I finished reviewing the last file the pattern seemed clear to me. I had taken notes on each case as I read it over, and came to the same conclusion Carol did. There was definitely a connection between Santa Ana police officer Gabriel Morales, his criminal brother Edgar, and his Santa Ana buddies. When they appeared in Judge Higuera's court on drug charges, the charges were either greatly reduced or dropped altogether.

I thought of Luis Hebron, walking out of court, all cocky and arrogant, charges dropped because the police witness didn't show. And my trying to reach him later with no luck.

I picked up the newspaper and looked at Judge Higuera as he was being led off. He didn't have the face of a guilty person who has been caught in his crime. His face reflected disbelief at what was happening to him. Yes, Tina figured in this prominently, but how?

David suspected she was using drugs. Was she supplying them too? How easy it would be to bring in cocaine from Mexico when you were assured your car wouldn't be searched. I let my mind free-float and put together the following scenario. Tina was a user and a supplier. She kept the "teflon six" in cocaine. Somehow the news was conveyed to Judge Higuera, maybe by Officer Morales who caught her under the influence. In exchange for protecting Tina, Judge Higuera was coerced into being lenient on Edgar Morales and his pals. Officer Morales brother was protected, Judge Higuera's daughter was protected.

But did Judge Higuera know about the supplier part? He didn't seem to. Maybe he thought she was just a user, perhaps even tried to put her into treatment. Maybe Officer Morales threatened to arrest her and held that over Judge Higuera's head. I could see him wanting to protect his daughter's reputation. I couldn't see him willing to smuggle drugs across the border. That would be personal and professional suicide.

The doorbell rang. I glanced at the clock and saw it was almost one o'clock. Gregory, right on time. I opened the door, eager to share my thoughts with him.

"Hi there. Quite a morning, huh?" Gregory greeted.

"Quite. Do you want some coffee, soda?"

"No, I had lunch before I came."

"Let's go in the living room then. I've gone through all six files and concluded Carol was dead on."

"Unfortunately," Gregory answered.

"I'm sorry," I gasped, realizing how tactless my comment sounded. "It just seemed to describe her feelings about everything, being so right, that is."

"I know. Let's talk about what we do next. What did the files reveal to you?"

Gregory listened while I told him of my conclusions, including my theory that Tina and her drug activity were at the center of everything. He pondered my story and nodded in agreement.

"Right now the federal authorities only have a car trunk full of cocaine," I added. "With Judge Higuera's truly surprised reaction, and Tina's ease at manipulation, coupled with their do-gooder reputation, they could say it was planted and probably get off. But the files we have show otherwise and tie them to a much larger crime, even murder. Somebody in that motley alliance tried to stop Carol from going to the Grand Jury, and intentionally, or accidentally, caused her death."

"On the way here I realized we needed to deliver those files to the district attorney. I'm more convinced than ever now. Only I have to be the one to do it. You've done enough Linda. I'm not going to have you lose your job over this."

"You think I can be kept out of it?" Hope rose in me for the first time since we found the files.

"Yes. I'm the grieving brother who couldn't accept that his sister's death was an accident. I searched the crash site looking for clues and found the files. I was contemplating what to do with them when the border incident occurred. It all tied in and made sense to me. Especially with Carol's letter. I can easily authenticate her writing if I have to."

"What a relief. I've felt like I had a ticking time bomb in my closet."

"You did. I'll detonate it for you. The D.A. can coordinate with the federal investigators. If Judge Higuera had a personal relationship with Carol, as her statement implies, then he must have been very upset at her death. Can you imagine his feelings when he learns her death was no accident?"

"Devastated, no doubt." I thought of Miguel Gonzales telling me he heard a second car stop and someone get out of it, then leave. Too bad he couldn't see who it was. We would have had an eyewitness to the accident, or murder, as it now appeared to be.

"I hope Miguel Gonzales doesn't read the news-paper," I said. "He might tell someone what he saw and heard that night, and how he told 'Miz Davenport' when he turned himself in."

"Didn't you say he was back in custody? He probably won't even hear about it. And if he does he won't want to admit he was there and didn't report what he saw." Gregory's thoughts on the subject made me feel better.

"I hope you're right. Otherwise I'll have some 'splaining' to do."

"I think I'll take the files and go on home. I'd like to look them over myself before I see the district attorney, and I plan to call him first thing in the morning. With what I have to tell him he should see me right away." Gregory stood and gathered the files.

"You know I'll see Jan tomorrow at work and she'll be wondering where all our stuff fits in with what happened over the weekend."

"I'll have to tell her I found the files but I won't bring you into it. I trust her but it will be safer for you if what I tell the D.A. is what I tell her. By the way, how's David handling this?"

"He's at Safe Haven, fending off reporters. He said he'd call me tonight."

"Good. Before I go, there's one other thing. I still have Carol's ashes. We always talked about having our ashes scattered over the ocean. We promised each other we'd do that. Whoever went first, that is. When this is all over, and I think it will be soon, I want to charter a boat and fulfill that promise. I'd like you and David to be there."

"I'd be honored. So would David. Good luck with the D.A. Call me tomorrow night."

After Gregory left I felt such relief to have the files out of the house. Now the information they contained would be brought forward. I busied myself while I waited for David's call, wondering how he was faring.

It was six o'clock before I heard from David and he sounded weary. I filled him in on Gregory's plan. He agreed that was the best way to proceed.

"Now tell me, how did it go for you?"

"It's amazing how many staff people came to

me and said they had thought there was something funny about Tina," David answered.

"Why didn't they come to you about it sooner?"

"That's what I asked. Their common excuse was that if they were wrong they'd be embarrassed."

"So what's the mood of everyone at Safe Haven?"

"Apprehensive at first, that the program would be affected, even closed. But I assured them we'd stay in business and reminded them that they are the ones who've made the program a success."

"I bet they liked hearing that. What about the New York office?"

"Not thrilled but satisfied with the damage control thus far," David sighed. I couldn't tell whether it was relief or fatigue.

"Were you hounded by reporters?" I tried to imagine what the newspapers would look like tomorrow.

"You can look for me on the nine o'clock news tonight."

"I forgot about TV." My heart sank at the notoriety this matter would receive.

"I gave an interview to the Times and Register. It'll be interesting to see how they spin it. I was very circumspect in my answers."

"Are you coming over?"

"I wish I could but I'm exhausted and I need to stay here a while longer. How about dinner tomorrow night?"

"How about if I cook it for you?"

"Sounds good if you don't mind. I can be at your place around seven. Does that work?"

"It works. See you then. Try to get a good night's rest."

"You too."

I felt better after talking to David. Whatever happened now, Safe Haven would survive, even though Tina's little game had been exposed. Unfortunately her dad had been dragged through the mud with her. How much mud could he slog through before he stopped protecting her? Hopefully the next few days would tell.

The Monday morning papers had a field day with the Higuera arrest. The judge's upright reputation was played against a backdrop of a "double life" scenario; "Judge Metes Out Justice During the Week, Defies Law on the Weekend," blazed one headline. An article focused on Tina, councilwoman and jurist's daughter, and how instrumental she was in bringing a needed drug rehabilitation program to Santa Ana. The writer opined that she was more in need of its services than the present residents.

I couldn't read anymore. After having watched David on the news last night giving a professional interview, not allowing himself to be drawn in by the sensational angle the reporters were aiming for, I realized the scandal would be the emphasis of the news reporting. But we suspected this all along. I had no sympathy for Tina but Judge Higuera was another matter. Whatever his involvement with his daughter's problems, I didn't believe he expected to be in this deep.

I walked into the office around 8:30 am. Most probation officers are in the office on Monday morning. Today it looked like no one was in the field. The halls were buzzing with conversations I could only catch snippets of. As I looked into offices on the way to mine I saw two or three people huddled over a newspaper, commenting as they read.

I went to my office and shut my door but within minutes there was a knock and then Jan peeked in without waiting for an answer.

"You've heard, haven't you?" It was more a statement than a question.

"Yes, unfortunately," I responded. I wondered how much she knew from the newspaper, and how much she'd heard from Gregory. I didn't have to wait long.

"Gregory told me about finding the files and what he plans to do with them. He said you knew too, otherwise I wouldn't bring it up."

"You haven't said anything to anyone here have you?"

"Oh no, never," Jan answered, with a hurt look on her face. "I know this is just between us."

"I'm sorry. It's been so tense since this all happened, finding the files, the arrest, David's damage control at Safe Haven, everything."

"I'm sure. Is David doing OK?"

"He is. Did Gregory tell you he's going to try to see the D.A. today?"

"Yes. Gregory thinks that finding the files and Carol's note, and the Higueras' arrest are tied in somehow with Carol's accident. I hope the D.A. takes him seriously."

"He has to. It's all so incriminating. He'll have to question Tina and her father." I thought of Miguel Gonzales telling me how he heard the footsteps of someone just after Carol's car plunged over the hillside. Someone who looked then left. Someone who would have offered help if they wanted Carol to survive. But who? The person following her, running her off the road?

"I guess I'll head back to my office. I have an interview at nine." Jan stood to leave.

"Take care Jan. Thanks for stopping by."

I stayed in my office for most of the day, avoiding the hubbub all around. By afternoon the novelty had worn off and most everyone had resumed their usual Monday routine. I went home relieved that I'd avoided any conversation about the Higueras.

I made dinner preparations, all the while anxious to know how Gregory had done. When the phone rang I raced to it. It was Gregory.

"It went well, finally. At first I was passed off to a deputy D.A. who seemed annoyed at my adding to his already busy day. Then when he saw what I had he suddenly had all the time in the world. He made a couple calls, and pretty soon I was in Bob Roland's office."

"The D.A. himself. Good for you." I imagined Gregory's tenacity.

"Anyway, I told Bob that I never believed my sister's death was an accident. I explained my foray into the brush around where her car landed as my effort to find anything belonging to her. I knew she always carried a briefcase and it wasn't in her office or car. When I found it, and the files inside with her incriminating note, I wasn't sure what to do. Then with the Higuera arrest the puzzle pieces began to fall into place."

"How did he react?"

"With great interest. He's already been in touch with the federal authorities. The word is that Tina is saying nothing but Judge Higuera is devastated, almost a broken man. After reviewing the files and reading Carol's note outlining her suspicions, he's willing to look into them, which will mean interviewing Tina and her dad about Carol's allegations." Gregory sounded pleased.

"Is he going to bring up the accident?"

"To the extent that the files and note were found at the scene and see where that leads. Any one of Tina's drug contacts could have been responsible."

"But did any of them know Carol was going to Rolling oaks to see the Grand Jury? Judge Higuera did." In my heart I knew he couldn't have been the one who followed her. This made the whole perplexing matter even more so.

"I know Linda. Let's trust the investigators for now. We've done enough. It's time to get on with our lives. What do you say?"

"I say I'd better get busy finishing dinner. David will be here soon. Thanks Gregory, for everything."

While David and I ate I gave him the latest chapter in our saga. He expressed relief that the files were in the D.A.'s hands and confidence that their investigation would sort everything out.

"I hope you're right. We're so close to the truth. I can feel it. They can't drop the ball on this one."

I began clearing dishes while David took a second cup of coffee.

"Safe Haven was pretty calm today. Amazing that after only one day it was practically business as usual. Made me realize that the staff will need me less and less, which makes me more comfortable with another decision I made."

I stopped rinsing dishes and turned around. David was looking at me with a mischievous eye.

"What decision?" I stood there with my hands on my hips, nervousness rolling over me like a draft.

"Part of my recent stay in New York had nothing to do with Safe Haven. I was gone as long as I was because I wanted to make certain Dad's law firm was in capable hands."

"Isn't your dad still working? I thought he was getting stronger."

"He is, but he's tapered off on his hours, gradually letting his partners take on more. The doctor was pretty emphatic that his workaholic ways would do him in. He works about half time now and actually enjoys the extra time he has with my mother."

"So, when will I hear the decision you've made?"

"I've decided to relocate to southern California, study for the bar exam, and practice law here. I'll still be a consultant to Safe Haven and any new programs that are opened, and I'll be able to handle their litigation as well."

I tried to take in what I'd heard. David, actually living here. The nervousness I felt gave way to sheer joy. My eyes welled up.

"I want you to be part of my life here too, forever, if you'll have me." David stood and took me in his arms.

"Is this a proposal?" I could barely speak.

"Yes. I've never done it before so it's probably not the most romantic way to ask you to marry me."

"It's perfect, just perfect," I cried as I laid my head on his shoulder, "and I accept."

Chapter Twenty Seven

The ocean was calm and clear and our boat seemed to glide on the surface with barely a ripple. No June gloom today. Sunbeams followed us along the water, a cheery accompaniment to our somber foursome. It was a year to the day of Carol's death.

David, Jan, Gregory and I sat in deck chairs, gazing at the water, each lost in our own private thoughts. The urn holding Carol's ashes rested on Gregory's lap. The events of the past few weeks had been both overwhelming and at the same time liberating; pedestals toppled, mysteries were solved.

Judge Higuera resigned from the bench and Tina was in custody pending federal charges of drug smuggling. Our belief that Judge Higuera was an unwitting accomplice to his daughter's activities proved true. Through the district attorney's investigation we learned that Judge Higuera first became complicit in Tina's drug use when she was arrested by Santa Ana Police Sergeant Morales in an undercover drug buy. Sgt. Morales's brother was one of the teflon six and he used Tina as a bargaining chip with Judge Higuera – he would let Tina go if the judge would be lenient on his brother and his cohorts. To protect his daughter, he agreed.

According to the D.A., Judge Higuera tearfully told him that he pleaded with Tina to get help for her cocaine habit, all the while dreading each time one of the Morales cohorts appeared in his court, knowing the devil's bargain he had made. He had no idea that Tina was using their orphanage trips to make contact with drug suppliers and using their car to bring cocaine across the border. He would never have gone that far.

When Judge Higuera was asked about the files and note found near Carol's car, he broke down. He had talked to Tina the night before Carol's accident, telling her of Carol's plans to see the Grand Jury, begging her once again to seek treatment. Instead he said that Tina told him she would go see Carol herself, talk her out of the trip. Tina promised to stop her cocaine use. After he heard about Carol's fatal accident he always wondered what had really happened. He said Tina assured him she had not seen Carol after all, tried to but missed her at the office. He took her at her word but she had obviously not given up her drug habit, so now he wondered if the rest of her account was even true.

This information was all the D.A. needed to talk to Tina about the accident. At first Tina denied trying to see Carol, then admitted she arrived too late, saw Carol pulling out of the parking lot and followed her, hoping to gain her attention. When they reached the Ortega Highway Tina said she started driving faster but the closer she came to Carol, the faster Carol went. Then Carol lost control on a curve and went over the side. Tina was horrified and stopped, stepped out of her car to look and was sure Carol was dead by the looks of the car.

Instead of calling for help she went back to her car and left the scene. As she drove off she saw another car stop and assumed they would call 911. Tina never told her father the whole story. Whether Tina would be prosecuted for this was still undecided.

Sgt. Morales had been suspended pending further investigation. The teflon six would be on their own if they continued their criminal activities.

Carol's death wasn't intentional after all but it was still the result of an accident that shouldn't have happened. At least it was out in the open now and

Gregory had some peace knowing the truth.

My thoughts drifted back to the present when I heard the captain speak to Gregory.

"We're far enough out sir. You can scatter the ashes any time."

Gregory looked at the urn, then at us. Silently we all stood and walked to the railing, bowing our heads and holding hands for a moment. Then Gregory began to slowly scatter the ashes. It was amazing to me that a vibrant human being could be reduced to a small amount of ash, but there she was, on the wind, falling gently to the sea.

With the last handful we said our good-byes. Gregory uttered the final words, "Carol, we left no stone unturned for you. I love you. Rest in peace."

We stood for a while at the railing. Suddenly a group of dolphins leaped out of the water in unison, disappeared underneath, the popped back up again. We laughed at their happy antics, so life affirming.

Eventually we returned to our chairs. Mission accomplished. As our boat headed back to shore we began to talk of dinner plans.

David whispered in my ear, "Should we announce our engagement tonight over dinner? This ring is burning a hole in my pocket."

"You have a ring?" I blurted. Gregory and Jan

jerked their heads in my direction.

"Let's just say we have a little announcement at dinner," David laughed, blushing.

"Let's just say," Gregory and Jan said simultaneously, giving each other a wink.

The four of us smiled as we watched the distance between Carol's resting place and our boat grow farther apart. The shore was coming into our vision. Soon we'd be there and on to the rest of our lives.

CPSIA information can be obtained at www.ICGtesting.com
Printed in the USA
LVOW13s0543241213

366686LV00001B/3/P